D0011147

THE
TALL
WOMAN

Books by Wilma Dykeman

Explorations

With Fire and Sword: The Battle of Kings Mountain

Tennessee. Text for Graphic Arts book

The Appalachian Mountains (with Dykeman Stokely)

Highland Homeland: The People of the Great Smokies
(with Jim Stokely)

Tennessee: A Bicentennial History

Too Many People, Too Little Love

The Border States. A Time-Life Library of America volume
(with James Stokely)

Prophet of Plenty

Look To This Day

Return the Innocent Earth

The Far Family

The Tall Woman

Seeds of Southern Change (with James Stokely)

Neither Black Nor White (with James Stokely)

The French Broad. A Rivers of America book

THE
TALL
WOMAN

by Wilma Dykeman

WAKESTONE BOOKS
Newport, Tennessee 37821

Copyright © 1962 by Wilma Dykeman Stokely

All rights reserved, including the right to reproduce
this book or portions thereof in any form

Library of Congress Catalog Card Number: 62-11580
ISBN: 0-9613859-1-X

First Wakestone Books paperback edition: 1982.
40th printing.

Published and distributed by Wakestone Books.
Originally published by Holt, Rinehart, and Winston.

For availability of our books in quantity at special discounts for
educational use, fund-raising, and other purposes, please contact
the publisher:

Wakestone Books
282 Clifton Heights Road
Newport, TN 37821
(423) 623-7394
http://www.wakestone.com

This book is for
the tallest woman I know:
Bonnie Cole Dykeman

"A tall woman casts a long shadow."

—*Mountain saying*

THE
TALL
WOMAN

1st
CHAPTER

The wind was a wild dark thing plucking at the trees outside, pushing at the doors and chinks of the house, then dying down still as death before another rise and rush and plunge. Listening to it, Lydia McQueen waited and shrank deeper under the quilts, until the corn shucks in the mattress rustled and settled into new shapes.

She thought about the wind—like the great fine horse Papa had owned once, strong and willful with no bit or stirrup that could tame it. Quiet for a spell, it would break with a sudden burst of energy and, as Papa said, "No man who walked in shoe leather could hold it then." Yet her father, a gentle man, had controlled the wildness in the horse as surely and invisibly as the sun controlled the plants in her mother's garden.

The wind came again and she felt the pleasure of her own body-warmth. Like a seed, she felt, one of those sun-warmed seeds in the spring ground, growing, ready to give forth new life. She was aware of the dry smell of the corn shucks. Her mind went back to the day she had sorted them, pulling the leaves off the hard stalk ends, working toward a soft stuffing for the mattress. She was making ready to be Mark's wife, to take this and a wagonload of other furnishings to her own home. It was a day last spring.

Spring was chancy, but she liked it best of all the seasons. One day would be still and soft with the sun flowing like honey along the hillsides, over the brown winter leaves and the tender green things peeping through, with time slow and the bees buzzing somewhere in the sunshine—forever, forever—and the next day fierce, with the wind tearing through the woods in gusts, shaking the last dry oak leaves, bending treetops, piercing every crevice of house and clothing with a bitter chill, and time rushing with it down the valley.

"It's a fair morning," she had said to her mother as they worked out in the yard beside the corncrib, where the shucks had been stored through the winter.

"Ah, fair enough today, but dogwood winter yet to come," her mother had answered.

And after the cold spell, when dogwoods bloomed, there would be whippoorwill winter and blackberry winter. The reminder cut through joy the way her father's knife cut through the living flesh of some animal on the farm, draining and deadening it. She set her mouth and determined to be stingy with her words the rest of the morning—until she spied the first flock of robins down in the new-cleared field. Then she cried out in pleasure again for her mother to come and see the plump, neat birds, for Lydia Moore was eighteen, and chancy too, like March. Anger would not hoard in her long.

But, "You're a girl turned woman now," her mother said. "No need for such wispy ways. Anyway, I'm of a mind they won't last long around Mark McQueen."

Lydia thrust a cornhusk into the sack so sharply that one dry blade cut her middle finger. She knew her mother had wanted her to marry Ham Nelson. "Ah, Hamilton's a well-turned boy, and the Nelsons are good livers," she had said when he brought Lydia home once from a sociable at the Burkes'. And Lydia had replied, remembering all that Ham had told her as they rode home that night, "Could he buy himself for what he's worth, and sell himself for what he thinks he's worth, he'd be princely rich overnight."

But Sarah Moore had not smiled. Neither had she smiled when her daughter came to ask her if Mark McQueen could speak to

14

Jesse Moore about their wedding. "With all the boys in the valley, Lydia, you must choose him?"

"Mama, I didn't choose."

But she had felt helpless to explain how it was since that first day she'd seen Mark at the mill, big and dark with the strength of a mountain in him as he helped James Burke grind the corn. From that moment there had been no peace in her. Everything was changed; what she had thought fair now became fairer, and the homely grew ugly beyond endurance. She ran when walking would do as well, sang to herself as she worked in the field because she was full of a strange confidence and beauty, and wept to herself behind the barn because she had so little confidence and was so lacking in prettiness. It was a time of days like spring, changeable and quick with life. She had no words to fit such feelings. "I didn't choose, Mama. It's like I was chosen."

Her mother looked at her then, steadily. Lydia could close her eyes now, this bleak winter night as she lay in bed alone, with the cabin small and empty around her and the great bare mountains outside, and remember precisely how her mother stood in the door of the corncrib, small, grave, brown hair streaked with grey drawn tightly back from her forehead and temples into a firm knot. For that moment it was as if Lydia saw her mother for the first time in many years. Her brown eyes were small, even in the small face whose delicacy had been only partly erased by years of hard work, but they were bright as minnows flashing in the brook. Her mouth's softness had almost disappeared behind a thin set line of determination. A fine web of wrinkles had settled around her eyes, across her high white forehead, along the once-smooth skin of her throat. When Sarah Moore looked directly and thoughtfully at someone, as she looked at Lydia now, she seemed to be gazing from some height or depth familiar only to herself. She wiped her hands on her apron in unconscious movements of nervousness, and spoke slowly.

"I've never held with craving women. Your papa can tell you that I never asked for more than he could give. But I have craved one thing: for you children to see better times than ours. Could I a-brushed every tangle-bramble and stumble-stone out of your

15

way, I'd have crawled to do it ere this. Wanting you to like Hamilton Nelson, I only wanted you to find the work of life a little easier."

She gestured to forestall any interruption from Lydia. "Your grandmother came from Virginia. She moved down from the Tidewater, through the Valley, into these mountains, after she was wedded. I was her eldest, born in the Valley. I was the only one remembered the softness and sweetness of her before the mountains wore it away. I learned the costs of new country to a woman—and to a girl-child. I'm not saying it's a cost beyond paying, Lydia, or beyond the worth. I'm a mind to set you a choice. Nothing's ever taken, or given, doesn't have its price."

Lydia nodded, suddenly shy, embarrassed by the intimate words passing between them, more than in any single day or year of all their lives before. And still her mother was not finished. Driving straight ahead, like a plowman behind oxen, she spoke again, fingers still busy with her apron.

"Living won't be easy with Mark McQueen. He's a proud man, with a restlessness on him that will be hard to still. Maybe he's not a body ever to find contentment this side the grave. I couldn't say. But such a man's life can hurt his wife, be he ever so in love with her or not."

For a moment she was quiet, looking no longer at her daughter but at the distant woods. Lydia heard the first spring insects humming out in the fields, heard their tiny rustling in the dry cornhusks around her where the warm sun was stirring them to life. But all she saw in her mind's eye was Mark McQueen's face and his stout sun-browned arms.

"It may not seem so to you now, being a girl only and a girl in love," her mother went on, "but there's something beyond even love, for a woman as well as a man. A body's personhood."

Her mother's gaze came back from the woods to the yard and the house and the garden patch beyond, and Lydia did not know how to answer all this strange talk. The insects ticked and droned even louder around them.

"Your papa has gentle ways not common to many men. Not many here in the back country look for what they're seeking in

16

books. But when your papa came from the Low Country, up into these mountains, and the load in the wagon had to be lightened, he threw out the household plunder and kept his box of books. Oh, he's cleared and planted and prospered enough to own his own land and decent home, but half his world has always been in his mind. He's never been a driven man. A man who is driven is not easy to live with."

The silence between them was longer than the words before Lydia said softly, "I never asked for easy, Mama."

"I know, I know." Her mother turned suddenly back to the crib and an armful of shucks. Her voice was muffled. "I'm beseeching the Lord to hold you in the hollow of his hand."

Lydia had told Mark her family would not interfere with their marriage. If he noticed that she could not say they were rousing happy over it, he made no sign.

Mark had spoken to her father. The older man was troubled by something larger than either of them. He asked, "And what about this war? What do you aim to do about it?"

Mark McQueen answered slowly, "I've heard it named a rich man's war and a poor man's fight. I don't feel strong one way or the other. If it comes to choosing, I reckon I'd have to stand by union."

"Well, Mark," Jesse Moore said, walking the length of the room and pulling his beard as he spoke, "if it's not making any greater difference to you than that, couldn't you see fit to go with me in the North Carolina troops? Since they've come to the pinch and are calling up the seed-corn young'uns and the old ones, too, I don't doubt I'll be going. But I can't turn against my state. The Yankees, even the President, got no right to tell us down here what to do. I couldn't fight against Zeb Vance and all my neighbors, and still I'd hate to think I was fighting my own son by marriage."

Mark's quiet face and dark eyes did not change. "I don't reckon I could fight for slavery," he said.

Lydia, listening in the next room, felt her stomach tighten with the sudden emotion of love for this tall, strong man and fear of the unknown stranger in him that could be so unyielding.

After a short silence he offered one brief explanation, with difficulty, as though his own past was something to be buried without words. "I worked for too many men when I was a chap, and after I come to manhood, I said no man ever again would own the strength of my muscles. That's my way of thinking: every man's stoutness belongs to himself."

"But that's for white. You can't set white and black alongside each other in worth——"

"I couldn't say about all that. I know they're men, no matter the color of the hide covering their muscle." There was a note of finality in Mark's voice. "I won't go to war unless it's a have-to. I've rented some fields from old man Nelson and I aim to make a home for Lydia and me. We'll move on land of our own as soon as I save money enough. That's all I come to name to you."

"Maybe the war will be over before we have to go separate ways," Jesse Moore said. He extended his hand to Mark. "If Lydia's chosen you, and you her, you're welcome to our family." He swallowed, still gripping the younger man's hand. "There's a passage in the Bible, you know, sets the value of a good woman beyond rubies. My oldest girl has always seemed something special to me, Mark McQueen."

Two months later, in June, when the Bishop rode through the mountains on his yearly pilgrimage, Lydia and Mark McQueen were married. The day was overcast, with thin sunshine and clouds threatening rain. Weather made no difference to Lydia. Her long slim body tingled with life and her grey eyes, so like her father's, glowed with warmth from inside. She wore the dress her mother had worn twenty years before, straight and simple with tiny buttons holding the high collar and the long sleeves at her wrists, but rich and elegant in its simplicity because it was silk. Silk sent down from Virginia, brought across the waters many years before, fell smooth and whispering around her, and she felt round and full and precious. The Bishop's words spilled gently over them —over Mark and Lydia, this man and this woman—binding them together with an invisible cobweb of words.

"I've nothing to bring you now," Mark had said to her the night before, gentle and angry, too, as he looked at her steadily, "noth-

18

ing but strength of muscle and something here in my heart. Do you but believe in me, though, Lyddy girl, and I'll get you a home and land and quench all your hungers. I bond my word to it."

Now they joined hands and after the minister's directions bonded their words and bodies and lives one to the other.

The Bishop had brought, in his saddlebags, a new book for Jesse Moore, and he gave it to him as soon as the wedding ceremony was over. "A copy of Gibbon!" and Lydia's father fondled in his large rough hands the volume telling of the decline and fall of a mighty empire.

"What good is Gibbon-what's-his-name in wrestling stumps out of new ground or making corn sprout two to the seed?" one of the Burke men present for the bridal infare asked with a great booming laugh.

Jesse Moore smiled. Lydia had seen that little secret smile of outer tolerance and inner pleasure before, and in this full moment of her happiness with Mark she wondered if anyone had ever really understood, or appreciated, her father. How much she had learned from him during those long winter evenings before the fireplace when he had read aloud to the family from one of the shelf of books behind the door. Her mother carding wool, knitting, sewing, and the children hulling dried beans for the next day's dinner or shelling corn for mill, while his voice built another world around them—of far places and other times, of laughter or bloodshed, history or poetry. She would never be sharing in these moments again, never be sitting again as a child before this fireplace weaving dreams, wrapped in magic. She laid her hand on her father's arm. He glanced at her and covered her hand with his own.

"Man does not live by bread alone," he answered Burke.

"Aye God, he don't for sure," James Burke replied for his brother. "He's got to have a little meat along with it!"

Jesse Moore joined in the laughter, and Lydia was pleased that this was a glad time, her wedding day a merry occasion for all. Even Mark was more at ease than she had ever seen him with a crowd of the valley folks. He accepted their good wishes and shook hands gravely, his tall dark head taller than the tallest of the men,

19

his big hands swallowing even the muscled hands of these hard-working people.

Late in the afternoon the bride and groom had ridden in their wagon, with such few furnishings as they owned, down to the rented house on the Nelsons' farm, this house where she now lay alone, remembering.

Their finest possession was the cow Mark had traded from James Burke. He had kept it a secret from Lydia till she came out to climb on the wagon beside him. "Mark! Whose cow?" she asked.

"She's all yours." And when Lydia exclaimed, he said, "There, Lyddy, it's just a cow." But his eyes were watchful and pleased.

"Mark, she's the daintiest beast I ever did set eyes on. . . ." Lydia went behind the wagon to where the cow stood and the pleasure of ownership filled her hands as she stroked the gentle square face and patted the brindle hide. "You bring us milk and cream for rich yellow butter and we'll see you get all the grass and fodder you can hold and a snug place to sleep nights when winter comes. You'll be a valuable to us. I'll call you Pearly."

She was proud as the ox team pulled the creaking wagon from in front of the house and turned into the rutted road that ran down the valley and to the Nelson acres, proud for the cow walking slowly behind so their friends at the infare could see that they might be a beginning couple, but they were beginners of substance. The little wagon was old, a castaway Mark had got from a man he'd once worked for, and it was not overly burdened with their belongings—but they had livestock. There, tied behind the wagon, was the beginning of their farm, the plenty and promise that they would make for themselves, Mark and Lydia, and their children.

The cabin they moved into was dilapidated; hay had been stored in it until the week before, when Mark had cleared it out, patched the shingles on the roof, put fresh clay between the logs on the west side where some of the chinking had fallen out and left gaps where cold and rain could seep in. There were two rooms with a dog-trot between. In one, a wide fireplace was crumbling, revealing age and slovenly construction. The cabin sat at the edge of a pasture, behind it a cluster of tall yellow poplars surrounding a spring of water. For the rest, there were only winding cow trails and tangles of blackberry bushes around the house.

At first its rooms had seemed bare as a bone picked by varmints, Lydia felt. Then one day Jesse and Sarah Moore and the five children younger than Lydia had come, bringing all that could be spared from their own home for furnishing: two iron kettles and an oven, a half-dozen pewter dishes and four bone-handled forks; a regular bedstead to take the place of the one Mark had built in against one wall, and extra quilts besides the two Lydia had pieced before her marriage; two chairs and a rough table Jesse Moore had helped Mark make from some cured-out lumber Jesse had been saving for a bookcase; several tools to add to the axe and froe Mark owned. Last, and finest of all, they brought the clock that had been Lydia's Virginia grandmother's.

Sarah Moore had held the clock, wrapped in the blue and white catalpa-flower coverlet, in her lap while the family rode in the jolty wagon as far as they could. Then she carried it, cradled in her arms, across the pasture to the cabin. Inside, she placed the clock on the rough slab of black walnut over the fireplace. Mark had promised to smooth and polish the fireboard for Lydia someday when the work outside was less pushing.

"There, Lydia," her mother said, while Paul and Kate and Robert and Annie Marie and Elizabeth stood and watched, making the giving of the clock a ceremony and a remembrance. "It's yours by rights. My mother had it from her mother because it was a thing had come across the waters with her from a village in Cornwall, and because she was eldest. It was passed on to me because I was eldest and had helped nurse it from breaking on our way from the Valley of Virginia. Now it's yours, a thing for your home, your dowry."

"What's dowry?" Annie Marie had asked, small and grave for her ten years.

"It's valuables a woman takes to her man when she marries," Kate answered from the wisdom of her fifteen years.

"What'll I have for dowry for my man?" Annie Marie asked their mother.

"We'll unravel that riddle when——"

21

"A spider and a flea, and a pinch from me, that's what Annie's dowry will be." Robert chanted the rhyme that spun out of his head as easily as a web came from a spider, and Lydia, lying now on the corn-shuck mattress, smiled to herself, remembering the gaiety of his mischief, the twinkle of his eyes, bright and small like their mother's.

Annie Marie had begun to cry.

"Don't devil the young ones, Robert," their mother said.

"Quieten down now," Paul warned, so that their father glanced at him and smiled, knowing that he was seventeen and, now that Lydia was gone from home, eager to show authority as the eldest. Robert made a face at Lydia, indicating his older brother.

Then they all stood for a moment, surveying the delicacy, the richness of this treasure from a far distance of waters and land, and from a time far back.

"No tell whose hands shaped and polished it," Lydia said.

"No tell what fine rooms it's seen," Robert agreed eagerly, always catching Lydia's meanings and moods more readily than any of her brothers or sisters, "or what important talk it's heard, weighty man affairs to make folks wonder and admire."

"All your days it's to keep time by," their mother said.

Lydia lay and listened to its tick over the fireplace this night. The wind had quieted and a great stillness came over the house. Her body was heavy and tired, but her mind would not drowse.

To keep time. But there was no way to keep time—or people. Last spring had run on to summer and summer had come into winter. Mark had filled the cabin and clearing with his presence, leaving his sign of order in the pattern of fence rail laid upon rail, his sign of permanence in stone laid upon stone for the tall reconstructed chimney built against winter. But from amidst their little patterns and permanences, Mark had gone, driven by the winds of war that rose somewhere beyond her knowing and would die somewhere beyond her reach. She thought about the winter.

Such a long cold this had been, tight and cruel, man and nature trying to outdo each other in their hardness. "Folks will live to date their winters from this one of eighteen sixty-four and -five," she heard old men predict.

What nature gave, the war took: grain from the fields, meat

from the smokehouse—and the men: her father, Paul, even her Mark. Wherever man proposed, nature disposed: up in Virginia and over in the valley of East Tennessee she heard of marches over frozen ground as hard and sharp as flint on bare, frostbitten feet. Early crops were blackened by late snow. Her mother's face grew tighter by the day. Her father and brother were out there somewhere, in butternut suits, hiding, running, fighting—she did not know. And Mark was up in Kentucky, in Union blue.

A man had come by her old home and left a spoken message. Her mother sent Robert to tell her about it the very next morning.

Mark McQueen sent word to his wife. He's well. He was on his way to the Gap when last I seen him."

"The Gap?" Lydia's mother asked.

"Cumberland Gap," the soldier answered. "Our troops got to keep a-holt of it till the Rebs surrender, ma'am. They're putting out word it may be any day now."

"And are any of the North Carolina Confederates around the Gap now?" Sarah Moore asked.

"Not as I know of, ma'am."

"Thank God," she murmured, and the young man looked puzzled, but none of the little ones clustered near, listening, knew to tell him that their papa might have been one of the Carolina men in grey.

"You stay now and take a meal with us."

"No, ma'am, I've got a long walk to the other side of the Craggies. But I thank you kindly." So she had found meat and a pone of bread for him to carry as he went, thinking of her husband and her son and her daughter's husband as she fixed the food and gave it to the bearded, weary young soldier.

Robert had been working outside, getting up firewood, and had not been there to hear the man himself, but he brought the conversation just as his mother had told it to him, including even the thoughts she had had as she wrapped the meat and bread for the stranger.

After Lydia had heard this message, third-hand now but nevertheless word from Mark, and after Robert had gone home, she went down to the spring and carried up buckets of sand and water and scrubbed the puncheon floor of the cabin until it shone. But although her body grew tired and ached, her mind was not stilled.

It was more than a month since she had received that message, but Lydia's unease grew. It kept her awake this night. The wind was no longer shaking the cabin, but her thoughts were. The ticking of the clock was like a human presence in the dark. She was thankful for its small steadiness. Then the baby stirred within her.

Could an unborn being know foreboding? she wondered. She sat up in bed, feeling the chill rush in to scatter the warmth of the nest she had made under the heavy quilts. The floor was icy against her bare feet. She walked in the darkness over to the fireplace and knelt on the hearth. The rough stones were cold under her knees as she bent forward and raked the ashes carefully aside. There, deep in the dead ashes, glowed a live coal. Lydia reached for some pieces of the rich pine she had splintered and carefully piled by the hearth before she went to bed. These she laid on top of the coals. Gently she blew, and the glow became brighter. The pine splinters reddened and burst into flame. The pungent odor of their resin filled the room. When the kindling was burning well, she laid a hickory log across the flames.

"Lydia's a master fire builder," her father had said once, and she had cherished the bit of praise for years now. Yet it had never seemed a chore to her to build a fire—to breathe warmth and light into being against the cold and darkness and watch it grow to vivid, splendid life.

She crouched on the hearth in her long nightdress and held her cold hands to the warmth. If only Mark were here, she thought, how content this moment would be. But now—he did not even know there was a baby. She folded her arms around her stomach: how precious she seemed to herself, carrying another life, and one that was part Mark's; carrying another design of nose and eyes and mouth, fingers and toes and tiny bones, all within herself.

"While Mark's gone, you can't stay alone, not another living soul with you," her mother had said.

"I can't do anything else, Mama," she had replied. "This is my home now. I've got to stay where Mark fixed for me. I've got to tend our fields and our cow——"

"You never did have fear in you," her mother had consented. "And you're a woman grown now. I'll send one of the young ones to see after you every day or so. And I don't reckon the Nelsons would let you want for anything."

"The Nelsons have nothing to do with it." Lydia had flushed both in embarrassment and anger that her mother would mention this. She had never spoken Hamilton Nelson's name to Mark and she had purposely avoided meeting him after they came to his father's farm to live. Memory of the evening they had ridden together from the Burkes' was still green in Lydia's mind. That night she had seen revealed Hamilton Nelson's true nature. He was a man who knew what he wanted, and that was simply everything he could get his hands on or around.

There was a little rise in the road just above the mouth of Thickety Creek valley, and Ham had stopped the horse and buggy just at the crest, so that they sat looking down on the fields and woods and sprinkling of houses lying there in the dim moonlight.

"Thickety Creek—that's mine," Ham said to her in his confident, deep voice. And she had thought for a moment that he meant this was his the way the flag was his—and hers, too, and everyone's who lived under it—or the way the air was his, and everyone's who breathed it. But then he had jumped from the buggy seat and had pulled her down beside him. Standing in the grass beside the road, he held her arm with one hand and pointed over the land around them with the other, and she realized that he meant this was to be *his*, the creek and earth a personal possession as though it were a land-deed to fold and put in his pocket, or a hat to keep in his closet.

She had looked at him then, looked to see the man she had known life-long but had never really beheld. He was not a tall person and this suddenly surprised her, for he seemed to be such a large man. His head was round and massive with a heavy shock of reddish-brown hair and the skin of his thickset face was slightly pock-marked. His neck was short and set between bulky shoulders. He stood with his feet planted squarely apart. Often he held his hands clasped behind his back. Standing so, he gave a powerful feeling of masculinity which could be at once attractive and repulsive. He spoke bluntly; neither nature nor need had inclined him toward thoughtfulness to other people.

Looking at his solid form looming above her in the moonlight, she recalled her father saying once that Ham's pride was his horse, a high-spirited Yankee horse that he had taught to perform certain tricks. A while back her father had been one of a crowd of men watching Ham put the animal through its paces. As it performed, it had thrown a shoe and its tender foot had caused the horse to try to pick its way more slowly and carefully on the rocky road, but Ham had whipped it on, then rode it home at a gallop along the rough, sharp road. The horse was permanently lamed.

Tonight, too, she had seen another side of Ham's selfishness, a humor carelessly cruel. During the party at the Burkes', she had wandered out into the yard where some of the boys had gathered in a circle. They were watching a boy named Sparrow. In truth, he was not a boy at all but a man who had never reached his full growth either in body or mind, and, since he was the child of an unmarried girl who had long since left Nantahala County, the community had made him their personal entertainer, their court fool.

"One more dance, Sparrow," she had heard Ham Nelson say, the flick of command in his voice as sharp as the flick at the end of the buggy whip he had been using. And she could see the poor witty's shuffling feet begin to move again.

Lydia had gone across the yard, forgetting herself in her sudden anger at this amusement. When she had reached the group of boys, she had not known what to say, however. Sparrow had stopped dancing. The others broke their circle and stood back.

"Here, boy." Ham Nelson had taken the situation in hand, offering Sparrow the choice of a dime or a cent lying on his outstretched palm. "Here, boy, take either piece of money you want."

And the witty had chosen the cent.

"Good boy, Sparrow"—Ham had winked at the others—"you

26

got the biggest." The men nudged one another and laughed. It was a familiar ritual in the valley.

A little later, when they were alone, Lydia had talked with Sparrow. "Why do you always take the cent?" she asked. "Don't you know a dime is worth more?"

And the boy-man had answered, "If Sparrow took the dime, they would stop giving him anything."

Then she had known that the witty understood more than people ever realized. He knew his position; the wretchedness of his life was real and raw to him. Just recalling the look in his eyes as he spoke with her, Lydia knew she could never respect anyone who had deviled him. She would never ride out with Ham Nelson again.

"Lydia," Ham was saying to her, his eyes bold and his voice easy, "it's always been in my nature to want the best, and I've not been often denied. I'd be proud if you'd be mine, too."

She was speechless. His proposal became mixed up with poor Sparrow's words back at the party. Ham mistook her silence.

"You and me, we could build things in this valley the likes of which it's never seen. You be my wife and——"

"No," she had finally gasped. "I—I couldn't."

He would not grasp her refusal. "Now you give it some thought and——"

But she wanted to be finished with this once and for all. "No." She pulled her arm loose from his clutch and was dimly aware of the bruise his tight fingers had caused. "I can't marry you, Ham."

"Can't?" he asked roughly then.

"I don't love you," she said.

"Won't, not can't," he said. "Well, you could learn that. I'd make it easy for you . . ."

She remembered the high-spirited, lame horse. She shook her head. Her hands were trembling and she held them behind her so that he would not know.

He was angered by her stubbornness. "I never have been beggar to anybody," he said. He reached toward her, but she dodged his grasp and climbed into the buggy.

They drove home at a trot.

After she had married Mark and they came here to live, Ham had ridden by their house one time on a fine sorrel saddle horse, spoken briefly to Mark about division of the corn crop, and left without speaking to her as she stood in the yard with a sedge grass broom in her hand. She wondered if his boots had been especially polished for this visit; they had never before looked so trim and spotless. . . .

Oh, no, it would not be the Nelsons who would look after her while Mark was away to war. And her mother had been wrong when she said Lydia was left alone after Mark had gone. She did have another living soul near, so near she could feel its every least move. The wonder and pleasure of this filled her mind, even as the firelight now filled the room; and her foreboding was lost. The heat of the fire baked against her face and her legs drawn up under the big nightgown.

She had not noticed the pale grey light at the window, perhaps she had even dozed for a little while, her head on her knees, she couldn't be sure, before she heard the sound of a horse's hoofs outside. They were quick, galloping. She realized all at once that she was in her gown, her hair loose, falling around her shoulders and down her back. Had she been dreaming so long that the day was already far spent or who could be coming so soon in the morning?

"Lydia, Lydia!" It seemed a familiar voice grown unfamiliar with breathless hoarseness.

She grabbed an old coat of Mark's off of a peg above the bed and flung it around her as she loosened the latch on the door and stepped outside.

Robert was hitching his horse, then running toward her, stumbling. "Lydia, you've got to come. They were there. They came in the night. Mama bolted the doors and told us they'd take what they wanted outside and then go away!"

"Robert! Who? Who came to Mama's?" Lydia shook him.

"That's what I'm telling you. The outliers!"

"Oh, dear God!" She had closed her mind against the stories of raiders who banded together under no flag but one of robbery and cruelty and took from helpless Unionist and Confederate alike.

"They rode around outside a long time; we crouched by the windows listening in the dark while they rounded up all Papa's livestock. They even got the saddles out of the barn. We could hear some of them driving off the cattle, shouting that they would sell them to the army. Mama thought that would satisfy them, but then they came to the house."

Lydia leaned against the door. "What did they do?"

"They broke down the doors. They had cloths over their faces, only their mean eyes could we see. They took Mama outside and asked her where Papa is. 'Where you ought to be!' she cried. Then they asked her where we keep our meat. She wouldn't tell them." Tears were rolling down his cheeks.

"Robert, what's happened to Mama?"

"They made us go back in the house, then they took Mama down in the field beyond the corncrib and barn, and we couldn't see even the lights from their torches any more. I left Kate to look after the others and I slipped out and went to the Caldwells, then came on down to the Nelsons. None of the men folks were home anywhere. The women were afraid when I told them it was the outliers had taken Mama. But Mrs. Nelson let me borrow a horse to ride up here for you. Lydia, you've got to come quick!"

"Oh, yes. Yes." Fear lay like a cold stone in the pit of her stomach. She moved as quickly as she could for all her heaviness, dressing, covering the fire without thinking what she was doing, mounting the tired horse behind Robert. And all the while her mother's face was plain before her.

2nd
CHAPTER

Lydia and Robert found their mother pinioned between the rails of a fence that enclosed the pasture beyond the barn. The rails had been used like stocks, the lower ones holding her feet while the two upper rails were pressed tightly together, as close as their roughness would allow, binding her wrists. They saw her at a distance, hanging in that awkward, disgraceful position, and they rushed to release her. A flock of crows in a field beyond, startled by their presence, cried shrilly and flew into the edge of the woods.

"Mama! Mama!"

"Hush, Robert, she can't hear you." Lydia was already kneeling beside her mother, tilting back the small wrinkled face that fell like a wilted flower. Sarah Moore's eyes were closed and her hair was loose in stray wisps and locks. "She's mercifully unconscious."

The boy struggled to lift the heavy rails while Lydia held her mother's limp body from falling. When they had freed her, they could see the bruises on legs and arms; her ankles and wrists were purple and swollen. "Look," Lydia said, laying one of her mother's hands in her own. The finger tips were raw and bloody.

"Why did they do it to her, Lydia?" Robert whispered, and al-

30

though there was no one near to overhear and no reason for it, Lydia understood why he had whispered.

"There's no why to it, Robert." She felt tears starting, hot and salty, behind her eyes. Her mother was so small, lying there on the cold ground in a torn brown dress. Hate surged through her for the men who had been so wantonly cruel. "They'll be punished. Oh, they must be punished, somehow, sometime!"

"I'll find them, I'll kill them myself!" Her brother sprang up from his knees. "If I can't go to fight in the wars, then at least I can fight for Mama."

"No, no!" What was she saying? What was happening that she could be making a boy talk of killing? And all while she carried a child. "We must get Mama home, Robert."

The body was a dead weight, but between them they carried their mother up the slope, through the barn lot and finally into the house. The three girls, Kate and Annie Marie and Elizabeth, ran to turn down the bed, unlace their mother's shoes, bring a cold cloth for her forehead and a basin of water so Lydia could bathe the bruised wrists and ankles. Once, when her raw finger tips brushed against the rough edge of the bed, Sarah Moore groaned.

"God be thanked, she's coming to. God be thanked," Lydia said to herself, over and over in a frantic silent litany. Outwardly she must remain calm. She was the oldest. She was a woman married now, steady and knowing. At least she must appear so to the little ones who had no one else on whom to lean. Their eyes were reddened by crying from the night before and wide with fright for what they had seen then and for their mother now.

Out of the silence of their watching and waiting, Annie Marie asked suddenly, "Have the men killed Mama?"

"No; oh, dear, no." Lydia turned and threw her arms around the shivering shoulders of the little girl. "She's unconscious for a little while, but she'll be awake in no time. She's been hurt, but we must help her get well. Robert, it's getting cold in here. You and Kate go and bring in more wood and build up the fire. Annie Marie, you take Elizabeth and tidy up the room so everything will be all fit and fine when Mama wakes up."

They busied themselves eagerly, glad to have some helping part to perform. And Lydia looked at her mother, working with her gently, praying inside herself, calling silently: "Wake up, Mama. Come back to life. Now, Mama. You've got to be all right. For Papa, for my baby, for all of us."

And at last her mother came to consciousness. Her eyes opened and she looked at each one of them and nodded slightly. When she started to reach out her hand, her whole body flinched. She lifted her arms slowly and looked at her wrists and fingers. To Lydia, the middle and fore fingers of her right hand appeared especially twisted and swollen. "Mama, they might be broken," she said softly. "Should I bind them up?"

Her mother looked at her without changing expression. The flashing brightness was no longer in her eyes. "My children need meat," she said. "With the stock stolen and winter still on us, my children would be hungry!"

"Hush, Mama, hush." Lydia choked in saying it.

"I didn't tell them," she said, but her look made it also a question. When Lydia could not answer, because it had never occurred to her to look and see if the men had got what they wanted, the hams and shoulders and sides of pork her father had helped salt down before he left, her mother was troubled. "I didn't tell. I didn't?"

"Skin up into the secret part of the loft, Robert, and make sure the meat's still there," Lydia said. She wanted to warn him not to tell if it should be gone, if in the last moment of pain their mother had whispered to the men the hiding place of the vital food. There was no way to caution the boy.

They waited as he went into the adjoining room where there were loose planks in the ceiling leading to the loft. They heard him climb up, then crawl along under the low eaves to a far corner where the meat was stored. Lydia remembered the many stories during the winter of people at nearby places, even at the county seat twenty miles away, being robbed of all their food. The beginning of this winter had found many families short because there had been few men at home to make a crop, and little seed left for those who were able to plant. The war had long since taken away real coffee and left instead parched grain and chestnuts; sugar had given way to molasses and honey for those who were lucky enough to have this "long sweetening"; for salt, however, there was no substitute. When the outliers rode, there was nothing left. The countryside was pillaged and stripped. Lydia had heard only a few weeks before that a group of women at the county seat stormed one of the stores there and made the ownei give up his keys. Then they took his barrel of salt and divided it among themselves, along with hidden coffee they discovered. Decent folks were desperate and there were marauders everywhere.

A log on the fire broke in two and one end rolled out to the hearth. Lydia was thankful for the interruption. She turned away from her mother's troubled gaze for a moment. She pushed the piece of wood back into the fire and laid on a fresh oak log. As she straightened up, a sudden dizziness swirled inside her head. Her stomach rolled and she felt saliva boil up in her mouth. She clutched the edge of a table.

Robert was back in the room. "Meat's all there, snug as a bug in a rug," he sang out. "You didn't tell them a form thing, Mama," he added triumphantly.

Their mother closed her eyes. "My children would be hungry," she said, just as though they were not standing around her listening, just as though they were strangers.

Lydia left the room. Outside in the yard she retched violently. The day had turned raw, chilly after last night's wind. Nothing stirred around the farm except a few chickens and guineas, huddled together in a protected corner of the garden fence. Then she remembered that now there was nothing left to use the farm but these few fowls. Oh, it had been a long night for sure.

Kate followed her outside. Kate was fifteen and looked like her mother. "She's the spitten image of your side of the family, Sarah," folks said. "But Lydia, she favors the Moores, tall like she is with those grey cat eyes that can turn green or blue. Of course, she's got your fine brown hair with the gloss on it, but she's really more her Pappy's girl."

Kate held her pretty plump hands in front of her mouth and the

33

fingernails were ragged where she had bitten them. "Lydia, are you all right?"

Lydia nodded. She put one arm around Kate and suddenly there were tears streaming down her face. The sound of crows crying in the distance and the quiet out in the barnyards was lonesome beyond measure. Papa and Mark—when would they ever return? And now the strange stillness in her mother's face, after this terrible night when none of them would ever know just what had happened. "Katie, Katie," she sobbed, releasing all the unease and loneliness of the night before—which seemed so long ago now—and the fear for her mother which had been only partly relieved, and the wonder and anxiety for the baby to come.

"Lydia, you've got to stay with us now," Kate said, and her voice trembled, too. "You're all we've got."

As her sister spoke of the staying, a picture of the little brindle cow flashed across Lydia's mind. No one had milked her this morning. Her udders would be stiff and heavy and she would be bawling in the pasture lot. And the children inside the house here, they had eaten no breakfast. She looked at Kate and saw the tired troubled harassment stamped on her round face. All these were Lydia's responsibility and she was standing out here weeping like a ninny. She must bring her cow up here, and even though the outliers had taken all the other livestock the children would still have milk. She must feed the children and restore order and help her mother get well. What had she meant by crying like a weakling? She wiped her face on the edge of Kate's apron.

"Well, that's a-plenty of tears," she said. "Now we'd best get some breakfast going. Then I want Robert to go over on Thickety Branch—if Mrs. Nelson will let him have the loan of her horse again—and bring Aunt Tildy over to stay awhile."

"Oh, yes!" Kate's face brightened at the thought of Aunt Tildy's arrival and the herbs and roots, the quarreling and the laughter, the tales and threats that would come with her.

"And while Robert's bringing Aunt Tildy, I'll have to go and fetch my cow. You must mind the house here, Kate. Now you come and sit by Mama while I fix some food."

34

She led the way back inside and set the big Dutch oven on the hearth. There was only a handful of wheat flour left in the wooden bin and Lydia knew her Mother had been saving it for her brother and father when they came in from the war, but with quick determination she decided there would never be a better moment than this to put it to use. Annie Marie and Elizabeth hovered close by, watching every movement as she stirred the bread.

"I'm plumb empty as a dog-sucked egg," Robert said with a little swagger, trying to sound like the men who gathered at Burkes' mill or elsewhere in the valley.

"Then take this knife and cut a piece off that side meat in the loft. Maybe if Mama smells it cooking, she'll know for sure she saved it."

Reminder of the night before cast another quiet over the room. "Lydia, will those men on horses with their faces hidden come back again?" little Elizabeth asked.

"No." She shook her head, stirring sour milk into the flour, kneading it, and her certainty was communicated even to herself. "When the bushwhackers first started riding, I heard Papa say they struck and moved on, cowards that they are. They get some neighbor in a community to turn traitor and lead them to those who are helpless, where the men are away, and show which places have the best stock for the taking."

Annie Marie asked the question that had also filled Lydia's mind as she spoke. "Which neighbor led them to our house?"

"I don't know, Annie Marie. I spoke in haste. Maybe they just chanced on our place. No one who knows Papa and Mama could do this to them." But conviction was lacking in her heart. Had someone in the valley really been with the outliers last night?

It was a long while before Lydia McQueen cried again. On that bleak morning in the yard with Kate, she knew that she had grown into problems larger than herself, into trouble beyond tears. If strength was what was called for, then she could be strong. She would be stout enough to carry every day as it came.

The room was filled with the smell of wheat bread baking in the oven on the hearth and pork slices frying to a crisp brown over a bed of coals. While the food cooked, she tried once more to arouse her mother from the stupor that held her. But the older woman would not speak. Once or twice she murmured a few disconnected words, "Virginia . . . my mother said it was always cool . . . high ceilings," and when Lydia tried to soothe the injured finger tips with some salve that had been on the mantel, she shuddered and drew her hands to the other side of the bed, next to the wall. Lydia was at a loss to know what to do. If Aunt Tildy could come—her mother's sister, two years younger than Sarah Moore but seeming ten years older—perhaps she could find a remedy.

Lydia took the meat off the fire. The bread needed to bake a little longer. She sat down in the rocker and rested, yielding to the movements of the baby within her. She knew they had a long walk ahead of them that afternoon and the sky was already threatening snow.

Somehow, with the last strength of her muscles and because she knew she must, Lydia rode back to the cabin behind Robert, on his way to fetch Aunt Tildy, and led the brindle cow to her mother's house. The road, little more than a frozen mud lane, was deserted. She walked as fast as she could, but her mind outraced her feet. A half-deaf old man from down the valley, hauling a wagonload of wood, passed her in the middle of the road.

She set her mind to thinking how it might feel to be deaf. This was a boon she had learned long ago when she was just a child working endless rows in the field, this putting of her thoughts on something else so that her mind did not share her body's labor. Now she would think of deafness. Immediately all the common sounds around rushed into her consciousness: a creek in the distance splashing over pebbles and boulders, the stirring of a slight wind in the trees beside the road, the thud and clash of the cow's hoofs as they rose and fell and struck a frequent stone. There was the rustling and scurrying of a hundred unseen feet and wings in the woods and fields through which she passed. Often before she had listened to these whispers of little hidden lives going forward with no need or knowledge of the man-world all around, and the thought pleased her. Under fallen leaves and bits of bark and log, through tufts of weeds in the fields and over pads of moss in the

36

woods, their tiny feet scampered, their noses sniffed, they ate and sheltered themselves and bore young and fought and died.

Sometimes at night at home, when she and Kate and Annie Marie had had to sleep three in a bed and she had felt she would smother from the closeness and the heaviness of their sleep (she had paid Kate and Annie Marie a trunkful of pretties over the years to take the middle and let her sleep on the outside), she would ease out of bed and go to the window and look out at the night. All would seem so quiet—the animals asleep in the barn or pasture, the chickens roosting in the cedar tree—but if she waited, she could hear the small rustles and settlings of the daytime creatures and the furry feathery rush and plunge of nighttime creatures. Once in a while, as she sat there, a whippoorwill would call under the window, an owl would hoot from down in the pasture, or out in the woods there would be the quavery little cry of a screech owl, and these were her favorite sounds. They bespoke the mystery of the night, not sweetly but hauntingly, half savagely, the way it was. Ah, the way it was even among humans last night. That's what the men who had left the nerve ends of her mother's fingers raw and naked, who had smashed her hands between the heavy rails and fastened her there in humility, had been: savages, beyond all the little wild varmints living by nature in the woods. . . . Now her mind had made the circle and she was back plodding with the cow toward home.

Farther on, a half-naked boy perhaps ten years old, coming around a curve ahead, jumped out of the road and hid behind a laurel bush until she was past. He was almost certainly one of the Bludsoe children: she had caught a glimpse of curly black hair. Any other boy hereabouts would want to talk, satisfy his curiosity as to where she was taking the cow.

The Bludsoes, they were as unfamiliar to the valley, as untamed, as the owls or the panthers she sometimes heard at night. Big Matt Bludsoe was the pappy of them all, although they said his mother, when she was still alive, had ruled even him. From scraps of talk she'd overheard, and the sound of his name, and her own imagination, Lydia had made up a picture of Big Matt in her mind. Someday she'd be glad to learn if he was really half a foot taller than any other man, with hands as strong and square as wedges and a great dark shaggy head. There were men who said Matt Bludsoe could lift singlehanded the copper tank for a full-sized still. Surely he should know how. For as long as she remembered or had heard, the Bludsoes, from their eyrie up on Stony Ridge and Creek, had supplied the valley and the county seat beyond with whiskey. When there were gatherings of any sort, it was Bludsoe corn that finally, as her mother said, "leveled it into a rough free-for-all."

Big Matt's boys, Young Matt and Morgan and Euell, were reported to follow every move he made and do whatever he ordered. Some said Morgan, the day he turned twenty-one, challenged his pappy's leadership and "they had a master fight." The story, like fire, grew by what it fed on until, at last telling, Matt and Morgan had fought all over the mountain, flattening bushes, uprooting stumps, bloodying the ground for yards around. And when they were finished and Morgan lay on the ground gasping for the breath of life, it was told that Big Matt went to the barn and got his bull whip and finished off the chore of teaching his son who was master.

There were many stories of Stony Ridge and Bludsoe cruelty and rage, withdrawal from the rest of the world for fifteen, twenty years, since Big Matt and Callie his wife, had first gone in there with his mother, Vashti, who was tall and strong as any man, although she lived only a year or so after they came. Lydia had often wondered about these women—they had been from the Low Country of South Carolina was all she ever heard—and she wished she could know the true story of their coming here and how they endured the wildness and the loneliness of the mountains and the hard men who ruled their lives.

Some folks in the valley said the Bludsoes on Stony Creek were rich with treasures few outsiders had seen, hauled in the wagons brought when they came taking up some vague land grant from the days of the old war, the Revolution. No one could say for certain about the riches or the claim to the land, but there was no call to dispute either. Who would want the land on Stony Ridge? Always for certain, however, was the evil aura around the Bludsoes, the shadow of blood. "They've got dark blood in them from somewhere . . ."

"They're mixed. They claim from Indian or Portugee, I'd say more likely from the Guinea Coast."

There was laughter.

So Bludsoe children darted off the public roads and men who wanted a jar of Bludsoe "stuff" had to go up to the mouth of Stony Creek and fetch it for themselves, and there was a wide distance of pride and arrogance and ignorance on both sides between the valley and Stony Ridge.

Lydia could almost see the craggy mountain there in the distance as she walked along now. A few low clouds hung over the rounded pinnacle in front of it. The clouds reminded her that it was growing colder. She pulled the cow to a faster step. Her legs throbbed with a dull steady ache. There was no need trying any longer to keep her mind off her weary, painful body. Determination carried her home. She half stumbled, half crawled the last mile in darkness.

Midafternoon the next day Robert and Aunt Tildy arrived. How welcome was the sound of the big woman's rough gentleness, beginning in the yard as she dismounted.

"Eh law, when the good Lord made my limbs he gave me a generous plenty and I reckon he meant for me to get over the ground on my own strength, not atop some critter and a fool piece of sidesaddle leather."

She stretched her stiff legs. By the time she came to the door the heavy grey shawl was already half off her head and shoulders. She thrust open the door and surveyed the big room.

"A fine fix! A pretty pickle you got yourselves into this time!" Then she flung out her arms and the least children rushed into her wide embrace while Kate and Lydia followed to kiss her shyly. They were not a demonstrative family; the first time Sarah and Jesse Moore had ever kissed in the presence of their children was the day he left for war. Displays of emotion had always embarrassed them, except with Aunt Tildy, who showed affection and anger, disgust and pity, as readily and naturally as weather changing. As she stood in the room now, holding Annie Marie and Elizabeth to her, she seemed to Lydia a tower of strength.

Matilda MacIntosh had never married. During the years when she was of marrying age, her father had been wrestling a farm out of the North Carolina hills to which the family had newly moved, and it was his hardship to have three older children who were girls. Sarah, the oldest, was her mother's favorite and the only one who showed no interest at all in things outside the house. When she worked in the fields, as they all did because they must, it was a heavy chore for her and nothing more. But Matilda saw ahead to what the farm might be someday, when tree roots were finally burned and rotted out and the stump-pocked fields were clear. She worked shoulder to shoulder with her father until the muscles in her arms were hard and her skin was tough and brown. Crow's-feet of laughter appeared early around her mouth and eyes, and the wrinkles on her forehead came from squinting against the sun.

"Matilda ought to be thinking about getting married," her mother said.

"Tildy's the best man I got around the place," her father joked. "Don't go talking me out of my help!"

The boys Matilda knew liked her. She bluntly said whatever came to mind, but there was no malice in her. They raced with her and skipped stones on the water and had close contests in throwing horseshoes, but the wish to marry her seemed never to occur to them. Her older sister, Sarah, married Jesse Moore, and Matilda gave them a piece of crochet work she had made when she was small and saved in her "wedding chest." Her younger sister, Adaline, married a man moving west, across the Mississippi to Missouri country, and she gave them a quilt out of the chest. Then the "set of boys," as her father called the four youngest children, came on, and she helped raise them and they married and after a while there was little left in her wedding chest and the years for her marrying had run out.

Tildy had never birthed children of her own, but she had cared for many when they needed her: her brothers' and sisters' babies, those of neighbors. "With no chick nor child to my name," she sometimes claimed, "I reckon I've washed more dirty little hippens

40

and nursed more croup than any mammy in this or a dozen valleys." No one could dispute it.

When Robert had come telling her about the bushwhackers and Sarah and the children, she had grabbed her shawl and her fat leather satchel that stood ready day or night. Now she set the small satchel on the table and looked at her sister on the bed. "What's she doing here in the kitchen room?"

"I wanted her close by," Lydia said, "so I could see after her while I tended to chores in here."

The shrewd old eyes took in the girl's drawn face and heavy figure. "Can't step so lively from room to room now, ha? Well, we'll help all that. Kate, go fix the bed in the next room so we can put your mama in there, let her rest up good."

Aunt Tildy was walking over to where Sarah lay. Her voice softened and finally faded away when she stood beside the bed. Sarah had heard the familiar voice and she looked up with the flicker of a weary smile around her pale lips. "Tildy." She went to raise one hand, then frowned.

"Eh law, Sally, I'm right here. I'd a-been here before if there'd been any inkling in anybody's mind that that scum of the earth was riding hereabouts. Could I lay my hands on them, I'd gut them like bantams . . ." and while she was speaking so harshly, she bent and gently smoothed the covers on her sister's bed, tenderly lifting each arm so that she could examine the swollen wrists and hands. "A poultice, I'll make a little poultice to rob the swelling and soothe the pain. Then a touch of spicewood tea to help tonic your appetite. He made the herbs and leaves for healing, He can——"

"Herbs." Sarah's voice was small but clear and the children waited to hear what she would say after her silence. "Tildy, do you remember Mother telling us about her herbs back in Virginia, and where she grew up how each big house had its own garden with nothing but herbs growing inside the picket fence?"

"Yes, Sally, yes." Aunt Tildy's voice was soothing, yet it was as though she spoke to a child, to Elizabeth, and Lydia felt a catch in her throat. "You rest now, Sally, and we'll visit tomorrow and the next days after that."

Aunt Tildy followed Lydia to the fireplace and turned the girl toward her to look her in the eyes. "She's had a rough go of it, Lyddy. Her mind's gone back to happier times for a spell; she'll be all right after a few days." One hand patted Lydia's cheek. "You look all tuckered yourself, child. Go rest. Aunt Tildy's here to see about everything."

There was a blessed relief in lying down and yet hearing the sound of the house's work going on all around her. Pothooks rattled and lids clanged. She dozed.

When she waked, the house was filled with a sweet aroma. She remembered the tea Aunt Tildy had mentioned and knew there was a pot of spicewood twigs steeping in boiling water on the back of the hearth.

Aunt Tildy's voice filled the house, too, not loudly but fully, a preoccupied mixture of humming and words:

"Now gather 'round, you ladies fair,
    And count yourselves quite lucky,
For 'tis not often that you meet
    A hunter from Kentucky.
Oh, Kentucky, the hunters of Kentucky . . ."

Lydia had heard Mark sing that selfsame ballad, telling the story of Andy Jackson and his men and the English and their defeat at the battle of New Orleans. One night—a week before he went off to war, it was—they were sitting outdoors under the poplars near the spring, catching a breath of air where a faint breeze stirred. September had brought a hot spell and Lydia and Mark had worked together through the long afternoon stripping leaves off the corn stalks for winter fodder for the cow. After a cold supper of food left from noon dinner, they walked down to the poplar grove to rest and cool and bring a bucket of fresh water for the night.

"I reckon I couldn't begin to name how lonesome I'll be for you while you're gone," she had said, stroking her fingers through his crisp brown hair.

"No more than I'll be for you," he answered, smiling as he stretched out in the thick, cool grass at her feet and looked up at the sky. "I'm sorry I had to go opposite to your papa and Paul in joining up," he said after a while.

"I wouldn't fault neither of you for it," she answered. Then, softly, "Should you be killed, seems I couldn't bear it."

He looked at her fondly, considering her face for several minutes. "You'd bear it, Lyddy."

A breeze rustled the high branches and scattered a few wide yellow leaves around them. Absently she picked up one of the fresh fallen leaves and put its stem between her teeth. The bittersweet taste and smell of poplar bark had reminded her of spring. After this evening it would always remind her of September—and this quiet moment when she and Mark drew so close. There were many kinds of closeness she had discovered: the kind they knew as man and wife in body in the fulness and happiness of their strength and youth, the kind they knew as man and wife in spirit when they shared each other's thought without words. She could not say which was better. It was best to have both: the gentleness out here under the trees, the passion later inside.

"Ever hear the tune about the Kentucky men and the War of Eighteen Twelve, Lydia?" Mark asked.

"No," she answered through the poplar leaf.

His voice was deep and clear. He sang softly, his strong body relaxed and easy on the grass, and as he sang she traced the features of his face with the leaf stem: dark blue eyes set far apart, the straight lines of heavy eyebrows, aquiline nose.

> "I suppose you've read it in the prints
> How Packenham attempted
> To make Old Hickory Jackson wince
> But soon his schemes repented.
> Old Packenham he made his brags
> If he in fight was lucky,
> He'd have our gals in cotton rags
> In spite of Old Kentucky.

But Jackson he was wide awake,
    He was not scared a trifle,
For well we knew what aim to take
    With our Kentucky rifle.
He led us down to Cypress Swamp,
    The ground was low and mucky,
And quickly 'round the General flocked
    The hunters of Kentucky.

They did not let our patience tire
    Before they showed their faces,
We did not choose to waste our fire
    And snugly kept our places.
And when so near to see them wince
    We thought it time to stop 'em,
It would have done you good I think
    To see Kentuckians drop 'em.

They found at last 'twas vain to fight
    Where lead was all their booty,
And so they wisely took to flight
    And left us all our beauty.
And now if danger e'er annoys
    Remember what our fate is,
Just send for us Kentucky boys
    And we'll protect your ladies.

    Oh, Kentucky, the hunters of Kentucky!"

The last light had gone from the sky by the time he finished and the evening star was shining directly above them.

"It's a gay tune," Lydia said.

"It's true words," Mark said. "And what happened in that war will happen in this one. We'll fight for the United States and we'll win. I'll be back home before you ever expect me, live and peart as the hunters of Kentucky."

She laid her head on the grass beside his and they looked up at the evening star together. . . .

Lydia buried her face in the pillow, remembering that good time, that evening, before he had gone to fight. In the next room, Aunt Tildy was humming the last verse of the "Hunters." Lydia heard her tell Kate to carry in more wood while Annie Marie and Elizabeth went to search the barn loft and corners for nests the hens had stolen out. "Your mama needs an egg for breakfast."

Lydia realized how she longed for a man's voice and footstep in the place once more. She wasn't low-rating Aunt Tildy who was salt and savor of their lives just now, but she was hungry for male voices and laughter, male appetites at the table, solid male footfalls on the floor.

During the next few days, as people in the valley heard of their troubles and came to see Sarah Moore and her children, Lydia's longing was scarcely diminished, for these were the women, too. In her buggy came plump Mrs. Nelson, Captain Cass Nelson's wife and Lieutenant Hamilton Nelson's mother, with her wide troubled eyes "as blue and blank as painted china," Aunt Tildy said after she had gone. "She's a poor, cowed creature, living with a grasping man."

Mrs. Nelson told Lydia she was sorry they were not on her farm now, she and Mark, but surely they would return when Mark came home from war. "It's fearful that Mrs. Moore should have been so mistreated. . . . Who could it have been? Everyone's so frightened to try to do anything . . ."

Emma Caldwell came, excitable, curious, peering into every corner, telling of her husband's exploits at Chattanooga, his wound at Kennesaw Mountain, making a boast even of her son Gentry's rejection from the Conscript Act for heart condition.

"Well, mercy alive!" Emma Caldwell exclaimed to Sarah and Aunt Tildy and Lydia and the children, "this was the most heathenish thing ever happened in our valley. 'Gentry,' I told my boy when I heard about it, 'Gentry, there's just one set of folks around here could do a thing like that to neighbors, and that's the savages that live up on Stony Ridge. You mark my words, when you get to the bottom of this—and I hope somebody'll keep on and find the truth or mercy alive none of us will ever feel safe

45

again—when the bottom's touched, I'd be willing to bet there's Bludsoes there. They're a canker sore on this community!' "

"That big, overgrown Caldwell boy's got heart condition all right, and dropsy, too," Aunt Tildy said when Emma had left. "He drops in a chair and can't find the heart to get out of it."

And Ida Burke came to see Sarah Moore. Old Lady Burke, some called her. She was old, for a fact, but she had lived hard, doing man's labor in the fields for days and years until she had long since lost important features of age or womanliness. Her feet and hands were splay and tough with calluses; her face was broad and flat with a scattering of whiskers on the chin. Her hair disappeared in a knot under a wide bonnet Lydia had never seen her remove. James and John Burke, who ran the mill, were her sons— big lusty fellows not overly burdened by thought for yesterday or tomorrow, enjoying every day as it rolled in, work and play alike. They convinced the conscription officers who came around that their keeping the mill open could do more to aid the war than their service, Union or Confederate. And every year the three of them, James and John Burke and their mother, Ida, came to look more alike—wide faces the color of sun-baked earth, wide mouths waiting to spread in a ready grin, shoulders a trifle stooped from the heaviness of all they hauled and lifted at mill and farm alike.

"It would be hard saying what wickedness loosed these bush-whackers on the countryside," Ida Burke said, holding a lump of snuff in her lower lip. "I knew something dreadful was to happen the very night they rode. A whippoorwill called right under my window. 'There's no surer sign of bad trouble, of death,' I said to James. We drove the bird away and he come back again. I knew then there was trouble somewhere sure that night." She spat a long brown stream into the fire.

So they came and comforted:

"Folks are frightened up and down the valley. Such fearful times and wicked men."

"That heathenish offspring of Big Matt Bludsoe, this is some of their doing."

"When that nightbird come right under my window and commenced its crying, I knew something wrong would happen."

At last Aunt Tildy broke the ebb and flow of their chorus. "Sally needs her rest. You-all were thoughty to come. Come back again and sit a spell."

Gradually the days passed. The nightmare of the outliers was dimmed by the needs of every day; there were rumors of battles over in the eastern Carolinas and up in Virginia.

Aunt Tildy cared for Sarah's hands with some of the concoctions she had brought in her satchel and finally even the exposed nerve ends at the tips of the fingers healed and were no longer painful with the screaming sensitivity of a hundred tiny conductors carrying the pain-message to the brain. It would be a long time, however, before Sarah could spin or sew again, her chosen household chores. When the children saw their mother around the house once more, even though she had little to say except for a lengthy reminiscence once in a while about Virginia, they settled into a routine of work directed by Aunt Tildy.

Knowing how his mother favored wild game, Robert combed the woods and brought in an occasional squirrel or rabbit. Twice there was pheasant and once he surprised them with a wild turkey, proud of the keen eye and steady shot that had made this prize possible.

"Could men set aside looking after the affairs of the big world long enough to stay home and look after their own little plot and parcel, appears to me things would be a heap better off, North and South," Aunt Tildy quarreled as she went about the house.

March came, time for spring plowing, but there was no beast to pull the plow. The fields stood covered in last year's stubble of stalks and weeds. Lydia could not bear to think of the spring passing without planting being done.

"Robert, Kate," she called one morning when there was a breeze from the south and she could smell the first fresh fragrance of blossoms, "we can't let everything run to seed like this. Let's try to hitch up Pearly and see what we can do."

"Your cow, Lydia?" Robert asked.

She nodded. "We can try her."

Kate went to the pasture to drive her in, while Robert searched the barn for the single yoke Papa had used on an ox they once

47

worked. Lydia petted the little cow and talked to her while the other two tried to put on the ill-fitting gear and hook the plow behind. Their efforts were only lamely successful. The cow pulled and kicked a few times, backed and balked as the weight of the plow became heavy in the field, but with Lydia leading her by the halter she made it down the length of one row and back again. Robert, guiding the plow, struggling to hold it to a deep furrow in the rough ground, grinned at Lydia as they looked back to see what the first round had done.

"We scratched it up a mite," he said.

"Enough for planting!" she answered triumphantly. "We can do the rest of the breaking up with our hoes when we drop the seeds. Come on, Robert, let's get our little muley-cow to work again." And Lydia led her up and down, up and down, until Aunt Tildy called that it was time for dinner.

"You've done a good man-sized job this morning," Aunt Tildy said at the table. "You mustn't go back this afternoon, Lyddy."

"But, Aunt Tildy, I've got to! We———"

"Your times's seven months, or better, along. You can't be jerked at any more, unless you'd rather have a corn patch than a baby."

"Yes, Lydia"—her mother laid one scarred hand on her arm—"we must have the baby and then we'll have it christened properly. I've saved the christening dress my mother made for me—so much lace, so many little stitches . . ."

"That will be nice, Mama."

"Robert, you and Kate and Pearly will have to go it the best you can the rest of the day," Aunt Tildy said.

"Pull Pearly easy but steady," Lydia told Kate, "and talk to her. . . ."

"I've nothing to say to a cow."

"Then say the alphabet." Lydia was sharp. "It's the sound of your voice gentles her. Don't you understand, Kate, she's all we've got? We've got to make her do, or do without."

The younger girl nodded, but Lydia knew the conviction of their need was not yet firm in her mind. Nevertheless Kate and Robert worked through the afternoon, resting Pearly after every round, and by evening the field showed a sizable patch of freshly turned ground.

When Lydia went to milk, she slipped out a lick of salt for Pearly. Salt was so scarce people had been scraping dirt off their smokehouse floors and boiling it to save the salt that had fallen there from the meat hung to cure during years past. She gave the little cow an extra nubbin of precious corn, too. There was not quite as much milk as usual that night.

By grinding no more corn for meal and feeding no more to Pearly, by hoarding every grain they shelled and scouring the corn-crib floor, they got together enough to plant the field. There was no seed for the other fields, however, and besides they were too rough, too filled with tough roots and stones, for the little cow and the boy and girl to break the ground. So they bent all their energies to this one spot, carrying off the rocks that seemed to appear and multiply overnight, breaking up heavy clods, laying off rough rows, and then, the last week of April when the ground seemed warm, dropping the seeds, covering them carefully.

"A hasty hand makes a wasteful crop," Aunt Tildy said, fearful that they had planted too early, but Lydia had been driven to get this crop in the ground before she was brought to her bed and had other work to do.

"It will grow," she said serenely. And Aunt Tildy stole a long look at the girl's confident grey eyes above her high flushed cheeks, the thick chestnut-colored hair, brown with amber and red high lights, falling in two heavy braids around thin shoulders thrust back to help carry the weight on her. Yes, Aunt Tildy felt sure the corn would grow.

And on the first day of May, Jesse Moore came home from the war. "We were whipped," he said, surprised that they had not yet heard of the Confederate surrender and halt of hostilities. "Some of us North Carolinians were with Lee to the end. It came at a place called Appomattox Court House."

He was sitting at the kitchen table and he looked at each one of them as if seeking some sign that one of them understood what had happened, what the day had been like, there on that distant farm in Virginia. But he saw that they did not know, could never know, and so he simply wiped one dusty sleeve across his bearded face, over his tired aching eyes. "General Grant let us keep our horses. He knew we'd have spring plowing to do when we got back home. I'd a-been here sooner, but I hunted up Paul. Found out he was at Richmond and come by there to see him."

"Why is Paul in Richmond if the war is over?" his wife cried.

"He's in the Chimborazo Hospital. Don't fret, Sarah; he's going to be all right. Paul had an accident . . ." He looked at Aunt Tildy questioningly.

She nodded her head. "Truth never hurt as much as suspicion," she said. "Speak your piece."

"Paul lost an arm, Sarah," he said quietly.

She gave one little cry. The children looked at each other gravely, wondering how it would be to greet an elder brother who had only one arm.

"Which one, Papa?" Lydia asked.

"His left," he said, unconsciously touching his own left arm, rubbing the sleeve.

"That's good, Mama," Lydia said. "He'll still have the use of his right." She was trying to clutch at any tidbit that would ease this blow.

"How did it happen, Mr. Moore?" Lydia's mother asked.

"We never talked about it, Sarah. There's been a heap of hard fighting over all these long months; the hospital was full and most were hurt worse than Paul. The little time I was with him we talked about getting home, the work we'd have to do. We didn't speak of any battles——"

"Had your craws full of fighting, I reckon," Aunt Tildy snorted.

Jesse Moore nodded slowly. "That's right, Tildy."

With a quick gesture she reached over and patted his shoulder. "Well"—she stood abruptly—"since you've come back to mind your own business and tend to what's yours, I reckon we'd better not let you starve."

"Papa"—Lydia leaned forward from behind the younger children, unwilling to mar the pleasure of the moment, yet unable to contain her question any longer. "Papa, you brought me no news of Mark? You never heard any words of him?"

A slight frown creased her father's forehead. "Nary a word, Lydia."

"Would he a-had time to reach home before you after the peace was made?"

"I couldn't say. Depending on where he was, it might take him longer than me. There's no need a-tall to give up hope."

She turned away from them and went quickly out into the yard. For the moment she could not bear their kind faces, their loving reassurances. She felt guilty for her sadness, her despair, at this moment when Papa had come home and Paul was alive, and truly she was thankful. But what of Mark? Mark must come soon. The baby would not wait much longer and Mark must be with her when their son was born.

3rd
CHAPTER

The days slipped into a new routine with their father home and a horse to work the farm. Robert, now that there was a man to band with, avoided the house and women and Aunt Tildy's endless requests for "one more bucket of water." Kate took over the chore of milking when Lydia admitted it was difficult for her to sit on the little three-legged stool.

"Pull easy on that left hind tit, Kate. It's been sore. But remember to keep milking it even if she kicks a little, or it'll cake and dry up and never be any more good. Just treat my little Pearly gentle."

"Do you be as foolish over your baby as you are over that cow," Kate said to her older sister, "he'll be rotten spoiled inside a week."

"I aim to take care of whatever depends on me," Lydia replied calmly.

The second Monday in May, a week after her father's return, Lydia awakened early. She got up with the first rooster-crow. Daylight was barely beginning to show outside in the open fields and the house was still dark. Aunt Tildy was often up and stirring by this time, but this morning she had overslept and Lydia was glad. She liked to move noiselessly through the quiet house and hear the heavy slumber of the family, peaceful, resting. She liked to open the door and step out into the new morning all by herself. There were fresh smells to drink in: dew on the grass and plowed ground, sweetness on the breeze blowing from the woods, and the sounds of early day: birds loud and clear, seeming busier than they would be again till evening, the cowbell, a guinea's pot-a-rack.

She looked up at the sky and it was bright and blue with only a handful of high clouds off at the edge of the horizon. This would be a good day to wash. She walked out to the woodyard and picked up a handful of dry splinters and chips to kindle a fire under the washpot. As she stooped to tilt the big black kettle over to one side, a pain caught at her abdomen. It was not a hard pain; it was slow and dull but very real, and when it went away, Lydia felt slightly nauseated and dizzy. She found a block of wood and sat down for a moment. Maybe this would pass and she could go on with her washing. She heard someone stirring in the house now.

The pain came again, a little like a cramp, not exactly like anything she had ever felt before. Then she knew for sure that this was the baby.

When the second pain had passed, she stood up slowly and looked around. It was a beautiful morning, a fine world into which to bring someone. She could not let even Mark's absence dim the joy her body and spirit felt in this moment. She had work to do, hard work. But it was something only she could do—she and the little body here within hers. Together they must bring forth life.

Dear God, she hoped that tiny being was perfect, with fingers and toes and limbs and features all in place—and eyes, oh yes, above all let the eyes be perfect. And she hoped the body was tough. Tough as a laurel burl to win through this struggle and all the ones to come. Another pain, longer, sharper, sent Lydia McQueen into the house where full daylight was just now dawning.

The baby was twenty-four hours a-borning. If Aunt Tildy had not been with them, Lydia knew she would have died, and the baby, too. During the days of pulling and lifting and hauling, sometime during the season of necessity and hard work, the baby had twisted. And when Robert rode in to the county seat for the doctor late that Monday afternoon, Mrs. Hornsby had sent word that her husband could not come. Dr. Hornsby was indisposed.

"Dead to the world with drink!" Aunt Tildy exclaimed. "That's how he's 'indisposed.' " Her voice made a mockery of the word. "In the meantime an innocent child can lay here and die for need of him."

"Surely Ralph Hornsby doesn't drink," Lydia's mother said, sitting in frozen helplessness by the bed which shook intermittently with the girl's labors.

"Yes, Sally, he drinks. He's drunk now. And if ever I see the wizened up little persimmon of a man again I'm going to give him some straight talk."

"No, Tildy, you mustn't do that. You mustn't feel hard toward anyone." A troubled look filled Sarah Moore's brown eyes. "Sometimes I think the worst thing I ever did to Mr. Moore was tell him about those outliers who came here, and what they did to us. He hates them and he's made terrible vows I must persuade him to give up."

Lydia writhed on the bed. Her moan was low, almost like an animal's. "Oh, child, child," her mother cried. "Tildy, what can we do? Old Mrs. Burke used to tell me a knife under the bed would help cut the pain. I never believed much in such things, but she's having such a hard time, anything that might help—what do you think?"

"We don't need Old Lady Burke's knife under that bed, we need it at old Hornsby's throat," Tildy cried in frustration and anger. She knotted one end of a sheet around the foot of the bed and gave Lydia the other end to tug on. "Sally, honey, why don't you go in there in the kitchen and be sure the men get a good fire going for the hot water we'll need after a little bit?"

"Why, yes, Tildy, yes."

When she had gone, Aunt Tildy rolled her sleeves a few inches higher above her elbow. "Looks like we're going to have to see this thing through by ourselves, girl," she said. "Let's do ourselves proud."

54

Better than two hours passed before she went from the bedroom into the kitchen, rubbing her neck and back wearily. Lydia's father and mother and the two older children were waiting, looking at her with wide eyes. Annie Marie and Elizabeth had fallen asleep on the kitchen bed where Aunt Tildy usually slept.

"Tildy, how's she doing?" Jesse Moore asked.

"Someone's got to go down to Hornsby's again, Jesse, and see if he can come. And if he's still 'indisposed,' then for God's sake bring me back his instruments."

"But, Tildy——"

"If he says I never used any instruments, you tell him he's speaking truth, but if he can't use them now, I will! Somehow, Jesse, we've got to help Lyddy get that baby turned so it can be born!"

"I'll go myself this time," he said. "I'll bring back the doctor or his instruments, one."

Lydia's labor wore on. Like wind she'd seen blow over a wheat field, rising and falling, the rhythm of her pain rose and fell. Years ago her father had read in one of the big geography books one night about volcanoes, how they erupted and subsided and erupted again, "all in the marvelous rhythmic plan of nature," the book said, and now she felt at one with those upheavals and those rhythms. The pain squeezed and wrenched her again, held on, then loosened slowly, and subsided. She wondered how long she could bear this. She wondered if she had moaned or screamed. If so, then she hadn't even been aware of it. Coming closer together all the time, the pains rolled in and lasted longer.

It was long past midnight when her father came back—alone. "Hornsby is drunk all right. I went in to see him for myself. But I brought the instruments. He tried to show me a little, in his stupor, how they should be held. Like this."

Tildy nodded. "I've helped two or three women when the doctor had to use these. I hope I've watched close enough to do Lyddy some good now." At the door she turned. "You and Kate better come to help me. Sarah's hands are still too tender."

Just after daylight the baby came, bearing two heavy bruises on its temples but headfirst, quietly, almost wearily, until Tildy held

55

its feet in one large hand and slapped its back with the other broad palm. Its gasp and cry was loud. The cry reached through the fog of pain and fatigue enveloping Lydia. Her heart leaped. "Aunt Tildy," she whispered weakly.

"It's all right, child. A big, fine, strapping boy. By the sound of him he's got a master set of lungs, too. Can you hear your son, Lydia?"

"I hear him. I see him, too."

"Let me get his eyes bathed out and swaddle him down and I'll let you see him up close."

"He's all right?"

"Nothing wrong with this boy! He just give us a hard time getting here. Now you go tell the others, Grandpa Moore, about their big fine boy, and directly my chores in here are done, I'll call them in to see."

So little David was born.

"A pure gladness he is, after all the troubles and destruction of this winter," Aunt Tildy said.

"We'll have to have a heap of birthing to make up for all the dying I saw this winter," Lydia's father said. "But a tad like this, that's special, he ought to make up for three or four ordinary run-of-the-mill lads!"

And Lydia's mother held him close to her and walked the floor. When he made the slightest sound, she took him from the bed and walked and crooned:

> "Oh, where are you going, Billy Boy, Billy Boy?
> Oh, where are you going, charming Billy?
> I'm going to seek a wife,
> For the pleasure of my life.
> She's a young thing, she cannot leave her mother."

To Lydia the baby was the sap of life itself. She had saved the name David for him, waiting before she spoke it to anyone else to make certain it was a name Mark approved and liked, but now she must go ahead and choose the child a name all by herself. She thought of the boy in the Bible who slew giants with his childish playthings, who went from a simple home and pastures to rule a nation in fine palaces, who wrote such songs of praise that they spoke down through the centuries to her own happiness this moment, and she said, "We'll call him David."

"It's a good enough name:" her father.

"Good as any. What counts is what he makes of it:" Aunt Tildy.

"David McQueen has a pretty sound. It will sound nice at the proper christening, whenever the Bishop comes back:" her mother.

Lydia regained her strength more slowly than she wished. For weeks the cords in her neck were sore and unknown muscles in her shoulders and legs ached from the long hours of fruitless effort before Aunt Tildy had been able to help her.

The bruises on the baby's head stayed blue and purple. She worried about this. After the first week, however, he began to eat ravenously, she let him nurse many times a day, and he grew rapidly. Sometimes she held him in her arms and exulted in her joy. Then she would think of Mark and how happy he would be to have this son—and she would wonder why no word of him reached her. She came to want to hear even the worst, if it was true, rather than have to keep on living with this silence.

When the neighbors came to see the baby, they remarked on Mark's absence. Some of them were not burdened by thoughtfulness.

"Quare thing and no doubting it, that Mark's never yet come back. My boys and I were naming the fact to each other yesterday and James he said, 'Nobody else I know of still out to the wars, except those that were killed.'"

"Oh, you mustn't give up hope, Lydia. My Hamilton only came back the first of May and this is just the first of June. Of course, I'd forgotten—perhaps I never realized—that Mark went with the Union men, until Hamilton reminded me of it. He might have a far piece to come back home, your Yankee soldier."

"Mercy alive, a man that's alive and not hurt ought to of given his wife some sign by now. Of course, you never know, but isn't this waiting, the not knowing, a grief to your heart?"

57

Sometimes at night Lydia remembered what they had said and then she held little David close.

As soon as she felt strong enough, she walked with her father out to see the field she and Robert and Kate and the brindle cow had plowed and the children had planted. The corn was ankle-high, a mite thin here and there, but unmistakably corn in unmistakable, if slightly uneven, rows. "You did a good job, Lydia," her father said.

"I'd a-done better if I'd had a chance to break Pearly to the plow," she laughed.

"Had the war lasted a turn longer, I foresee you'd have had the old Dominecker rooster helping in the fields!"

"Papa!" They laughed together.

"Your Aunt Tildy says she's leaving us soon," he said, as they walked back toward the house. "She's seen us over the hump of our trouble and I reckon we can't beg her to stay. But I'm happy you and the baby are here with us right now. David seems to mean a special something to your mother."

"I'm glad, Papa."

They looked up.

Someone had come around a corner of the house: a tall, gaunt, bearded man with a face so sad he appeared at first glance to be a mummery of President Abe Lincoln's ghost. But he wore no tall hat or long coat, only thin, ragged trousers and a jacket. "Lydia!" He spoke as she took an uncertain step toward him.

"Mark!" She was no longer uncertain. He was holding her as close as breath would allow.

4th
CHAPTER

Lydia awakened early the morning after Mark's return. For a moment she could not remember where she was—in the little back room she and Kate and the baby in the trundle bed had shared until last night when Kate went to sleep with Aunt Tildy—and she could not recall immediately why a warm coal of happiness glowed deep inside her. A rooster crowed in the distance. Then all was silence and darkness. She heard Mark's heavy breathing beside her. Mark! She came fully awake.

After the weary months of loneliness and responsibility, how sweet it would seem to share the burden with his broad shoulders, to follow his long, sure footsteps. Only the faintest grey streaks of first daylight filtered into the room, but she could see the dark growth of his hair and beard, the cavernous hollows of his cheeks, all seeming quiet and at peace now. She realized that he seemed like himself, the self she had known, now that he was asleep and his eyes were closed. Yesterday the flame of his eyes, in those bony sockets, had kindled his face with disturbing fierceness. His eyes had made him a stranger to her. And slowly the warmth of her joy in his return had been shaken by a chill of foreboding.

The baby stirred in the trundle bed beside her. She waited to see whether he would wake or settle back to sleep. Gently she turned on one side and with her right hand drew a coverlet over the sleeping child. The chill within her grew as she recalled Mark's first sight of David yesterday.

In the beginning, he could not seem to believe he had a son. "The stink of death has been so strong around me I reckon I forgot there was anything else in the world."

Then she took him in to the bed where the baby lay asleep. He stood for a long interval. "What name did you give him?"

"David." She spoke it hopefully, watching to see if he would approve.

He only nodded. His face did not change.

Aunt Tildy's entrance into the room broke the silence. "You've got a heap to be thankful for, Mark McQueen, that the boy or his mammy either one be here today. They had a tough time of it——"

"Ah, Aunt Tildy, that's all past now." Lydia was uneasy with praise for doing what naturally had to be done, with retelling of old troubles.

But Mark was paying them no heed. He leaned over the bed and scooped the sleeping baby up in his arms, awkwardly as a person unaccustomed to this special sort of burden, but with the firmness of one determined to fill a sudden need. The baby, startled awake, cried shrilly. Mark held him in the dangling blankets. The small feet kicked and the tiny fists beat against the air.

"David," Mark said to him. The dark bearded face bending above him increased the baby's screaming. "David—it's your pappy come home."

"Eh law, man, don't you know that a swaddling infant don't understand the King's English?" Aunt Tildy demanded roughly. She stretched out her arms.

But Mark did not yield the screaming, kicking baby. "You had all these weeks, now it's his pappy's turn to know him."

Flustered, Aunt Tildy fled the room.

Lydia stood motionless. The moment was somehow important, but she could not bear either the sound of little David's crying or the look of Mark's blue eyes. "It's just you coming sudden like that," she said. "Sometimes he has a mite of colic when he first wakes up. Let me quieten him and then he'll be ever so proud to see his father."

Mark looked at her. All at once he thrust over the bundle in his arms. She turned the baby across her shoulder, laid her cheek against him and patted gently. "There, little David, there." Abruptly the sobbing quieted.

"What color are his eyes?"

"Blue. The image of yours. Everybody sees him, names it to us how he's the spit of his father."

But Mark left the room and did not look at them as he went.

"Oh, little David," she crooned softly, "why couldn't you a-let somebody dandle you just this once without raising such a storm?"

That had been before dinner, and afterward for the rest of the day and evening Mark had barely glanced at the baby.

Lying now between the dark tousled head on the pillow beside her and the small bruised head (the purple marks were fading, she was certain she could see a difference every day) on the bed below her, Lydia wondered how she could contain the abundance of love she felt for each of them. She wondered if all that love could not help but bring them an inch closer together in spirit.

The sound of their breathing filled the room; the baby's even rhythm only a whisper against the heavy rise and fall of Mark's slumber.

There was no denying—she must meet it here alone before she got up to face the others for the day—that the Mark who had come back to her was not the Mark who had left. The Mark here with her last night had been a strange, greedy, knowing man, alien to the affection of the Mark who had lain with her and sung to her under the poplars by the spring a long time ago. She touched his hand gently in the growing light. He still brought excitement with him, but tenderness had disappeared.

In crowds, in narrow rooms, Mark had always been awkward and yet it was this awkwardness that had been most appealing in him, revealing the gentleness of his strength. There had been a shyness tempering his determination, a timidity before the weakness of women and words and small delicate things, that endeared him to Lydia and made him seem more powerful. But now Mark's quiet had been transformed into a brooding. The power in him seemed to Lydia to be coiled like the spring of a clock wound too tight to function, but ready at the slightest touch to break loose from confinement.

Perhaps this tension was prison born. She tried to recall all those terse, important words by which he had sought to bridge the gap between them yesterday. He told Lydia and the others only that he had been in prison at a place called Andersonville. Under the blazing suffocation of late autumn's sun and in the chill drizzle of winter rain he had watched a herd of men, been one of the herd, twisted from humans into grasping, craving animals—yet not quite beasts: sub-humans, super-animals, ashamed in their cunning, insufficient in their tokens of kindness that still flashed through the welter of humiliation and starvation.

Twice he had come close to dying. When he left the stockades there and set out on the road home, he discovered he was too ill, too irresponsible to make the long journey. A family along the way, somewhere in middle Georgia, had taken him in, granted him shelter, shared such food as they had, and given him time to recover a measure of health and sanity.

"Bless them, whoever, wherever they are," Lydia murmured.

When he was able, he had set out for home and now he was here. Beads of sweat stood on his forehead when he had finished the telling. He wiped them away with the back of his hand. "I've been to hell and seen the hellions men can be."

"I know, son." Jesse Moore reached toward Mark, but the younger man pulled back his hand.

"Nobody can know, wasn't there." His eyes, above the rim of the cup from which he drank scalding gulps of parched-corn coffee, were scalding, too. "There'll never be a forgetting. Not of that place, not of that man sent me there."

They looked at him.

"What's your meaning, Mark?" Lydia's father asked.

"Somebody here in the valley give me away to the enemy. Somebody here betrayed me, got me sent, alone out of all my outfit, to that hell-hole they called a prison."

62

"That don't seem likely, son," Lydia's father said slowly. "What makes you think——"

"They told me. When an outpost of us was captured near the Gap, one of the Reb officers said they had special word on me, word on how I'd gone against my own family, and they'd learn me a special lesson."

Lydia's fingers twisted tight until her knuckles stood out sharp and white. "Somebody here in the valley betrayed me . . ." he had said. She was remembering the dreadful morning she and Robert had found their mother at the rail fence. Somebody had led the outliers to this farm. "No, Mark, surely it was nobody here had told them."

"Who else would know so much about one common soldier out of thousands but a person from his own home place?" Mark leaned his elbows on the table, the children staring at him without a word or movement, fascinated by the singleness of his look and purpose, as he said, "I aim to find him."

No one spoke for a moment. Then Robert asked, his voice high-pitched and boyish with excitement, "What'll you do to him?" There was no answer and the words hung in the air around them like smoke that had drifted from the chimney and stung their eyes.

At last Lydia's father said, "Our ways that separated in war are coming together again in peace——"

"Not peace," Aunt Tildy said sharply, "be you holding in your mind what I think is there!"

They told Mark then about the night of the outliers—plunderers and destroyers directed to the Moores' by some neighbor whose name they did not know. They chose words carefully so that Lydia's mother would remember as little as possible. When they had finished, Sarah Moore only said, from the long silences she kept now, with the subdued voice that would have been so unlike her a year before, "We must not feel hard toward anyone. Mr. Moore, promise me——"

He laid his hand on her thin arm. "I can't pledge my word to anything, Sally. But I'll honor your wishes the best I can. It's nigh impossible to forego vengeance for wickedness to those we love, to disremember——"

"I'll not disremember!" Mark pushed back his chair and the ragged leg of his trousers caught in it and tumbled it over as he stood up. "I don't aim to speak of all that's past again, but it'll lay in my mind until the time ripens."

Thus briefly, sharply, with only a picture or two etched in her memory—of Mark in the brutal stockade, of his stay with the strangers who had given him shelter along some dusty road in Georgia—the war ended for Mark and Lydia. Ended but was not finished.

". . . until the time ripens," he had said.

The first pale daylight filled the little bedroom now and there was a loud melody of birds singing and twittering in the early dawn outside. What was this deep-gouged inner scar Mark had carried home with him? Out there in some strange field or corner of a prison camp the Mark she had known had been lost. Forever? Or could she find him, lead him back to David, to herself, to himself?

The baby stirred and let out a hungry cry. She bent quickly to bring him to her breast, but not before Mark had sprung from the bed, startled, unsure of his surroundings, crouched to defend or attack. Then he saw her in the long white nightdress from throat to floor, with the long, rich hair falling around her shoulders and down her back, and the baby in her arms, and he breathed a long, shuddering breath. For the first time since he had returned, he tried to smile at her.

During the days that followed, Lydia turned some of the time and attention she had lavished on David to healing Mark as well as possible. The girls, Kate and Annie Marie and Elizabeth, had often wished to have the baby more to themselves, to fondle as a play-pretty. Ever since the night she had helped fetch him into the world, Aunt Tildy had spoiled David as she had never spoiled anyone before. Now Lydia let them bestow their love. After she discovered that she could help care for the baby, Aunt Tildy decided to stay on a few weeks longer at her sister's home. "I want to brew him a good tonic tea before I leave," she said. "It'll see him through summer and fall ailments."

And when the others were busy with chores during the day, it was Lydia's mother who rocked the baby, hour after hour, singing in her clear, gentle voice, clinging to the infant almost as if he were the protector and she the child. Lydia nursed him and cared for him at night, but she knew there were many others who could care for her David the rest of the time, and only she could care for her Mark.

She did not know whether she should try first to fill out the gauntness of him with such food as she could scrape together, or whether to try to cover the gauntness with such clothes as she could hastily make. And so during the day she prowled the fields and woods, searching out every wild green she could find and every patch of berries. She found stolen hens' nests that the children had overlooked around the barn lot, and she salvaged the last nubbins of corn in crib and barn. She picked the first beans in the garden before they were fully grown. Mark had always had a special taste for blackberries and she tore her ankles and heavy skirts on briers and brambles as she went day after day, taking the youngest children with her, to pick the juiciest, sweetest berries she could find.

"We've had no loaf sugar for a coon's age," she said at the table, "But the old sun-ball itself sweetened these berries."

"He's a master sweetener," her father said.

But Mark said nothing; he ate ravenously and stopped suddenly, and left the table as anxiously as he had come to it.

At night Lydia knit and sewed, her needles flashing in the dim candlelight. From a piece of cloth her mother had woven the winter before, Lydia managed to find enough material for a pair of trousers and a jacket. She unraveled an old shawl to knit Mark some socks. When he protested at her destroying the shawl, she laughed and said, "I guess there's nothing sacred about it, even if the moths have made it holey!" But she could not draw out his old easy laughter.

Those evenings while she worked and most of the family sat together—unless Robert had struck off down the valley somewhere looking for companionship his own age, or the girls were playing out in the yard, catching fireflies in their cupped hands—

Lydia tried to make as jolly as possible. She sang all the songs she could remember, not the many ballads of unrequited love and death and killing, but quick, gay songs. Sometimes the others joined her, but never Mark. Sometimes her mother even sang alone, and these were the lonely tunes, the tragic tales, created on many a wind-swept moor, up many a rock-bound cove, shaped and lengthened beside many a lonely hearth, remembered across many an ocean mile. Then Mark might sit and listen with never a motion, or he might stride from the house and be gone for hours, walking in the night.

Sometimes they spoke of events in the nation: "I hear a whole passel of the Confederate people are moving down to Brazil, South America, to get away from reconstruction government."

"But I thought we already lived in South America," Annie Marie said.

"No, child. We live in the southern part of North America."

Or: "It's rumored some in Washington would impeach President Johnson——"

"Only old Abe could a brought us through these dark days without sowing the seeds of more trouble."

"You can say that, Papa, even though you fought on the side against him?"

"I can say it. He was a man to look up to."

"Eh law," Aunt Tildy would conclude, "everything is gaumed up, all over this country. It's beyond figuring out for the likes of me. I just hope they'll have it all straight by the time that little tad grows up." And she nodded toward David.

More frequently, Lydia would set the older ones to telling tales in the evening, hoping for the funny stories that would join them all in laughter. "Like the time . . ." her father would begin, and some escapade of his youth or long-ago friends would be forthcoming. Or some more recent foolishness would bear retelling.

"Like the time the Burke boys decided everything here in the valley was too smooth and peaceable, and so they got up before day one morning and Jim took out up the road and Johnny went down, and they stopped at every neighbor's house. They'd tell the first one that some man 'way down the road had sent word to come and see him as soon as he could. A little farther along, they'd leave the same message, supposedly from the first man they'd called on, with another neighbor. After a while, they had everyone stirred up, invited a mile or so away to some house of 'a feller who wanted to see him.'

"They hooked me proper. I went trailing all the way down to old man Caldwell's, caught him just as he was going out the door. He said he'd had word to step down the road a piece, but it could wait till after my visit. So I went on in and we sat around awhile, me a-waiting for him to say why he'd sent for me and him a-waiting for me to say why I'd come. Finally I asked what was on his mind and he said he reckoned nothing special. Well, I could agree with that. Far back as I can remember the Caldwells haven't had much of anything on their minds."

Aunt Tildy snorted with laughter and the others smiled, but the twinkle in Jesse Moore's eyes kept malice from the words. "Anyway, I asked Caldwell why he'd sent after me by one of the Burkes, and when he said he hadn't even seen Jim Burke since the last time he was at mill till Jim stopped in that morning and told him he was wanted down the road—well, then we begin to see what was happening. I tell you, those Burke boys sure played hob with the work in this valley that day!"

"Speaking of the Burkes," Lydia said, "there's a new mill being built down at the lower end of the valley, Mark."

"What's the matter with the Burkes? They stopped grinding?" Mark asked.

"No. This new man just come in. Papa, you talked to him. What did he say?"

Jesse Moore pulled gently at his beard, a habit he had when he was troubled. "A man by the name of Hawkins, Mark. A shrewd sort of feller. He figures that before too long the main county turnpike is a-going to run down there along the road near where Thickety Creek joins the river. Be a regular crossroads. If he builds his mill there, folks not only from the valley here but from all around will come to him. I reckon he's got it figured pretty straight."

"But what about the Burke boys?"

"They were bad wrought up when they first heard about it. Old

Ida vowed she'd go down herself and crack Hawkins' skull with one of his fancy millstones if he fooled with her boys, took their customers."

"Papa says the man is building a great dam right near the mouth of the creek so he can get a good head of water," Lydia went on, pleased that Mark had shown interest in some of the news in the community.

"He'll need a powerful head of water if he aims to use four sets of stones, like he named to me," her father said. "He even claimed one set was coming all the way from France."

"And what's the need to haul stones all the way across the waters, from France or wherever," Aunt Tildy demanded, "when we got nothing but stones throughout these mountains?"

"This Hawkins have a family?" Mark asked. "Where's he from?"

"Only a daughter with him," Jesse Moore said. "A frail thing named Dolly. Hawkins said her mother died back on the coast, where they come from."

"Quare-sounding folks to me. Dolly!" Aunt Tildy reached for the little round snuff tin deep in her apron pocket and took a pinch. "Must have more money than sense if he can haul stones halfway around the globe."

"He seems to be a man of means," Jesse Moore said.

So they talked and sang, and Lydia sought to bring Mark back home in mind as well as body.

If the children were out in the yard in the evening and heard Aunt Tildy's voice beginning a story, they dropped their playthings and came quickly, for hers were neither ballads of love nor recollections of old pranks, but tales of ghosts and witches and all manner of unnatural occurrences.

"Eh law, who's to say whether there be ghosts or not? I can't say spirits walk this earth. But who's to prove they don't?"

"Did you ever hear tell of a spirit walking, Aunt Tildy?" Robert would prompt.

"Well, I know my mammy, the day before she died, told me she saw the figure of her least 'un that had been buried years before during an awful siege of the bloody flux. The child figure that come to her was all in white, Mammy said, standing at the foot of her bed, and the light off its face filled the room. It just smiled at her, turning its head ever so slightly to one side, a habit it had had when it was an earthly baby. And then it went away, slowly, like fog a-lifting."

There was silence in the room except for the click-click of Lydia's knitting needles. Annie Marie huddled closer to her big sister Kate. "The next day my mammy went away, too," Aunt Tildy continued. "And when she was laid out in her coffin, it seemed to me like a light was on her face I hadn't never noticed there before. That made it a heap-sight easier to say good-by to her, knowing she went happy in her mind with somebody she loved to meet her out there in the dark."

Lydia's mother nodded.

"I've seen men go out into that dark a-screaming for their mammies or their wives," Mark broke in harshly. "Was there somebody out there to meet them?"

No one spoke. Then:

"There was the love of God, and Jesus," Sarah Moore said, but her voice seemed small against the terror of his question.

Finally Jesse Moore said, "Yes, I've seen them and heard them, too, Mark. Men on my side of the line, in butternut suits, and men I did not know, on the other side, wearing blue—all dying the same way under their different-colored cloth."

And all at once the two men who had been to war were bound together in a world none of the others could enter, isolated in memories of shattered bones and severed limbs, blood turning a stock pond red on some farm in Virginia or Tennessee and soaking the ground soggy on some forgotten field. Lydia sensed their closeness at such moments, even though they had fought so far apart, and she was thankful there was someone in the house who could share this world of Mark's that she would never know.

There was another to share it, too, when Paul came home. He arrived in midsummer, three weeks after Mark. His hair was close-cropped; they had done that in the hospital, he said, to make him cooler and keep down lice. He had grown from a boy into a man. He greeted them all calmly, disturbed only by the change he found in his mother. At first, they were all uneasy before the dangling empty sleeve, but he looked at them boldly and told them not to fret.

Lydia felt the sureness of Paul's reconciliation to his loss when he said to her, the morning after his return, as he walked with her to the barn on her way to milk the cow, "Better an arm than a leg or an eye." He let down the bars leading into the barnyard, deftly using his one good hand. "Besides, I had two arms. If the bullet had strayed a little closer, I might have lost the onliest heart I've got!"

She laughed with him, marveling at how the months had matured him. As she milked, she thought about Paul's lost arm, comparing this inevitably to the lostness of Mark. Surely it was a strange thing how people could recognize a wound of flesh and never see a maimed spirit. Friends who had come to welcome Mark home and ask him when he'd be taking Lydia and David back to the house on the Nelson farm had found it hard to reconcile the Mark they had known with the moody man who now walked the house and fields, working spasmodically, preoccupied and unsettled. Lydia leaned her head against the cow's warm side and bit her underlip in a vow to give Mark the only gifts she knew to help him: love and time.

How hard it was to be patient. She had waited so long for Mark to come back so they could have a home again, with David this time to make it complete. How she longed to set her own few dishes on her own shelf, to wind the clock on her own fireboard, to work with Mark in their own crops. Time . . . time. Time would surely bring it to pass. If only her patience could endure to fill the time he would need.

A few days later a new fear arose to confront her. Mark left early in the morning, riding her father's horse, to take the last scraps of last season's corn for grinding at Burkes' mill. The new crop was already filling out in the fields, and they were luckier than many people in the valley who had not been able to plant any corn that spring. By sundown Mark had not returned.

"He wouldn't have had to wait long for his turn at the mill, I know," Lydia fretted. "Hardly any folks with corn left to grind these days."

"Maybe he's visiting a spell with the Burke fellers," her father said. "After all, he's just seen them once since he come home. They've got talk to catch up on."

When supper was over and the dishes were washed, however, and Mark still had not come back, Lydia asked Paul if he would go and make sure there was no trouble.

"You oughtn't to ask him to set out at night, Lydia," Aunt Tildy objected. "Mark can look out for himself."

"Of course he can." She did not want to betray any lack of confidence in her husband. "But accidents happen——"

Paul grinned at her. "Never mind, Aunt Tildy, I've made worse marches than this, and after night, too. With bossier generals to command me!" He nodded toward his sister.

When Paul came home around midnight, bringing a Mark whose head was swathed in bandages, Lydia learned that there had been trouble. It was no accident. Paul had had the story from the Burkes.

Mark arrived at the mill a few minutes after Ham Nelson and a man named Tilmon Haddon had come with half a wagonload of prime corn to be ground. James and John Burke had talked with Mark a little while, until Ham Nelson asked them if they would be getting to his corn that day or had he better take it someplace else? As they went in to start the grinding, Jim Burke heard Ham introduce Mark to the short, red-bearded man with him. "McQueen, this here is Tilmon Haddon. He and his family are living down on our farm. They been wanting the cabin you and Lyddy Moore had——"

"She's Lydia McQueen now," Mark interrupted him.

"Well, now, it don't make no never-mind. I'm not a-speaking about her, but the cabin." Ham Nelson spat in the dust at Mark's feet. "Haddon here's been a-wanting that place, but Pa made him wait to see if you was coming back to tend crop for us."

Mark acknowledged the introduction to the stranger, but made no other answer.

"Tilmon, this is Mark McQueen," Ham said then. "McQueen is one of our big victorious home-grown Yankees."

The man looked up sharp as a ferret. He surveyed Mark from head to toe with his squinting eyes, and then he too spat a long stream of ambeer into the dust.

Mark turned and went to water his horse and carry in the half sack of nubbin corn he had brought to the mill.

It was an hour or so later when Morgan Bludsoe rode by. John Burke saw him through the open door of the mill. He was sitting easy in the saddle, wide black hat pulled low over his face, looking neither to right nor left. Ham Nelson, whittling in the yard, called something to Bludsoe who reined in his horse and slowly pushed back his hat, still sitting half slumped in the saddle.

Suddenly from around the corner near the millrace came Mark, obviously drawn by whatever Nelson had said. He paused a moment, then walked toward Bludsoe's horse. Deliberately, almost casually, as Mark walked past, Ham stretched out a foot. Mark stumbled, tried to regain his stride, failed, and fell sprawling on the hard-baked yard. He sprang up in the very moment of his falling, it seemed, and leaped toward Ham. The impact of his first blow struck the whittling knife from Nelson's hand and he staggered backward.

As the Burkes told Paul, a regular Donnybrook followed. Nelson's new tenant entered the fight next, felling Mark with a short, heavy blow from behind as he went toward Ham again. No one had seen Morgan Bludsoe leave his horse, but before the Burkes could reach Mark, Bludsoe was there, pulling Tilmon Haddon off and landing him a straight right punch on the jaw. The Burkes' first intention had been to separate the men, but even as they tried, Ham Nelson's fist crashed into Mark's face, bringing a spurt of blood from nose and mouth. Mark's foot caught Nelson in the stomach and sent him flat on the ground. Jim Burke leaped to pin him there, but Haddon tripped him. Then, while John Burke and Bludsoe took on Haddon, Mark and Jim turned to Nelson.

"I got nothing against you, Burke," Ham Nelson said between clenched teeth as he sparred for time. "You know what's good for you, you won't meddle in what's not your business."

"Ah, meddling in a fight is always more pleasure than business," Jim Burke roared as he struck at Ham, who side-stepped him and made another lunge for Mark. They locked in an exchange of savage blows.

Bludsoe and John Burke pinned Haddon to the ground. "Redheaded people always peppery-tempered," John grinned at the angry thickset man.

Mark held Nelson's arms twisted with the grip of a vise behind his back. "I've seen better men than you lose arms in a fair fight, Nelson"— Lydia reached out to touch Paul's good right arm as he told her this—"and do I ever see your ugly face or hear your weasely voice around me again, I'll break you like a tallow candle."

When Haddon and Nelson had left in the wagon, shouting to the Burkes that they would be back for the full measure of their ground corn the next morning, Ida Burke took one look at Mark and insisted on caring for him. Mark managed to hold her at bay for a little while; he said there was something he must speak to Morgan Bludsoe about at once, and the two men stood by Bludsoe's horse and talked quietly for a while. Then Morgan mounted his horse and rode away and Mark went into the house and let Ida Burke bandage a cut on his head and wash the blood off his split lip and swelling nose. Thus Paul had found him.

Mark would not talk to Lydia about the fight. He only said with a calm that made her tremble, "Next time, I'll kill Ham Nelson. High and mighty Rebel."

"Mark, there can't be a next time!"

He nodded. "That's right, Lydia. We're going away from the midst of this valley."

"Where will we go, Mark?" She was kneeling by his chair, bathing his bruised hands.

"We're going up on the mountain. I've had enough of the swinish ways of men. We'll take to the woods and the beasts that have natural cruelty and cunning. We'll build us a home up under the Devil's Brow."

The Devil's Brow! A great grey slab of granite at the headmost part of the valley. As a child she had often looked up at the hard, unchanging face of stone cropping out from the tree-covered mountainside and she had wondered if it marked the beginning of time, the creation of the world. "But whose land, Mark? How will we live . . . ?"

He leaned toward her and took her hands and for the first time since he had come home from the war she saw confidence and expectation in his face. "I'm making arrangements, Lydia. I've spoken to Morgan Bludsoe."

"What about?"

"We'll buy a patch of land from them. They won't cheat us in a trade. No matter what else may be said about the Bludsoes, nobody ever gave them a name for anything but straight-out honesty. They own all that upper cut of mountainside, and Morgan said he'd ask Big Matt and the others about selling us a piece."

The dark, strange, terrible Bludsoes. Would they be neighbors then? Should she repeat to Mark Emma Caldwell's judgment that the Bludsoes had been among the outliers when they raided her father's farm? Would she have to leave the familiar valley for their wildness?

Mark misunderstood her troubled look. He stood up and paced the floor. "Oh, the land's not all steep up there. I recollect when I used to hunt with the Burkes over those ridges, before ever I set eyes on you, Lydia, and we run across many a nice little level bench and cove. I'll choose a rich neat spot for us. I told Morgan Bludsoe I'd come up tomorrow to see him and his pappy, maybe make a trade."

"The Bludsoes, Mark . . . there's David——"

He was rushing on. "I'll have a speck of war money coming to me, Lydia, once the papers get cleared through. Maybe we can buy us some peace with it."

But there was no peace in her, only consternation. Yet if this was what Mark wanted, she must do it. She was no longer only herself. She was already divided into three: herself and Mark and David. And now it was Mark who needed her most and she must give the other two parts of herself to this.

"Somewhere in this valley there's a person betrayed me in war; and there's the devilment of Ham Nelson and his new henchman

74

turned against me. I won't live amongst it!" He slammed his fist against the wall. "I'll find peace and satisfaction if I have to blast these mountains open to their eternal core!"

"We'll find it, Mark." Lydia stood up beside him and laid her hand on his arm to calm him before the others, all except Paul, came up from the field where they were working.

The following weeks stretched Lydia's nerves thin and taut. She had not expected her father to react so stubbornly to Mark's plans. "When you married, you seemed a settled man," he said to Mark. "You promised me to cherish Lydia like a woman above rubies. Now you want to take her to the backside of beyond. There's nothing more than an ox trail up under Devil's Brow."

"We'll make out," Mark said. There was neither triumph nor defiance in his voice, only dogged determination to run the course he'd set. Mr. Moore had always been a man apart, in Mark's mind, combining the farmer and the scholar, to everyone courteous, yet practical and hearty, too. It did not go well with Mark to turn aside from this friend, this father by law.

"Reconsider," Jesse Moore pleaded. "Don't take Lydia and the baby and yourself up there to become mountain boomers!"

But Mark only answered, "They don't have to come. I do——"

When the men understood there was no purpose in talking to each other, they went their separate ways, preoccupied and grudging during the summer days. When the family came together at mealtimes, the atmosphere was strained and none of them—not even the big-eyed, watchful children—fully enjoyed the bountiful food yielded by the garden. The table that had been so light all winter and early spring now grew heavy again with steaming cabbages and sweet potatoes and beans. The rich, satisfying smells of their boiling and frying filled the house and spilled out into the yard, yet no one came running eagerly to table as they all had earlier in the season.

Mark was gone for days at a time. He told Lydia he had made a trade with Big Matt Bludsoe for a tract of land. The two men went in to the county seat and drew up papers.

"Have you fetched all your belongings from Nelson's place?" Lydia's father asked the next day.

"I'll not step foot on his acres again," Mark said. "Be he an honest man, he'll not want to keep what's not rightfully his."

"I'll go tomorrow and bring your tools and the rest of your household plunder," Jesse Moore said.

"I'm not asking you to——"

"I know," the older man said impatiently. "But you'll be having need of every scrap that's yours. We're in for bad times after this war; no need to pay a pauper's price for pride."

The next day he hitched up his horse to the wagon and went down the valley to Nelson's. When he came back, Mark was gone, but Jesse's mouth was drawn in a thin white line and the flesh was tight across his jawbones.

"You may be leaving at a right time, Lydia," he said, "even though I still don't foster the plan. Seems the war's not over here in the valley. Plenty of men dead back on all those battlefields we come through, but war's slower a-dying."

"What do you mean, Papa?"

"The night after Mark's fight at the mill, a man by the name of Taylor, a Unionist who lived down the river, was called out from his house and shot in cold blood. Died before his wife could get across the yard to him. Nobody knows who did it."

"Poor, poor woman," Lydia murmured.

"Then last week, to pay back the debt—leastways that's what the talk is—word got out that Hawkins, the new miller, had been a Confederate, and he was dragged out in the night and beat up and left for dead."

"What's happening to everything and everybody, Papa?" Lydia cried.

"We can't go on like this, that's sure," her father said. "The law's broken down. But it's hard to know how to begin to put the pieces back together."

"I wish I was a law-man," Robert said.

His father turned his head and looked at the boy. "Why yes, son. You might be someday." Robert had grown taller during the summer—"shooting up like ragweed in a wet season," Aunt Tildy

76

said—and there was manhood and quietness growing in his face. More than any other child in the family, he looked like his mother and acted like his father. "Yes, son," Jesse Moore repeated thoughtfully, "you might make us proud one of these days, help bring law and order back to this community. We'll think on it some more."

The boy flushed with pleasure and looked quickly at Lydia. She smiled at him, but it was such a pale, fleeting smile that he knew her mind was not on what they were saying. "Papa, you see —Mark is right to want to get out of the thick of it for a while. We'll be able to start all over again, together, up on the mountain —and besides, it's not an ocean away. Oh, Papa, do try to understand."

"I try, daughter." He looked at her smooth young face shining with hope, her direct grey eyes, the loose bundle of hair knotted at the back of her neck. "I guess I keep forgetting," he reminded himself rather than speaking to the others, "that you're not my little girl any longer. You're Mark McQueen's wife."

"Oh, Papa!" Lydia's eyes suddenly swam with tears, bright glistening tears.

And it was as Mark's wife that she went through the next weeks of preparation to leave her father's house forever. Jim Burke left the mill to his brother for a week and went up with Mark to help clear land for the new dwelling. "Ah, there's little enough grinding to do now," he said, when Mark protested. "Besides, don't I recollect the time before you married when you worked at our mill, and the many a heavy sack you lifted on your days off, when you didn't have to by contract?"

Paul and Robert and their father went, too, taking the horse to help snake logs out of the clearing or to bring them in for the cabin. "It's a fair enough situation Mark picked out," they said when they came home, dog-tired and dirty after their days of grinding, sweating labor.

"Menfolks!" Aunt Tildy muttered. "Such a clear picture they paint with their tongues that I can fairly see every little bush and pebble-stone on the place!"

Lydia laughed. She waited for Mark to ask her to go up the

mountain and see the site. At last she could wait no longer and on one of the hot, sultry summer mornings that settled over the valley she asked Robert to go with her and show her the way around Devil's Brow.

The walk they had together was good. When they were children they had often explored together, liking the woods more than Paul or Kate, who preferred the pasture-lot or hayfield and playing house or preacher or store. Many a creek bank Lydia and Robert had searched during long summer days, enjoying the cool shade and the quick water after long hot hours of helping in the fields. In winter, too, they had walked the woods, breaking the silence of a grey day or a heavy snow with shouts and songs. Sometimes just the silliness they were not allowed at home broke through and they leaped and tagged each other and called words that had no meaning but their sound as they echoed through the leafless trees, or under the branches of evergreens bowed with snow. Those days were ended now, and they walked sedately, steadily, toward a sober destination. Yet the bonds of those former times still held them close together and when Lydia had to stop and rest, after they had begun the long pull up the mountain, she found that it was not difficult to tell Robert why.

"I didn't eat much of a breakfast," she said, wiping the skirt of her dress over her hot face.

"My legs don't object to sitting a spell," Robert answered. He pulled a thick stem of grass and stretched it between the two thumbs of his cupped hands for a whistle. It made a loud, sad shriek.

The shade of the beech tree bending in a long leafy limb over the level spot where they sat was like a cool hand stretched to shelter them from the sun's burning heat. Lydia lay back on the ground and looked up through the thick green leaves, absorbing into her body the coolness of the shade above and the ground beneath. "I didn't eat much at breakfast," she repeated, "because I couldn't. I reckon I was what they call morning-sick."

Robert looked at her quickly, then looked away. As a family, they did not talk about such things. With Lydia it was different, however. She spoke to him about this as freely as she spoke about the heat or the cold, walking or breathing. He tried to speak easily, too. "You going to have another—baby?"

She nodded. "I'm pretty sure. Don't nobody know yet, but you. Properly, its father should know first, but Mark's been away so much the last few weeks—and I feel so happy I have to share my news with somebody. You hold your silence till I give you word, you hear?"

"Who would I be a-talking to about such things?" Robert asked. His face did not reflect his sister's happiness. He blew again on the grass in his hands and stared off through the woods. "I recollect what a bad time you had a-borning little David."

"Oh, that was one time in a thousand. Even Aunt Tildy said so. David came after we'd been through—all that other . . ." Their eyes met for a moment and then they looked away. Lydia sat up abruptly. "This time Mark's here, and there's not any war going on, and we'll be in our own house——"

"You'll have to stay at home, won't you, till after this?" Robert asked.

"I'll be at our own home," she smiled, drawing her knees under her chin. "Come the end of fall, Mark and David and me will be moving up here and I'll have all winter to make this place ours before another baby comes in April." She laid her cheek on her knees and said softly, "April. Won't that be a lovely month for a birthing?"

"April's all right," Robert said. He did not know quite how to respond to her mood that had acknowledged him to be a man, grown up, by the nature of her confidence, and yet also demanded that he admit tenderness and affection. In a sudden burst he met Lydia more than halfway. "To my mind, April's one of the finest months of the whole twelve. If a body's going to get born and live a spell on this earth-ball, I can't think of no better time to begin it all than in April. Nor"—he stammered slightly—"no better way to begin than with you for a mama."

"Why, Robert Moore, what a fine thing to say. What a fine, splendid thing." Lydia looked at him with such pleasure and love that he flushed with embarrassment from his thin little neck to the roots of his dark brown hair. "I'll cherish what you spoke to

79

me . . ." She paused, thoughtfully considering him before she said, ever so softly, "You've a way with words, Robert."

He threw away the grass in his hands and looked off up the path. "Well . . ."

But Lydia had not moved. "Maybe that's what Papa had in mind when he said you might go into the law."

"You reckon maybe so, Lydia?"

She nodded slowly. "You do it, Robert. You understand? You take Papa's advice, and mine, and you amount to something— for this community, for us, for yourself."

"Lydia, I want to——"

"Then do it! You're the only scholar in the lot; you make it count for something." Impulsively she leaned over and picked up his hand and squeezed it and looked at him intensely. "Oh, Robert, did you ever think how wonderful to have so much ahead of us? There's a whole lifetime to be lived, all sorts of undreamed surprises to come, people to know, things to be done—and we're here! Sometimes I come right up against thinking about it and I'm so full of joy it fills plumb to the brim, like the psalmist's cup that just runs over."

"Well, I guess I——"

"That's the way I feel about this second little one, Robert. It'll be a blessing to us all; you'll see. I feel so rich, Robert, rich as cream with nothing but pure happiness, and this little one will make Mark view life different, too. I know, I know it will."

They were silent. The woods around them lay still in the noonday sun. Robert knew he would never forget this moment. Something had passed between him and Lydia that was rare and although couched in words was yet wordless.

"Do we reach the house-place before dark, we'd better get back onto our path." Lydia stood up and brushed her skirt and smoothed the back of her hair where she'd lain against the ground. This was one of the characteristics Robert loved most in his sister: she could be carrying him off in big dreams and plans somewhere beyond the everyday world they knew, and then all at once her mood would shift and she would be plain and practical again, the brightness in her eyes lowered before the busyness of her hands.

80

Long ago Aunt Tildy had once said, "Eh law, the Lord gave that child Lydia a heap of common sense, and then He turned around and gave her a matching heap of nonsense, and ever since then it's been an even draw as to which would win out." Robert remembered what Aunt Tildy had said and hoped they both would win; her sense and nonsense, her light laughter and hard labor.

"Here's the path," Robert said. "It won't be long now before we get there."

The last part of the trail was the steepest, climbing sharply up the mountain, under and then to one side of the great exposed outcropping of rock called the Devil's Brow. At a spot almost even with the rock on the left, a new path branched to the right. It had been gouged out of the hillside recently. Robert nodded yes to Lydia's unspoken question.

"If we held to this way, we'd get to the top of Stony Ridge," he said. "You reckon the Bludsoes really have a chest of gold pieces stored away up there where they live?"

But Lydia was in no mood to think about the Bludsoes or their gold or their whiskey or their wild ways. Her steps quickened, and Robert followed, as she took the freshly made path and so came around the side of the hill to a full view of the cove that lay just beyond.

The site Mark had chosen lay in a little ravine, hills folding in on either side, with trees covering and surrounding it. Only at one spot was a tiny scar now visible, and Lydia, searching for some sign of where her house was to stand, saw this first clearing. Her heart seemed to be in her throat. The clearing looked so tiny. Could the three of them—a man wounded in spirit, and a woman and a baby—make their mark on this domain? Moving closer, she began to see the level patches, the clump of tulip poplars around a ledge from which a stream of water flowed and made its way down the ravine. The sight of that stream reassured her and she hurried toward it. As she reached the ledge, someone spoke. "That'll be your spring," Mark said. "And a fine bold one it is, too."

"Ah, you startled me. I—I wanted to come and see where you're a-building, Mark." She watched his sweaty face for any sign of reassurance or reproach, but there was neither.

81

"It's good you come," he said. "Robert, I'm beholden to you for bringing Lydia up here. Your pa and Paul are hauling some rocks on the sled for us to set up the chimney right away."

"I'll go help them," Robert said, and walked toward the clearing.

"It's a-coming along fine, Lyddy," Mark said, when they were alone. He took a long drink of water from the spring. "You'll see this place is right for us, once we move up here."

"I see it now, Mark."

"Do you?" He looked at her, gripping her arm so that it hurt, a deep longing in his eyes. "I hope so, Lyddy. I hope so."

She felt that that one look lowered the invisible barrier between them. "Yes, Mark, it's so." And she was happy as he showed her the spring where they would get water, and the rich level square of ground where wild pea vine for the cow was already growing tall and plentiful and where they could plant a garden next year, and when, at last, he took her to the protected spot where the house would sit. The cabin was already under way—a one-room skeleton with a gaping hole at the north end for the chimney. Directly in front of it stood a tall, straight pine, the only tree remaining in the stump-pocked area that would serve as a yard. Broken limbs and tree tops littered the ground. "I spy what I can do!" she cried.

It was up in the afternoon and they all ate ravenously the food Aunt Tildy had sent up by Lydia and Robert. When they had finished, Lydia began to drag the brush and pile it in one enormous heap at the edge of the clearing. The green limbs were heavy and many of the treetops she could not even budge, but while the men went down the ravine and heaved rocks for the chimney onto the sled and hauled them back up to the cabin, she lifted and pulled and piled the debris out of their way.

"You've made a sight of difference already," her father said, when they came up with their second load.

"Rest a spell now, Lydia," Robert called.

"No need," she called back. "I've not run out of my first wind yet."

By the time they had to start for home, the brush heap had grown into a small mountain and it was possible to pick a pathway across the yard. "Do we get to living here, I can pretty all this up in no time," she announced triumphantly. Her hair had come loose around her neck and shoulders, the hem of her dress was torn where it had caught on a sharp edge of stump, and her hands and face were grimy with sweat and stain from wood and bark. Her skin was red from the day's heat. She took a deep drink of water from the gourdful Robert brought from the spring. It was cold and sweet. Tired as she was, she walked again the little distance up to the spring to watch it bubbling forth from its sandy cup beneath the three trees and the stone ledge. Surely any settler was blessed who had such a treasure of water. "It's a fine place you chose," she said to Mark again, as they all turned to go out the new path that led to the trail down the mountain.

"We'll see," he said.

"Maybe we could have a housewarming, once we get it built," she said happily, then paused at the silence with which he met her words.

During the days that followed, Mark worked with a frenzy of determination that kept him on the mountain day and night alike. The last hot spell of summer passed. Evenings and mornings grew chilly, although the sun still blazed fiercely. Fall, and a hint of the winter to come, left the grass dry and thick with grasshoppers and crickets. Lydia did not listen to Aunt Tildy's arguments that Mark was cutting the logs for their cabin at the wrong time of the moon and season, but she made ready for her move to the mountain. Time she could spare from work in the valley, she made the long journey up to the clearing and helped Mark on the cabin.

Her father and Paul and Robert and Jim Burke had to leave off their building and clearing for Mark and Lydia and get on with their own harvest for a long winter. Lydia tried to help in their places. Her hands were torn and mashed and hardened by handling heavy rocks and rough logs. Once when she and Mark were lifting a hearthstone into place, her fingers slipped and the stone fell across her toes, bruising them. The pain lasted for days, and she was crippled for weeks.

Then she could not go and help Mark and the loss of time distressed her. She knew that he wanted to be moved before winter came, and with the rumors of fighting and bloodshed that flared up every week or so, the war vengeances and new feuds that filled the valley and even the town beyond, she, too, was eager for them to move before another season. That was why she suggested the barn-raising.

Lydia could not bear to think of the cow shivering in a makeshift lean-to during the winter to come, but Mark would have no time to build a barn before snow fell. Why not invite some of the folks in the valley for a barn-raising? Several had already been asking about the place Lydia and Mark were building.

Emma Caldwell, stopping to see Sarah Moore on a Saturday afternoon, had wanted to know if it was true that they had bought land of the Bludsoes. "Mercy alive, ain't you scared they'll burn you out—or worse?"

"The mountains ought to be big enough to hold us all," Lydia replied.

"Gentry said he seen record of the deed when he went in to the courthouse last week to buy his own farm."

"Your boy a-buying land?" Aunt Tildy sniffed.

"River-bottom acres down next to Hawkins' new mill," Emma Caldwell answered promptly. "But he mayn't farm for a spell; may rent it out. He's been talking of taking up preaching."

Aunt Tildy nodded briskly. "I'd say preaching would set better with him than farming. Harder on the lungs, but a heap easier on the back!"

And Ida Burke had asked one day, "You dropped any dishrags lately, Lydia? A sign somebody dirtier than you was a-coming to visit? I been aiming to go up on the mountain and see that new farm you and Mark are making."

Their curiosity would be satisfied, and Mark would have many hands to help put up a barn, if they could have a community building. After a while Mark might even find some reconciliation with the people he had avoided and rejected. She and Aunt Tildy and the girls could fix food for all, and when the tight stalls for Pearly and her feed were finished, the men could come and join their wives in a big dinner set under the trees. Her eyes shone at the prospect.

Everyone in the family seized the idea of a barn-raising readily, everyone except Lydia's mother and Mark.

"We'll ask Willoughby Hayes to bring his fiddle," Robert said.

"And I might bring Dolly Hawkins," Paul added. They all turned to him in surprise, not knowing till now that he had even met the girl.

"Please," Sarah Moore said, "I wouldn't want to go. All those people . . ." She twisted one hand in the palm of the other.

"There, Sally, there." Jesse Moore patted her stooped shoulder. "There'll be no call for you to do anything you don't want to." He turned to the others. "But Lydia's thought on a good plan, I'd say. Wed profit to pleasure. . . . How about you, Mark? What say you?"

Mark glanced at Lydia. His face seemed drawn and tired. "I don't hold with a feller asking other folks to shoulder his labor."

"Nor I," said Mr. Moore, "but this is a different sort of undertaking. Almost every farm in this creek-valley has some house or barn or fence that was partly built by neighbors' hands. Nobody here but would be glad to turn in and help you get a start——"

"You're wrong," Mark said. "You're forgetting that there's somebody here wouldn't want me to prosper, could he have his way——"

Jesse Moore's face clouded. "Maybe you're right, son. Maybe there's some here would do us all hurt—have already done it."

"Would to heaven I knew who it was!" Mark flung his chair away and paced the room. "Whenever I walk in this valley, I look at every man I pass and think to myself: Was it him? Was he the one? . . . And I don't know."

"I wish I knew, too," Jesse Moore said. "But we can't let the not-knowing poison the rest of our days. We can build in spite of them."

"Or to spite them!" Mark said.

The words froze Lydia where she stood by the hearth, covering the coals for tomorrow morning's fire. Was this why Mark worked so restlessly, why he seemed strengthened by some inner source of energy? As she had watched him lift those heavy stones into the chimney and daub the chinks between with wet clay, as she had seen him fell great trees and strip them of bark and swing the adze to flatten one side for puncheons for their floor, as he had strained and lifted and pushed and mauled their cabin together—"by main strength and awkwardness," as Aunt Tildy said—had it been because he was against, and not because he was for: for their home, for Lydia and his child, for life itself? "Or to spite them." The words lingered in the room and echoed in her mind.

Even Mark's consent to having a barn-raising, when he announced a few days later that the house was almost finished, did not completely dispel the blight of those four words. Lydia plunged into the work of moving. Several mornings she was wretchedly ill and had to leave the breakfast table and her father looked at her tenderly. Robert flushed and looked at his plate, but no one noticed him. Mark was not there; he stayed the night on his own farm now.

It remained for Aunt Tildy to ask for the family, as they molded candles for Lydia to take with her to her new home, "Lydia, you expecting again?"

The girl nodded.

"Eh law, it never stops, I reckon," the older woman said. She poured a ladle of hot tallow carefully into the mold. "Hating and dying and loving and birthing, all creation penned up in one man's breast, one single body's breath." There was no question of pleasure or sorrow over the baby's coming, although Lydia longed to share her anticipation. It seemed that a child was as inevitable as morning, as sure as spring.

Again Lydia took her furnishings into a strange room, as she once had done—long ago, it now seemed—at the Nelson farm, but this time it was fresh, a room where no one else had lived. And it was her own. Hers and Mark's, built by their labor. The kettles and the oven, the bedstead and the quilts, the chairs and table: they filled the log-scented room with familiar coziness. Pearly was tied at the edge of the wild pea-vine field, close by the overflow stream from the spring. One thing alone Lydia missed at her new home: the Virginia clock was still at her mother's house. Mark had not yet fixed a mantel for their fireplace.

Although it was fall and grinding at the mill had increased, Jim Burke came up for two days to help Mark fell logs and make ready for the barn-raising. "Aye God, folks are looking forward to this-here frolic," he boomed with hearty pleasure. "What victuals you going to set out for us?"

Mark lifted his head suddenly from the shingles he was splitting. He looked at Lydia. "Papa and Aunt Tildy are bringing up some of the victuals tomorrow," she told Jim Burke hastily, "and I'm making ready to fix corn pudding and bake a batch of stack pies——"

"Just make sure you've a plenty, Lyddy girl," Burke laughed. "Men that fetch hearty labor eat from a hearty stomach."

"That's truth," Mark answered slowly.

He watched closely the next day as Lydia made ready to prepare the stack of orange pumpkins and long, plump sweet potatoes Paul and Robert had brought up on the sled. There were crisp, juicy Winesap apples and corn with the milk thickening to sweet hardness in the kernels that would yield to a homemade grater. "What amongst all this is for meat?" Mark asked.

Triumphantly Lydia led him to the table before the fireplace. There lay two broad hams. "They're fresh," Mark said.

She nodded. "Papa butchered three days ago when the signs were right, before the moon changed——"

"Before we had our barn-raising, you mean," he interrupted. "Everybody up and down the valley will be saying your pa had to butcher his hogs early this year to furnish the table for them that come to furnish us a barn."

"That's no way to view it, Mark," she cried.

"How else?" He left the house.

The day wore on. Lydia peeled apples and pumpkins until her fingers were stiff with tiredness. Years before, she would have wasted half this time throwing long curls of apple peel over her left shoulder, to see what initial they would make, foretelling whom she would marry. She smiled, remembering, and wondered if she had ever seen an "M" among all the letters the apple peelings had shaped.

She milked and brought a bucket of fresh water from the spring.

For supper she warmed over the stewed squirrel Mark had liked at dinner, but he did not come to eat it. She nursed David and put him to bed. In the loneliness of the shadowy room she saw for the first time in weeks how he was growing. His fingers were clenched into tiny fists on either side of his face on the pillow. Tenderness, and pity for him now that the new baby was coming, swept over her. "David, little David," she crooned, hardly aware of the words she said, knowing only the meaning she intended. "I'll never let any harm come to you . . ." Her lips touched the small damp fists. The baby stirred, and she stepped back.

The night outside was dark as a cave. What had happened to Mark? Once she thought she heard his footsteps, but he did not come. In the distance she heard a shriek that must have been a wildcat's cry. She wondered if Pearly was frightened, if she would be safe from wild animals? It would be good to have her a tight, warm place for winter. Day after tomorrow the barn would be built. Aunt Tildy would be coming up tomorrow to help with the day's stewing and baking.

Lydia stirred the fire, put on a fresh log and went back to peeling and cutting the hard crisp pumpkins. Sometime before midnight she had them all ready in the big iron pots. Tomorrow she would cook and mash them and . . . Her mind rebelled. She could think only of Mark. Where had he gone? Could he have been hurt? She went to the door and unlatched it and stood listening in the darkness, wondering if she could hear him if he called. Even the stars in the autumn sky overhead seemed different from the stars in the valley.

Lydia let the fire die down and carefully covered up the coals to kindle tomorrow morning's blaze. She plaited her hair in two long braids and made ready for bed. She had not eaten much supper and she was hungry, but there was nothing in the house she craved to eat. Her thoughts were fitful as she dozed, then lay awake, and dozed again.

Sometime just before morning Mark returned. The fact of his presence and that he was all right eased her mind and she heard him only vaguely as he said, "Come barn-raising day, we'll have meat to roast in style and plenty," before she fell asleep.

The sun was almost over the hill before Lydia was out of bed the next morning. Fog lay heavy in the narrow cove, but Mark said the sun would soon burn it away. Hot water boiled up with the saliva in her mouth and she felt at once famished and nauseated. She dressed quickly and hung water to heat over the fire Mark had built. Some of Aunt Tildy's herb tea might settle her stomach. She changed the baby's diaper and soaking nightgown and fed him.

"Tomorrow they'll all be a-coming up to view our home," Mark said. "I hope you'll be proud, Lydia."

She looked around at him. "I'm proud, Mark."

"And there'll be no call for you to be ashamed of the food we have to offer. I'm going to build us a turning spit today on a pattern I've held in my memory from down in the Low Country——"

"But we've only the hams, Mark, and they're not for cooking on a——"

"Hams?" Mark laughed. "You fix the hams. I'm talking about beef. I butchered our beef last night."

"Our beef?" Lydia asked.

"The cow."

The words seemed to drop like thunder in the room. The silence that rolled after them was total, engulfing her, stifling her. Lydia gave one cry and clasped her hands to her mouth. Turning, she ran out the door and down the path to the field where the wild pea vine grew. At the edge of the field between it and the spring, swinging from a heavy beech limb, hung her cow, hung Pearly.

She could not look at the carcass. In the back of her mind somewhere she paused to wonder how Mark had managed to pull it up on that limb all by himself. What had happened was beyond belief. A dozen memories flooded her mind: of mornings when the milk foamed into the bucket and promised them nourishment for one more day; of Robert guiding a plow behind the strangely harnessed creature as Kate coaxed her along; and of the sound of dainty hoofs as Lydia led Pearly down a long hard road on a bleak late-winter day before David was born. She was more than a cow: she was the high confidence Lydia and Mark had shared on their wedding day when he had said, "She's all yours," and they had driven away from the infare to their first home. She was the hope that had carried Lydia through the suspense and destruction of war. And she was a gentle beast that had fed them, nourished Lydia's baby when food was scarce, and had been ready to do so again—until last night.

Lydia turned and ran toward the house. Tears streamed down her face. Mark met her halfway across the stump-filled yard. "How could you ever a-thought it, or a-done it?" she cried. For the first time since their marriage she turned on him in full hot anger. "Something that never harmed you, something gentle, how could you go out in the night and kill?"

His face reflected a mixture of startled incomprehension and shame. "A feller learns such things," he said more slowly, "learns more than he bargains for, I reckon, when he goes off to war."

"War! When will we ever be done with the war? Mama's life has been shattered, and Papa and Paul are changed, and you—it's like the mark of Cain had been set on you!"

"Lydia! It was just a cow."

Tears still ran down her face, but Lydia's voice was firm as rock beneath a waterfall. "She was a living thing. Killing and thinking of killing has got to stop sometime, somewhere. And no better time than now and no better place than here."

"Life's not a play-pretty, Lydia," Mark said sharply. "It's a fight. That's one thing a man learns."

"Well, I'm fighting! But to bring strength into this world, not to sap and squeeze and blast it. And it's partly your life, too, Mark McQueen, whether you care or not."

"Speak plain, Lydia."

Her voice faltered slightly, then steadied. "I'm trying to tell you, we're going to have another baby. And we could a-used our little cow's milk."

He turned away. "I didn't know. I wanted us to stand proud at our own table——"

"Pride's a poor bone to gnaw on an empty stomach."

"I said I didn't know about the baby, Lydia. But a man's got a right to make what peace he can with his pride, his own spirit——"

"It's a costly peace, for sure," Lydia said.

He nodded. "But somewhere there's got to be answers, too, to some of the questions a man asks. There's got to be an answer to the why."

Suddenly, seeing his lean and haunted and miserable face, and wrung by her own misery, Lydia flung herself into his arms and held him close. How strange, she thought, that she could hate and love in the same breath. She felt his arms tighten around her.

"Lydia, I know I've been a hard-natured man to live with since I come back home," he said. "But I never, none of the time, stopped holding on to my love for you."

Out there beyond this brief charmed circle, all around them, invading even their own minds, was something that disbelieved and destroyed and defeated. She knew it and recognized its power and yet she would never cease to deny it. In this moment of large weakness she suddenly knew large strength, a core buried deep within her that would refuse to be daunted by the outrageous blows or the niggling trifles human life was heir to.

5th
CHAPTER

In April, a year after the end of the war, Dr. Hornsby delivered Lydia of a girl. Since she had chosen David's name, Lydia asked Mark to name this baby. He called her Martha, after his mother, remembered only briefly from his childhood before she had died of smallpox.

Two summers later, Dr. Hornsby rode up the mountain again, and Burnett Moore McQueen was born. These two births were easy compared with her first one, when only Aunt Tildy had been there to help. Each time Lydia thought of that earlier time, and so did the doctor.

During his first visit, when he was waiting to bring Martha, while Lydia was still in early labor, Dr. Hornsby saw David for the first time. The child lacked two weeks of being a year old. His light hair still held its infant curl and baby chubbiness rounded his arms and legs. He crawled ponderously from the door to his mother's bed. The doctor stooped and picked him up lightly and trotted him on his knee.

Hornsby was a handsome man. Lydia delighted in the ease and precision with which he moved. He was of medium height and somewhat heavy-set, his dark brown hair was laced with streaks of grey and there were hints of dissipation in the lines around his mouth and deep blue eyes; yet intelligence—keenness of mind, quickness of wit, aptness of learning—was the first and strongest impression given by his looks and actions. Lydia had often wondered how he came to be in this corner of the world; it was said he had received training for medicine in the great city of Philadelphia. His wife, a short, plump, tightly corseted woman, with a pale tight mouth, seldom mingled with the valley folks. Mrs. Cass Nelson was her only friend. But everyone admired and enjoyed Dr. Hornsby and although his heavy drinking was the subject of constant gossip, it afforded that rare enough thing, the gossip of concern and affection rather than malice.

His fingers, Lydia noticed, as they moved deftly over David's head and temples, were short and thick, covered along their backs with hair, unlike her expectations of how a doctor's hands should look; but they were infinitely tender. "These bruises been here from birth?" he asked.

Lydia nodded. "But they're ever so much better now. When I brush his hair just right, a body would hardly notice."

Dr. Hornsby glanced at her sharply, and Lydia did not understand the expression in his quickly averted eyes. Then a pain of labor with the new baby broke into her thoughts and when she looked again, the man was playing some game with the child's hands and tapping him on one knee where it crossed his other knee. David looked at his mother, the blue eyes wide and round— the way Mark had used to look at her when he first came back from war, before he had turned to building up this farm and home with all the energy he possessed.

The boy gave a quick crow of laughter, clapped his pink hands and turned back to the doctor. Through closed lips he made a humming sound, and Lydia found herself hoping, as she had so many times lately, that the sound might develop into a word, "Mama" or "Man" or "Moo." It died, however, shapeless and meaningless.

From one of his saddlebags the doctor drew a small empty box. He removed the lid and fitted it back on several times, carefully and patiently. Then he handed it to David. As Lydia yielded to another pain, she saw him take the child to the other end of the room and leave him there on the quilt where he played until his father came in from doing the morning farm chores. When the doctor returned to her bedside, she squeezed his hand impulsively. "Can ever I love another one the way I love him?" she asked.

Dr. Hornsby smiled. "I guess there's never been a mother expecting her second baby who didn't wonder about that." He patted her hand. "You'll manage to multiply your love just as often as you multiply your family."

"It always seemed that David was sort of special. Coming when he did and all——"

"I know. And I want to tell you, Mrs. McQueen, many's the time since that night when I've bitterly regretted what happened."

"I never faulted you for it," Lydia said.

He turned away, self-recrimination deepening the lines in his face. "I—a doctor—it was unforgivable."

That brief conversation and understanding seemed to weld a bond of friendship between Lydia and Dr. Hornsby. And when Mark went to pay him for helping Lydia have their little girl, he refused to name a fee. "I owe your wife and your son and you something I can't repay," he said. "At least I can refrain from letting you pay me."

"But I came for you, you looked after Lyddy so well, you brought us the finest daughter a man could want," Mark said. "I wouldn't want to be beholden——"

"Please. I beg you never to mention it again."

Even Mark was put off by the contradiction of authority and pleading in his voice. They looked at each other across the battered wooden desk of the doctor's office—the tall, lean, mountain farmer with the blazing eyes, and the keen, skillful professional man with the stamp of dissatisfaction on his face—and they sensed their kinship. It was the kinship of mutual mortal hunger for knowledge beyond learning and certainty beyond doubt.

"Then I'm much obliged to you," Mark said indistinctly, turning to the door.

"And I to you," Dr. Hornsby replied. "Oh"—he delayed Mark—"next time your wife expects a baby, if you'll be so good as to

warn me ahead of time, I'll try to be sure that everything is
—ready."

"I'll bring you word."

In July, two years following, he was ready when Mark rode
down to fetch him one rainy morning. "You've got to take good
care of Lydia, Doctor," Mark said. "Before I come, her eyes stared
so big and full of pain as she lay there against the pillow. Did anything bad happen to her, I reckon we couldn't stand it."

Dr. Hornsby was startled at this strange man's sudden lack of
customary reserve. "Nothing bad will happen," he said.

When they arrived at the cabin, the doctor sent Mark to take
David and Martha down to their grandmother's and bring back
one of Lydia's sisters to assist him. A little while after he had gone,
Lydia's labor, instead of intensifying, gradually eased off. "False
alarms are not infrequent," Dr. Hornsby said. "We'll wait a little
while and see."

He gave her medicine from one of the dozen round bottles fitted in his saddlebags, and they talked with a friendliness that had
carried over from two years before, as if there had been no interruption. He questioned her at length about David and she shared
with him her concern over the fact that her first-born had not
learned to walk as soon as she had expected, that he spoke only a
few of the simplest words. At the same time, she allowed Dr.
Hornsby no opportunity to explain what the cause of her worry
might be. "Most likely he's slow because everyone—Mama and
Aunt Tildy especially—always spoiled him rotten. Everyone but
Mark, that is. You see, not knowing David when he was a new-
born baby must have made a difference with his papa. Somehow
they never seemed to take to one another. It's been Martha that
made the difference with Mark. She's such a good child."

"And so pretty, with those big brown eyes," Dr. Hornsby said.

Lydia smiled. "Thank you, Doctor. Mark's always speaking of
her eyes, too; and the way she clings to him, the way she's so quick
to walk, and talks already like a jaybird chattering—well, he thinks
she's mighty nigh perfection itself."

"There's no denying you've fine-looking children."

"I want them to *be* fine, too, have a chance in life. Dr. Hornsby,

95

you reckon we'll ever get a school worthy of the name on Thickety Creek?"

"I hope so, Mrs. McQueen."

"My father's had schooling," Lydia said thoughtfully. "He learned all of us children what reading and writing we know. And a little ciphering, too. But I want my children to go to a school-house and have a proper teacher. I long for them to amount to something. You know, my brother Robert has gone off to school. He's been away better than a year now. He wants to follow after the law."

"He spoke to me about it once, when he came for me to extract an abscessed tooth. I remarked to my wife that he was an unusual boy."

"What about your children, Doctor? What do they do for schooling?" Lydia asked.

Dr. Hornsby stood abruptly and walked to the open door. He stood looking out at the summer rain falling on the clearing around the cabin. "My daughters? Fortunately their mother was once a teacher. She's been able to tutor them at home. In a few years I think she wishes to send them to some female academy. Only one of them really enjoys her books, however. Lenore. The oldest. The other two—well, perhaps they're too young yet."

His tone puzzled Lydia, but she could tell that he was pleased when she repeated the girl's name. "Lenore. It fairly sings," she said.

"Yes." He almost seemed to be counting the raindrops, he stared out the door so intently. "Lenore. She was named from a poem. A student I met once at the University of Virginia wrote strange, haunting sort of poetry. Later I found some lines he'd composed to a 'lost Lenore.' " The sound of the rain was loud and insistent. Lydia hoped the storm would not beat down the fragile tomato plants she and Mark had set out in the new-ground day before yesterday. "Well, Mrs. McQueen"—the doctor walked back across the room—"we'll have to see what we can do toward getting free public school in the valley one of these days."

Something in his voice made her look up. "Surely there's none would stand against it," she said.

"Well, now, I wouldn't be so positive," he answered. "You know, taxes are needed to pay for such improvements."

"Who'd hold back taxes for their children's schooling?" Lydia asked.

"I don't know. I do know that Hamilton Nelson is the biggest taxpayer in the valley, now that his father's dead and he inherited all the property. And he's not married, has no children."

"But I meant everyone's children——"

"I know what you mean. Do men like Ham Nelson and Thomas Hawkins?" Dr. Hornsby demanded.

Lydia was silent, then she said, "But Hawkins has—a family."

"Yes. And I beg your pardon, Mrs. McQueen. When I spoke Thomas Hawkins' name, I had forgotten for the moment that his daughter is married to your brother."

"Dolly and Paul." Lydia twisted her fingers and even as she saw her bony knuckles whiten and grow red again, she was reminded of the countless times she had watched her mother perform this gesture. "Paul losing an arm in the war . . ." She hesitated. "I guess he had a yearning for something to protect."

"It's a natural need," Dr. Hornsby said.

"Maybe I oughtn't to say this," Lydia went on, "or maybe the only reason I can say it to you is because you're outside the family and it's preyed on my mind for all this past year: out in the woods, Dr. Hornsby, I've seen stout trees hung with the green leaves and white pearly berries of mistletoe that's ever so pretty to look at. It feeds off the sap of the limbs and the trunk that support it; and sometimes I've seen a tall strong tree drained of its life because of that mistletoe clinging to it."

"Mistletoe *is* a parasite. You're an observant woman, Mrs. McQueen."

"No. Just loving. My brother means a lot to me. And it's hard for a one-armed man to work in a mill." Tears stung her eyes. "I've not felt I could speak to anyone about these things . . ." She paused. "You see, my brothers, Paul and Robert, have always stood in my mind sort of like the opposites of mountain and ocean. Paul is steady and quiet and slow-changing as the hills, and although I never saw an ocean, I've always thought it to be quick and never-the-same and yet strong and constant underneath, like Robert."

"And each necessary and loved." Dr. Hornsby smiled.

"Oh, yes. A body couldn't spare either the land or water." She smiled back.

"I've seen your brother Paul at his father-in-law's mill. I believe he'll make out all right. You know his Dolly is expecting a baby?"

Lydia nodded.

"Your brother spoke to me about it. I believe he was worried because he said his wife did not want me to attend her. Sometimes young girls get notions. I told him she would probably be ready for me to come when the time arrived."

"I hope so," Lydia said, feeling a quick, returning discomfort of her own.

"There's enough waste in that community without adding another unnecessary iota to it," the doctor said abruptly, sharply, and as if removed to some distant observation point above his usual familiar territory. "Rains have about drowned all the early corn plantings; somebody burned a barn on Gentry Caldwell's new place night before last. And we buried the Haddon baby yesterday, dead of nothing but neglect. You know the Haddons?"

Lydia nodded, remembering the fight Mark had had years ago with Ham Nelson and Tilmon Haddon, the fight that had helped send them up here to the mountain for their home.

"They're trash of the earth—slovenly, ignorant, filthy—and yet we're told they're made in the image of God." Dr. Hornsby's face was troubled. "I can't understand why Nelson keeps them on his farm if he feels they're animals to live in a house not fit for a fox den, or why he doesn't admit them as human beings and try to give them a decent chance."

Lydia bit her lip against a sudden thrust of pain. It occurred to her that this apparently calm and self-sufficient man had found comfort, even as she had, in being able to talk of important hidden things here in a place removed from the valley in an unexpected suspended moment of waiting. "You've a lot to look after, Dr. Hornsby," she said.

98

He gave a short mirthless laugh. "When half the time I'm incapable of looking after even myself?" he asked, not of her but of himself.

The rain was slacking. "I hope Mark and Kate will get here before the baby comes . . ."

He became once more all efficiency and knowledge. "We shall make out all right either way, my dear," he assured her.

Kate and Mark did arrive before the baby. Kate, now eighteen, plump and easygoing, tidied up the room, heated water over the fire Mark started under the washpot in the yard, and bathed Lydia's sweating face with a cool cloth. Just after dusk the boy was born, with a lusty cry and a head as bare and white as an egg. They named him Burnett Moore McQueen, after Lydia's grandfather, who had been a preacher.

"Little Burn," Mark said, gazing at him fondly a few days after his birth. "I reckon he's a regular ripsnorter." Both the nickname and the reputation clung to the child.

The children thrived. Martha, trim and sure as a tiny wren, coaxed David, a year older and larger, into walking rather than crawling. David was devoted to his two-year-old sister and followed her every move, with his eyes if not his actions. Between them they greeted the new baby as a plaything, but they were each touched by jealousy at the time and attention he demanded from their mother. When Lydia saw this, she bent her thoughts to devising a way by which they could all be drawn together.

Whenever it was time for her to feed little Burnett, she sat in the only rocker and placed David and Martha at her feet. There, while the baby nursed at her overflowing breasts, she read aloud from the only book she owned. Psalms of praise and simple teachings of Jesus, thunderous words of creation and bittersweet wisdom of Ecclesiastes, these and dozens of other passages she read, knowing that, although they could not yet understand the meaning, the beauty and rhythm of the words would hold them captive if her voice could perform the proper magic. At such moments she recalled her own father reading some of these same melodic lines, these tart instructions and proverbs, and how his enchantment in their beauty, his concentration on their meaning, carried him away from the room where his family sat listening. Now she understood what he had experienced.

There was majesty in these words, sympathy in these parables, brief and vivid—ah, the young lambs lost in the dark, cold hills. The children's eyes grew large as she told of the shepherd's faithful search, as she bleated like the lost, strayed lamb. They all looked forward to these times when they could sit together in the embrace of her voice. Even Mark, sometimes when she nursed Burnett in the early evening, before David and Martha were in bed, sat and listened, too. Then Martha might climb up in her father's lap, and David, deserted by his sister, would creep into the rocker beside his mother. Then Lydia, holding the infant with one hand and the Bible in the other, wished for a third arm to encircle this strange, loving, older child.

During these years Mark worked with all the strength that was in him. He cut the trees and split rails, hundred after hundred, enough to trade in the valley for a cow to take the place of Pearly and use the barn the neighbors had helped them raise. Then he split more rails, enough to fence their fields. When his war money came, he took all that was left after he paid Big Matt Bludsoe for his land and bought a horse, a splendid black animal, tall and sleek and spirited.

"I'm sick of having everything second-best and scanty," he told Lydia when he took her out into the yard to see the stallion. "His name's Black Deuce and there's not a finer piece of horseflesh this side of the Blue Ridge."

"We could have bought a team of oxen," Lydia ventured.

"Oxen are dull, slow beasts," Mark said. "I wanted something with spirit. Like my wife," he added, and Lydia flushed with pleasure at his look.

Later she felt disloyal, but she could not help comparing the prime years and bearing of the horse with the old and withered look of the cow Mark had bought from Gentry Caldwell, almost dry of milk, expecting a calf in the spring. But later the cow had had her calf and had gone back to giving the wooden pail three-fourths full of milk twice a day; the calf had grown into an excellent heifer. And Black Deuce had earned his keep, snaking logs out of the clearings, pulling the bull-tongue plow to turn new-ground, jerking at tough green roots and stubborn stumps, hauling in crops.

Lydia helped Mark in the fields, taking the children to play on a grassy spot, or a quilt spread at the edge of the clearing, where she could watch them. Once, in winter, when she left them in the house alone while she carried water from the spring, David burned his left hand badly in the hot coals on the hearth. After that she was mortally afraid to leave the children out of her sight for long.

In the fields she planted and hoed, picked and harvested, piled stones and dug out roots from acres newly cleared. She pickled and dried and saved every scrap of food available. Their first winter on the mountain was long and meager, and memory of it drove her afterward to horde food with miserly passion.

Within the house, she worked from before-sun till after dark. The daily routine of making fire, fetching water, milking, cooking, sweeping, cleaning, sewing, caring for the babies, was augmented by other regular chores: churning, washing and boiling clothes in the big black kettle in the yard, ironing, making soap from ashes collected in the hopper Mark had built for her at one end of the house—and caring for baby chickens, ducks, pig, kitten, or pet squirrel someone had given her, or she had found. From the first setting of eggs and an old hen to hatch them that her mother had given her that first spring after she moved on the mountain, Lydia developed a flock of chickens. Foxes and weasels raided them, hawks carried off many of the young ones, but enough remained to provide all the eggs the family needed, except in the very coldest part of the winter. As for the pig, it was a runt Mark had traded from Ida Burke, but it was a female and Lydia was determined to make it live and grow into a sow that could bring them a litter, build up a regular drove.

David particularly enjoyed Lydia's care for all these young, and he helped her feed and doctor them. When Aunt Tildy—who had gone back to her own home from her sister's as soon as David moved—sent the child a stray kitten, he played with it constantly and let it sleep beside him. Lydia was pleased with his happiness in the kitten. It seemed to demonstrate to her that he was just like all other children, and it helped quiet the ripple of worry that crossed her mind with increasing frequency as she watched David and compared him with her younger children.

When Mark first came home from the war, Lydia had mistaken his silences for indifference to herself. Slowly she came to realize that they were the result of a loss of faith in his fellow man and a questioning of God Himself. Aunt Tildy had taught her how to treat many illnesses, where a poultice would help and what sort of root or leaf would brew best tea for a certain fever, but this was a malady beyond such simple cure. The time and love Lydia had vowed to give Mark had been helpful—but they were not enough. They had not made him whole, had not quieted the rages into which the simplest difficulty sometimes sent him, although the understanding of which Lydia's gifts were born bound him to her more steadfastly than any romance or quick pleasure they had known during the earliest days of marriage. The savage starvation of the first weeks after he returned from prison gave way to normal hunger, and he and Lydia found satisfaction in each other. They were young and strong, they drove their bodies to labor to the limit of endurance, and they brought themselves to love with the same fullness and freedom.

Lydia did not see her family often. Robert went away to school, Kate courted several boys but chose none for wedding; Annie Marie, delicate of bone and size but tough of tongue and spirit, gradually seemed to become more like Aunt Tildy, taking Sarah Moore's place in work and care for the household, while she retreated more and more into a private world of reflection and memory. With increasing frequency, Jesse Moore turned to his books for companionship. Paul's marriage to Dolly Hawkins had disappointed him, not because of any personal dislike but because of the hope he had held for his son's future. And looking at the pretty, silly child who had become Paul's wife, he felt a foreboding that between these two, weakness would overcome strength, the protected would lead the protector. His feeling was confirmed when Paul protested at first but finally went with Dolly to live at Thomas Hawkins' and help him run the mill. With Lydia and Paul and

Robert gone, and only the girls, Kate and Annie Marie and Elizabeth, and his sickly wife at home, Jesse Moore found challenge and pleasure only in the books he cherished.

He did make arrangements for monthly Sunday services at their home. There was not yet a church building in this remote valley and various handfuls of congregations depended on traveling circuit riders or missionaries to stop at intervals and preach a sermon, perform weddings for those who had become engaged, conduct funeral services for those who had been buried, baptize or sprinkle or accept into membership anyone who professed faith. Sarah Moore spent a large part of each day reading her Bible, or merely sitting with it open on her lap, and it occurred to her husband that the visits of a regular preacher, the fellowship of a church group meeting at their house, might bring her happiness. When he spoke of it to her, she smiled and tears filled her eyes.

"Mr. Moore, you're a good man," she said.

"Now, Sally, don't tell me something I already know," he jollied her, "but what about my idea? Would you like to have church here for a while?"

She nodded. "It would pleasure me a heap." She wiped her eyes with one corner of her neat print apron. "I know how you hold your privacy dear, too, Mr. Moore. I know you're doing this for me."

"Partly for you, Sally, but maybe in part for Thickety Creek, too. Get a regular preacher bringing the word of God to this place, maybe some of the bitterness and enmity and strife left by the war will be stamped out."

He turned his handiness with carpenter's tools to building, at the gable end of the house, an outside stairway and door to the loft. The loft room was large and ample, but its ceiling sloped sharply from the roof-pole and a grown person walking anywhere except in the middle of the room had to stoop to keep from bumping his head. The door and a tiny window in the opposite gable afforded the only light. Despite these drawbacks, however, there was much enthusiasm for "the Prophet's Room," as Sarah Moore had named it right after her husband started work on the loft. Several neighbors, including Paul and his father-in-law, came and helped

103

build benches for the congregation and a crude Bible stand for the minister.

The Moores' loft soon became familiar as the Baptist meeting place. On the first Sunday of each month, elderly Elijah Gudger rode out from the county seat. Gudger had been born in England and brought to America by his father when he was a boy of ten. He had won a reputation throughout North Carolina as a mighty laborer for the Lord and the Baptist faith, and had built numerous churches in the Piedmont area of the state before he came to the mountains and built his last and largest Baptist church in the only town in rugged, beautiful Nantahala County. British accents still clung to his speech, and it seemed to Lydia that Old World dignity and elegance came into the valley whenever she glimpsed his tall, spare frame, crowned by a shock of white hair and covered by a long black frock coat of fine, meticulously brushed, English material.

By 1870, Elijah Gudger was becoming a familiar figure on Thickety Creek and he and Jesse Moore had formed a warm friendship. After the Sunday services each month the minister ate a midafternoon dinner at the Moores' table and he and his host discussed the sermon, the Bible, church doctrine, and worldly events of the weeks just past. When the girls had finished eating, they either slipped away from the table or sat nodding drowsily with full stomachs and empty ears, while the two elderly men compared knowledge and clashed wits. Frequently, Gudger stayed overnight, having broken off discussion with Moore too late in the afternoon to begin the long ride back to town, and then they talked late into the night.

"I'll provide you nourishment of the body while you nourish my mind," Jesse Moore said to him in jesting truth.

Lydia felt the need to bring her children to some companionship this summer when David was five, Martha four and Burnett, two. They were fine children, she thought, but shy as partridges. They needed the sight of strangers and groups of people, and the services at her parents' home provided her with an excellent opportunity to take them to the valley.

The trip down from the mountain was long, but they rode in

104

the jolty farm wagon, pulled by Black Deuce. At first Lydia had hesitated to drive the big stallion, but Mark refused to go to the sermons, assured her she could control Black Deuce if she never let him have his head, and so she did what she must.

The first Sunday in July was hot and humid. As soon as she reached her father's house, Lydia put Burn to nap on the bed in the cool back bedroom. She loosed the collar on the new shirt she had made for David and pushed up the sleeves on Martha's dress; both the shirt and dress, so fresh and carefully ironed at home, were dusty and wrinkled from the children's long ride in the wagon.

She could hear people gathering upstairs and suddenly she wondered how she herself must look. She had been thinking only of the children and their appearance before family and friends. Hurriedly she glanced in the narrow mirror above the washstand. She had not realized before how sunburned the skin on her face and arms had become during all her work out of doors. When Kate came in the room to tell her that the rest of the family was waiting for her before they went upstairs to the services, she smiled and said self-consciously, "I guess I haven't been taking the pains we did when we were girls, Kate. Remember those old stockings pulled over our arms to protect them when we worked in Papa's fields, and the big hats to shade our faces? Seems like I don't have time for all such as that any more."

Kate's glance flicked over her. "You don't look very stylish," she said, "but then nobody around here does since the war. Unless, of course, you count Dolly." She took Lydia's hand. "But you look mighty good to me any time."

Later, as they sat in the Prophet's Room, listening to the measured flow of Elijah Gudger's message, Lydia realized what Kate meant when she spoke of Dolly. Paul and Dolly and their child, Timothy, sat two benches in front of Lydia. The boy, born three months after Burnett, was not quite two years old, and Lydia had not seen her sister-in-law since the day of the baby's birth. Paul had been up on the mountain during this past year and a half, always with a legitimate reason for his visit—Ham Nelson was wanting to know if Mark would trade Black Deuce for some land in the valley; or Paul's father-in-law, Thomas Hawkins, was wondering if Mark would like to bring his corn down to the new mill, and since he was now a relative the toll would be only half charge. But Lydia knew that her brother's real purpose in coming was to see her and Mark and the children and make certain they fared well.

Mark welcomed Paul each time but gave him short answers to carry back with him: To Ham Nelson, "Tell him I have both the land and the horse I want. No need for trading." To Mr. Hawkins: "Tell him I've been a friend to the Burkes and they to me, since long before he moved to the mouth of Thickety Creek. I couldn't go back on them now."

Paul received the messages with the same patient humor in which he had brought the inquiries. As he played with the children and ate the food she fixed for him, Lydia sensed a growing reserve and sadness in her brother. The confidence he had appeared to muster when he first came back from war was subtly changing into subdued acceptance. Lydia always asked about Dolly and Tim. She was careful to choose the right words, words that were commonplace and could have no hidden meanings, for ever since that day spent helping Dolly bear her baby, Lydia had had much to hide.

She looked at Dolly now, fragile and white, sitting on the hard, square bench near the front of the room, her face lifted attentively toward Preacher Gudger. Dolly was dressed all in white, the material of her dress soft and fluffy. Like a summer cloud that has no meaning, Lydia thought. It doesn't bring rain, it doesn't interfere with the sun—it's just a pretty, loose thing floating up there in the high blue sky.

Dolly had meaning, however. She was Paul's wife. For that reason, when she had sent Paul to fetch his sister that chilly October night, Lydia had left David and Martha and taken her infant and gone to help.

"It's a notion Dolly has, maybe because her time's come a little early," Paul explained apologetically, "but she won't let me get Dr. Hornsby, or even Aunt Tildy. She grew plumb hysterical when I insisted. You were the only one she'd even let me mention bringing to the house, Lydia. I hate like mischief to ask you———"

"Nothing to hate about it, Paul," Lydia reassured him. To herself, as she dressed, she admitted her fright at the responsibility of serving as midwife, but she hoped that, once she had seen Dolly, she might persuade the girl to let Paul go after Dr. Hornsby.

She made sure there would be food enough ahead for Mark and the children during the next day and night. "I'll have to bring little Burn with me, to nurse," she told Paul.

The three of them rode down the mountain in the cold moonlight. Far away, in some valley the other side of Stony Ridge, Lydia heard the baying of hounds on a fox chase. That would be the Bludsoes and their notorious pack of dogs. Lately, Mark's only diversion from work had been an occasional hunt with Big Matt and his boys. When Lydia asked him about the company he kept, he replied, "They're as good as any," and refused to say more about his friendship with those men. In the summer he had brought home a black-and-tan pup from a litter of one of Morgan's dogs, and in spite of herself Lydia had grown attached to the awkward, flop-eared hound. It had already developed a deep, distinctive bark that led Mark to name it Big Bass. As they turned aside near the Devil's Brow to the trail that led to the valley, Lydia wondered if she had remembered to tell Mark where she kept the corn bread for Big Bass.

When they reached his father-in-law's house, Paul and Lydia found Thomas Hawkins pacing the floor in despair. "She ordered me out of the room. There's no one in there with her and I can hear her groaning. Something's got to be done. She'll die!" For once, his sallow face had found a tinge of color.

"Don't fret, Mr. Hawkins," Lydia said, more calmly than she had thought possible. "You and Paul tidy up everything out here, put some water to boil. I'll see after Dolly." Then she had pulled off her cloak and bonnet, washed her hands and gone in to help birth a baby and bury a secret forever.

She closed her eyes now, trying to concentrate on Elijah Gudger's words so that the memory of that day would be erased, but she could not hear the new words addressed to her for the old ones ringing in her ears.

107

"You won't tell? You won't, will you, Lydia?" Dolly's fingers were small, but they scratched and clung like a bird's. "Lydia, I couldn't bear to have any of those others come, those strangers. I've heard of women bearing babies and how they chatter queer things, and often the truth, and I know I'll speak his name before this day's over. But you'll have to forget you ever heard. You will, Lydia?"

"Dolly, what are you saying?" Lydia was puzzled and frightened at her incoherent talk.

"Lydia, you mean you're not going to help me?" Tears rolled down the round pale cheeks, pretty even in her distress. "You were my only hope. Ever since I knew Paul's folks, I've thought of you as the one to turn to in need, the one who would know what to do. And now I can't ask you what to do! Oh, I couldn't lay blame on you, Paul being your brother—but Lydia, I have no one."

"Hush, Dolly, hush. You've Paul and your father and me——"

"And thought of him! Oh, he said he'd always be here, too, but now none of you can help me."

"Him? Who are you talking about, Dolly?" Lydia asked.

"If you won't tell, if you won't ever tell. . . ."

The two women stared at each other. Dolly whispered a name. "Ham Nelson."

Lydia felt a chill run through her. "What about Hamilton Nelson?"

"Oh, he talked so sweet to me, Lydia, gave me goods from his store, whatever I wanted. I'd never had so many pretty things before. I thought he really cared for me—till he found out I was going to have a baby. Then he asked me how he could be sure it was his. He said a pretty girl like me might have a lot of beaus. Oh, Lydia, he knew it was his, but he told me I could go find a pappy for my——" Her voice broke off in hysterical weeping. Her teeth chattered.

"And you found Paul?" Lydia said slowly. "Then the baby's not early at all."

Dolly could not answer. Her crying was uncontrollable.

Lydia wondered for a moment if the room itself showed signs of any of the wreckage wrought by the words she had heard here in the last few minutes. It seemed odd that the walls still stood and the furniture remained in place, that Dolly's silver-backed mirror and comb and brush still lay in a row on her dresser. Yet nothing was changed. Lydia remembered a childhood chant: "Sticks and stones may break my bones, but names will never hurt me." She knew that if Paul ever heard the words Dolly had just spoken, they would break something that sticks and stones had never managed to touch. She took the hysterical girl by the shoulders and shook her as hard as she was able.

"Hush! Do you hear me? Hush your caterwauling!" Lydia commanded. "Lay by your selfishness just this once and see what you can do for somebody else."

The crying broke off into several long sobs. "Then you won't tell? You'll help me bear my secret?"

"I'll help you bear your baby." Lydia forced her to lie down in the bed. "No, I won't repeat what you've told me. How could I, knowing what it would do to my brother? If you can live with your secret, I can."

Dolly's crying had become a whimper. "But I'm doing it for Paul, too. Oh, I'll make him a good wife hereafter, Lydia. You'll see."

Lydia wondered, especially when Dolly whispered Ham's name several times during the labor just before the baby came. Lydia thanked God, during the long hours of that day, for all that Aunt Tildy had taught her. She sent Paul to Dr. Hornsby to get some drops for the baby's eyes. At last, in the early evening, both the boy and his mother were resting. Dolly had had a comparatively easy time. Lydia was exhausted, both in spirit and body. But when Dolly's father insisted that she spend the night with them, she begged Paul to take her back home. No matter how soft the Hawkinses' feather beds might be, she could not lie under this roof. She wanted time to think, and compose herself, before she tried to talk with an earnest and happy Paul, who thought he had just become a father. She wanted to be with Mark.

Studying their backs as they sat there before her this hot, still Sunday, Lydia wondered how life in their house had been during

Tim's infancy. He was squirming now on the hard bench and in a moment he turned to look around him. Lydia could see that his face was small and pale, like Dolly's. She tried to reject the thought that his black eyes, small and round as shoe buttons, were Hamilton Nelson's eyes. Slowly and carefully she smiled at the unhappy-looking child, but he did not smile back. And later, after the sermon, when Paul was lifting him up to kiss her and Dolly said, "Tim, this is your Aunt Lydia," he pecked at her cheek and wriggled to the floor, where he stood holding Paul's hand.

"That's a fine suit you're wearing, Tim," Lydia said. "You'll have to show it to your cousins David and Martha, over there with their grandpa."

"Such—such healthy-looking children you have, Lydia," Dolly said. "Here, Tim, let me straighten your jacket, then you run over and see the little boy and girl with your grandpa Moore."

The child walked away reluctantly. "No need to tidy him up to play with my children," Lydia laughed. "I just loosed their collars and made them comfortable before we came up to the preaching, in this July heat. After all my work before daylight to scrub them and neat them up so nice, too!"

"It's good to see you down here, Lydia," Paul said.

"Oh, yes," Dolly agreed, and Lydia wished she would not push so hard with her chatter, "it seems like a Methuselah age since we've seen you."

"You been well, Lyddy?" Paul asked.

"Oh, yes."

"Of course she has. She looks as strong and sturdy as the children," Dolly said, and Lydia was uneasy at the undertone of resentment in her voice. Lydia's father had always said that the quickest way to lose a friend was to give him good advice or the loan of money; there was another sure way: possess his secret that must never be told.

"I wish Mama looked half as strong," Lydia said. She searched Paul's face. "How is Mama? She seems so frail."

"Dr. Hornsby says there's something wrong with her blood," Paul said. "He's giving her tonic, but I can't see that it's helped her any."

110

They grew silent as they saw their mother coming toward them, her arm around the waist of a wizened, white-haired woman dressed all in black silk, even to the gloves covering her tiny hands. "Children," Sarah Moore said in a happy, excited voice, "here's someone I want you to meet, someone I haven't seen in a long, long, long time. . . . Naomi, these are my children, Paul and Lydia and Paul's wife, Dolly. Paul was in the war, you know."

The stranger gave them each a brief, sure handclasp. "Sarah's children!" she said. "Paul, Lydia, Dolly," and she bowed her head in a brief regal nod of acknowledgment.

Their mother turned to them. "Naomi was a friend when I lived in Virginia long ago. Of course, I was just a child and she was the prettiest young lady along the Shenandoah, but we were neighbors, and when she and Willoughby Hayes were married, she saw to it that I received an invitation to their splendid wedding. And now, just imagine, Naomi and Willoughby living here, down on the river just below Thickety, after all these years!"

"Of course, Mama," Paul said gently, "everyone knows Mr. Hayes is the finest fiddle player in these parts——"

"You'd better mind your tongue here at church service," the little old lady interrupted. "I've heard it's rumored that some think Willoughby's music is the work of the devil."

"Oh, I just love to hear it, Mrs. Hayes," Dolly said.

"Of course, I'm sure I'd heard their names spoken," Sarah Moore was saying in preoccupied bewilderment, "but I suppose it just never entered my mind that this would be my old, my dear Virginia friend."

"And when I heard of Sarah Moore," Naomi Hayes said, "the few times I've been out in the community since we've lived here, I had no idea it was the little Sarah, the pretty child, who'd once been our neighbor before her parents took her traipsing off to the wilds of North Carolina."

Then Jesse Moore came up with Preacher Gudger and the three grandchildren, and other neighbors who had not seen Lydia for a long time stopped to greet her.

A little while later, while Lydia helped Kate and Annie Marie fix dinner on the table, she sent the children outside to play, under her younger sister, Elizabeth's, supervision.

"Be careful with Tim," she told Martha. "Remember, he's younger and you're a big girl."

She experienced a quick nostalgia for the long hot Sunday afternoons, not too many years past, when she and her brothers and sisters had been the ones going to play and let "older folks" visit, with the parents' soft, monotonous voices rising and falling as they talked inside the house or out under the sugar-maple tree in the yard. "Seems hard to think we're the grown-up, settled ones now," Lydia laughed, as she handed Dolly a bowl of gravy to set on the table. "Here, you'd better have an apron to protect that pretty dress."

Dolly tied the wide checked apron around her narrow waist. "Don't reckon I'll get to wear it much longer anyway," she said.

"Will you pass it on to me then, Dolly?" Elizabeth, lingering near the door, asked quickly, trying to compare her thirteen-year-old size with Dolly's.

"Lizzie, mind your manners," Annie Marie said sharply and slapped at her younger sister's wrists. "Go on out and tend to the young'uns."

But Dolly was speaking only to Lydia. She did not notice the others in the room. "Paul and me—we'll be having a baby along about the end of spring."

Lydia noticed that she did not say "another baby." She took Dolly's hands. "I'm glad," she said. "Ever so glad. You let me know if I can help."

A light flush crossed Dolly's cheeks. "That's mighty kind, I'm sure. But I hope I'm more grown-up this time, not so notionly, as Paul says. We'll call on Dr. Hornsby."

"I'm glad," Lydia said again.

"You can leave little Tim with us while you're abed," Kate told her.

"I don't know," Dolly hesitated. "We'll see."

Jesse Moore's voice from the next room interrupted them. "What about food in there, you womenfolk? You running anything but your tongues?"

112

"Yes, Papa, it's 'most ready; we're taking up dinner," Kate called.

Just as they were ready to sit down, leaving the children until a second table, there were shouts and cries outside. "I'll see about it," Lydia said. "The rest of you go ahead. Just some childish trouble."

Out under the maple tree, the children were in a scramble. A frantic Elizabeth was holding Martha with one hand and Tim with the other, trying to keep them apart as they hit and kicked at each other. David stood apart, against the tree.

"Bless us, whatever is the matter?" Lydia said as she ran to them. "Martha, what are you doing to your little cousin?"

The child's carefully plaited hair had come loose and there was a streak of dirt mixed with tears down each cheek. "He kicked David," she screamed. "He doesn't like my brother; he'll hurt him."

"Martha, hush!"

"Moo. Baa. Oink oink," Tim said, and Lydia realized that unconsciously he was mocking David. His pale cheeks were lively with spots of pink, as he pointed his finger at David and laughed gleefully.

Lydia looked at her five-year-old, his back against the tree trunk, eyes wide and full of troubled wonder. "What happened?" she asked Elizabeth.

"They were playing make believe," her sister said, "and Martha was to run the house and Tim be her baby and they were letting David build the farm. He was putting pebbles inside the twig fences he'd built and making noises, like Tim just made, for each animal. While he was putting one batch in, his hand slipped and I guess he knocked over something Tim was building—I wasn't paying too close mind to it all. First thing I knew, Tim had kicked David and before I could get to him, he kicked David again. David never did fight back, he just sat there sort of stunned, like he looks now. But that little Martha, she come at Tim like a whirlwind . . ."

Lydia looked full-face at her son. The midday heat out here in the yard had brought beads of sweat to her face, but that sweat

113

was turning clammy. Her hands were cold. Once, long ago, she had found a hummingbird flown into the house by mistake, and before she could rescue it or guide its way back through the open door, it had beaten itself to death in a corner. She could almost see those fragile frantic wings beating behind David's eyes at this moment, or in the pulse at his throat. She knew that a moment she had avoided for years had finally arrived.

Tim, released from Elizabeth's grip, was running around the tree, lisping the same animal noises he'd imitated before and laughing with strange childish cruelty. Was there something of the pack in every individual, then, even in innocent children? The pack, the hunt, the kill, turning on the weakest, nipping at tendon, slashing at the jugular?

"Take Tim on inside to his mother, please, Elizabeth," she said in a tight voice. "Martha, you go along, too—and be a nice girl the rest of the day."

When they were across the yard, she bent down and slowly examined the twigs David had arranged for fences. "About as good rails as your daddy could split," she said aloud. Where one had been knocked down, she carefully rebuilt it.

She stood up and David was beside her. He buried his face in her apron and sobbed. Slowly, trying to keep from doing any of the hasty, startling things her impluses cried out for, she folded her arms around him.

The boy's tears fell on her hand. If only *she* could cry and relieve any fraction of this pain. She knew—all along she had known, somewhere back in the cave of her mind, but she had locked the fear away, never allowed it into daylight. How foolish to blind yourself to a precipice ahead.

"Little David. Hush," she whispered. To herself, "Something happened when he was born, that long night of his birthing . . ." A numbness spread through her as she admitted all the mounting suspicions and the single sweeping fact she had steadfastly refused to confront. "David's not right!"

"Lydia," someone called from the house, standing in the door at a distance, "is everything all right? Your dinner is growing cold."

The cold of her dinner, even if it were chunks of ice lying in her stomach, could never equal the cold settling over her heart. She could not even bring a reply from her throat to answer the someone who was calling her.

Why her David? Why the child who had already known too much love from the old women, and too little from his father; whose very expression frequently bespoke a wonder, a need, a bewildered lostness she had tried not to see. And now she knew these had been more than fleeting glances. They were revelations of David himself.

Paul came across the yard. "What is it, Lydia? Is David hurt?"

She looked at him and he was startled by the pain in her drawn face. "Lydia——"

"Hitch up Black Deuce for me, Paul," she said in a tense high voice. "I've got to go to Mark. I've got to go home. Tomorrow we'll have to go and see Dr. Hornsby——"

"Did Tim hurt him, Lydia? Little Martha said——"

She shook her head. "It's not that, Paul. Tim didn't hurt David any more than we've all hurt him before. Or will again, I expect." The child had stopped crying and she wiped his eyes and smudged face on her apron. "Why don't you go in and eat a piece of Grandma's chicken now?" she asked, and nodded toward the house. He smiled at her, and went.

"I'm glad you're taking him to the doctor——"

Lydia looked at Paul. "Then you've seen this? You and the others have talked about it—about David?"

He nodded unhappily. "Just the past year or so. We didn't know how to name it to you. Mama says it's just——"

"Don't!" She put her hands over her ears. "We'll go to the doctor and learn the truth—tomorrow."

But even Dr. Hornsby could not tell her what all of the truth might be. When Mark and Lydia brought David to see him, he peered and probed and examined, spoke of injury at birth and lack of certainty as to how much damage might be done.

"Isn't there something we can understand—or do?" Mark asked.

"There's nothing we know to do for him," Dr. Hornsby answered. "Someday maybe someone will explore the secrets . . ."

He ran his hands over David's temples. "You remember, Mrs. McQueen, those bruise marks he still carried when I came to deliver your second baby?"

Lydia nodded. "They finally went away."

"But they left their mischief behind. Believe me, Mr.—Mrs. —McQueen, if there was anything on God's earth I could do . . ." His eyes even now, as he talked to them, were bloodshot, Lydia noticed. His handsome face was haggard. Perhaps she could hate him; she didn't know. His was the largest responsibility for what had happened, for the fact that people would call her firstborn foolish, crazy, an idiot. She had heard them use the words before. She had heard folks talk of Sparrow, the witty. She buried her face in her hands. But she could feel only pity for the doctor. Pity for him, for her child, for Mark, and herself.

They left the doctor's house and began the journey through the valley and up the mountain.

6th
CHAPTER

The next day was not different from the day before: the morning light came early along the mountaintops, shedding a pearly summer glow over the narrow valley; the chickens fluttered down from their roosting trees like plump, feathery leaves; the cow bawled once in the pasture before Lydia went to milk her, and the heifer gave an echo; Black Deuce tossed his head and pranced proudly as Mark made ready to harness him for the day's work on the mountainside. The little stream splashed over its bed of rocks and matted leaves; birds were busy in the nearby woods; the children dressed and ate and skipped out into the soft, warm morning. Lydia carried ashes from the fireplace and dumped them into the ash hopper behind the house; she picked beans in the garden and sat down by the cool spring to string and break them: everything ran on just as it had the morning before they went down to see Dr. Hornsby, just as it had every day before that—and yet nothing, to Lydia, was the same.

The next day came and the next week. A month passed and summer became autumn. The anger that had burned in Mark when he first returned from war was rekindled. He could not bear to see David's awkwardness. Once, when the boy fell from the top

117

of the rail fence that enclosed the pasture, and they carried him indoors to make sure no bones were broken, Mark said to Lydia, "Had I been home before he was birthed, you wouldn't a-had a man's work to do, the boy might never have been—the way he is."

He watched while Lydia felt carefully over the boy's legs and arms. When she was satisfied he was all right, she gave David a tickle in the ribs and joined in his laughter as freely as she could. "That old fall didn't hurt this chap," she announced. "Now you run on out and play, but don't climb any more for a while."

He nodded and climbed slowly off her lap.

"Same as if he had been out on the battleground," Mark said, watching him go through the door, "he's victim to that war—and to those hellish outliers!"

Lydia's throat was tight with suffering held inside herself. At first, she had tried to believe that the doctor was mistaken; after all, he was only human and men could be wrong about these things; David had already shown improvement since he was a baby: he was the sweetest-dispositioned child she had. But her common sense would not let her escape the truth so easily. Then for a while she had let her work and the rest of the family and everything else go, while she worked with David, teaching him words, coaxing him to talk, doing all she knew to make his walking and running easier, more like the other children's. But her conscience would not let her neglect the rest of her family indefinitely, so she turned back to them and tried to divide her care as justly as possible. During these small reconciliations with the truth, however, she had not been able to share her desperate evasions with Mark, with her husband, with the one person who could have shared them if only he had not been ridden by his own question: why? And by his own need to bring justice out of what seemed unjust. He had convinced himself that this was the last and ultimate outrage bequeathed them by the bushwhacking band that had wrought such harm during the war.

"Seems as if a man could have got some lead by this time as to their names," he said to Lydia, "but all the folks down in that valley are thick as thieves. Did they know who the renegades were, they'd never tell me." He slapped his hand on the table. A pewter trencher and the water dipper one of the children had left there jumped and rattled. "A Union man's got no show among all these Rebels."

"Papa was a Rebel," Lydia said, in a tight voice, trying to be calm, to be reasonable, "and he can't learn any more than you about those raids." The war seemed very long ago. Perhaps Mark was right, however, and it was still alive—in David, in Paul's crippled arm, and Mark's crippled view of life.

"They needn't think I'll be forgetting," he went on. "Long as there's breath in me I'll be seeking out the traitors that caused me to be in that Andersonville death-hole, caused you and your ma to be robbed and ruined——"

"Mark!" It was a choked cry. If David's affliction meant a renewal of Mark's old bitterness, how could she bear them both? "I don't know—I don't know——"

Misunderstanding, he squeezed her hand. "We'll find out, Lyddy. We'll find out."

So misery clung to them like a stale odor that could not be banished. And words could not span the gulf between them.

Work went on. Sometimes it seemed to Lydia that work was the only certainty, the only lasting truth in a human world of fitful change. Work and the mountains remained. Joy was deceitful and as brief as a summer rainbow. Love was a spear upon which you hurled yourself in ecstasy—to discover pain and bear the wound forever. A man in your heart, the child of your flesh, a dream of your spirit—you gave yourself to them, wholly and in wonder, and they never knew you. They looked at you with longing but with the eyes of a stranger, and you looked at them out of love and knew they saw in turn only the eyes of another stranger.

She watched David grow—his brown, slightly curly hair always too long because he would not sit still long enough to have it cut, so she trimmed it only now and then; his wide-eyed, puzzled gaze; his heavy gait—and numbness froze her. Sweat rolled down her neck and body as she helped Mark in the August haying, the October stacking of fodder, the winter hauling of wood—but inside herself she remained rigid with cold. She drove herself to work

119

and her body ached with fatigue; still she felt only that inner, clammy chill.

Little Martha played with David, the oldest, and Burnett, the youngest, and Lydia marveled at the instinct that made the child treat her brothers as if they were the same age. Watching them roll together on the floor or hide her thimble in a game or make a playhouse of twigs and bits of broken crockery, content and absorbed in their make-believe, Lydia could almost forget the shock and dread of David's difference.

But then suddenly the thimble would be lost—Lydia's precious thimble, given to her by her mother, stored with her needle in the small wooden box that had a tiny painting of a beautiful lady's head—black hair and red lips and a rose behind her left ear—on the inside of the lid. And one day, while they were still searching franticly, Mark came back early from a trip to the blacksmith's with Black Deuce. Lydia could hear the stallion's new shoes striking against the stones in the yard.

Whenever Mark went down to the valley, he returned home uncertain and full of suspicion and hate. Lydia dreaded each return and now, before she had time to tell the children to postpone their search and play at something quieter, while she herself was still on her knees beside the table, Mark strode through the door. His hat sat far back on his head, his face was tight and uncommunicative, his mouth was set in a thin line.

"What ails you-all?" he demanded. They looked up. Only the baby tottered toward him across the uneven floor.

Lydia stood up and brushed her skirt; her hands trembled. Before she could speak he went on, "What in thunder has gone wrong now?"

"Mama's thimble," Martha answered in a small, high voice from under the bed. "Mama's thimble's gone."

Mark knew Lydia's need of her sewing tools, knew how hard a thimble was to come by in the mountains. "Gone? How could it be *gone?*"

She heard the burden of meaning he laid on the word and knew that he had brought some outside trouble home to make the moment larger than it was in truth. "Of course it's not truly gone."

She made her voice as light as possible and scooped little Burn up from the floor, where he was pulling at Mark's trousers. "Sometime when we're not expecting or looking, that silly old thimble will turn up——"

Mark scowled at her. "I don't rest easy when things are lost. Enough been taken from us already, and money everywhere scarce as hen's teeth. How come the thimble out of its place anyway?"

"We had it for a play-pretty." Little Martha crawled from under the bed and stood in the center of the room, smoothing her tousled hair in a gesture exactly like her mother's, calmly unaware of the threat in Mark's voice.

"Your mama's sewing plunder wasn't meant to be used for play-pretties," he said. "You shouldn't——"

"Oh, it's all right. Mama said we could——"

"You disputing me, miss?" Mark demanded.

"Sh-h, Martha," Lydia said. "You see, Mark——"

"No, I don't see and I'm trying to find out if this——"

"I wasn't 'sputing, Papa," Martha interrupted earnestly, in a smaller voice, uncertain now in the tense atmosphere that suddenly surrounded her. Her lower lip quivered.

"And don't break in when older folks are talking! I won't bring up a houseful of disrespectful young'uns. Be it in your minds to turn spoiled-rotten like your cousin Tim, recall that Paul Moore ain't your pappy or that fancy Dolly ain't——"

"Mark!" Lydia cried.

At that moment David darted from a far corner of the room where he had stood half hidden. He snatched Martha's hand and pulled her toward the fireplace. Behind a crock of cream that stood at the edge of the hearth souring for the churn, he pointed out the thimble. But as he brought it forth from the hiding place, he let go of his sister's hand and one of their feet—whose it was impossible to tell—tripped against the big crock. With a crash the jar struck the hearth, shattering to fragments, spilling thick cream over the stones and into the fire.

"Watch what you're doing!" Mark was on the children in two strides. He did not look at David, but his left hand caught Martha's arm and with his right he gave her a heavy blow on her little backside. Startled, the child cried out, then stared up at her father, blinking back tears, shrinking away from him.

"Why don't you look after your brother?" But his sudden action had released the tension in him and now his voice broke. "You —we've got to help him." He let loose of Martha's arm. His temper cooled as quickly as it had flamed.

Lydia knew how troubled he must be if he was driven to hurt without reason the very child he loved best. Oh, nothing was what it seemed any more and the ways of God and man alike were beyond all understanding. She could have wept for the realization and misery growing in her husband's face. The strong smell of spilled cream soured the room.

She set Burnett down by the table and took the sedge broom from its hearth corner. With long hard strokes she began to brush the thick cream into the ashes. "Mama." Martha ran to her and clutched her apron. "Mama, Mama, Mama."

Lydia tried to make her voice matter-of-fact for the child. "All right, Martha." She stooped down and straightened Martha's pinafore and wiped away, as though it were an afterthought, the tears brimming in her eyes. "Like your Papa says, we've all got to try to help each other. Now why don't you and David put on your coats and go out to the barn and see if you can find a nest some old hen's hid out? Bring me an egg and I might make us a little sweet-bread cake for supper."

David, who had stood immobile beside the broken crock, walked over now and took his sister's hand. She pulled away from him, but when he took down their jackets from the pegs along the wall and brought hers across the room, she put it on. Without a word, gravely, as though they must carry without spilling it some invisible cup full to the brim, they went outside. The door closed carefully behind them.

Mark slumped down in a chair by the table. He threw his hat down beside him and rubbed the back of his hand across his forehead. Lydia swept the hearth. Then she went outside and brought in a bucket of water and a handful of sand. She scrubbed the stones and the floor around the fireplace thoroughly. The baby watched her.

122

"They's to be no more credit allowed down at the store," Mark said suddenly.

Lydia stopped her scrubbing. "The store" would be Ham Nelson's, down at the forks of Thickety Branch and the turnpike—but how would all the folks get along without credit from one season to the next, till they could make a cash crop, find some way to earn a dollar in these hard days after the war? There were things Lydia and Mark had to buy—coffee, salt, an occasional tool or cooking pot—but they were better off than many others who needed food from the store. "How can he do that?" she whispered.

"Oh, he can do it, all right," Mark said bitterly. "Times are tight; the man has the money can call all the tunes."

She remembered that her father had said he had plenty of money—smiling faintly, as though the subject did not concern him—enough Confederate currency to pave his way to the poor house! And with Robert gone and his own mind preoccupied more and more with another world of books and ideas, he had been able to harvest barely half a crop during the past fall. How would he and her mother and the girls make out through the winter if Ham Nelson refused to accept his name, written with such elegant penmanship, on those regular bills of goods?

"Of course, Nelson has sent out word that he'll take in most anything for barter. I reckon he aims to gobble up the whole valley afore he's done." Mark paused, then added, "They're telling, down at the mill, that Weatherby Hayes was whipped last week."

"Oh, no!" Lydia could see the erect, proud figure of the woman her mother had hugged at the church service up in the Prophet's Room last summer; the slightly stooped, merry-faced man who owned the only fiddle in this part of the mountains. "Why ever would they whip him? He was too old to see service on either side."

"Seems there's been some barn-burnings on the farms of Unionists that won't sign a petition asking for the vote to be given back to those fought for the Confederacy. So the Federal men had to have their revenge. Hayes being a Virginian, he was marked as a Rebel sympathizer, most likely. Anyway, it's all bound up with politics in at the county seat. I just aim to have done with it all!"

Lydia laid aside her scrub broom and wiped her hands on her apron. She came to the table and pulled up a chair across from Mark. She knew all that ruckus, a few minutes ago, hadn't been raised because of any thimble. "And now the Confederates will make vengeance on some other Unionist," she said quietly, "and we never know when they'll come here."

"I wish they would come!" he cried. "Did they show their sneaky, greedy faces on my land, I'd be proud to instruct them how a loyal man defends his own. I told them as much down at the mill——"

"Burkes' mill, or Paul's and Hawkins'?"

He looked at her sharply. "You thinking I'd go to that Hawkins' place? It was at the Burkes'."

She was relieved. Not many men brought their grinding to Ida Burke and her sons any more. Maybe no one but his friends had heard Mark's dangerous boasting. Her relief shamed her, however, and she reached out to touch Mark's hand. "It's a time of living under a shadow——"

"I can't stand up under it any longer. It's like I was smothering. Not to know the truth . . ." His eyes burned and his fingers caught her arm in a vise. "Do you know what I'm saying?"

She nodded. "There's others of the same mind, Mark. You take it harder than most. . . ."

"Last night I had a dream I was in the prison camp again. Under that blazing Georgia sun we was digging for water, some of us clawing it out of the ground with our bare hands, but every time we struck a spring some fiend would come along and stamp it out. And that man was supposed to be a friend of mine; somehow I knew that, though I couldn't ever glimpse his face. I never knew who to fight. I was parching to death, but I didn't know my enemy. Lyddy, it was setting me crazy!"

"Mark, it was only a dream."

"But the truth's the same. Lyddy, somebody here in this valley helped darken our lives—aye, even to that boy playing out there in the yard—and I can't even bring him to justice. I can't forget it, but it don't help to remember."

"Mrs. Caldwell told us she believed it was the Bludsoes," Lydia said desperately. Mark must end this obsession somewhere, some-time.

"Why did she say that? What did she know?"

"Nothing. She knew nothing for sure, but she said the Bludsoes were strange and bloodthirsty plunderers——"

"Because they're strangers? No, it won't do." Mark sank back in his chair. "If I thought it was the Bludsoes, I'd go up there on Stony Ridge and rip that den apart, clean them every one out. But I don't know. I've got to *know*."

"Of course you have, Mark."

"With money so tight, things the way they are since the war, we'll never get a true chance here."

"We'll make our chance. We're on our way, Mark——"

Silence a moment. Burnett was playing with Mark's hat under the table.

"Lyddy, Jim Burke named to me about a feller come through a little while back, stopped overnight with them. He'd been quite a traveler."

She waited for him to go on.

"This feller—he told them about the West."

Thus Lydia first heard Mark speak about the West—the wide sky, the open lands, the opportunity.

"You mean the gold fields?" she asked. Tales of California luck, good and bad, had been drifting back to the mountains ever since the rush for riches started in forty-nine. A Caldwell boy—older brother to Gentry—had gone from Thickety to find his fortune. The last word his family had heard left him at the gold diggings sick with a strange plague, and there was no response to later letters his mother wrote—even when Emma Caldwell sold her best cow and sent the money to him out in the country where wealth was supposed to be plentiful for the taking.

"The stranger stopped at Burkes' wasn't no prospector. He knew the land, was interested in farmers, settlers, anybody that will help take a long view of that country and make it a fitten place for folks and their families to abide."

She had heard there were people moving West. The weekly paper her father got from the county seat told of a party there that had bought new wagons, schooners, and gone to join other families heading across the Missouri. "Why were the Burkes a-telling you about this traveler from the West?"

"Reckon they thought I'd like to hear."

But a few weeks later Mark said, "Jim Burke might go out to see for himself what the West is like. Now that they don't have much call for their milling . . ."

All at once Lydia's grey eyes twinkled as they had not done for months. She looked directly into Mark's face. "Would Jim Burke be a-going all that long journey by himself?"

Mark flushed. A little grin creased the corners of his mouth and eyes, so that she was reminded of the way he looked on their marriage day, the way he looked under the poplars before he went to war. "I reckon Jim'd like it well enough to have somebody else along for company," he said. "Lyddy—I might go West for a look."

She nodded slowly.

"I wouldn't go till after the baby comes. I ain't a-leaving you till you're in good shape. Aunt Tildy could come and stay while I'm gone. I wouldn't be away but a season at most——"

"Reckon you've been giving it considerable thought," she said. She did not say that she, too, had been giving his mention of such a move considerable thought. During several long sleepless nights she had anticipated this conversation and had tried to determine what she should say when he was ready to name that he would be going out yonder. Should she tell him of the dozen fears that would gnaw at her while he was away? Or that she hated to see their little farm, without his work, slip back to wilderness because she might not be able to hold it in cultivation by herself? Should she tell him that sometimes now, carrying their fourth child and knowing the full dread of what had happened at David's birthing, she grew anxious and tired beyond belief; that as she sat down by the spring or beside the fire to catch her breath, she wondered how it would be after this baby was born?

But now that the moment of Mark's telling her about the trip West had arrived, Lydia realized the needlessness of saying any of these things to him. It had already been settled—back in nameless time, somewhere, as Aunt Tildy would say? In God's own

126

good plan, as her mother would say? If there could be no other way for Mark to find peace, she would not throw hindrances in his way.

"Lydia," he was asking her, "would you be holding it against me?"

She was not sure what words to choose, what the truth was. But she could not hold Mark here in the limbo he had created for himself. They would all be poisoned by his unspent hatred, his unnamed need. "No," she said. "It's already settled in my mind for you to go, Mark."

He took her by the shoulders and drew her to him. "I'm thankful you've an understanding heart for how things are with me, Lyddy." His big hands patted the thinness of her shoulder blades under the linsey-woolsey dress. "When I come back, girl, do I have a gold mine or a big spread of river-bottom land all free and clear, titled to my name, we'll make us all a fresh start." For the first time in a long while she saw something akin to eagerness in his face. "Can we make it through this winter, I'll get the spring crops in the ground for you—and then Jim Burke and I will go and have a look out yonder." He gripped her shoulders. "Can you get along?"

She nodded. "I can do whatever has to be done." But she thought how sweet it was to stand folded in his arms like this for a little snatch of time, of even false security.

After this, Jim Burke tramped up the mountain and talked with Mark beside the fire during long winter evenings, while Lydia spun and wove and sewed and the children listened with wide eyes and finally fell asleep under the fire's warmth and the drone of adult voices.

Lydia went down to her father's house only twice during the winter, once to attend church and once to mourn.

The first time, her mother presided, as always, over the narrow room in the loft where Elijah Gudger preached; presided was the only word Lydia could think of, although Sarah Moore did nothing official. But her welcome enveloped all who came and her attentiveness to the service affected everyone gathered there. Yet she seemed so fragile that Lydia was shocked. Her skin was like transparent wax stretched over the network of tiny blue blood vessels running underneath.

"What does she eat?" Lydia drew her sisters off to themselves for a moment. "Are you looking after her?"

Kate shrugged their helplessness. "We do the best we can."

"Papa nor Mama either one, they won't pay a mind to any of us the way they do to you or Paul." Annie Marie's voice was older than her years. Lydia looked again at her younger sister. Already Annie Marie's hair was drawn tightly back from her face, and although she had a ribbon like Kate's, she had made it into a necessity, while the older girl had made her ribbon into a plaything decorating her dark, loose hair.

"What should we do?" Elizabeth asked gravely.

Lydia threw her arms around them. "I don't know. But she looks so frail . . ."

Later that day her father said, "Don't be too hard on the girls, Lydia." He pulled gently, reflectively, at his carefully trimmed beard. "It seems all of us in this house love one another, and yet there's nothing we can do for one another. Your sisters need— well, all those pretty things and the gaiety young girls need before they're married, and we can't give it to them. All I need is someone who would wish to discuss my books, but why should my daughters care about books when living itself is so exciting to them now? And your mother—we none of us can seem to provide what she needs."

"Like my David," Lydia said.

Her father nodded. "How is he?" he asked gently.

Mark had insisted that she leave David home with him today. "No need to expose the boy to outsiders," Mark said. And she had understood that he did not want people to see his wounded child. All at once she saw how their own pride was part of the hurt they felt for their child's affliction. She had thought about it as she came down the mountain with Martha and little Burnett: How selfish we all are, even in our loving and caring. We think it's only for him we grieve, but it's for our own stricken pride in our first-born; our humiliation, too, and our helplessness.

"David's like always," she told her father now, "sweet and clumsy and adoring of Martha. . . . Papa, Mark says he was told that Ham Nelson is cutting off credit at his store."

Jesse Moore shook his head. "The world is changing. Men are becoming mercenary beyond all reason. . . . You remember this book, Lydia"—and he went to the shelf above his bed and drew out a thick volume—"this one the Bishop brought me on your marriage day? Well, in its pages are lessons for all of us to read. They're lessons learned in blood and the fall of empires that have gone before us."

"The book by Mr. Gibbon about Rome?"

He nodded eagerly. "And the rise of mercenary . . ." but he saw that she could not share his meaning with only a moment's explanation and already Kate was calling for Lydia from the next room. He replaced the book on the shelf. "Ham Nelson is very unwise," he said, "to place cash above good will."

"But can you and Mama get along?" Lydia asked.

Her father took her hand. "My dear, dear Lydia," he said. "With all of your own to look after, you would try to care for us, too. Yes, child, we'll get along. There's nothing Ham Nelson has to sell we can't do without."

Kate called again. "Mama's asking for you, Lydia."

"It's improvement in your mama's strength we need most," Jesse Moore said. "Hearing of Weatherby Hayes's trouble upset her a heap. She's got Naomi Hayes all bound up in her mind with happy days back in Virginia."

"Oh, Papa, did she have to know?" Lydia asked.

"I managed to keep it from her for a while. Then some of the women came to call and told all about the whipping——"

"Oh, I declare! Sometimes I wish we could be spared our comforters."

Her father smiled. "Lydia and Job," he said. "Folks mean well, I suppose, but she's been in bed most of the time until today. Dr. Hornsby prescribed a powerful tonic for her, but it hasn't seemed to even touch her yet. . . . Well, I'll go and wrestle over the Scriptures with Preacher Gugder while you visit with your mama a spell."

129

Sarah Moore was sitting in a rocker by the window when Lydia came into the small bedroom. (It was the same room where David had been born. Lydia could remember how many planks there were in the ceiling: she had counted them back and forth, back and forth, during that long night.) The narrow window looked out on the front yard, the muddy road and the bare winter woods beyond.

"Lydia, did you ever take a root from my rose-of-Sharon bush?" Sarah Moore asked. Her brown dress, dyed from walnut bark, matched her brown eyes, and a white starched cap covered her white and brown hair. Her hands, burrowed into a nest on her lap, twisted and pulled at each other like tiny bird claws.

"Not yet, Mama——"

"Then you must take one today. I want you to have a rose of Sharon to comfort you—there's something about their soft blossoms—this is the time of year to set out shrubs, they take good root before the summer dry spells—you will take one today?"

Lydia nodded. Her mother looked at her heaviness and said, "You mustn't dig it out yourself." Worry clouded her face. "Are you—are you all right, daughter?"

Lydia sank down on the floor and laid her head on her mother's knee, as she had done so often when she was a little girl. She smiled up into the finely wrinkled face she loved so dearly. "Yes, Mama, I'm all right."

The gesture seemed to please her mother more than Lydia could have guessed. She stroked her fingers through her daughter's hair. "You were my first-born, you know," she said softly. Then, "Why didn't David come with you today?"

"He wanted to stay home with his papa." They had never told Sarah Moore what Dr. Hornsby had said about her favorite grandchild. She and the boy seemed to have a special understanding when they were together. "David's growing like a weed."

The fingers never missed a stroke through Lydia's hair. "You mustn't let him go like a weed, though. David's more like a woods plant, wild and tender and not hardly ordinary to grow, you know."

Lydia looked up at her mother in surprise. Sarah Moore's pale

130

face was impassive. Her daughter could only guess at what she knew, or was trying to say. "We're doing our best, Mama."

"Of course you are, child. Of course, of course," her mother crooned. They sat quietly for a little while. The sound of voices from the next room was a meaningless hum. "Lydia . . ."

"Yes, Mama?"

"Your papa, and Mark. Do you think they're happy?"

"Oh, yes——"

"No. Don't give me rocks when I've asked for bread, Lydia. I must know. Have they forgiven bitterness and remembrance? Hate can waste away a whole life. Have they let it go?"

"Papa has forgiven, Mama." She hoped she spoke truth.

"I'm thankful. It seemed to me he had found some content."

"It's been a crueller hardship for Mark." She tried to laugh lightly. "I'm not of the mind that the word 'content' will ever suit Mark."

Her mother took Lydia's face between her hands. "Is he good to you, child?"

She nodded.

"Then you're not sorry for the day you told me you'd been chosen out by love?"

"No, Mama." She could answer without hesitation, firmly. But she must add something else: "Come spring, he's going West for a spell. I'll stay with the children and the farm. But I won't make love into a tether-rope holding Mark back."

Her mother touched her cheek gently. "Surely a woman has strange ways. The heart makes its own logic, I reckon; nothing like the logic your papa talks about from all his books. It's made known to anybody who gives herself to being loved and bringing children. And who can ever tell what it means to have given yourself in these mountains? A mountain mother——" She broke off Tears glistened in her eyes, making her face appear even more wan and otherworldly. "You're our mountain girl, Lydia, and our natural-born mother," she said.

Lydia brushed her own eyes. It was good to have woman talk again after being so long up on the mountain away from other women. It was good to talk with her mother, as they had not talked for years, and sweet to hear her mother's praise. She remembered the times as a little girl when she had done a tough job well and her mother had smiled and said simply, "I can always count on my Lydia." Now she recalled the inner glow of secret strength and satisfaction in her own being, her own self-fulfillment.

"And when Mark goes away, you must bring the babies and come down here with us," Sarah Moore was saying. "It will seem good to have little ones around the house again. Oh, I've missed David, and we hardly see Paul's boy and girl. You'll come with us?"

Lydia knew she would never leave their own farm, but she could not further upset her mother. She squeezed the small clasped hands. Her mother nodded. "You won't forget your rose of Sharon today? There's nothing like a flowering shrub to lift a body's heart . . ."

Lydia did not forget to dig a root that afternoon and plant it early the next morning, just before the first snow of winter came. And Lydia did not forget her mother's words, either, when she made her second trip of the season from the mountain to the valley. At the end of February, 1871, five weeks after her third boy, Gibbon, was born, she went down to her mother's funeral.

Robert came after her. Ida Burke had been up three days before, brought by her son so full of his talk of the West that both he and Mark seemed to find the world around them unreal while only those distant hills and canyons beyond the horizon held any interest. "I've been taking turns sitting up with your ma during the weeks past," she said, "and I've been a-watching her sink lower and lower. But your pa wouldn't let anybody bring you word; said you weren't stout enough yet to take on the hardship of nursing your ma. I been a-heeding his wishes till last night."

"And what happened?" Lydia asked.

"Just at dusk last night, when I was on my way to the milk-gap to do the evening milking, a snowy owl, the likes of which I never seen hereabouts before, flew right across my path and perched in that old pine that marks our line fence."

"But, Mrs. Burke, if Mama——"

"I'm a-telling you, Lydia, that was the biggest, whitest bird I ever laid these poor old eyes on. Its wingspread seemed wide as a pillow sham fluttering in the wind whenever it sailed past me there in the half-light with a whispery rush. Directly I got home I said to the boys, 'Come daylight, I'm a-going up to Lydia McQueen's and carry her word about her ma. Sarah Moore's not long for this world. I've had a sign, and her daughter's got a right to know.' "

"I thank you for your thoughtiness, Ida Burke," Lydia said.

"No more'n I'd want you to do for me," the rough old woman replied gently. Then, "Jim Burke, on your feet! You and Mark McQueen done talked your way to yon side the Great Divide and back again. Afore you get down to making the journey in fact you'd best turn off a mite of work at home."

But Lydia could not bring herself either to leave or move her baby, the scrawniest of limb, the strongest of lung, she had yet borne. Gib, as they had promptly nicknamed him, cried almost without ceasing during his first three weeks. Mark had helped all he could, pacing the floor with the tiny bundle hour after hour until Lydia had wondered if the puncheons wouldn't finally be worn smooth. He built great roaring fires against the bitter January cold that crept between the chinking in the logs; he heated quilts for Lydia's and the baby's bed and soaked bits of cloth in warm sweetened water for the baby to suck on and find temporary satisfaction. He saw to it that Lydia had the most and the best of their meager fare of food, for she had told him she thought the baby cried because he wasn't getting proper nourishment from her milk. She was weaker than she had ever been before in her life. Every morning she awoke to the hope that the old reliable strength would be returning to her legs and back and arms, and every day she succumbed to helplessness as she tried to take up the familiar chores.

Dr. Hornsby had told her, the morning he left after delivering lusty, long-legged Gib, that she must not give way to despondency, now that this big fine boy had come, although he had seen it happen with mothers often enough before. "You pamper yourself a little now, Lydia," he had said. "You be that Virginia lady your mama talks about." His beefy, knowledgable hands had covered her own for a moment. "Are you all right, Lydia McQueen?"

She nodded, feeling deep unconscious pleasure in his concern, in the sure grip of his hands on hers.

And during the weeks that followed she tried to remember what he had said, but the older children's noise and the baby's crying and Mark's attempts at cooking and milking and tidying up, plus his own work, kept her tense and drained. When Gib was about four weeks old, however, he seemed to find increasing substance in her milk. He cried less. With more sleep, her strength began slowly to return. Then Ida Burke came and the brief peace was shattered. Lydia could not go to her mother—surely Papa would let her know if worst came to worst—but when she was asleep at night, her mother's face came to her, and sometimes her mother's thin, sweet voice mingled with the baby's crying just as she was waking.

At last, when Robert came in the door one day just before noon, she knew his message. She hugged him for all the months they had not seen each other, and Mark gripped his hand cordially. Slowly and deliberately she gave him some coffee from the pot on the hearth and began to gather her things. "Tell us how it happened, Robert," she said.

"You know?"

"Why else would you be away from your precious law school-ing? Yes, I know Mama's dead." Her voice trembled slightly on the word; she clenched her fingers.

Robert told them about her last days in bed. Sarah Moore had slipped away as quietly and naturally as a leaf swirling along on a stream, neither able nor wishing to delay the journey. Neighbors had been kind and constant: they brought in food and took turns spelling the girls at their mother's bed. The family had done all they could and at the beginning of the week they sent word in to Robert at the county seat for him to come home. "She was asleep when I got there yesterday evening and she never waked up. Just at daylight she stopped breathing. That was all."

"It was a peaceful enough way," Mark said, "after the torment she'd been through."

Lydia nodded. Somehow it seemed to her that Mark had spoken of his own life as much as her mother's death. She hesitated about the children. David and Martha and Burn did not ask to go with her, but their faces grew bleak as she prepared the baby's things, and Mark said, "Would it be best, I could stay here and look after the other young'uns, Lydia."

Suddenly Robert spoke up. "There'll be enough old women a-hustling around. Why don't you bring the children on down to the house and give the neighbors something to do?" And Lydia could have hugged him again. As when they were children, he had read her secret mind.

She told them they could come along and Martha led her big brother and her little brother over to the table and said solemnly, as they stood in a row, "Thank you, Uncle Robert."

He bent before each one of them in turn in a playful bow. They went to let Lydia comb their hair and wash their hands.

"When's the burying set for?" Mark asked.

"Tomorrow at one o'clock," Robert said.

"Then I'll look after the stock here tonight and in the morning," Mark said. "I'll come down about noon tomorrow. She was a fine lady, Miss Sarah was. I'll grieve for her—and help avenge her someday!"

"What happened to Mamaw Moore?" Martha asked, as Lydia braided her hair. Before she could answer, David had pulled at his mother's sleeve, looking at her with a wide, urgent questioning.

Lydia knelt beside the children. Her legs were weak and shaky. "You remember the squirrel we had last spring, and the kitten Aunt Tildy sent you, David, how they died and we had to bury them out yonder in the woods under that big pretty dogwood tree? Well, folks die, too." Tears were suddenly streaming down her cheeks. She tried to remember preachers' messages she had heard, or things her father or Elijah Gudger had said, so that she would know what words to speak to her children now, but no ready explanation came. "Mamaw has died, but her spirit will live on——" Lydia's voice broke; she could not see her mother on streets of gold in heaven, wearing a crown, and yet that was what Lydia had been told of heaven. "Mamaw will live on as long as we remember, as long as we cherish her."

David put his arms around his mother's neck and laid his face against her own. That he should be her comforter flooded Lydia's heart with contradictory grief and satisfaction. She clung to him. Surely the ways of God to man were beyond all knowing and the diminished mind of this gentle child might hold some secret unknown to the rest of them.

Mark helped her to her feet and took the children to put on their coats and the wool caps she had knitted. He talked with them matter-of-factly and took them outside to show them where they would ride in the back of their grandpa's buggy.

"I didn't mean to break down so," she said to Robert as she put on her coat. "It was David—he and Mama——"

"I know."

Thin February sunshine shone on the bare trees and the ledge of the Devil's Brow as Robert drove his father's buggy around the mountain and turned down the road that was little better than a trail. Robert glanced at Lydia, humming to the baby in her arms:

> "Down in the valley,
> Valley so low,
> Hold your head over,
> Hear the wind blow—"

After a while he spoke. "You like it up here on the mountain, Lydia?"

She broke off her song. "It's my home," she said, as if that would tell him all he needed to know. "You see the ledge up there, Robert?"

"My eyesight is still pretty fair," he said, "in spite of all that legal fine print."

"Right under it, there where the bank is so steep, is a bed of arbutus, the finest I ever did see. Hidden like it didn't want to be found by prying mortals"—she smiled at him shyly—"but I know its seasons. I can even rake away the late snow and find its blossoms."

Robert had thought, back at the house, that Lydia seemed thin-

136

ner, more subdued, than the quick older sister he had always worshiped. But now he saw the brightness still in her eyes, although they were swollen from tears; the eagerness still in her voice. She sang to the children and she spoke of spring arbutus under the snow, and he knew that she meant to tell him that not only the cabin that sheltered them but this whole mountain was her dwelling place. "Good!" he said.

Lydia finished the song and the baby was asleep. "Had you seen Mama lately?" Robert asked.

"It was the first week in December. I came down for preaching." Lydia treasured the memory of sitting by the window with her mother. "There's some of her rose-of-Sharon roots taking hold right now in the ground beside our front door."

Robert nodded. "She—was she the same——"

"Mama never really started living again after that night during the war. That's why I won't cry any more now, Robert. We've been sorrowing for her for a long time."

"She never got used to the mountains."

"No. She said, that last day, that I was her mountain girl—a mountain mother."

"Mama knew." He smiled, but his eyes, so like his mother's, were full of sadness. "I wish she'd had it easier . . ."

"That's what she wished for us, exactly," Lydia said. Beneath the dark shawl thrown over her hair, her eyes peered forth clear and grey. Almost to herself, she added, "It's not the ease to do less that we need; I reckon we need strength to do what we can."

"Was I studying for the pulpit in place of the courtroom, I'd squirrel that away for one of my texts," he said. "But I'll recollect when I come to wishing for my own——"

"Oh? You found a girl there in town, Robert?"

"No. Trouble's been sharp enough on my own; I got no cause to double it just now. But one of these days . . ."

She asked about his law. He told her that he had had to give up his course for the time being and go to work in the town's main livery stable to earn enough for bed and board and a little extra now and then that he was hoarding for the time when he would go on with his study.

"I wish I could help," Lydia said. "Does Papa know you've run out of money?"

"We've not talked it. I reckon he suspects. But there's nothing he can do about helping me; it would be an embarrassment to have him name it to me."

"I know."

"Oh, come sooner or later, I'll be a lawyer, Lydia, never fear," he said cheerfully, and she realized how tall he had become, and self-confident, and that he had turned eighteen. "Things are tight in town, too, Lydia. The war left every business pretty crippled up, folks divided against one another. But you wait, conditions are going to begin to improve one of these days. When they do, this mountain country will grow and there'll be no limit to what we can do. I aim to be ready for that day."

His enthusiasm, his certainty, was a tonic to her.

Neighbors had gathered by the time they drove into their father's yard. "That's the oldest child," Lydia heard someone whisper as she came into the house. All the people standing around made it a strange house. David came close to her and clutched her skirt as she started toward the bedroom. Emma Caldwell stopped her. "They're washing her up and laying her out in there now, Lydia. Won't be but a few minutes till you can see her. I declare, it's dreadful to have Sarah go so young."

Lydia turned to the kitchen. She must find someplace where she could let the baby nurse. The other three children kept close beside her. In the back of her mind, she considered Mrs. Caldwell's words and realized that she had never thought of her mother as young. Yet forty-four was probably not old.

The kitchen was full of women scrubbing pots, sweeping the floor, dusting the mantel and washing the food safe, arranging and tasting mounds of food on the table. Two of her sisters, Kate and Elizabeth, were standing helpless and uncertain with grief in the midst of this activity. They ran to Lydia, and embraced her so tightly that the baby began to cry. "Oh, Lydia, we didn't mean——"

"It's all right. Where's Papa?"

"He went with the men who're going to make Mama's coffin." Kate's tears flooded her face. "He said he wanted it of cedar wood —Mama always loved the smell of cedar."

"And Annie Marie?"

The girls looked at each other. They had just then realized she was not with them. "We don't know."

"Then go and try to find her."

She looked at the groaning table again. Everyone in the valley was pinched for food at the close of a long winter after a slim harvest, but they had brought dried-fruit pies and one-layer cakes, puddings, dishes of cooked vegetables, pots of stewed chicken with flaky dumplings, slices of ham. How many times had Lydia watched her mother fix a basket to take on just such an occasion to someone in the valley? Seeing this food now, on her mother's familiar table, brought her at last face to face with the loss and sadness and reality of her mother's death.

The air was rich with fragrant smells and she was overcome with homesickness. The women swarmed around her, watching for signs of her grief, seeking to care for the children. They lured Martha and Burnett with them, but David still clung to Lydia. She saw a familiar figure come from the closed bedroom. "Aunt Tildy!"

"Lydia." The big arms were around her. "Lydia, child. We've got your mama laid out neat and pretty in the white dress she wedded in."

"Aunt Tildy, I want to see her, but first I've got to find someplace where I can let the baby nurse . . ."

"Land sakes!" Aunt Tildy waved her broad, work-reddened hand toward the women. "Shoo! Let this child have a minute's peace so her babe can suck. You're a kindly passel of folks to share like this, but Lydia's got to have a chance to collect herself."

So she lay on the old bed in the kitchen and Gib nursed. Her legs trembled with weakness and fatigue. She heard the murmur of voices from the next room as the people went in to view her mother's corpse. Aunt Tildy sat in the rocking chair near the bed, with David on her lap. His legs dangled to the floor. "Sally was glad to hear about your big new boy," she said.

139

"I'm proud she knew," Lydia whispered.

"Oh, she knew all right. 'The Lord giveth and the Lord taketh away, blessed be the name of the Lord'—that's what she said the day before she went." Aunt Tildy's rocker creaked for a few minutes across the uneven floor. "Now," she said, and her voice had changed, had sharpened, "why didn't you let me know when your other babies come?"

"Aunt Tildy you'd done so much for us already. I figured we'd worn you out."

"Likely! Better wear out than rust out, that's my belief." Aunt Tildy looked at the baby, kicking and squirming even as he finished nursing. "Reckon I better help you out with that one. He's going to be a major for sure. And my boy here"—she stroked David's hair—"appears like he's not plumb forgotten old Aunt Tildy."

"No, how could any of us?" Then Lydia understood that what Aunt Tildy wanted, needed, here in this moment of her favorite sister's death, was not comfort but assurance that she would still remain part of a family. She needed to be loved and provoked by children, consulted and quarreled with by their parents. She needed to be needed, and used. And Mark had wondered if she would come while he went West.

"Aunt Tildy, David and the baby need you, and so do the rest of us. As soon as crops are in the ground, Mark and Jim Burke are heading West for a look-around. Could you be staying with us while he's gone?"

"A body could hardly promise to last that long!" the older woman snorted. "What I hear, it's a far piece West and back. But I'll stay till something else calls me away." She could not quite conceal the pleasure and relief in her voice. "Now, let me go hunt up some extra little tidbit for this-here boy of mine . . ."

Several of the women went home at nightfall, but many of them stayed and were joined by their husbands wearing fresh linsey-woolsey shirts and newly scrubbed faces. They all ate of the food and enjoyed a fellowship together. Jesse Moore moved among them with bewildered dignity, saying little, eating nothing.

Annie Marie came in the house and told her sisters she had

140

been showing one of Tilmon Haddon's boys what chores had to be done outside. "Mama wouldn't like us to neglect the stock," she said abruptly, but her eyes were red with crying.

Through the long night the watchers sat in living room and kitchen, stoking up the fires, recalling other deaths in the valley and other occasions of watching. They told familiar jokes on their neighbors and chuckled quiet, intimate laughter. They spoke soberly of politics and President Grant in Washington and secret societies that were reported organizing in neighboring states and towns. In the small hours of morning a few of them dozed, but Lydia, in bed with the children, could still hear a few of the voices, soft and reassuring, talking on and on. . . .

At first rooster-crow she aroused from her dozing. Breakfast was already being cooked on the big fireplace and there was a general stirring throughout the house. For a moment she could not recall where she was, or what had happened. Then she got up and rinsed her face at the washstand. She combed her hair a long time before twisting it into the soft, heavy knot at the nape of her neck.

Shortly after daylight there was a loud knock at the front door. The men who had sat up during the night were out in the back entryway washing up for early breakfast. Emma Caldwell, sweeping the floor while the room was temporarily empty, called, "Come."

But only the knock sounded again. She went to the door and opened it. Outside stood a boy, tall and thin under a shock of midnight black hair. "My grandpap sent this to Mrs. Moore's folks." And he held out a side of venison.

"Who be your grandpap?"

"Big Matt Bludsoe. My Pap's Young Matt."

Without a word she fled into the house. "Young Matt Bludsoe's boy is out front offering a side of deer meat," Emma Caldwell cried to the startled women in the kitchen.

"Bludsoes? What are they——"

"Deer meat? No deers around here any more."

No one moved toward the door. At last Lydia went to the front of the house. The boy still stood, offering the venison. "Why— why did your grandpap send this?" she asked.

141

" 'Make them the gift without any palaver,' Grandpap said. 'Say only that Mrs. Moore done the Bludsoes a good turn once. They recollect her kindly. There's few for us to speak such words about.' That's what he said."

Lydia took the heavy chunk of meat. "Then tell your grandpap in return that Mrs. Moore's folks send him thanks for his kind remembering."

Those who had overheard the exchange were tight-lipped when Lydia returned to the kitchen. There were headshakes of displeasure at her unseemliness. "I'd a-told him to take that meat back to wherever he stole it from," Emma Caldwell whispered to Dolly, who sat by the fire buttoning her new high kid shoes with a buttonhook.

Dolly glanced around at the silently disapproving women and her pretty chin quivered. "Lydia, do you think we should be trafficking with trash when your poor mama and Paul's poor mama is laying in there——"

"Button your shoes, Dolly," Lydia said calmly, stirring a pot of mush that hung over the fire. "Then go get your Tim and Pru and we'll feed all the little ones together."

Thus were the first murmurings about the conduct of Sarah Moore's funeral turned aside for the moment. The second murmur came when it was learned that Weatherby Hayes would play his violin at the service. The elderly wizened couple arrived an hour before the funeral was to commence—she in her fine black silk dress and tiny hat and black silk gloves, he with his violin tucked under one arm. They spoke only to Jesse Moore and his daughters and then they climbed the stairs to the Prophet's Room where Sarah Moore's body had been moved in the rough, oblong, fragrant cedar box. They sat and waited, staring straight in front of them, while the flurry of protest broke and buzzed downstairs.

"Be he aiming to play that fiddle today?"

"I ain't heard-tell, but why else would he a-brought it to a funeralizing?"

"Jesse Moore"—Emma Caldwell confronted him—"what's the meaning of that fiddle up in Sarah's Prophet's Room?"

"Why, Weatherby Hayes is going to play one of Sarah's hymns," he said. "I think it will please her if she can know about it, Emma."

"I never heard of a heathen fiddle at a Christian burial," Mrs. Cass Nelson said, in a high voice more puzzled than belligerent.

"Nor I." It was Mrs. Dr. Hornsby, sitting stiffly beside Mrs. Nelson like a fat, trussed-up baking-hen. "It's the devil's instrument and I'm surprised your Preacher Gudger would allow it." Mrs. Hornsby was a Presbyterian.

"Yes," one of the Baptist women said, "we'd better ask Brother Gudger about it——"

"Ladies, neighbors"—Jesse Moore held up one hand and gave a little smile that only revealed his sadness more clearly—"I have already asked good Brother Elijah if this music would offend him at the service. He has agreed that the circumstances are unusual, that it may serve a righteous purpose at this time."

"But a fiddle that's played for dancing——"

Mr. Moore interrupted, "Besides, I didn't ask this thing of Weatherby Hayes and his wife just for Sarah, or for me. I want it for them, too."

There was silence.

"I would reckon you all know my meaning. A humiliation of the flesh can sometimes be cured by salve to the spirit. Thickety Creek stands in need of some of that salve now." He went to the door. "If you'll excuse me now, I'll wait out in the yard for our preacher."

Paul came into the kitchen where Robert and Lydia sat. His face was harassed. "Is it all right, Lydia?" he asked. "Do you think Papa's done wrong?"

She shook her head.

"Papa knows what he's doing," Robert said.

"Dolly's upset about it," Paul went on.

Lydia bit her tongue.

"What's upset her?" Robert asked.

"She's afraid folks won't understand."

"Who cares about 'folks'?" Lydia burst out. "I'm caring about Papa, and Mama's friends who need to be shown they're still respected in this community and part of it, and you—how do you feel about it, Paul?"

143

But Robert rescued his older brother from misery. "I feel plumb satisfied," he said. "Let me see if I can't ease my sister-in-law's troubled mind a mite."

He went after Dolly. Paul stayed with Lydia only a second and then went in search of his children. When Robert came back after a few minutes, he was shaking his head. "It's a shame to think Paul's empty sleeve drove him to sacrifice himself to an empty head, too."

"Robert, don't twist words around," Lydia protested, but she knew what her brother was saying.

"All right, all right. But my twisty words have brought her around to accepting the violin playing at the service in a few minutes."

Lydia went to inspect her children. They were all neatly scrubbed and dressed. Mark, too, who had just come, was in his black suit and cleanly shaven. No one could deny he was a handsome man, with strength in his limbs and a dark, tormented fascination in his face. He stood awkwardly at the edge of the room and sat uneasily on the benches upstairs, unfamiliar with the form and ceremony of what was taking place. The only moment he relaxed was when Willoughby Hayes played the violin.

The room was hushed with more than a usual silence as the slightly stoop-shouldered little man set the instrument under his chin and put the bow to the strings. He drew it gently, insistently, and a strange, sad, peaceful music poured across the room. It seemed to Lydia to be pure liquid, sweet as the juice they sometimes drew from the sugar-maple trees, clear and limpid as the water from her mountain spring. No other sound from outside reached the listeners; there was no motion in the room. Like vassals frozen under a spell in some fairy tale, they sat and the music flowed over them.

Then Elijah Gudger preached. His white beard was trim as ever, his long black coat as brushed, his English accents as elegant, but Lydia felt that she had already heard her mother's funeral message, in the purity, the beauty, the everlastingness of that violin music. Something larger than the voice of man had spoken to them.

144

She heard only the final words of his eulogy. They lodged in her mind. Leaning toward them across the open Bible, with his large, veined hands clasped in front of him, Elijah Gudger said: "There be those that fall like an oak, struck by a flash of lightning straight from the finger of God. There be others that fall like a barren fruit tree with its roots nibbled away by the little mice of time and fret and fear. Then there be those that go like a leaf picked in its greenness, a flower in full blossom, wilting slowly, dying gently, leaving fragrance on the air.

"There be few oaks in this old world. There be many empty fruit trees gnawed to death by the petty, persistent teeth of destruction. But Sarah Moore was one of the few who are gathered by some higher hand beyond our knowing.

"Good friends, today, which kind of death are you building for yourselves? For in the time of our living is the making of our death."

They sang a hymn there and at the little cemetery on the hill above the big bend in Thickety Creek. A cold February wind cut across the brow of the hill and the procession of people shivered. A prayer was offered and grains of red clay symbolizing dust-to-dust filtered through Elijah Gudger's fingers onto Sarah Moore's coffin. Then neighbors lowered the cedar box into the raw red earth. . . .

As Lydia and Mark and the children rode in the wagon back up the mountain late in the day, in the gathering darkness, she repeated the preacher's words. "Mark," she said softly, "I don't want our lives to be nibbled away by fret and fear, like Brother Gudger said today."

He clucked to Black Deuce. "Thunder, no! If I've got to go one of these days, I mean it to be with the oaks, with a crash and a loss, not like choked-up broom sedge trampled underfoot."

"I mean," she said, "we want to leave behind our children, stronger and knowing more than we. We want to leave some mark on the place we've been, this corner of the earth we've used."

"Yes, I reckon. But we can try to find better places; we

145

can strike out to make new corners. That's my meaning to going West."

"But wherever it is"—she was looking at the high clouds overhead, scudding across the face of the moon just rising behind the mountain—"we can leave our mark for better."

"You and Robert," he said, grinning slightly, "you got your papa's way with words."

They jolted along in silence. The children were asleep after a long day filled with unfamiliar faces and events. Black Deuce moved steadily and strongly. They watched the moon clear the mountaintop and disappear, then reappear, behind swift clouds.

"Lyddy, we could go West together," Mark said. "Lots of families going out in these schooner-wagons."

His words stunned her; then she said, "Was I footloose I might go rambling with you. Like the Preacher in the Old Bible says, there's a time to go and a time to stay; it just come about that now's your time for a-going and now's my time for a-staying put. There's the baby and David, and"—she had to be honest—"I don't rightly know could I ever leave these mountains."

He did not press her. "There's times I look for it to be mighty lonesome out there."

"And times I look for lonesome back here," she said.

The wind grew quieter for an interval and the clouds moved more slowly. The moonlight revealed the road ahead almost as clear as day. "It favored Aunt Tildy to be asked to come and stay with us while you're away," she said.

"She'll help you out. I can't be around the old woman; she bosses and angers me, but I know her worth."

"It crossed my mind this morning," Lydia said, reflecting on the day, "how Annie Marie is growing to be like Aunt Tildy, bristling when she wants to be kind, fearful she'll be beholden to somebody."

"I heard Paul say to your pa, when we were making ready to leave, that Annie Marie was going down to live with them for a spell."

"With the Hawkinses?"

146

Mark nodded. "With your brother and Dolly and old Hawkins and the young'uns, however you name that," he said.

"But Dolly will make her into a servant," Lydia cried. "Poor Annie Marie——"

"Paul told your pa she was wanting to go, that she could have the run of the house——"

"He meant she could have the running of it! She can scrub and churn and milk and wash while Dolly prettifies."

"She's a worthless woman," Mark said. Lydia looked at him sharply, wondering what he might know in his own man's way of knowing about women, but he only added, "Paul's hobbled, for sure."

"It's for him Annie Marie's going," Lydia said. Then, "Maybe I'm harsh on Dolly because I'm jealous. She's got a pretty white skin and plump little arms and a rosebud mouth, and foolish clothes. Maybe it's me and not Paul or Annie Marie I'm pitying."

Mark was not often demonstrative. Now he put out his arm and gathered her closer beside him on the wagon seat. He laid her head on his shoulder. She could smell the good wool masculine smell of his rough coat beneath her face. "Pity will never be your due, Lyddy," he said. "Pride and joy and sorrowing, maybe, but not pity. Don't ever name the word again."

"I promise, Mark." Gladness grew within her. No matter what might happen, they belonged to each other.

It was a strange gift to bring home from a funeral. And yet it would have pleased her mother to know that mourning—for her, dead, and for David, living—could rest side by side with flashes of happiness.

The mourning and the happiness went hand in hand throughout the rest of winter and the spring. Before he went back to the town Robert brought her the clock their mother had given Lydia at her marriage. "It was on my mind you'd like to have it up here," he said.

"It'll be company to me, with its ticking and its chimes," she said.

Robert helped Mark put up the length of black walnut he had

saved for a mantel since they built their home. Lydia set her clock on it proudly and said, "A fireboard needs a clock."

"I remember fetching you this once before," Robert said.

"So much has happened since then," Lydia said, looking at her children.

"Well, it's back to the livery stables and the law books for me," Robert said. "Good luck, Mark, on your Westering."

"Good luck to you, Robert, in your learning." Mark shook his hand.

When it came time for Mark and Jim Burke to start West, the first week of May, Lydia could hardly believe the day had arrived.

"I've made arrangements with John Burke for plowing your crops in the summer and harvesting them come fall, if I'm not back by then. You know the rest to do if you get in need."

They had spoken of all this before, several times, yet each knew that the thought of things they could not foretell or prepare for was what lay heavy between them. Lydia cooked a bountiful breakfast. Only the children ate. She fixed food for Mark to take with him, and he slipped it into his saddle roll.

He mounted Black Deuce. Except for that tightly rolled pack, he might have been going to mill, or up on the mountain to cut wood, or any other of a dozen commonplace journeys. She held each of the children up to him for a last good-by. Black Deuce tossed his head and bucked at the delay. Then he went. He turned once, where the trail led around the side of the mountain and took him from sight, and waved to her.

7th
CHAPTER

For the rest of the week she could not let herself think of the West. She would imagine his going to the store for a sack of salt. Or by night of his going to the Bludsoes' for a fox hunt. She tried not to see the half-keg of salt he had left in her kitchen or the limp-eared hound that lay under the steps waiting for a whistle.

It was May and work did not stay done. Weeds came overnight in the fields; milking was morning and night; sassafras and locust sprouts she and Mark had thought they had grubbed out of the pasture during the winter put out tough new shoots. The runt sow had lost her first litter of pigs, but she was due to have more in the next week or so, and Lydia kept a sharp eye on her pen. The cow was ready to freshen again any day, too, but her young heifer had not yet begun to give milk, so temporarily the children were without. Lydia picked wild greens and gave the children the pot likker in which they were cooked. Aunt Tildy said it would provide all sorts of nourishment.

Heedless of protests, Aunt Tildy dosed everyone in the house, including herself, with sulphur and molasses.

"Aunt Tildy," Martha asked, after she had squirmed and swal-

149

lowed, "why does everything that comes out of your funny little satchel taste so strong?"

"The better to make you strong, my child," Aunt Tildy said, and pounced like the wolf on Red Riding Hood, to the children's delight.

The ground had been too cold for corn planting before Mark left, but when Lydia went down to see John Burke early in June he was surly and would not promise when he might come and help her plant a corn patch.

"I don't know what heathenish notions have got into him," Ida Burke said. "Since his brother left, seems like he's just sulled up like a possum. Him and me work around the mill here all day and sometimes nary a word but 'Hand me that sack,' or 'Loosen up them grinding stones,' passes between us."

Lydia comforted her. But the old woman spat a stream of brown snuff and wiped her hand across her mouth. "It's a sorry way to live. Puts me in mind of the story of that prodigal son in Bible days. Your man out traipsing—that's a sorry way to live, too."

Lydia left then. She knew that Aunt Tildy shared Ida Burke's opinion, but she would not listen to her—or anyone—speak it. As she climbed back toward home, she wondered how she would get the corn planted. But she could not remain downhearted, for it was June. Where the trees crowded close beside the road their new green leaves already made a heavy shade, and it was welcome under the warm noon sun.

Fresh, sweet smells of late spring rode on the gentle wind. Bees used the air like a giant room. Above her and beyond her and all around, the mountains were stirring with life, thrusting up shoots and leaves and blossoms, feeding roots, soaking up pockets of spring rain for dry times ahead, yielding small animals that had burrowed away for the winter. Lydia felt the surge of life—as she had felt it in previous springs. No matter who came or went, what crops were planted or unplanted, who was meted justice or injustice, this would always return. She felt as small as an insect curled in the leaf at her foot, knowing that all of this went forward without knowledge of her. And yet she felt large, too, as great and grand as the green peak of the mountain looming above her because she was part of it all. She was here and now and alive!

When she was a little girl, she had loved to run. Now she ran again, lightly on her toes, feeling the spongy earth beneath her feet and the warm air flowing around her. Her breath came hard and when she fell down to rest, her lungs burned and ached with the effort of breathing. She could not run as she used to. It didn't matter. Her spirit was the same. Come what would, she would remember that spring, too, always came again.

During the next weeks she set chickens and guineas and ducks and geese, and when they hatched, David helped her look after them. The cow dropped her calf and hid it behind a locust thicket on the far side of the pasture hill, but the children helped Lydia find the wobbly white-faced little thing and bring it in to the barn. The runt sow brought four pigs and in a few days they were almost as large as their mother. Lydia was happy with the thriving increase of livestock.

Then one night she awoke, startled, to hear shrill squeals from the farmyard. By the time she had got Mark's rifle from over the door and lit the lantern and stumbled out into the thick darkness, the squeals were growing weaker, retreating up the hillside. She ran to the pigpen. The top logs on one side had been knocked loose. She could see quite easily the long scratches fierce claws had made. She held the lantern high and leaned over to look inside the pen. The little sow was backed into a far corner, uneasy but belligerent. Behind her, standing very still, hovered only three pigs.

"Lydia, you all right? Whatever is it?" Aunt Tildy called from the door. The two long braids of her hair hung down the back of her tentlike nightdress. She rubbed one bare foot against the other.

"A bear, Aunt Tildy," she called. "It was a thieving varmint of a bear. But it's far away from here now—with one of my pigs for its breakfast."

For three nights after that Lydia waited by a window with the loaded rifle. On the last night the bear returned. She was aroused at first by a feeble bark from the hound pup before he retreated under the steps. Then, as she strained to listen, she could hear the bear's clawing as it tried to tear down the logs she had put back in place. She did not know what to do. A light would scare the bear away and yet without it she could not see a step in front of her.

She turned the wick in the lantern as low as it would go and opened the door carefully. Behind her everyone lay sound asleep. Before her there was silence and everything in the barnyard seemed sound asleep, too—everything except this big black beast she could not even see, and herself. Fear knotted her stomach and tightened her throat until she could not swallow. But she knew that she had to get this bear or he would come back again and again until he had taken all the food she had. Mark had tried to teach her how to handle the rifle; he said she had a good eye, but she had never shot more than a dozen times. Why hadn't she practiced every day while Mark was still home? she wondered now, desperately.

She moved forward softly and slowly. There were pauses in the scratchings and gruntings around the pigpen, and then she stood still. When the noise began again she eased forward. She could smell the acrid odor of the pen, the sour remains of swill in the feed trough. She was hardly breathing. What if it shouldn't be a bear? There were other varmints caught pigs. Then one of the logs was dislodged, and fell with a thud. She turned up the wick and lifted the lantern high.

The bear was standing on its hind legs. Its forefeet raked the top of the fence around the little pen. Its black bulk loomed up in the night, the largest animal, Lydia thought, that she had ever seen. Uncertain in the sudden light, its head weaved back and forth for a sharp, suspended minute. Its nose seemed to sniff the air.

Lydia swung the handle of the lantern over an end of a log and took hasty aim along the barrel of the rifle. But the movement had alerted the bear and more quickly than she could have expected from its deceptive appearance of heavy awkwardness, it began to back away. Another second and it would be part of the darkness. She pulled the trigger.

The gun kicked against her shoulder and she fell against the pen. There was a grunt from the opposite side, then silence. The pigs stirred restlessly. When she picked up the lantern, the bear was gone. She circled around the fence. Where it had stood, there were blotches of blood staining the ground. At least she had struck it, then. All at once she was weak with fear that it might come from the darkness, enraged by its wound, as she had heard hunters tell in their experiences, and attack her. She ran across the yard.

The next day Lydia let David go with her when she followed the splashes of blood and bear tracks for a long distance up the mountain. Aunt Tildy warned her against going: "It's a flouting of Providence for a female like you to go stalking after bear." But she had to make sure that the plunderer wasn't still around her farm.

They did not find the bear; she never knew what became of it. It did not come raiding again. Sometimes, a long while later, she would wonder about the fine, free, wild animal she had confronted there so briefly. She hoped it had died quickly—or better and more likely, that she had only flesh-wounded it. And ever after that night alone in the barnyard, Lydia knew a little less fear. "I declare, Aunt Tildy," she said the next afternoon when they were mixing up a batch of sour milk and corn bread for the newest hatching of baby chicks, "it's a sight how a body grows. A year ago you couldn't a-told me I'd go out in the black-dark and try to kill me a bear." She giggled softly.

"Maybe you was smarter a year ago," Aunt Tildy said. "Foolhardiest thing I ever heard of, out in the night——"

"I couldn't just sit by and let it eat up all we need so bad. Could I, Aunt Tildy?"

"Course not. Course not." The old woman knocked her spoon against the kettle and started outside.

"I reckon we shed fears all along the way," Lydia said as she followed her, "like a snake shedding his old skin every year, we let go of them. And finally we're plumb grown up and free."

"That's a 'finally' not many folks ever live to see," Aunt Tildy declared.

At last John Burke plowed her cornfield, but the growing season was poor. Not only corn but all her garden crops had a thin yield. Kate came up to see her one day in fall and brought news that, although the season had not been quite so rainy in the valley as up here on the mountain, crops there were short, too.

But Kate was not dwelling on grim matters. She had come to tell Lydia that she was going to be married. Alec Thurston—Alexander Hamilton Thurston—was the man's name. He was younger brother to Clay Thurston, who had moved with his wife and family down near the mouth of Thickety Creek.

"Clay Thurston is a lumberman and Alec will be a-helping him. To begin with, they've bought a big tract of forest from Ham Nelson."

"Not that virgin stand that runs along by the river?" Lydia asked.

"May be. I don't know for sure just where it is. They say it's easy to reach." But Kate was not thinking of trees. "Oh, they're fine folks, Lydia, gay and hearty."

And so Lydia heard for the first time in the valley and on the mountain the name of the Thurstons.

"We'll have the ceremony the next preaching Brother Gudger holds," Kate said. "You'll be there?"

"I wouldn't miss it for a pretty," Lydia assured her. "My little sister getting married. Children"—she swung Burnett up in the air and put him on the floor again—"how would you like to go to a marrying one day before long?"

Martha agreed they would like it. She rattled off a dozen questions while the little boys looked on and nodded and Burnett begged to be tossed just one more time. And Aunt Tildy dandled the baby on her knee so that it seemed that even he was joining in their merriment.

After Aunt Tildy and the children were in bed that night, the sisters sat up and talked together by the flickering firelight. "How's Papa, Kate? I'm just hungry to see him. What does he think of your marrying?"

"He's the same as always," Kate answered, preoccupied with brushing her thick hair in long steady strokes. "And he likes Alec—even though Alec's not a reading man. Papa likes all the Thurstons, I think. They're likable folks."

"You're witness to that," Lydia teased. "And what about the

154

rest of my family, besides my new brother-in-law: Elizabeth and
and Annie Marie?"

"Papa's tutoring Elizabeth in Latin," Kate said. "Papa says
she's quick to learn it and he claims it might help her become a
teacher sometime."

"Oh, I always wanted to learn some Latin," Lydia cried, "especially if Papa could teach it to me. I wanted to read Caesar. 'All
Gaul is divided . . .' That's the way it begins." She thought of
Papa's rows of books and how she had always meant to read them
all, and others, too, someday, and how Papa had said of her,
many an evening when she was working out a lesson he'd given
her, "You're a quick scholar, Lydia. I'm counting on you having
proper teaching one of these days. Hadn't the war come, we
might have brought a mission school in here by now." But she had
forgotten books when she saw Mark McQueen at the Burkes' mill,
and there had been no time since. She looked at the clock on her
new mantel. Where did it go, all that time ticked off by tidy seconds?

"I never could see the use of it," Kate was saying, and Lydia
realized she was still speaking of the Latin.

"Why, I reckon no special use right here on Thickety," she said.
"It's just the *knowing* that's good."

"I'd as soon know other things," Kate said. She shifted the
brush to the other side of her hair and continued the faithful
strokes. Yes, she was pretty enough and happy enough and am-
bitious enough; Lydia could guarantee what an easy, pleasant
wife she would make to Alec Thurston.

"And what about Annie Marie?" she asked.

Kate's smooth forehead wrinkled in an unaccustomed frown.
"She stays with Paul and Dolly. They were always favorites to
each other, Annie Marie and Paul, sort of like you and Robert
always were."

It was said without rancor, but Lydia flushed. She had not
known that the rest of the family felt the bond that was between
her and her younger brother. She had not intended to exclude any
of them and yet, looking back, she could see that was what she and
Robert might have done.

155

"Oh, Kate, I didn't mean——"

"It was all right, Lydia. Mama once told Elizabeth and me there were ties nobody could help, ties between like-natured people. Paul and Annie Marie were shy and deep-running, she said, and you and Robert took a-hold of life, whatever come, and she told us we were part of all of you and to be our own selves. Her explaining made everything all right with Elizabeth and me."

"I'm glad, Kate. I didn't love any of you the less——"

"But now that Annie Marie's gone to Paul's, seems like she's helping Dolly most."

"Dolly's Paul's wife. Maybe that's what pleases him for Annie Marie to do."

An odd expression crossed Kate's face. "She sleeps in Dolly's room, you know, and Paul sleeps with the young'uns."

Lydia's face grew pink. "But why?"

"Dolly claims she has nightmares and she's afraid of keeping Paul awake and making him lose sleep. What she's afraid of is having more babies and losing her little waist."

"Oh, Kate." Lydia turned her head away and began to weave her hair into two long braids. "Then I don't wonder that Paul was so quiet at Mama's funeral."

"He works like a dog at that mill. Folks say those big French stones of old man Hawkins and Paul's careful grinding make the nicest, liveliest flour in all Nantahala County. I reckon they'll be rich someday." Kate laid her hairbrush aside.

"Rich wouldn't count for much if you had to live like that," Lydia said.

"One good thing Annie Marie's done, being there," Kate went on, "she's straightened out little Tim and Pru." (It had always struck Lydia as passing odd indeed that Dolly wanted to name her little girl Prudence. "Prudence Moore—it has the sound of a lady," was Dolly's explanation.) "At least they've learned not to sass grown folks."

"Kate"—a thought had lain heavily on Lydia's mind ever since her mother's death—"was there any more talk, any unpleasantness about the fact that I took the Bludsoes' venison, or that we had Weatherby Hayes play his violin at Mama's funeral?"

156

"There was talk, but Papa says talk is like a grass-fire, big and showy but soon gone out. Does he ignore such things, it's easier for him than for his girls. Somebody even named about our quare ways to Alec while we were courting."

"Oh, Kate——"

"You come to know Alec, you'll know that didn't bother him as much as a mosquito buzzing. He just turned off that tattle-mouth. 'Reckon the Moores know there's a lot of kinds of music in a fiddle,' he said. 'And what about the Bludsoes?' she asked. 'Why, I've yet to make their acquaintance,' Alec told her."

"Seems I'll like your Alec, Kate."

"Oh, Lydia, wasn't it one lucky day for me when the Thurstons moved to the valley?" Her plump face glowed with the beauty Lydia knew only love could kindle.

"Lucky for Alec, too," she said.

While they put on their night clothes before the fire, Lydia said, "It troubled me some, Kate, that I had flouted the folks that came to mourn Mama. I don't know why sometimes I just naturally seem to go against the ways others follow."

"While they're worrying, you're doing," Kate said calmly.

"Maybe there's times I'm doing the wrong thing," Lydia said.

"Leastways you're not blaming others—or the Lord."

"Katy"—Lydia sat down on the warm hearth and pulled her knees up under her chin—"you know I'm not a-tall sure what I really do think about the Lord. It may sound heathenish, out in words like that, but it's truth. While I'm working around, when the children aren't deviling me with questions, I get to studying about it. Be Heaven a place like the preachers say, I don't know as I'd be easy amongst all that gold and silver. Seems like it might get wearying on the eyes."

"Lydia, you're a sight." Kate giggled uneasily.

"I mean every word. I'd take more pleasure in Heaven if there was a wide green field and plenty of woods, with streams and all manner of flowers and birds and living things to discover. I've thought about Mama there, and I hope they've found some corner where she can tend her flowering shrubs—and all her cuttings will take root."

"I never put much thought on it, one way or the other," Kate said, interested but uninvolved.

"And the preachers be so wrapped up in the glories of that next world," Lydia went on, looking into the dying fire, speaking to herself as well as to her sister, "that they're missing half the glory of this world. I can't believe the Lord meant us to be heavyhearted every minute here when He made so much to lift our hearts. . . . Katy, am I wicked for such talk?"

The younger girl shrugged.

"The words I remember from the Bible mostly, they're about the waters of life—and I think about my spring out here, bubbling up pure and plentiful—and about losing your life to save it. I believe I know what that means, Katy. I know it true. It means to lose your littleness in bigness, your own self into the all of living."

"Why I reckon so, Lydia."

"That's not the salvation the preachers talk about, Kate." They sat silent while the hot coals in the fireplace crumbled to ashes. "But it's the only salvation I've ever had any true experience of," Lydia said.

"We were all baptized together. It pleased Mama. I remember that," Kate said.

"That's not the same thing," Lydia answered.

She heaped ashes on the final coals so that she would have fire to begin the morning. After they were in bed and the house was quiet, Lydia lay awake a long time. She wondered if Mark was finding whatever he needed for salvation out there on the Western waters.

8th
CHAPTER

Three weeks later, on a Sunday morning, Paul drove his white team and carriage up to fetch Lydia and the family to Kate's wedding. But the three older children were sick with colds and croup; they had coughed most of the night before.

Aunt Tildy was nursing them with hot flannel cloths she had torn from one of her own petticoats, and poultices on their chests. A kettle of water steamed on the crane over the fire. She insisted that Lydia should go on to the wedding.

"We'll get along. Young'uns always have one thing or another ailing them, but a marrying don't come along but once in a coon's age."

Lydia was too tired, however, to find much pleasure in the wedding. All week she had worked out in the fields, digging potatoes and cutting late cabbages to store away for winter, and then the children's sickness had kept her up during two nights. On the way down the mountain with Paul, she fell asleep in the carriage. She was chagrined, for it had been a long time since they had had a chance to talk together and there was much she would have liked to say.

The wedding itself was a blur of people. The Thurstons were

the ones Lydia remembered most clearly: tall, dark-bearded Henry Clay Thurston, who spoke with authority but stammered slightly; his wife, Sue, a small, wiry woman with a firm chin and merry eyes; and their three boys, Tom Jefferson and Jim Monroe and Ben Franklin, seven and six and five; and an infant, Nellie. Then there was Alec, not as tall as his older brother, Clay, but carrying the same square shoulders, enjoying the same hearty stamp of freedom.

"I aim to keep your sister proud she saw this day," he said to Lydia, and she thought it was a nice thing for him to say.

She saw her father only briefly, but before she left he piled Paul's carriage with apples and fresh-ground meal and other provisions. And after Paul had unloaded them for her at home that night, he slipped a bill into her pocket.

"No, Paul," she protested, "I can't take it. It wouldn't be fair to Mark. He's left me provided for——"

"I know he has," Paul said. With his one good hand he reached out and took her arm. "This is for something extra. Hire help for the harvest while Mark's gone. It'll bring me satisfaction if you let me do it, Lydia."

"But it's too much——"

"Please?"

She was embarrassed. She was not accustomed to receiving such gifts. "I'm much obliged," she said. "Now, how about staying the night here and making that long trip home in the morning?"

Paul shook his head. "Dolly will be waiting for me."

"Annie Marie's with her," Lydia said, then added in hasty embarrassment, "and the children."

"I'd best go." Paul did not look at her. After he was in the carriage, he leaned out and said softly, "Lydia, you needn't ever mention that—that little present to anyone."

"No, Paul," she said.

"If you should ever want for anything, you'd let me know?" he asked more cheerfully.

"Of course, Paul. I understand." She reached up and squeezed his hand, then hurried inside to see how her babies were.

Their colds were better, but the croup came again and again

during the winter. As Lydia went about her work—wearing an old coat and hat of Mark's and a pair of his big brogans through the slashing rains and cold days of fog and finally the snows shoe-mouth deep—feeding the fowls, tending the calf and heifer and milking the cow with stiff chilled hands, carrying water, keeping leaves in the pigpen, bringing in armfuls of green firewood, she wondered whatever she would have done without Aunt Tildy.

Aunt Tildy showed her how to improve her carding and how to make her weaving move faster through the loom. She taught Lydia several new dyes, and some old medicinal remedies. During the winter evenings, when darkness slipped down over the mountain by five o'clock and there was only the rushing of the wind through the cove to remind them of the outside world, Aunt Tildy dipped into her fund of stories and told of spirits from another world or people from her memory world. The children listened, rapt and motionless. Family history repeated itself as Lydia remembered nights at her father's house when her mother was still alive and Mark was home and she still believed that David might be—well, whatever he chose to be.

Aunt Tildy's stories carried them to other times and places, bridged the world and made them part of it. Words, thought Lydia, were magician's tools.

It was on one of these nights that the idea came to her of how to use Paul's money. She had determined that it should not be dribbled away in bits spent here and there; such a sum, the largest she had ever had in her own possession, must buy something meaningful. And then she thought of a fitting purpose for it: she would send the fifty dollars he had given her to Robert. And Robert could go on, now while he still cared, to find the words and substance of law. It would be a gift not only to Robert but to them all —to Papa, who had wanted a child of learning; to Mark, who needed to see that there were rules for meting out justice.

Once decided, she carried the happiness of her secret close. After that, throughout the winter, when the weather was bitter or her back ached with steady, wearing misery, or Gib cried in the night and she got up to rock him, she drew her purpose forth, like a jewel, and thought about Robert receiving the money, his surprise, his pleasure. She smiled to herself, imagining the moment. She was impatient to get to the store so that she could mail the money and have it on its way.

The winter dragged on. By the end of January the hay was all gone and she was doling out any corn she could spare to the cattle. The cow's milk decreased. She warmed the slop for the pigs and even gave them the dishwater from the house. One sunny day when there was no snow on the ground, she went into the woods with the children and picked up mast for the hogs. When David found a half-frozen baby rabbit, she let him bring it home and put it in a box near the hearth. Aunt Tildy sniffed but did not quarrel about the new arrival because David had brought it.

Their own supply of food dwindled. Lydia tried to think of different ways to cook cabbage and potatoes and dried apples to make them tasty. When she wanted to fix the children a special treat, she fried individual apple pies, folded in triangles, the crisp dough sprinkled with spice. Then the room was filled with a delicous aroma that suggested warmth and richness, and they were enveloped in a sense of coziness within the cabin—the little cabin that, seen from the mountaintop seemed a flimsy landmark, indeed, set in the hollow of these everlasting hills. When she had used up all the grease, however, and when the last sprinkle of the cinnamon her mother had given her was gone, they had no more of the little pies.

In late February the spicewood bushes around her spring began to swell, but that was the only sign of spring she saw. She had no word from Mark. She killed a possum in the barn one night, but she was not so lucky with the foxes that lurked around her chickens and barked up on the hills. She was disgusted with the hound, full grown now but useless, it seemed, when it came to keeping marauders away from her livestock.

"If those flop ears were fit to eat," Aunt Tildy announced, "I vow I'd have that hunk of worthless meat in the pot before you could shake a stick and shame the devil."

When the calf—a young yearling now—wandered out of the barn one night just before a late freeze set in and got its head caught between two rails in the back pasture fence, Lydia grew

162

desperate. It was all she could do, using all her strength, to bring the poor animal home. They nursed it with Aunt Tildy's potions beside the fire. David crooned to the yearling and cradled its wild-eyed head in his lap all day. It was too far gone. Just after supper it died. Tears ran down David's face. Martha put her arms around her older brother and cried because he was crying. He insisted on going with his mother to drag the calf into the woods. As they left the carcass under the trees, Lydia knew she should have tried to skin it and make use of the meat. Beef would taste good to them all. But she shuddered and knew she could not do it this time. She would have to be more hardened—or in even greater need.

Their wants were pressing enough. "Aunt Tildy, I've got to do something." She would not consider using Paul's—now Robert's—money. It had never really been hers. Fifty dollars would do a great deal, but nothing as important just now as setting Robert's feet back on the path of the law. "Aunt Tildy, help me think!"

Aunt Tildy chewed on her black-gum-twig toothbrushes and thought and one day she remembered what the old man at the herb house in at the Nantahala county seat had said to her: "You know a good root digger out in your country, send him on in to me. Was he a-mind to, a feller could turn a right good sum selling herbs."

Lydia was excited about what Aunt Tildy told her. She quizzed the older woman again and again about roots and herbs and their uses and which were scarce and which brought the highest pay. She knew the mountains and their plants; such gathering would be no hardship to her! And if the buyers wouldn't do business with a woman, why then, she would borrow Robert from his studies and make him transact the trading for her. She was full of plans and new confidence.

On the first fair day in March she got out her best dress and bonnet and her high-button shoes early in the morning. She put Paul's fifty dollars in her pocketbook. David and the baby stayed with Aunt Tildy and she took Martha and Burnett with her. She reached the valley in time for early dinner with her father and sister Elizabeth and left the two children with them. "Stop by the mill and see Paul," her father said; "he'll drive you in to the herb dealer's."

It was some distance from her father's down to the turnpike where Thickety Creek entered the river. By the time she came to Hawkins' mill, her legs were weary and her feet were burning from the unaccustomed tightness of her dress shoes. Paul was alone in the mill. He was surprised to see Lydia, but even more glad than surprised.

"Dolly and her pa have gone down on Turkey Creek for the night to some kind of celebration," he said. "Just me and Annie Marie here with the children. You can stay the night. It will be like old times again."

She could have wept at the evident pleasure he felt that the others were not there, at the old man's stoop of his shoulders. Instead she took his right arm and laughed and explained about how "lady's feet" cramped an old mountain woman like her, and they went across the road to the house.

This was the same fine house Lydia remembered from the time she had been midwife at Tim's birthing. Everything was neater now, however; the windows shone, the floors smelled of soap and water. When Lydia saw Annie Marie she knew why the house was different. The thin girl in the faded dress and mended shawl, with her hair knotted on top of her head, might have been ten years older than Annie Marie's seventeen. Paul came in, the children were eating their supper and Annie Marie was telling them a story. She kissed Lydia almost savagely, and made Tim and little Pru shake hands politely with their aunt.

"Annie Marie works too hard," Paul said, when he took Lydia upstairs to the spare bedroom where she would sleep. He spoke as though he had suddenly seen his younger sister for the first time in several months, and had seen her with Lydia's eyes. "I can't seem to make her do less."

Lydia did not know what to answer. The little bedroom seemed crowded to suffocation with furniture. "Is it all right if I open a window after while, Paul?" she asked.

He nodded. "Dolly doesn't like the night air in the rest of the house, but she won't mind what you do up here." He rubbed his

164

arm across his forehead and leaned against the doorjamb. "Lydia, I do the best I can by them all," he said.

"Yes, Paul. We know you do. You've always been good to everyone."

"It will seem nice for us to talk like old times," he said, and went back down the stairs. His steps were slow and heavy.

Lydia turned and struck her fist on the middle of the bed. The downy feather bed underneath absorbed her angry blow and fluffed back again, soft and yielding—and unyielding. She bit her lip. She would not think about Dolly. She should not sleep in her house and despise her. But memories of that other visit kept coming back. She had cheated Paul before they were married, and ever since then she had drained him, and now Annie Marie. Oh, what was it Dr. Hornsby had called the mistletoe that day— a parasite? Yet Dolly was a parasite of Paul's choosing, a parasite he loved, his wife.

Paul's hopes for "an evening like it used to be" were not fulfilled. Annie Marie put the children to bed and then the three grownups ate together. But Annie Marie, in her eagerness to mark the specialness of the occasion, had set the dining-room table and used a fine linen cloth and flowered china. There seemed to be other people at the table with them. Lydia knew that the three of them would have felt more at ease in the kitchen, in front of the fire, with plain plates and the kitchen clock ticking as it always had in their mother's kitchen. A verse of scripture floated across her mind: "Better is a dinner of herbs where love is, than a stalled ox and hatred therewith." The verse reminded her of her purpose here and she told them about the plans she had to trade with the herb buyers in town.

"Lydia, I could help you out," Paul began, and she saw that he was embarrassed for this home when she was on such a mission. "Digging is no proper work for——"

"Paul," she said, "you look after your family—and you know Mark and me, we're of a mind to look after ours."

"Why, yes, Lydia . . ."

"We're not asking charity. And any kind of honorable work I

165

can do is proper." She had spoken sharply for she must settle this once and for all—in her own mind and in theirs.

"I'll take you in tomorrow," Paul said. "I know where that warehouse is. I went there a long time ago when I was a boy with Papa and Aunt Tildy. She was getting some golden seal, I remember. She'd had a spell of rheumatism and hadn't been able to go out and find any for herself."

The stiffness still hung between them, cramping conversation.

"You're as good a cook as Mama," Lydia told Annie Marie when they had finished eating.

"The bread had too much soda," Annie Marie said brusquely, pushing back her chair and commencing to clear the table.

"She's always faulting herself or her cooking," Paul teased.

"Long as Paul likes it," she said to Lydia, "that's what matters. When I first come here, he was skin and bones."

Paul frowned. "And now *you're* skin and bones," Lydia wanted to say, but she did not.

Lydia found a rheumy-eyed buyer of herbs at the warehouse on the edge of town. His office was a square cubbyhole cut out of the big plain of floor covered with mound after mound of assorted roots and leaves and plants. She told him that her husband and boys wanted to try some digging for him. The old man peered at her and grunted, then took her through the dusky building. He told her the names of varieties he could use. She knew them all but one—a twisted root with a queer shape, called ginseng. It brought more money than any plant on the list he gave her. He said it was shipped all the way to China.

"Just be sure everything you bring me is done dried out good and proper, like I showed you," he called as she left. "Roots to break with a snap, leaves and plants easy to crumble. No cheating on the drying."

She would have protested his implication against her honesty, but under the worn and filthy hat his yellow eyes blinked at her like an owl's. She hurried to be out of their range of vision.

When they turned down the street from the warehouse, she asked Paul if he could take her to the livery stable where Robert might be at work. She looked at the new houses and stores in town as they drove past. They went by a hotel with a wide veranda running around three sides. Lydia imagined how it might look in summer, crowded with ladies and gentlemen in Sunday clothes. Today, however, it appeared deserted. The streets were muddy and not crowded. Planks for ladies to walk on had been laid across some of the worst puddles along the side of the street. Lydia looked at names on offices and wondered at which lawyer's Robert would be going to study. The livery stable was not far from the hotel. They found Robert currying a big bay mare. He greeted them in high spirits.

"You see this mare? She's getting ready to carry one of the biggest businessmen in the North on a little trip out into our mountains. I couldn't say what he's hunting for, but one thing pretty sure, it spells money. I aim to keep my ears open."

"You're looking peart," Paul said.

"Peartens a feller up best to see homefolks." Robert grinned at them.

Lydia told him why she had come to town and about seeing the merchant. "Good as you know plants," he said, "it won't even be a hardship on you, will it?"

When Paul went to water his horses, she slipped the money to Robert. His face grew red. He shoved it back toward her in his clenched hand.

"No!" she said, and her eyes blazed at him. "I didn't bring this over here to take it back. Now you keep it and stop this stable work tomorrow and go back in that law office. Maybe you can find some handyman jobs to help board you when this runs out, but nothing that will interfere with your studying. You understand?"

He stood looking at her. "You don't doubt I can do it."

"More likely I'll be struck by lightning than you'll fail at law. That's my belief." She pushed his hand, with the money in its fist, into his pocket. "Here comes Paul. Don't ever name this to anybody—or to me again."

"Name it or not, I'll not disremember," Robert said.

And so it was all done—the giving and the receiving, the surprise which she had pictured in her mind so many times as she

167

went about her drudgery. It had happened so quickly; she felt a vague disappointment at the consummation of her dream. Perhaps she had cherished it too fondly. Maybe some dreams were like some people, unable to carry too heavy a load of affection lavished on them.

On their way home Paul was very quiet. "You think Robert will make good at lawyering?" he asked.

"Yes. Of course he'll make good." She wondered if he suspected what she had done.

"Could I find a way, would he let me help him out?"

She sighed. "Not likely. We're such a proud, stubborn, pitiful tribe. . . ."

"We are that," he said.

She blew her nose. "Just like all those old Scotsmen and Englishmen and Irishmen laying in their generations of stony graveyards back on the Isles. Papa says they lived and died by a code set down in no record, but in our blood."

"May be," Paul said.

"As long as we keep on trying to climb, in pride and pain, I reckon they'll be alive."

They stopped by the mill and Paul's house, and Lydia said hello to Dolly, who had been home since noon. "It was lonesome, coming back from all that frolicking to find nobody here," she pouted to Paul. "Nobody but little ole Annie Marie and the children, that is. Lydia, honey, won't you stay tonight, too?"

"I thank you, Dolly. The children will be a-needing me. You bring Tim and Pru and Annie Marie and come to see us when the weather fairs up."

Paul took her by her father's, where they picked up a sleepy Martha and Burnett, and once again Paul brought them home late in the night. But this time he stayed on the mountain until morning and had breakfast with them. Before he left, he brought a sack of flour and a twenty-pound keg of lard into Lydia's kitchen. "This is special ground wheat flour," he said. "If I do say it as oughtn't, I'm right proud of it, Lydia."

She understood then that it was not work at the mill that had aged Paul. The work was his only satisfaction. "Many a day since

168

we've had wheat bread," she said in delight. "We'll think of you with every mouthful."

"You and Robert and your words," he said, but he was pleased.

"We could thank Uncle Paul in our blessing," Martha spoke up.

"Acorns make oaks," Paul laughed. "She's already taking after you, Lydia. Here, Martha." He took some licorice from his pocket. Lydia suspected he had bought it in town for Tim, but now he handed it to Martha. "Divide with David and Burnett," he said.

"I will, Uncle Paul. But I'll thank you for us all. You see, my older brother doesn't say 'thank you' very well."

Paul did not look at Lydia. "You're a good child, Martha." He patted her head. "Well, it was good to see you, Lydia."

"I'm much obliged for all you've done for me, Paul."

"Only wish it was more. Good-by, Lydia."

"Good-by."

The next afternoon, after her morning's work was done, she took the older children and went up on the mountain to begin her gathering. It would take a while for her to learn where everything had its best growing spot. But she would spy out their secrets— bloodroot and yellow ragwort, snakeroot and wild ginger, the cohoshes and lady's slippers, and most particularly that root of the ginseng.

After supper she told Aunt Tildy about the ginseng and how much money it brought.

"Eh law, where you been, girl? Haven't you heard about 'sang before?" Aunt Tildy asked.

Lydia shook her head.

"Well, it's a pretty enough plant with five leaves, grows about so tall"—she held her hand ten, twelve inches above the table— "and most places it's pretty scarce. Now and again, though, you can run up on a good-sized bed. And you have to take care digging not to break the root."

"What's it good for, Aunt Tildy?"

"Nothing."

"But it's bound to be——"

"Nary a thing," Aunt Tildy chuckled. "But I've heard tell the heathen Chinese set great store by it because it's shaped sort of like the figure of a man. They wear 'sang roots around their necks. Like Indians, I reckon they claim it keeps away evil spirits."

"Well, you claim assafoetida around a body's neck keeps away bad sickness," Lydia laughed.

"That's different."

"It might not seem so to a Chinee. But I hope this 'sang doesn't smell anything like your assafoetida. Did it stink so, it might keep off *any* spirits, good or evil."

"Judging from that price list the man handed you, 'sang just smells like money," Aunt Tildy said. "But won't do any good to hunt it now, not till it leafs out this spring. Then I'll teach you how to spot it.

And so she did. Through spring and summer, using a sturdy seasoned stick to lean on and point with, Aunt Tildy went with Lydia and the children through the woods, teaching them her knowledge of all that grew and lived there. Tiny plants and towering trees, a fragment of fungus on a stump and a new bee-swarm; nothing seemed to escape her sharp eyes. Why she's as much a scholar here, Lydia thought, as ever Papa with his books.

They found a few scattered ginseng plants, and then—high up above the Devil's Brow—they located a bed. At first, Lydia hesitated to tear it up, but then she taught David how to dig the forked roots out gently and they worked for several days, filling their sacks. Aunt Tildy had said the patch would come back again big as ever if they left some of the plants for seed. So Lydia left a wide swath of ginseng in its bed, and as she went down the trail, she wondered if the plants that were still there in the woods didn't give her mind more satisfaction than the ones she had carried away.

That spring came late and left soon. Mark had been gone a year. When she thought of him, as she did throughout the day— when the hound came wagging its tail to be fed, or she brushed against one of Mark's old coats hanging along the wall; when she saw an abandoned horseshoe of Black Deuce's on a peg above the barn door; when she cooked blackberry cobbler or smelled a poplar leaf on the ground—she closed her mind against both hope and fear. She only repeated the questions over and over: When would she hear? When would he come?

John Burke, still surly, nevertheless plowed the fields and helped her plant a crop. The season was good. Everything flourished. The hogs were fattening. Eggs were plentiful. The children worked, too, carrying water from the spring, pulling arms full of plantain and other weeds for the hogs, hoeing in the fields. In midsummer, when the crops were laid by, Lydia and the children went back to the woods. They brought in sacks of plants and roots and spread them in the sun to dry. Lydia made a game of the gathering: Whose eyes were keenest? Who could find the most, the largest, of each specimen? Whose hoe could dig the easiest but sharpest? They chattered and ran like squirrels, and they laughed a great deal.

David and Martha and Burnett grew brown and tough as hickory nuts, and Gib was eating more than any of the other children had at a year and a half; his long baby legs had been carrying him on explorations since he was ten months old, and he was talking well. Lydia crawled into bed at night weary in every muscle. She slept deeply and awoke with first light and stretched to meet the day. The routine flowed on, salving the raw wound of knowing about David, easing the sharpness of Mark's absence.

With her first herb money she marched into Ham Nelson's store and bought a wagonload of hay to do her through the winter. Ham was the only man on Thickety who owned enough level land to have spare hay for sale. "Hay fields not producing so good up on Stony Ridge?" he asked her, as she counted out the money to him.

She ignored his reference to Stony Ridge where the Bludsoes lived, not she. "The crop on our place is better than common, thank you. But we've got more stock to feed this year."

He raised his heavy eyebrows.

When they had completed their transaction, Lydia stood for a moment and looked around the murky interior of the store. Shelves to the ceiling were filled with bolts of cloth, shoes and boots of various sizes, horse collars and blankets, pails and dippers and all sorts of tinware, coffee beans and coffee grinders, hammers, saws, bolts, and screws, threads and buttons, turpentine and kerosene and castor oil, a hundred and one assorted things—and around the floor were kegs of crackers and nails and other necessities. The light in the room was dim and a haze of dust hung in the air. The smell of new leather mixed with the smell of dry goods and linseed oil and strong cheese. She had not been in the store before since Ham Nelson owned it.

He interrupted her survey. "Something else I can get for you?"

"A little candy," she said. "Some licorice, I guess. Five cents' worth."

In one corner she saw shelves full of an odd assortment of things: dishes, quilts, seed corn, axe handles, a nub for a sneed. One brass kettle seemed familiar to Lydia. When she looked closer, she saw that it was Ida Burke's; every woman up and down Thickety had used that kettle to make her apple butter. Lydia realized that these were things Ham Nelson had taken from his neighbors in place of credit. Ida and John must have been hard-pushed since James was gone with Mark.

Ham measured the licorice out on the wooden counter. "How many young'uns you got now, Lydia?"

"Four."

"Nice even number," he said. She had never liked Ham's eyes. They were set too close together. She was always uncomfortable when he looked at her. "Doc Hornsby's brought me news of you a time or two."

She glanced at him quickly. Would Dr. Hornsby have told Ham Nelson about David? "Here's your nickel," she said.

"Said you and him had been talking something about a school for Thickety Creek," Ham said.

"Oh." She laid the money on the counter. "Papa's been writing some of the Presbyterian folks up North. They might start a school here if we could get them some central place——"

"Some church outfit aims to bring it in, that's all right," he interrupted. "Let them that wants a school build it, I say."

"But even this would have to be the community," she said.

172

"Ham, you own so much land down here at the center of things, wouldn't you——"

He shook his head. "Thought you'd come around to it directly, just like Hornsby. No siree, schooling ain't my line."

"But we've got to build——"

"*We* ain't got to do a damned thing! You settled that yourself several years back."

Lydia's face burned. It made her angry that she blushed—but she knew there must be a school on the Creek. "I was speaking about we the community, Ham Nelson. And you're part of it, whether you like it or not."

"I be that," he said. "It's not much of a puddle, but I'm a pretty big frog in it."

"Then you're a-wanting to see it prosper."

"Not with taking away all our money for school taxes. Oh, I've read what some of the big talk is over at the state capital—free education for everybody. Free for them that gets it, but who's to 'give' it to them?"

"All of us . . ." Lydia faltered. She did not know what was being discussed at the capital; she did not know about tax plans. She only knew that her children would be educated, if she lived, and every other child had the same right. There ought to be some way they could all go to school.

"Not all of us. Not me!" Ham shouted.

She put the candy in her pocketbook. "I was hoping—" she began.

"Well, now, I know something about that," he said. "Once upon a time, I was hoping, too. And it wounds a feller's pride to have his high hopes scorned."

Lydia fled to the door. Behind her she heard him say, "You're still a fine figure of a woman, Lydia, to be living without your man. Maybe I could bring that load of hay up the mountain myself?"

She turned and confronted him. Her face, with its sunken cheeks and blazing grey eyes, was pale. A stray wisp of hair curled over her forehead and gave her a girlish look, but there was nothing girlish about the timbre of her voice. "Ham Nelson, what

173

call have I ever given you to speak such a way to me? This is Lydia McQueen, and don't you ever forget it again. And Mark McQueen is not my man. He's my husband. And we're together whether he chances to be in Andersonville prison, or in the Western country, or here!"

The tension, the exhilaration, of her anger carried her over the threshold, but at the steps she turned once more, briefly. "And we'll have a school here, never fear. Greed can't keep down folks with gumption."

"Well, Mrs. McQueen, you ain't lacking for spirit." His laughter followed her down the steps.

Tilmon Haddon, ragged and dirty and slow-moving, brought the hay up to her farm a few weeks later.

"Eh law, that man moves like the dead lice was falling off of him," Aunt Tildy grumbled as she fixed a pone of bread for him to eat. "He's taken all day to get up here and now he comes just at supper——"

"It's not his fault," Lydia said. "He told me that Ham Nelson didn't start him up here till a while after dinner. Does Ham pay him by the day, reckon he gets his money's worth this way."

"But he'll be way after dark getting home."

"He told me Ham was a hard driver," Lydia replied. She had not told Aunt Tildy or anyone about her talk with Ham Nelson at the store. But she could sympathize, as Dr. Hornsby had once sympathized with this poor creature who was tenant on Ham's farm. When she took Haddon out a plate of supper, she had an idea. "The first good cold spell we have, how about you coming up here to help me butcher two of my hogs, on shares?" she asked.

For the first time she saw him move with something approaching speed. He grasped her hand and pumped it up and down. "That be a sealed bargain," he said. "I'm much obliged, ever so much obliged."

Twice in October he came, ready for the butchering long before the weather was ready. Lydia knew that the real cold had not set in yet and the meat would spoil before it cured. At last, in November, when they finally did get one of the hogs killed, it developed that he knew little about proper butchering. He dipped the hog

174

before the water was hot enough and they could not scrape its hide. The job was to do over again. When that was finished and he tried to cut up the meat, Aunt Tildy exclaimed, "I never saw such a mommicked-up job! Give David yonder a case knife and he could a-done better."

So Lydia divided part of the precious pork with Haddon, letting him take the liver and head and a piece of loin. But she did not let him try to butcher a second hog.

With hay in the barn, corn in the crib, meat in the smokehouse, and the knowledge of how she could earn a little cash along, Lydia met the winter with more satisfaction than she had known in a long while.

The days were uneventful. She had only two callers through the long months of December and January. The first was one of the Bludsoe children, a little girl this time, with long, uncombed hair and skittish ways. She had come to say that her pappy, Morgan Bludsoe, offered to butcher Mrs. McQueen's other hog for her, did she wish it.

"But how did you know——" Lydia stammered.

"Papa saw that other man's work," the girl answered readily. "Papa said that man couldn't even kill clean."

Lydia suddenly wondered if she and Mark had been under surveillance ever since they moved here. Had the eyes of the Bludsoes, like hawks, been watching her all the while Mark was gone? The thought chilled her.

But she did not ask that question of Morgan Bludsoe when he came, at her word, and with quick, sure movements dispatched a morning's work of butchering. When he had finished, he rode out of the yard, slouched again easily in his saddle, his hat over one eye. He would take no pay, no share of the meat. The unexpected generosity, without explanation, made her uneasy.

"Don't be looking a gift horse in the mouth," Aunt Tildy advised. And during the cold days they enjoyed the rich flavor of sausage and ham swimming in gravy and ribs baked to a sweet crisp, and succulent loin roasted over the open fire.

One night late in December, Lydia was awakened by a noise in the yard. She went to the window and stood there for a long time, but the night was dark and moonless and she could see nothing. Once she thought she heard another muffled noise, but it might have been one of the cows moving around in the barnyard. The next morning she discovered that a ham and shoulder were missing from the smokehouse.

"What comes of living up here close by heathens," Aunt Tildy muttered. "No wonder they come by offering to butcher for a body."

Lydia was troubled. With Mark away, anyone who had a mind to could thieve her out of house and home. But there was no more stolen, and after a few weeks she and Aunt Tildy began again to sleep easily at night.

Their other winter caller was Dr. Hornsby. Lydia was down by her spring the last day of January. The afternoon had been somewhat warmer than usual and she had come to dip out any leaves that might have blown into the water since the last storm. She had brought along her hoe to deepen the bed of the overflow stream that ran from the spring. The smell of the wet leaves and the soaked ground and the chilly day gave her a feeling of being under water, of drenched lungs and body.

When Dr. Hornsby rode into the yard at the other end of the path and up the rise, she called to him. She did not recognize who the visitor was until he dismounted and she saw the heavy saddlebags across his panting horse. Before she could get her hoe and start down the path he was striding toward her.

"And what are you doing this bleak day on this godforsaken mountain?" he asked.

She laughed at the gloom of his words, belied in part by the heartiness of his smile. "Cleaning my spring."

"And pray tell me, Lydia McQueen," he said, "how do you clean a spring? Do you wash the water?"

"Don't be making fun of me! There"—she pointed with the hoe—"look under the ledge where the roots of those poplar trees are, and tell me if you ever set eyes on a bolder, finer spring than that? Or a cleaner one?"

He went and looked. The natural bowl of water, surrounded on three sides and overhead by a ledge of rock and tangled web

176

of roots and earth, stood clear and cold as glass. Around the spring and beside the stream that flowed from it were beds of moss and galax, a luxuriant winter green, and the vines of other carefully preserved plants that bloomed in summer. On the far side and overhanging the spring, were a dozen wild blackberry stalks. There were no other briers or dead weeds or fallen limbs around this spot. Someone had worked here lovingly and well.

"I never set eyes on a bolder, finer spring," he repeated. "Or a cleaner."

"This is my favorite place on our farm," she said.

He looked at the well-worn path that led to the house. "Water, water everywhere," he murmured pensively. "And how that albatross doth stink!"

Lydia did not know what he meant. She was surprised at herself, too. "Here I've stood talking foolishness about my favorite places," she said, "and not even greeted you properly. We must go up to the house."

"No. No need to stop your work," he said.

She saw then that this face was red and heavy-looking. Like his hands, it had become a strange blend of grossness and delicacy. Dissipation had stamped the skin to smoothly shaven leather; dissipation was in the heavy eyelids, the too-knowing eyes. Yet the torment, the eagerness, the flickering of hope Lydia had seen before was still there, too.

"I was at the upper end of the valley," he said. "Old lady Burke got her hand crushed in the mill——"

"I hadn't heard. Was she bad hurt?"

"Bad enough. She'll be all right. She's one of the tough old locust roots of this world; you'll have to blast her to get her out. But since I was that far along the way, I decided to ride on up the mountain and see how your David is."

"That was thoughty of you," Lydia said. "Dr. Hornsby, he does talk better now, and he's not been sick all this winter."

But still he did not move toward the house and seeing David. He looked at the spring and the mountain and the sky, tapping his leg with the light riding switch he carried. "No," he said finally, "I didn't come to see David. I know how he is—a little improvement for him, a little hope for you, and then when he's twelve or fifteen physically and six or seven mentally, the standstill: as advanced by then as he'll ever be——"

"Dr. Hornsby!" she cried.

"I didn't mean to hurt you. Oh, believe me, I don't mean to hurt you. I just can't bear to think you'll go on hoping."

"If not David," she asked, "then why did you come?"

"Sometime," he said, and he snapped the leaf off a galax plant with a sudden angry flick of his switch, "just one time I wish I could bear you word of something good. Now I've got other bad news."

She clutched the hoe. "What?"

"Ham Nelson will fight you on getting your school for Thickety Creek," he said.

She waited for him to go on.

"Was that your news?"

He nodded and she threw back her head and laughed. Her shawl came loose and her hair fell around her shoulders. The news might have been of Mark. She laughed as though she could not stop.

"But I thought it meant so much to you," he said stiffly. "I misjudged——"

"Oh, no!" She took a step nearer to him. "A school means everything to me. It's just Ham Nelson that doesn't mean anything."

The doctor looked at her. Laughter and sarcasm and amazement were mingled in his look. "Nelson's a powerful man," he said.

"The power of a rock," she said.

"Then——"

"But there's something stronger than rock. You see that ledge over my spring? I've seen it cracked by the stem of a little vine that had to come up to sunlight through it. There's nothing strong enough to stop for long the strength of growing things. And children are stouter than any vines."

She knew she must look wild. With that sudden shift of nature that shunted her from dreams to realities in the space of a breath, she pushed back her hair and pulled the shawl over her head. Dr.

178

Hornsby gazed at her. Then his mouth flickered in a faint smile. "I brought you no news at all." He bowed slightly, as if conceding defeat in an important tournament.

"Oh, Ham Nelson and I never did hit it off," Lydia said. She started up the path ahead of the doctor. "I didn't expect his help."

"And what will you do about your school now?" he asked.

"There's always the Presbyterian folks up North."

"Then let us lay up for ourselves hopes in the North, where neither moth——"

"Doctor!" Was he making fun of her or the church or the school, or all three?

When they reached the yard, he mounted his horse and sat for a moment looking down at her. What a handsome figure of a man he would have been, Lydia thought, except for his drinking. And somehow he had always managed to make her feel—she groped to understand what he had made her feel: like a woman, capable of her best. That was it.

"I'm glad to have seen your fine spring of water, Lydia McQueen," he said. He smiled down at her. "I'm glad to have seen you."

"Thank you, Dr. Hornsby. I'm sorry you won't stay for a bite of supper or some . . ."

But he had turned and was galloping out of the yard. That was the last time she ever saw him alive.

And in February, when Gib was two years old and David was sick with pneumonia fever and the last snow was thawing on the Devil's Brow, Mark came home from the West.

Once, the tight confinement of prison had catapulted him into the world on a stormy search for some nameless freedom. Now, wide-ranging freedom returned him home with contentment in the confinements of family and community and love.

9th
CHAPTER

The day would be hot. Although the clock had not yet struck seven, the air was already heavy and suffocating. It lay still as a blanket stretched over the mountain and valley, stifling every breeze and human breath. Out in the farmyard, chickens wallowed in the dust on the shady side of the barn, the pigs sprawled on their bellies in the cool mudhole of their pen, and the cows had already sought the north side of the hill in their pasture.

In the house, Lydia, baking bread in the Dutch oven on the hearth and stewing a kettle of rhubarb over the fire, paused and wiped sweat from her face with the edge of her apron.

"Again the bread's baked, we ought to be ready to leave," she said to Martha, who was straining the morning's milk into two big crocks. "With us wanting it to turn out extra good, I've most likely left out salt or some necessary."

"Is the pieplant tender?" Martha asked. She gathered up the foam-filled straining cloth and went to rinse it out in a pan of cold water on the back porch.

"Just fine," Lydia called after her, "even if it does take a heap of sweetening." This was the first year since she had planted the roots Robert brought her from town that she had had enough rhubarb, or pieplant, to make a decent dish. She wanted to give all the people on Thickety a chance to taste it at dinner today.

There was to be a July Fourth celebration at Clay and Sue Thurston's. After some speechmaking, everybody would spread a family dinner on the grounds and there would be a time for good eating and sociability, leisurely exchanges of food and news. For weeks the children had lived in excited anticipation of this day, and this morning they had finished their outside chores by the time it was full daylight. No one but Mark and Lydia and the two babies, Lafayette and Jessica, had eaten any breakfast, and Lydia herself had to admit that excitement choked the food in her throat when she thought about the full day ahead of them. With Fayte, born in January, 1875, two years old, and Jessie, born in May, 1876, and now just a little better than a year old, Lydia had seen little of the valley and its people during the past few years. The six children, her house and garden, and the constant care each required, meant that every day was filled to overflowing with demands on her attention and patience and stout muscles.

Martha, now eleven, was a small replica of Lydia: alternately gay and grave, quick and hard-working, responsible far beyond her years. But she was not long of limb as her mother was. She was short; and she did not like the outdoor world as Lydia did. She helped her mother milk and cook, wash and spin, and her small hands could handle four steel knitting needles and turn out a sock as neat as anyone's. If she worked in the garden or fields, however, the sun was apt to give her sick headache, and her father had said that she was not to try to work outside with David and the little boys, Burnett and Gib. Indoors, she was her mother's third arm and ear, and her second pair of legs. After Aunt Tildy had delivered Fayte and Jessie, she had gone to stay awhile with Lydia's father and Elizabeth, and odd as it seemed, Martha had taken the older woman's place in many ways, especially in caring for the younger children. She rocked and crooned and changed diapers, and when the time came, helped the babies crawl and walk and begin the effort to make words. And in all this she did not shut out the older brother for whom she had always shown such instinctual protection: David adored her and helped as he could with all her chores.

Then, of course, there was always Lenore to help with the babies, too. Lenore Hornsby, with the fair skin and wide, dark, liquid eyes, and her father's sensuous mouth, who had lived with them for almost a year now. But although she was past twenty, she was really less help than little Martha at eleven. Lydia sighed and wondered how Lenore would get along at the celebration today. It would be the first time she had been out in public since that summer day—that terrible summer day—that morning last August. . . . Lydia shuddered.

"Mama, you'd better call Gib." Martha was taking a crock of milk down to the spring-run where it would stay cool. Under one arm she carried a big wooden lid to cover it. "He's trying to walk around outside with the bandage off his foot."

"Tell him to come in here this minute!"

Gib, trailing his father like a shadow everywhere he went, had been up on the mountainside where Mark was cutting timber last week, and he had stepped on the sharp stob of a sassafras bush. It had punctured his bare foot like a wedge driven into soft pine. When Mark had brought the boy home, Lydia had opened the deep wound to make it bleed, drenched it in turpentine, and bandaged it. During the next days it had been difficult to know which hurt him more, the throbbing flesh of his swollen foot or the fact that he could not be active. Now, followed by Burn, he limped in the door, barefooted, dusty, his face eager and inquiring as he rested his weight on his good foot and balanced with the toes of the other.

"Where's the bandage?" Lydia asked.

He did not blink an eye. "It came loose. I was helping Burn drive the cows and did I stop to put it back on, he'd be mad at me." He knew, and his mother knew, it was not Burnett that bothered the younger boy but the thought of being left behind.

"Let's look at it." Lydia took him in her lap and held his strong little foot in her hand. A good scab had formed over the wound, but the flesh around it was still bruised and angry. "A wonder you didn't break it open again. I'm a good mind to leave you home today!"

He looked at her in such astounded speechlessness that she could not remain severe. She warned him against losing another bandage, scrubbed his feet and legs, and bound up the gash again.

When Mark and David came from the barn, Lydia put the children to loading up the food for the day. There was a succulent stewed hen and a baked ham, the fresh bread wrapped in a white cloth, corn pudding, pickled beans and vinegar pie, berry cobbler and fruit cakes: plain sweet layers with applesauce between each layer. Lydia remembered a time when Mark had been fearful of being shamed by their food before the valley folks; she was determined he would not be shamed today.

During the four years since he had come home from the West, Mark had been a changed man. Lydia did not know the cause behind his change, whether it was born in the long spell of fever he had endured in the California country when he lay near death day after day and finally recovered to learn that his partner, Jim Burke, had died two weeks earlier of the same sickness and that Black Deuce had been traded to pay doctor's costs; whether it came from the awesome sight and knowledge of a vast new land of canyons deeper and mountains taller and plains more vast than anything he had dreamed of, or whether it was wrought by his slow realization that this far country was a place of action but not yet of answers. A man might become rich overnight or remain a wanderer—he had seen both—and still be lonely and full of gall.

"For a while," he told her, "I resolved not to come back home till I could bring you a sack of money or deed to a boundary of that Western land. Then, one day, on a wagon train, I saw a little girl about the size of Martha. Some sort of little apron she had on—it was blue—and her hair, in two braids over her shoulder, and she was helping her ma cook supper. Then and there, I knew it was time to come back."

Once, when they were sitting by the fire and Mark was speaking again of the West, he had said, "It's not a place to ask questions, out there. It's a country where you do or die."

"Then I'm glad you went to see for yourself," she said.

183

"I regret the trouble I've brought you, Lyddy, the years I was gone—longer than I meant. But I've come home now to find what satisfaction I can—to bring what satisfaction I can to you."

"Oh, Mark, welcome home!" The firelight illuminated the pleasure that lit her face.

And he had "taken hold," as Aunt Tildy said approvingly, working with almost maniacal fervor, clearing ever-widening patches of new-ground, growing more and more corn, accumulating livestock. He was still reticent with the people of Thickety, but the greatest change in him was reflected by the amount of time he spent with Lydia's father. Jesse Moore taught him to read and write and understand arithmetic beyond the elementary rudiments he had known; he talked with him about politics, religion, history, philosophy.

Sometimes Mark had taken Martha or Burnett or Gib—and once or twice all three of them together—down to their grandfather's for a lesson, too. At home Lydia had sharpened goose quills and squeezed out pokeberry juice, helped them learn to form the letters of the alphabet and the numerals, to read and write and cipher a little. After Dr. Hornsby—after the tragedy, when he had left some money to bring a teacher to Thickety, for two terms the children had gone to school for three-month sessions.

But Riley Scroggs, who had come out from the county seat to teach in an empty shed on the old Burke mill place, had seemed to Lydia a queer teacher, indeed. She knew that to spare the rod was to spoil a child, but the excess of Scroggs's temper sometimes led her to wonder if someone should enter a plea to spare the child or spoil a scholar. The stoop-shouldered, wizened schoolmaster seemed less interested in what the boys and girls learned than in what they did not learn: a misunderstood lesson called down as heavy a punishment from him as a mischievous trick or fault of character.

His tool of punishment was a combination paddle and switch, and worse than either: a slim, seasoned piece of board with a handle at one end and four thin, tough lengths of leather at the other. He had perfected a method of cutting those leather strips around a child's legs until the flesh stung and was broken and sometimes bled. Of all the students who sat on the hard benches in the bare single room, ranging in age from five years to twenty, none feared Mr. Scroggs as deeply as did Lydia and Mark's children. Perhaps because they had known less of the harshness that was customary to their time, they were less prepared to accept or understand the teacher's outbreaks of anger and "correction," as Mr. Scroggs called it.

Gib was the youngest child in the school. When the teacher whipped him one day for shuffling his feet while the second-book readers were reciting, he came home and announced to Mark and Lydia, "I hate that old teacher. Never another day am I a-going to his old schoolhouse."

And in spite of his father's punishment and his mother's cajoling, he would not go back to classes.

"I've set such store by a school," Lydia had said to Mark and her father, "but it seems like Riley Scroggs is turning the children against their books."

"He's a little free with his whippings," Mark agreed.

"Most likely scared of the older boys," Jesse Moore said, "and he's taking it out on the little ones, using them as lessons to the rest."

"But what will we do about Gib, Papa? He's mule-stubborn about not going back."

"For a little spell, let him be. Knowing that chap"—her father smiled—"he won't want the others to get ahead of him for long."

Before he could be proved right or wrong, however, Scroggs's teaching career on Thickety Creek came to an abrupt end near the close of his second teaching term. Scroggs's departure was the result of revenge on the part of some of the larger fellows he had punished. Tilmon Haddon's oldest boy agreed to pass by the school during a dinnertime recess and call out, "School butter!" At these words, as everyone in the mountains knew, the whole school was supposed to give chase to the intruder. During the course of the chase, Riley Scroggs, in a furious attempt to get the students back to their recitations, was tripped by a hidden deadfall the Haddon boy had made. He fell down a steep embankment and broke his right leg. There was no doctor on Thickety, and Paul had had to take the teacher in to the county seat.

"I won't be intimidated by those mountain boomers," he had said. "I won't be subjected to them. In town I am, in town I'll stay."

He never returned. For the past season there had been no more attempts at education in this part of the mountains. Ham Nelson circulated word that events had turned out about as he had expected.

Folks talked of pay schools and free schools and church schools, and Lydia wondered if her children would be grown up in ignorance before one of these institutions reached Thickety. She never doubted it would come eventually. But she wanted to help make it come in time—as Dr. Hornsby had wanted to. How could she ever forget?

"Lenore," she called across the dog-trot now, into the two-room addition Mark had built on their cabin when the last two babies were born and this girl came to live with them.

Lenore Hornsby, pale and fragile, wearing a muslin summer dress, came leading little Fayte. He wore a plain baby dress the children before him had worn when *they* were two years old, and high shoes, but this morning Lenore had sewed a ruffled white collar on the dress, giving it a special festive air, and had tied a tiny black ribbon in a bow where the collar fastened, for all the world like a man's string tie.

"We started the shoe buttons wrong," Lenore said to Lydia, "and had to begin all over again."

Lydia exclaimed over the new collar and Fayte preened like a peacock. Then she asked Lenore to take charge of their food baskets when they arrived at the Thurstons'; the baby, Jessie, would be taking much of her own time. She did not say that she wanted Lenore to stay busy today, to be useful, to seem an indispensable part of the celebration.

"Oh, yes, Lydia, of course," the girl agreed eagerly, but her wide eyes seemed to Lydia still vulnerable and full of pain, not yet free of the horror they had seen.

Martha came out on the breezeway. "You look pretty," she

186

said to Lenore. Confused and blushing and pleased, Lenore helped put the last food in the wagon.

What was it the girl's father had said about her name—Lydia tried to remember. Checking the bandage on Gib's foot to make sure that it was tight, and the baby's diaper to make sure that it was dry, covering the fire in the fireplace, giving a last look around the kitchen to see if anything necessary to the day's celebration had been forgotten, she tried to remember Dr. Hornsby's words. Lenore—the lost Lenore—part of a poem, he had told her when Martha—or was it Burnett?—was being born. And now he was gone. So fine, so able, how could he have done it? She would have to put such questions out of her mind. Today was July Fourth. The dead could not hold back the living. Surely her children knew little enough of celebrations! They were all out there at the wagon, Mark lifting them in like squirming sacks of feed.

She called out to them, "Fee, fum, foe, fie. All's not ready holler I."

"Not I! Not I!" they screamed back happily, returning her gaiety with interest.

"Fee, fie, foe, fum. All's not ready now can't come!" she answered, and closed the door behind her.

The clock was striking seven. "We're getting a soon start," Mark said.

They arrived at the Thurstons' in good time, a little after ten, but most of the people in the valley were already there. The big yard, sloping down to the river, was filled with clusters of men standing in awkward, midweek leisure, spitting ambeer, talking together with hats pushed on the backs of their heads. Women bustled in and out of the big unpainted frame house, calling to children, carrying baskets and pots and pans of food to and from long tables made of double widths of lumber laid on saw horses and covered with unbleached muslin. Smaller children clung to their mother's skirts or sat on the grass near the steps and watched with wide, solemn eyes the coming and going of their elders, while the larger boys chased and wrestled in the road and grass beyond the yard, and the girls walked arm in arm together along the picket

187

fence or sat under a big old lilac bush, whispering, giggling, self-conscious, confident, and fearful. The lassitude of summer heat, the quiet flowing of the river, the greenness of earth and goldness of sunshine enveloped them all.

Inside the house Lydia found Sue Thurston showing the women her new cookstove. "This-here's the firebox, and under it there's this ash catch to keep your floor from getting gaumed up when you clean out the ashes. You open the oven here at one side. It's a sight how it bakes bread, so nice and even."

Lydia was intrigued by the flat-top stove with four eyes. "Reckon it would be like cooking on a play-pretty!" she exclaimed, and the other women laughed.

"It don't have a movable hot-water reservoir like Mrs. Nelson's," Sue Thurston added, "but Clay said he's afraid I'd be rotten spoiled did he get me everything all to once." Her brown eyes were merry. Although her voice was deep and rough, at times almost like a man's, Lydia thought it was Sue Thurston's voice that gave her an air of easygoing good will and integrity.

"Papa says he's aiming to get us a cookstove with nickel-plate trimming right away," Dolly said. Glancing at Lydia she added, "Papa and Paul."

Aunt Tildy, unpacking the basket she and Elizabeth and Jesse Moore had brought, snorted audibly. "Paper and print don't write a book. Fire and food don't make a cook."

Just then old Ida Burke appeared in the doorway. The stove was forgotten. The women rushed to greet her.

"Mercy, Ida, it's a month of Sundays since we heard word of you and John!"

"You be a sight for sore eyes."

"Ever since you sold out and left Thickety, we been wondering when you'd find your way back."

The wrinkled leathery face under a bright new split bonnet beamed with pleasure at this attention. "Well now, John and me, as we come along today, we seen a redbird alongside the road and I made me a wish and throwed a kiss and I said to him, 'John, it's a-going to be a good day out here with old friends.'"

"It's a treat to see you," Lydia said. She recalled the day, only a few weeks after Mark had returned from the West without James, that their friends, Ida and John, had given up trying to hold on to their mill.

Some of old Ida's nerve had weakened when she learned that her loud, joking elder son was no longer alive. Ham Nelson had closed the mortgage on them. After all the years they had labored and lived in the valley, the stout woman and her dour son left it with only their livestock, a wagonload of meager household furnishings, and the memory of a few friends.

Mark had tried to do what he could for them; he helped find a farm at the other end of the county where they would make a crop on shares. "My being a raw, scared stranger, the Burkes were the first folks in Nantahala to give me work," Mark told Lydia. "This won't seem the same place without them." And then, with a flash of the old anger, he had struck his fist against one knee. "What's Nelson going to do when he's gobbled up all of Thickety?"

"He won't get it all," Lydia said. And she was able to offer Mark some proof a short while afterward—when they took Dr. Hornsby's money and bought the mill land for a school.

"You paid too much," some folks in the valley said.

Even the town lawyer, Wheeler, who helped Robert draw up the papers, said the price seemed outrageous. "Land must be high as quinine out where you live, Mrs. McQueen."

"No," she had replied. "But there was more than land in this trade. Looks like the man that owns can set his terms and the one that buys can accommodate to those terms—or do without. We want our school on Thickety to be on that place."

The Burkes had been more reconciled to leaving when they learned about Lydia and Mark's plan. Now Ida Burke was telling Lydia, "Never crossed your mind, did it, that we'd let Robert Moore give a speaking out here and us not come to hear it? Why, he brought us with him today. He's getting to be a regular, fine, well-known gentleman in town. And him the son of Sarah Moore, as fine a neighbor as ever lived."

"Robert's here now?" Lydia asked.

"Right out there under the trees."

So she went to find her younger brother. The years were dealing kindly with him. She was proud of the progress he had made in the Wheeler law firm. Old Mr. Wheeler had said that come fall Robert could have his name put up on the sign in partnership with the three Wheeler names.

"Well, our lawyer has fleshed out some," she said to him as they stood under the spreading limbs of a big beech tree at one side of the yard.

"And our mountain girl hasn't fleshed out," he said. He held her at arm's length and looked at her carefully—thin face, lean body, brown arms, and work-worn hands. "You're well, Lydia?"

"Mercy, yes! You know what Aunt Tildy used to say, a lean hound for a long race."

"Haven't seen you for a while, Lydia. You've not brought any herbs in to the warehouse?"

"Mark has taken a little 'sang. I'm saving for the children's subscriptions, do we get our school started up again."

"One of these days, Lydia—well, blast it all, I've been saying that so long now I'm shamefaced—but someday maybe I can be some help."

"Hush up, Robert Moore. Tell me what you've been doing."

He told her about the exciting things that were happening in town. "There's a man from up North going to open some mica mines right here in Nantahala County," he said, and Lydia smiled, thinking that his eyes shone like the isinglass he was talking about. "He's a full-blooded Englishman, but he likes these Southern mountains. He's been poking around here a long time. I'm going to try to raise some money to put in his company. It could amount to a big thing one of these days. Lydia, this is the sort of thing our state has got to have before she can ever pull herself out of the mud."

Lydia was not familiar with this talk. She knew nothing about companies and what might be "good for the state" and such.

"Do you think I could ask Paul if he'd like to get in, too?" Robert asked.

"Why not? He can say yes or no well as anybody. You're his own brother. He can listen."

"I might name it to him. This country's going to boom some-

190

day, no need for old Paul to spend all his life grinding other folks' food." Robert looked like a lawyer, she thought, with his vest and watch chain. He had told her, the last time they saw each other, at the Hornsbys' funeral, that the eldest Mr. Wheeler gave him the watch.

"The better to watch out for that old-maid Wheeler daughter?" Lydia had teased.

This might have been in both their minds now, for Robert suddenly said, "Lenore Hornsby, she's still with you?"

Lydia nodded.

"Is she—all right?"

"I think so—almost." At that moment they caught sight of the girl over near the tables; Fayte toddled along beside her; Martha hovered near, waiting to help spread the food. "That black moment of finding them both, father and mother—it's been just blotted out of her remembrance. Mercifully. She's lost now like a fawn or a——"

"She's not a child, Lydia. She's grown."

"You're never too grown to be lost, Robert."

He grinned at her. "I guess all there is to know isn't in law books."

She smiled back at him. "Well, it's a heap," she said.

And when she heard him read the Declaration of Independence at the July Fourth ceremonies before dinner, she knew Robert had learned "a heap." His voice was deep and deliberate, and he had a flair for the dramatic.

" 'When, in the course of human events, it becomes necessary . . .' " he began, and all his old neighbors and friends grew still. They moved in a bit closer to the little platform Clay Thurston had put up in his yard.

" 'We hold these truths to be self-evident . . .' "

Several of the older ones nodded agreement to the words.

" '. . . among these are life, liberty, and the pursuit of happiness . . .' "

Remembered tales handed down from those days of the Old War, the Revolution, came back to them: hateful taxes, arrogant Tories, death to patriots as likely by Indian tomahawks as by

English gun or sword. This Declaration to which they listened was more than ink scrawls on a piece of paper. It was a dream set down in plain words for all time—for men to read and ponder. More than that, it was a fact, a truth, as certain as tomorrow's sun—and as necessary to a human's growth.

"'. . . we mutually pledge to each other our lives, our fortunes, and our sacred honor.'"

People had groped toward this truth during ages past; they would struggle to keep it during generations to come. Yet for a brief glorious moment on that July day there in the yard by the river, surrounded by mountain ranges, the vital reality of democracy's document quickened and came to throbbing life. It was a moment none there would soon forget.

When Robert sat down, they applauded. It was an odd, indescribable sort of applause, tribute not only to his voice and reading which had moved them deeply, not only to the Declaration which they had always revered, but also, perhaps, to the unknown defenders who had gone before them, unnamed, and those who would come long after, quiet, anonymous, but constant as breath itself.

Preacher Gudger brought them a sermon next, shorter than most he preached, and one of the Sons of Temperance delivered an oration, longer than was necessary. Weatherby Hayes made music for them to sing by: "Dixie," and "The Battle Hymn of the Republic," and "America." Some would not sing "The Battle Hymn of the Republic" and a few would not sing "Dixie." Lydia looked over at Mark, wondering whether he still carried revenge in his mind. But all joined together on the words, "from every mountainside, let freedom ring." Animosity was not all dead yet, but unity was beginning to be born.

Dinner was bountiful. The people who came to table had risen early and were eating later than usual, and they heaped their plates, then returned for other helpings. The children finished first and went back to their playing. But the older ones sat in comfortable immobility, digesting the heavy food in oppressive heat, and only talk moved between them. It flowed as lazily and steadily as the river in the near distance.

192

Among the men the talk was of weather and crops, taxes and the price of necessities, railroad routes into the mountain counties from the lowlands—and politics. The Thurstons were politically minded men, rabidly Republican yet able to deal with Conservatives, with Democrats, and remain friendly. That was more than could be said of many of the county's voters of both parties. Still, Clay Thurston, stammering and poking the air with a forefinger in his excitement, loved to argue politics. And Clay's oldest boys, Tom and Jim Thurston, thirteen and twelve, left off their racing with the other boys and hunched on their ankles near the men and drank in the talk of conventions and candidates and elections.

"Aye, our state's finally got back sovereignty of its own affairs," Gentry Caldwell said. His fat, puffed face reddened as everyone looked at him. He mopped his forehead with a fresh bandanna handkerchief. "We'll have white leadership again. No more nigger rule."

"Er-ah"—Clay Thurston nodded vigorously—"and who did it take to bring this fine state of affairs to p-pass?"

"Why, the President——"

"That's right, er-ah, that's right, boys! Recollect you when some of them city Conservatives published a p-plea in the newspaper back a couple of years ago—asking the white men of Western North Carolina to rebuke 'the corrupt civil rights radical party'— that is what they called us—by v-voting down our candidates and putting in instead the Conservative men who would return to 'our old landmarks of a cheap and honest government.' That's about what they said, if memory serves me. And now it's P-President Rutherford B. Hayes, one of our good old radicals, who's recalling the Yankee soldiers and finishing up this 'reconstruction' business."

"There's talk he made a deal——"

"Er-ah, there's always t-talk. It comes cheap. Boys, just remember, you want something right done, get you a good old 'radical' Republican——"

"Soon's we get them all back up North where they belong," one man joked.

"Did that happen, some of the best men in this part of the state

193

would be pulling out," Alec Thurston said. He slapped his brother-in-law, Paul Moore, on the shoulder. "Even Paul here would admit that."

"Well spoken, Alec," Jesse Moore said, winking at his son-in-law. His hair had turned white during the past half-dozen years, and his body seemed more fragile than ever, but there was vitality in his countenance whenever he spoke. Today he did not wish this political discussion to grow too serious. At the county seat recently there had been killings growing out of just such arguments —nourished, too, by a little Bludsoe whiskey, no doubt. "You fellers heard that story about old Zeb Vance and the rabbit during the War?"

Most of them knew the story, but they were happy to hear it again, and to laugh again. "Tell us, Jesse."

"Robert here knows it better than I do. Tell them about it, son."

"Well, it seems Zeb Vance, he was there in one of those battles and he'd got a little more into the thick of it than he meant to. Bullets were flying all around and men were falling like leaves, and some of that fire was grazing a little too close for comfort. Well, Zeb's company started across this sedge field, and just as they were about halfway across, they started a rabbit. The little cottontail jumped and lit out across that field for the woods. Zeb watched him a minute, then said, 'If I didn't have any more reputation to lose than you, I'd run, too!' "

The men's belly laughter filled the yard. Robert joined in and winked at Mark, and Mark joined them. The Thurstons slapped their legs and led the laughter.

"Say," Alec Thurston asked, "Ham Nelson didn't come down today?"

"He's keeping store," someone said.

"Good Lord, don't he ever take a holiday?"

"Sabbaths he usually closes down. Reckon it goes mighty hard with him to do that," Mark said.

"Er-ah, you folks know then, that although Nelson is our new postmaster out here, although he's an office holder in our government, he's not as loyal as he should be."

194

"No, Clay," Gentry Caldwell said. "What you talking about?"
Suddenly serious, the men looked at Thurston. "What's your meaning?"

"Why every feller here knows that Ham Nelson has got a wonderful animosity toward the American eagle. Whenever he sees one on silver currency he tries to squeeze it to death."

Their laughter erupted again. It filled the drowsy afternoon.

On the wide porch overlooking the yard, the women sat and rocked and nursed their babies and talked together, weaving a pattern of words. Their conversation rose and fell around Lydia as she rocked little Jessie, and it seemed to her that each woman contributed her bit of brightness or darkness to the pattern—or just the filler that set the other pieces together in one big design.

"Eh law, I ate too much, for a fact. So many good victuals, it's hard to pass any of them up."

"Now that's a fact. Lydia's pieplant was a pure treat. And Sue, all you said about that new cookstove baking fine cakes was gospel truth."

"Shucks, my cake wasn't a whit better than Kate's here."

Lydia glanced at Kate. Her placid face was bent above the sleeping boy in her lap. Her figure was even rounder, plumper than ever, and her contentment with life was evident as she smiled at the generous praise of her older sister-in-law. "Why, thank you, Sue. Did I try to be the cook you are, it'd make me a hard run. Guess I just manage to do good enough for Alec and me and Alec Junior."

"And Dolly here"—Sue Thurston laid her rough hand on the dainty flowered skirt of Dolly's dress—"she brought as fine a dish of pickled beans as ever I tasted."

Dolly smiled. "I'm glad you liked them." She glanced at Lydia. "Annie Marie and me—we both fixed them."

"Why ain't Annie Marie here today?" Ida Burke asked, looking around.

"She's got a bad cough," Dolly said. A tiny frown puckered her smooth brow. "It come on her late in the winter and to this day she can't seem to shake it off. I gave her tonic Lydia made, we been doing all we could, but seems like she just keeps dragging around, coughing her head off. I told her to stay in bed today, while we were gone."

They were all quiet. There was only the sound of the children shouting in the distance and the men murmuring out under the trees. Then Aunt Tildy said, "Consumption."

Their silence deepened. The dread word threw a pall over them. The word had been in Lydia's mind for months whenever she thought of Annie Marie, but she had not openly spoken it.

"Maybe not." It was Sue Thurston's kind, rough voice. "No need to run to take trouble in your hug. A cough don't always mean the worst."

"Whatever it is, trouble don't spare no man, that's sure as shooting," Emma Caldwell said. "All we can do is take it to the Lord."

The women nodded.

"Neighbors," Sue Thurston said, "speaking of the Lord, it's a great grief to me that I can't get Clay Thurston to join up with the church. Now that we've moved our congregation from the meeting room at the Moores' house and built our own little church house down here near the forks, it would pure pleasure me if he'd become one of us."

"He gave the lumber for the church house, Sue," Lydia said.

Emma Caldwell nodded. "That speaks good for him." She had brought a palm fan with her and she fanned her broad hot face with energetic strokes.

"Oh, he's a good enough man," Sue Thurston agreed, "a little tempery—but nobody wants a blob of dough for a husband. It just frets my mind for him not to be in church communion."

"Maybe he's not seen enough different in church folks to make him think joining would be worth his while," Lydia said.

Sue Thurston sighed. "He does say that it looks to him like we're willing to fight for our religion, or die for it, or do about anything but live by it."

Lydia smiled.

"That's a good excuse"—Emma Caldwell fanned a little faster—"but it don't relieve him of blame. Why don't he join up and change things?"

Martha came up on the porch to speak to her mother. "Would

196

it be all right if I took David and we went down to the river? Some of the young'uns are going wading at the edge."

Lydia nodded. "But don't let David wade. Tell him I said he wasn't to go in the river. You keep a sharp eye on him, Martha."

"I will, Mama."

"That child's a jewel beyond price, Lydia," Emma Caldwell said, as Martha went back across the yard. "She puts me in mind of her grandmother."

"She's worth any other two her age." Aunt Tildy had enlarged the affection she felt for David to embrace Lydia's next oldest child, as well. "Already she can turn off a day's work almost as good as any woman grown."

"My Pru," Dolly said, "was so sickly when she was little, it's hard for me to make her do things now. But she can sew as fine a seam as ever you did see."

"Why now, that's nice," Sue Thurston murmured.

"And beginning the eleventh of the month, we're sending Tim in to town to the Nantahala Classical and English Academy for Boys."

"Oh, Dolly, how fine!" Lydia said. At least one child in the family would be going to school this year. "How long will the term run?"

"Till November. Oh, it's all set up according to the state laws providing for four-month schools in every county."

"Seems like they just overlooked that rule far as Thickety Creek's concerned," Kate said.

"Oh, Colonel Westmoreland says it's overlooked everywhere," Dolly assured her. "But at the academy Tim will get all he needs in the classics and physical sciences and mathematics. Colonel Westmoreland, from Virginia, he's in charge."

"What's the cost?" Aunt Tildy asked.

Lydia blushed at the old woman's lack of manners, but she was eager, too, to know what the Colonel charged.

"Twenty-five dollars for the full term," Dolly answered.

Then it might as well be twenty-five hundred, Lydia thought. With Martha and Burnett and Gib ready now, and Fayte and Jessie coming along, she and Mark would never have enough cash to

197

school their children. Most of the others there were in the same situation.

"Lydia," Sue Thurston asked, "what about our school here on the Creek? Can't we find nobody to take Riley Scroggs's place?"

"Papa's been working at it, writing up North——"

"Papa had a letter this week," Elizabeth interrupted. Her voice was so soft the other women had to listen attentively to hear all her words. "He was going to tell you today, Lydia, when he got a chance, or maybe announce it to everybody here. There's a Presbyterian preacher coming down sometime this summer to look us over, see the school site and the folks and all. And if he carries back a recommendation, the Presbyterians will set up a permanent school here."

"You don't say!"

"Well, seems like you and your pappy were long enough giving out the news."

"Elizabeth!" Lydia cried. "Why didn't you tell me before dinner?"

"I figured it was Papa's news."

"I don't know, I don't know." Ida Burke was shaking her head. "I'm just an ignorant backwoods woman, but it appears to me like a bad omen hangs over this school here. First, it being on our old mill place, and I know what the luck of that place is. And then the money that bought it from Ham Nelson for twice the honest price, look how that come to the community. . . ."

Lydia looked around quickly to be sure that Lenore Hornsby was not on the porch but saw she had taken Fayte out to look at some lambs in the upper pasture. The women were silent, grave at remembrance of the money.

"It was a quare thing," Aunt Tildy said slowly.

"Blood money, some called it," Dolly said.

Oh, there had been blood and to spare, Lydia knew that. She shivered, in spite of the afternoon's heat. The carpet on the floor in that elegant living room had been stained red, a darker red than the flowers in the design, and the folks who found the bodies of the doctor and his wife said both were crumpled on the carpet there, in pools of their own life blood.

198

Lenore, clutching her two younger sisters by the hand, had run to a neighbor's with the terrible news. Then she had collapsed and for days had been in a state of shock, speaking to no one. The other two girls had cowered together in their fear and ignorance of what had happened—they had not seen the sight in the living room, as their oldest sister had—and could provide no explanation for their parents' death.

The Sheriff had pronounced the two deaths murder and suicide. Dr. Hornsby had been drinking heavily for weeks and he had spoken to Clay Thurston, the last person to see him alive, some incomprehensible words about an albatross around his neck, and being an albatross to those whom he loved best. The morning he had shot his wife and then himself had been dark and gloomy after a rainy, wind-swept night. No one in the house had had breakfast; in fact, by the time the neighbors arrived after the girls' flight, they had found the coffeepot boiled dry and the fire in the kitchen stove gone out. "Mrs. Hornsby's eyes were wide open, even in death," Emma Caldwell later reported, "and her face had a look of the most surprise I ever beheld."

Dr. Hornsby had left three notes, and the wavering, poorly written lines in which they were scrawled indicated the agitation which had prompted them. One was to his sister in Philadelphia; the second was to his oldest daughter, Lenore; and the third was to Lydia McQueen. This last note had surprised the people of Thickety, but no more than it surprised Lydia when her father brought it up the mountain to her. When he told her what had happened, she found it unbelievable. "But he was so alive, so smart; folks needed him. . . ." What could she say?

"There was something inside Ralph Hornsby that nobody ever knew," her father said, "eating him away like a canker. I used to think, back when he was coming to doctor Sarah, that he might overcome it. Then lately, I'd begun to realize that it was overcoming him. But nobody could have foreseen this. There's no dark like that of a man when the mind's light shuts off."

She had read the note: "Lydia McQueen, For the first and last time, I bring you good news. You are to have your school. The people of this little creek don't deserve the likes of you, but you deserve a school. Fifteen hundred dollars of my estate is to be set aside for this purpose. You, and your father, if a man is necessary to the legalities of the transaction, are to have sole control. You've got the wellsprings of life in you, Lydia McQueen. May they never run dry. Your friend . . ." and the signature had run off the page.

But it was found that the doctor had, indeed, made legal provision for the school money he had mentioned. The rest of his estate was put under trusteeship of his sister and her husband for the education of his daughters and their inheritance when they should come of age. When their aunt had come from Philadelphia, however, and made ready to take the girls back home with her, Lenore had refused to leave the mountains. "I can't go," she sobbed, "this is my home."

In desperation she had appealed to Lydia and Mark to take her into their family. "I know my father counted you his friends. I'll never be a bother to you, I swear it. But don't make me leave this country. Father loved it, I know, in spite of all he used to say about its being godforsaken. Please; oh, please."

And Mark had remembered how it was when he was an orphan bound boy, and Lydia remembered a rainy day before one of her babies was born when Dr. Hornsby had stood in the door of her cabin and spoken of his oldest child. They remembered the care with which he had brought Martha and Burnett and Gib, after his regret and guilt for David. "You'll ever be welcome in our house," they told the troubled girl.

The aunt had warned that if Lenore refused to submit to the care and guidance of her legal guardians, she would see that the girl did not share in her father's money. But Lenore had never known the meaning or hard need of money, and Lydia was half frightened, half admiring, of the apparent carelessness with which she laid it aside. "Do you ever feel a panic for a few dollars you can't raise, or see the day you want a pretty dress when all you can have is linsey-woolsey, you'll rue this," Lydia said. Then, seeing the startled questioning in the black eyes, she had embraced the girl and added, "But long as you're with us, you'll never want for necessities if we can help it."

The women on the porch talked on, recalling the gruesome details of the Hornsbys' deaths, wondering at the money the doctor had left their school. Emma Caldwell had never been sure that all the money should have been spent on buying the old mill site. She named her doubt again this afternoon.

"But we didn't spend it all," Lydia said calmly. "Ham just asked us fourteen hundred and fifty dollars. We had fifty dollars left over to pay Mr. Scroggs his two terms."

Mrs. Caldwell laid down her fan impatiently. "Well, if you want to strain at a gnat——"

Lydia forced a smile. "I don't," she said. "You're right, we may not have been wise to use everything we had—but it's such a lovely site, on the stream, and it has some buildings we can use. Why, if a Northern schoolmaster comes, he might want to live with his family in the Burkes' old house, and maybe we could redd up the old mill house. Who knows what those outside folks might decide to do?"

"Now that's right," Sue Thurston said.

"I didn't mean to say outright it was a mistake," Mrs. Caldwell interrupted. "I was just wondering——"

"Wondering don't make the mare trot," Aunt Tildy said.

"When's this teacher coming?" Kate asked her sister.

"I don't rightly know," Elizabeth said. "We could ask Papa."

They went after Jesse Moore and he told all of them the news, explaining that he had waited about the announcement until after the main program was finished and dinner eaten. "I didn't want to take the edge off my own boy's public speaking, or your appetites." He smiled slightly at Robert.

"Who?"

"When?"

"Where?"

The questions tumbled at him. He held up one hand. "Hold on. Hold on. This Presbyterian fellow, name of Harmon Duncan, will be along sometime this summer to look over our situation here. On his recommendation, maybe the church will help pay his salary to be a teacher here."

"And if he don't like it here?"

"I hadn't even figured on that," Jesse Moore said.

201

"He married?" Dolly Moore asked.

"I don't rightly know. May be. May not. Main thing is, will he think we can make good use of his teaching?"

"Somebody better make certain he don't have a chance to talk with old Scroggs in town," Alec Thurston said. "He wouldn't give us a very high name for learning."

"And we wouldn't give him a very high name for teacher," Lydia added.

They broke up into little groups, discussing this news and the day in general. Sue Thurston took Lydia to the back yard to show her the garden and a snowball bush she had planted last year. Robert found them there.

"You did yourself proud today, little brother," Lydia said.

"I'm trying." He shoved his hands in his pockets. "You ought to see me before a jury. Old man Wheeler says I'm getting better all the time."

"Reckon if that boy keeps on he'll rival Zeb Vance on the stump," Sue Thurston said.

"Say, Lydia," Robert asked abruptly, "where'd Lenore get to?"

"She took Fayte up in the pasture to see some lambs; they ought to be on their way back by now."

"I'll go see," he volunteered, and left them quickly.

"Those two got up a case?" Sue Thurston asked.

"Not that I ever noticed before," Lydia said. "But wouldn't it be fine if they did come to like each other?"

"Some would say it's risky. What with the bad blood of her father's past——"

"And what about the good blood? I remember his doctoring; Mama always said there aren't many as good as Dr. Hornsby."

"You're right, Lydia." The other woman patted her shoulder. "Nothing as risky as life itself. Too many afraid to try it. Now, come fall, I'll send you a root of that snowball."

"I'd be ever so much obliged."

The afternoon grew late. The children came back from their frolic by the river. Paul and Dolly's little Pru had slipped on a stone and fallen in the river. Her flouncy dress was ruined and she was soaked to the skin, and so Paul and Dolly and the children went home.

"Tell Annie Marie I'll come to see her the first chance I get," Lydia told Paul as they left. "Or tell her she should come up and visit with us for a turn."

"I'll see after her the best I can," Paul said.

Lydia knew she and Mark should leave, too, and yet, somehow, the long afternoon shadows on the grass, the blue haze hanging over the hills in the distance, the easy companionship of all the folks they knew, made her loath to break away.

When she saw Lenore and Robert walking down the slope behind the house, she sent Burnett and Gib to bring Fayte to her so that the couple could walk alone. How nice they looked, she thought, walking there together—he in the good black suit, she in a thin summer dress, with the mellow light of late summer afternoon falling around them.

When the two youngest children were in the house asleep, and the older boys had gone off somewhere with Mark, Lydia walked around to the front where the other women were gathering up their baskets and pans.

Across the road, on a level stretch of ground, she could see Mark and Alec Thurston and some of the children. They were getting ready for a last foot race of the day. Mark was showing the boys how to stand so that they could make a quick start at the go signal.

Lydia paused, surprised to see David there with the others. She watched as Mark bent David's knees to give him the feel of a crouch, ready to spring forward. For the first time in many months tears stood in her eyes. Ever since he had been home from the West, Mark had made special inconspicuous little efforts with their eldest child. This had been fortunate, for David had transferred some of his single-minded devotion from Martha to his father and thereby come in closer contact with a man's world. Mark had taught David how to harness up the ox teams he used in his timbering and how to curry the pair of mules, and the boy had learned to handle the animals with patient skill. His pleasure at being part of the daily work was evident in every line of his face. This ready evidence was only another way Lydia had come to know he would always be a child: as he had grown older he had not also grown knowledgeable in ways to camouflage his feelings, his innermost self; he had not learned secrecy as self-protection; he had not acquired the guardianship of withdrawn eyes and immobile face.

Sometimes she wondered what would become of him when she and Mark were no longer there. Where would his vulnerability find refuge? The possibilities for his being hurt—not only in body, as she had dealt with so many times (falls, burns, bruises, even a spider bite) but in spirit—dismayed her. She thanked God she was strong. She must stay strong for a long time for her children, for this child in particular. During all the years since she had admitted his affliction, she doubted if a single day had passed that she had not asked God to continue the gift of her strength, especially for the one of her children who was weak.

Alec Thurston was toeing the boys up along some line that was not visible to her at this distance. David seemed frozen in the crouch Mark had shown him. All at once, prompted by some signal that was not audible at this distance, they leaped forward. She could not make out identities until suddenly she realized that the boy in front was David. But he had never won any contest, even at home among those who would try to let him win. She clasped her hands together at her chin and strained to see the meadow. Others were close behind David. Two seemed to be gaining on him. She closed her eyes for a second. When she opened them, the boys in the distance were surging over the finish line. Someone was standing beside her. It was Sue Thurston.

"He come in first," she said.

"Who?" Lydia asked.

"Your Davy." The other woman put an arm around her waist. "And that Tom of ours right behind. I'd a-skinned that young'un alive and nailed his hide to the smokehouse wall if he'd a-beat out Davy in that race!"

"Ah, Sue . . ." Lydia did not finish. She loosened her hands

204

and was surprised to find them wet with sweat where she had wrung them together. "Sue—Sue, nobody knows . . ."

"Course they don't!" Sue brushed her hand across her eyes. "But I believe you got somebody coming yonder to tell you the news."

David, followed closely by Burnett and Gib, was coming toward her. When they reached the yard, he was almost out of breath, but he panted hoarsely, "David—won the running." He always spoke of himself in the third person.

"David ran a good race." She put her arms around him. "I saw."

The younger boys were embarrassed by her hug for David, but they were prouder of his achievement than if they themselves had won. "He was way out in front of everybody!" Burnett said.

"Nobody ever even got close to him!"

Gib's exaggeration touched Lydia and amused her. "Now for a fact," she said.

And David's face was still like a light as they all climbed in the wagon to go home a short while later.

Lydia squeezed Mark's hand. "I saw you teaching David how to start his race."

Mark smiled at her. "He won."

"Yes, I heard," she said.

After they had thanked the Thurstons and told everyone good-by and settled the children and made Lenore comfortable and started home, they looked at each other. Lydia sighed.

"It was a good Fourth," Mark said.

"The nicest I ever recollect," she agreed.

10th
CHAPTER

The next morning while Lydia and Lenore were chopping cabbage to make sauerkraut, Lydia heard the girl humming a song for the first time since she had come to live with them. And presently she asked, shyly, almost in a whisper, "Lydia how old is your brother Robert?"

"Let me figure a minute." Lydia stopped her chopping for a moment and wiped her face with her apron as she calculated the years. "Why, I guess he's twenty-four."

The girl nodded.

"I declare, how the years fly! Seems to me like he's still just a shirttail boy."

But Lenore was not really listening. "Lydia," she said presently, again finding the words hard to speak, "is twenty-three a plumb hopeless old maid?"

Lydia considered before she answered. She must not say too little or too much. "I reckon not." She picked up her chopper again. The pungent smell of the fresh cabbage filled the kitchen. It had a sharp cleanness that made her think of the brine in the pottery crock when the kraut would be finished and she could dip out tart juicy helpings. "No," she said slowly to Lenore, "Mama used to tell us girls that some flowers bloom in April and some in September. I never had reason to doubt what she said. And I guess they can bloom all seasons in between."

Lenore's pale cheeks were tinged with pink. She would not look up from her work. "Thank you, Lydia."

Several weeks later, on a lazy day in August, Lydia took Lenore and the children one day and went on the mountain above the Devil's Brow.

During the years she had lived up here, Lydia had found in this rocky crag a deep source of comfort and inspiration. Its effect on her was something she could not explain and therefore she had kept it secret to herself. Sometimes on winter days when the noise of the narrow cabin, congested with so many people, their laughter and crying, their walking and running and shuffling, their constant need of her, seemed to close in with stifling pressure she would slip out and climb to this precipice. There, standing with its hard firmness beneath her feet, her head and face bared to the wind that swept up from the deep valley below and broke in torrents against this ledge, she regained an inner quiet, a stillness she could not name or identify. It was as essential to her existence, however—had been even when she was still a child—as water or food itself. And as the wind struck her like a wave, taking her breath for the moment, beating and breaking against her, drowning her in an ocean of air, she was revived. And so she went back home, but returned to the rock again and again.

Today she brought the children.

They found crevices at the edges of the great solid mass of stone and clambered up and down in these footholds. Pockets of moss with clumps of ferns and flowers brought cries for their mother to come and see.

"Isn't it a pretty sight, for a fact?" Lydia would respond with all the joy they had come to expect. "Now that's called wild geranium. Look at its leaves"—taking one of the leaves in her hand, not pulling it but leaving it alive on her palm—"don't its veins look for all the world like the veins in your grandpa Moore's face, or your mama's hands?" And she would turn the back of her other hand over to compare the blue tracery of blood there with the finely

207

webbed lines of the geranium leaf. The children clustered close to see and compare and then dashed to find more veined leaves, but were disappointed that their own young hands did not reveal such prominent webs as Lydia's.

"Only young leaves and old folks show their workings so." She laughed, but there was a tightness squeezing her throat as she spoke it. She wished there had been someone close by to deny her words, to protest her identification with "old folks." But no one spoke up. She knew they felt no reason to deny what she had said. They were already playing at another game. And Lenore was daydreaming, as she did frequently these days.

"David, you and Martha lead the way," Lydia called after a little while, "and we'll go look at our 'sang bed."

They led off gaily, Burnett and Gib close on their heels, Lenore and Fayte walked behind, while Lydia carried the baby. "Digging 'sang," she explained, "you have to leave some roots to make new plants for the coming years. Otherwise, pretty soon we could have the mountains scoured and there wouldn't be any more to come."

Lenore's gaze turned to the mountains towering all around. "Appears like it would take considerable time to scour all this land of anything," she said.

"Not when folks set their minds to it," Lydia replied. "It would be a surprise to you how quick a thing can be killed out. And 'sang's one of the scarcest things there is, to begin with."

Before they reached the bed, they heard the children shouting. Martha came running back through the trees. "Mama, Mama! It's all gone! Everything's tore up!"

They stood and watched in wide-eyed concern as she came to the spot where the green leaves of the ginseng plants had been thick a few months ago. None remained now. There was only gouged-up earth where roots had been dug out.

"Mama, who you reckon did it?"

"What you going to do now, Mama?"

"Will any of the 'sang come back?"

Lydia was heartsick. The money from this bed had been important to her, but it was not of the money she thought now. It was the complete destruction of this beautiful thing that agitated her. She had come to think of it as her secret, her special treasure of nature. And now it was torn up and trampled and destroyed. "Aunt Tildy says they won't come back unless you're careful to leave good roots," she told the children. "And whoever was here took everything but care."

"Then this bed's gone forever," Martha said mournfully.

Lydia realized that tears were rolling down David's face and the others were on the verge of crying. "Well, we'll just have to look someplace else." She made an effort at cheerfulness. "There are other 'sang beds playing hide and seek around these hills, I reckon. But I'd sure like to get my hands on the blackguards that ruined this one."

"Who was it, Mama? Reckon who?"

"I couldn't say."

As they walked solemnly back down through the woods, however, she could not keep suspicions out of her mind. Who else but the Bludsoes, as far as she could tell, would be roaming these hills? And God knows, from what she had always heard, they would not hesitate to take what they wanted, and in any way they wanted. Maybe Emma Caldwell was right, in spite of their accommodations to her, perhaps they were a scourge on the valley. . . .

They all sat down to rest on the ledge before going home. It had been such a gay day, up till now. Lydia was sorry to see it end in disappointment. She suggested a game of drop the handkerchief. After they had played for a few minutes, they begged her to join them.

"Aunt Lenore's playing."

"It's more fun with you." That was the argument she could not resist.

"All right," she said, "but it will be hard for me to make a showing when I'm against champion runners," and she winked at David.

She laid the baby on her thin blanket under the shade of a tree and circled up with them. She ran when they dropped the handkerchief behind her, and when it came her turn to drop, she made certain everyone had a chance to play. They laughed and jumped up and down in excitement. And suddenly, as she came around the circle, holding her dress above her knees, hair loose and free in the breeze, she saw Mark and a stranger standing just at the corner of the ledge.

The newcomer was a man of medium height but so thin that he seemed quite tall. His hair was brown, tinged with the slightest suggestion of grey. High cheekbones emphasized his eyes, cat's eyes, green the color of deep spring water or a bird's eggs she had once found where white and green and blue were all merged into one rare, pale, clear color. He wore a suit such as she had not seen before; a city suit, she supposed. It was in sharp contrast to Mark's rough work clothes.

For one suspended minute they faced each other, while the children and Lenore looked to see what was happening, then dropped their circle of hands and came to inspect the stranger, too.

"This is my wife, Lydia McQueen," Mark said, stepping forward with the man.

Lydia let go her skirts and clutched at her hair. She was embarrassed and confused.

"And this-here's Harmon Duncan, Lydia," Mark went on.

The teacher! She gasped. She had planned to make such careful arrangements for their meeting, for his introduction to the school and to Thickety folks. "Professor Duncan"—she held out her hand—"I'm proud to make your acquaintance."

He shook her hand with equal firmness. "And I yours. Everyone in the valley has told me you are the moving spirit behind a school here."

"You've been in the valley—awhile . . . ?"

"Only since yesterday morning. But I've talked with several people."

"Yes." She had her hair smoothed down a little now. She straightened her apron. "These are our children. David, Martha, Burnett, Gibbon and Fayte—Lafayette. And this is Miss Lenore Hornsby, who is part of our family, too. Our least one, Jessica, is on the blanket under that little dogwood tree." She went and fetched the baby, holding her astride one hip.

He shook hands with the children and Lydia was thankful that they remembered their manners and said "Sir" when they spoke to him.

"He was anxious to talk to you, Lydia," Mark said.

"Your husband insisted on leaving his work and showing me the way up here," Harmon Duncan said. "I didn't mean to bring inconvenience to him, or to interrupt your games, but I have so little time here——"

"It was just foolish frolicking," she apologized.

"But all of you seemed so happy." He smiled at the children and his face crinkled into dozens of little lines. He spoke very rapidly. Lydia thought she had seldom seen a more pleasant face than the Professor's. "Maybe, if we have a school, these young folks can help teach the other scholars some games to play during recess."

At this the children smiled, too, and Martha stepped forward. "We'd do our best for you," she said.

"And that's all that is required." The Professor accepted her child's pledge as seriously as she gave it. "Neither God nor man could ask more."

Watching him, Lydia felt an upsurge of hope and confidence. "Well, now," she said to the children, "if we're to have company for supper and the night and as long after as he cares to stay, we'd best be getting home."

As the children ran ahead of them down the mountain, Mark grinned at the newcomer. "I told you she'd want to see you today." The way he said it, Lydia knew Mark liked the Professor, too.

Thus Professor Duncan came to Thickety. He looked over the school where the mill had been. He talked with people at the county seat and up and down the valley. Then he called them to a community meeting at the little church and told them that if they would repair the house where the Burkes had once lived, making it usable for his dwelling, and if they would change the millhouse into a schoolhouse with a good floor and a tight roof, two windows and two doors for light, a fireplace at one end, benches for the pupils and a table for his desk, he would come to this place and open a subscription school. In the beginning it

211

would run only six weeks at a time: through July and August, when folks had told him their crops were laid by and they could spare their children from the fields, and in December and January, when farm work was slack. His sister Octavia would come down and live with him and take as boarders any boys who could not otherwise attend school. At first the school would be only for boys. Professor Duncan asked them to vote on the proposal.

"And who's to pay for all this?" Ham Nelson rose to his feet. "Who is to pay your wage?"

"Your community can be responsible for fixing up the school site by any plan it wishes," Harmon Duncan replied. "My own salary will be paid in part by my Presbyterian church group in the North, and in part by subscriptions of the students I shall teach."

"That's all right," Nelson replied. "But I'm giving you fair warning tonight, there'll be a fight the first time land taxes for this so-called free-school foolishness is mentioned in these parts."

Mark stood. "I donate logs and labor to make benches for the young'uns seats," he said. Lydia was proud of that quiet determination in his voice.

"Er-ah"—everyone recognized Clay Thurston—"me and my brother, we give all the good stout shingles needed for the roofing."

Alec Thurston nodded and Kate looked at Lydia and smiled.

Other volunteers spoke out. A good school was finally coming to Thickety!

Through the fall, after Harmon Duncan had returned home to make his arrangements for coming to the mountains, during spare time from their harvesting and other work, the men labored on the house for the Professor and his sister and the building for a school.

One day in October, Mark yielded to the boys' pleas and let them go with him while he was hauling down logs for the benches he had promised. "Come to think of it," he had said to Lydia at supper the night before, "they might be a right smart help to me." And they sat with straight manliness as they rode beside him down the road—even Gib, whom his mother had thought too young to go but who refused to stay at home.

That night they returned full of tales of the day's experiences. Tim had been along with Paul at the school-raising, too, and they had all played together. Just as they crawled into bed, Burnett said, "Tim told us his sister is sick."

"What's wrong with Pru?" Lydia asked.

"Measles," the boy said.

"And Tim was playing with you, when he's probably coming down sick himself? Oh, that Dolly!" Lydia had not meant to speak so sharply in front of the children, but when Mark came in from feeding the stock and she questioned him about Paul's family and found that Pru was, indeed, in bed with measles, she felt her resentment was justified.

Gib was the first one to take his bed. The morning after his high fever began, Burnett was sick, too. Two days later David was ill with measles. Lydia moved Martha and the two babies into the room across the dog-trot, with Lenore. It was well that she had just weaned Jessica.

During days and nights of their fretfulness and fever, she gave the sick children hot brews Aunt Tildy had taught her would "bring out" the measles and keep them from "turning in." She doctored and crooned and hung a quilt over the window when the light hurt their eyes. The two younger boys broke out in scanty patches, their fever went down, and they began to recover rapidly.

But David's face and chest were covered with measles. His fever would diminish and then, unaccountably, it would suddenly soar again. For a while he could not even keep Lydia's tea on his stomach. She had nursed him through many illnesses; this was his worst.

At last, after so many days and nights that she lost count, when weariness dragged at her like a millstone, his fever seemed to be broken for good, and although he was weak, he no longer ached or was nauseated. She was thankful for the change. The next morning after Mark had taken the other children to help pull fodder in the cornfield, and Lenore was looking after the baby, Lydia stretched across her bed and was asleep immediately.

When she awoke, someone was speaking to her.

"Where's David?"

She was stupid from the heavy sleep.

"Where's David?"

213

The words suddenly penetrated her consciousness. She sat up with a jerk.

David's bed was empty. Lenore was standing in the room. It was she who was asking where he was.

"I don't know," Lydia cried. "David?" There was no answer in the house.

She ran out into the yard. A chilly autumn wind tugged at her skirts. "David!"

Still there was no answer. Unaccountably, she ran toward the barn. "David!"

She heard a muffled answer then. It seemed to come from inside the barn. She found him slumped against one of the mule's stalls.

"David wanted to see," he gasped weakly. "Somebody looking after David's mules and cattle . . ."

She went into the barnyard and screamed for Mark. He came at a run and carried the boy into the house. David had a chill even as she covered him with quilts. A smoothing iron stood heating on the hearth, and she wrapped it in a cloth and put it to his feet. She gave him a hot drink.

"Pneumonia-fever," the other children whispered to each other as they tiptoed around the house during the next few days. At last, no matter which room they were in, they could not escape the sound of their brother's labored breathing.

Mark went for Aunt Tildy, and when she came she and Lydia tried every remedy they had ever known for dread pneumonia-fever.

"I can't sit here and watch my child strangle to death!" Lydia cried. "There must be something a body could *do*." Her eyes were dry. Mark, looking into the drawn anguish of her face, knew that he felt more sorrow for her than for the unconscious child struggling on the bed.

David died that night. When at last he could breathe no more, Lydia buried his head against her bosom and rocked back and forth in silent, stricken grief.

Her first, her weakest, her gentlest . . . the one she had named for a shepherd and a king and a singer of songs.

214

"David is dead," she told the others.

Mark stumbled out into the night to collect himself before he faced them all.

"Child, child," Aunt Tildy said.

"Oh, Lydia!" Lenore cried.

"Mama . . ." The children did not know what to say, or what was expected of them.

Lydia's mind repeated over and over a few words of the ballad she had heard her mother sing a long time ago:

"We must walk this lonely valley,
We must walk it all alone,
Nobody else can walk it for us;
We must walk it for ourselves."

11th
CHAPTER

Her mother's clock ticked off time second by second, minute by minute. Hours built into days and weeks lengthened to months. Seasons passed.

Years withered grief from its first green burning sap to a dry stored husk, tough, with sharp unexpected cutting edges. Lydia lived with the seasons and the pain. Her other children had a right to joy; she knew that. And no matter how many days she or Mark or any of them had upon this earth, the time would be too short.

When Annie Marie died, two winters after David, coughing up her strength in a bubbling fountain of blood, Lydia watched by her sister's bed throughout long nights and remembered how brief the years had been since they were children, before the war, and Mama had braided her daughters' hair and said time and again, "Be mannerly now. Remember: the greatest respect due a lady is her self-respect."

They had grown up so quickly, and none of them had really known Annie Marie. Lydia was the oldest and her father's favorite, Kate was pretty and easygoing, Elizabeth was the youngest with the sweetest disposition, and Annie Marie had had only her helpfulness, her loyalty to her family, to give them. Annie

Marie, who had stolen out to the barnyard to be alone when their mother died, who had kept grief and happiness alike locked up inside herself and had stifled both. Lydia thought, if only she had talked with her sister there at Paul's the night she was on her way to town to see the herb buyer, if she had only spoken with her then, perhaps something would have been different, the consumption avoided. But other needs always seemed to be pushing them, there was not enough time, and now time had taken Annie Marie away without the right word spoken between them. Lydia learned again that there was a time for holding and a time for letting go.

Summer and winter, Mark worked from first daylight till after dark, clearing, planting, harvesting, clearing a little farther up the mountainsides every year, harvesting a bigger—or a lesser—crop. The children grew and the boys became tough and tan helping in the fields. Sometimes Lydia looked at them and the girls as they all sat around the dinner table, and she wondered at these strong young creatures who were her children. Then she would smile at Mark across the table and their look would be secret and intimate as a touch.

The boys, especially Burn and Gib, were full of energy and mischief. They joked and wrestled, played tricks throughout the community and were liked by everyone in the valley. Harmon Duncan despaired of their ever being scholars, but declared they were smart as crickets when they had a mind to be. With the Thurston boys, they became the gossip and fun of the valley. Martha, being older, was ashamed of their escapades, while Jessica, the baby of the family, adored them.

New years brought new deaths. There were new births. Robert and Paul invested in mica mines opening in the mountains and the investment prospered. Lydia did not know much about these transactions; she did know about Robert and Lenore Hornsby. Her brother had been in love with the girl for years—Lydia suspected it was that pale flowerlike face, so different from any he had known in his own family, that captured and held him—but a year after the school came to Thickety Creek, Lenore Hornsby married Harmon Duncan.

217

Soon afterward Lydia made it a point to go and see Robert several times at his law offices in town. She pretended each time it was a casual happen-chance that she was there. She asked him to come for Christmas and other holidays with Mark and the children and herself. But he never spoke of Lenore or asked after her. His face, once so expressive in its eagerness, grew guarded and Lydia saw the mask of manhood settle permanently over the handsome features. He moved as easily in the town as in the country now and he was spoken of as an able young lawyer who won his clients' cases. Lydia was filled with pride when she looked at him, but it was a pride tempered by knowledge of something lost, too.

The children had chicken pox and mumps and colds, bruised toes and burned fingers, and once Gib jumped on a pitchfork and pierced his foot to the bone. Lydia, fearful of the dreaded lockjaw, let the wound bleed heavily before she drenched it with turpentine and bound it up; it was a month in the healing. Mark had a stomach ailment, begun a long time before in Andersonville prison, and she doctored and fed him as carefully as she knew how when the pains attacked him. Aunt Tildy, twisted and tormented by rheumatism, lived with them most of the time.

One morning in June, Lydia and the two youngest children, Fayte and Jessie, were carrying water up from the spring to fill the great black washpot in the yard.

"How come women be so partial to water?" Fayte asked, after his fourth trip. "Looks to me like we got enough here to start a plumb Noah-flood." He was twelve and suspicious that it might have been an insult to be left to help with household work while his older brothers went to the cornfields with their father.

Lydia blew on the fire under the pot. When it had caught to a bright blaze on the kindling, she stood up and brushed off her apron. "Reckon it's not that we like water so much, son, but that we hate dirt more. Now you wouldn't want your own sister to be a-celebrating her marriage day in any but the tidiest, shiniest house, would you?"

"Makes no differ to me," he mumbled, but he went to fetch another bucket of water.

218

Lydia had always liked to wash. She enjoyed working out of doors and seeing clearly the results of her labor. Most of all, she liked to hang clean things out to dry. Today she soaped and scrubbed the shirts and dresses, socks and underwear, pillow shams and curtains. She boiled and stirred and rinsed and wrung each piece with her strong hands until the muscles stood out in her arms. Extra dirty garments she laid on the battling block and rubbed with soap. Then she beat them with a wooden paddle until all the water and grime was worked out of the cloth. Jessie watched closely as her mother dipped the dripping pieces, one by one, from the rinse tub and wrung them into long twists that curled out of her grip and around her strong forearm.

"Jessie, you best go tend the dinner beans," Lydia said at last. "And ask Aunt Tildy, if she feels like it, to stir us up a pone of bread. Your pa and Burn and Gib will be coming in directly and I want to finish this wash early as I can."

"Why doesn't Fayte——"

"He's fetching firewood," Lydia said. "Now go on and do as you're asked." The child went slowly into the house.

Lydia straightened her back for a moment. She leaned thoughtfully on the washboard. Ten years between her two daughters' ages, with three older brothers for Jessie, had made the girl into a regular tomboy. She rode like a demon, joined in pranks, worked in the fields, and hated household work. After Martha and Tom Thurston were married, Lydia wondered if Jessie, as the only girl left at home, would become more domesticated.

She smiled gently to herself. Jessie was built like her, long and lean, as the boys said, but it was Martha—small, weighing under a hundred pounds, earnest to fulfill herself and at the same time pleasure the people around her, whose ways were most like her own.

Ten years ago, when Professor Duncan's school had first opened on Thickety, it had been Martha who took up the chance to learn in much the way a hungry man draws up to a table filled with food. As soon as girls were admitted, she had attended the school each year, and during the other months she had read every book she could find: her grandfather Moore's volumes, the boxes of books

219

Harmon Duncan and his sister brought from up North. She practiced her penmanship and perfected her spelling, poring over the dictionary until her brother Gib asked her with a grin how she could find a book so interesting when the words of the story were all disconnected. Martha told him she aimed to learn how to spell and figure. And she helped her father when he needed to compute lumber measurements on timber he sold to the Thurstons, or in other arithmetic around the farm. When Harmon Duncan had asked her to help him at the school, Mark's pride almost outran Lydia's. For three years Martha had taught the first two readers while she continued her own studies. She read Caesar and Virgil. With the first money she made from her teaching she wanted to buy her mother a stove, but Lydia insisted that she get something for herself.

"You're a thoughty girl, but wait a little while on something for me," Lydia had advised. "Your first money never comes but once. Find something to remember it by."

And so Martha, saving every penny, had surprised everyone and bought, the first year, a little parcel of land near the county seat. Robert had been telling Mark about the brisk way land was selling in the vicinity of town, how a little investment there now might grow through the years as the city grew; Martha had heard them talking and asked her uncle to buy a little piece of land for her.

The second year she had purchased an organ. It was a small thing with pedals that wheezed rhythmically as she pumped them, but the whole family enjoyed the hymns she learned to play on it.

Land and an organ. Lydia nodded unconsciously, thinking how much the combination spoke about her oldest child. (Her oldest child *now*. Even after ten years the sudden remembrance of David's face and curly hair could twist her heart like a knife.) And, of course, for the past school season Martha had been saving for her hope chest.

Last Christmas Tom Thurston, tall and jolly, with wavy brown hair that wouldn't stay slicked in place, and blue eyes that wouldn't stay solemn, said, "Martha, I'm past twenty-three and you've turned twenty-one. You've had all the book learning a body needs, and more. It's time we had done with this courting and got ourselves married."

"June is a nice month," Martha had said softly, leaving him suddenly speechless.

And June had come quickly, or so it seemed to Lydia. Now she was making the house ready for the infare after the wedding next week. At her suggestion, the young folks were going in to the county seat to be married. Although Gentry Caldwell had had the call to preach and was the only minister in the valley, Lydia had wanted Martha and Tom to find a judge or preacher in town. She rebelled at the thought of her child's wedding vows being spoken by Gentry—red-faced, excitable, and somehow not to be trusted, with his darting eyes that could not hold your direct gaze. She had never been overly fond of Emma Caldwell, with her steady gossiping, but she was half ashamed of the doubts she felt toward Emma's son. Everyone else on Thickety, except her father, thought him a fine and stirring preacher with his exhortations and tears and sweat. Nevertheless she was glad Martha would be wedding elsewhere. And she had not yet let herself think that her daughter would soon be a married woman.

She wrung out two curtains and hung one of them to dry on the big rose-of-Sharon bush by her kitchen door. There the sun would strike it till up in the afternoon. Looking at the bush, she remembered a talk she and her mother had had before she and Mark were married. At the time, Lydia had thought it a strange conversation. Now she understood so much more that her mother had tried to say—and had left unsaid.

"I've never held with craving women." She could remember her mother saying that. And, "Nothing's ever taken, or given, doesn't have its price."

She flung the other curtain over the paling fence that surrounded her garden. It occurred to Lydia that Martha looked like Sarah Moore: small and grave, but with Mark's dark brown eyes beneath her smooth white forehead. And what, of all that she would like to impart to her, would Lydia find to say to her own daughter?

She thought about the family Martha was marrying into. The Thurstons were fine people, "good livers," as folks said, with their busy sawmills and fat livestock and plentiful tables of food. They were politically minded, fiercely partisan, and they did not shrink from arguments about President Grover Cleveland in Washington or the local sheriff of Nantahala. But they were also folks of high good humor and no one could stay angry with them long. They were tale-tellers and they liked to make music; they worked hard and played hard in the physical world that was their domain. Lydia suddenly wished that Martha, a beautiful seamstress and an apt scholar, was a little more interested in cooking. She had never given any attention or care to kitchen work, beyond getting it done as quickly as possible, and Lydia wondered how Tom Thurston would fare, after the good food he was used to at home. Sue Thurston was noted for her cooking. "She cooks with a heavy hand," the women said, meaning the quantity of butter and lard she used, but no one ever frowned at the result. Perhaps Martha would be more interested in food after she had been around her mother-in-law for a while. Lydia felt that the girl's shortcoming in some way reflected her own.

Early this morning Martha had gone down to her grandfather's and Aunt Elizabeth's to spend the day and night. Friends were gathering there for an all-day quilting bee, as their gift to Martha and Tom. It was a beautiful quilt they were making, the Double Wedding Ring design, and Martha herself was the best quilter of the lot. Lydia could imagine her now, head bent attentively over the quick neat needle as it dipped in and out of the material and left behind a trail of tiny, even stitches. Lydia had had too much work to do at home; she had not tried to go to the quilting party, but now she wondered if perhaps she should have made a special effort. Martha would be gone from her forever so soon; they would have had a little while alone together going down the mountain. She stirred the washpot.

Mark's and the boys' Sunday shirts were boiling out to a gleaming white. She had been afraid they might be dingy, but that last run of soap she made had been extra good. Aunt Tildy had told her it would be hard and pure white if she made it during the light of the moon, when it was turning toward the full. After the shirts had bleached in the sun all day, they would be as white as new.

She straightened her back again and wiped her forehead with the edge of her apron.

It was a deep satisfaction to her to smell the boiling, soapy water and the smoke from the fire, to hear the blue jays screaming in the woods and the mourning doves calling in the pasture, to see her clothes emerging bright and clean from the clear rinse water, to feel the sun on her neck and arms and know the strength of her wrists and shoulders as she wrung and lifted and covered every inch of fence and bush in her yard with fragrant wet laundry. She listened again to the blue jays. Their crying would worry Aunt Tildy if she heard it. "A jay's the devil's own bird," Aunt Tildy always said, "and when they flock around your place, it's a bad omen. Old folks always told me that the blue jays was talebearers for the devil, telling him all the evil things folks do. And on his trips to the devil every Friday, the jay bird carries him a grain of corn, if it's during planting season." Lydia hoped none of these birds today were stealing Mark's corn.

She had finished hanging out all the big pieces. Last, she squeezed out her little midwife cap and wondered if she should lay it aside till she could make some flour starch. Aunt Tildy had made the cap for her. Even though it was growing a little frayed around the edges, Aunt Tildy's big, impatient stiches were still visible. And yet it was Aunt Tildy who had told her, "Take time when you go to help a woman bring a baby, Lydia. Remember, getting born will be one of the two importantest things that ever happens to that baby. And it takes patience and hard work."

Tilmon Haddon had been the one who started Lydia to being a midwife. The spring after David died he had come ·pleading for her help and she had found solace in the hard, satisfying task.

"Since Doc Hornsby killed hisself," Haddon whined, "there ain't nobody left to look after a woman on Thickety. And we ain't got the money for a town doctor. You've had young'uns, Mrs. McQueen. I heard tell you helped bring your sister-in-law's baby. You've downright got to help us out."

It had been in Lydia's mind to ask Aunt Tildy to go instead, but suddenly she saw how the older woman had broken in the months since David's death. Aunt Tildy had fairly worshiped the boy and his loss had been a heavy grief to her. Rheumatism, too, had already begun its first twisting of her muscles. So Lydia had said, "Tell me what I must take, Aunt Tildy, what I must do."

And Aunt Tildy brought out the little case she had used for so many years and explained its contents to Lydia piece by piece. She snapped it shut and handed it to the younger woman. "Better take along a clean quilt, too, this time," she snorted. "Never know what you'll find at a place like that." Her glance defied Haddon, with his dirty clothes and bearded face, to reply.

Lydia had found the worst: a miserable house full of dirt and disorder and pale-faced children, the oldest a scrawny girl of seventeen named Ruby, the youngest a baby under two years old. There wasn't a bed in the cabin. Ruby had tried to fix her mother's pallet as well as she knew how; Lydia could see that she had stripped the other pallets of their coverings in an effort to make her mother more comfortable and was glad Aunt Tildy had advised her about bringing the clean quilt.

Before she was through, Lydia had torn up her own white petticoat for cloths and diapers. She had also solved a little mystery. Just before she shooed their father and the children, except Ruby, into the other room, one of the little boys had said, in a clear, loud voice, "Be you the lady raises such fine hog-meat?"

She had paid no attention to his words until he asked again and Tilmon Haddon said, "Shut your mouth, boy." Lydia looked at him. His face was flushing purple with anger and chagrin.

She looked at the boy. "Why, I don't know, child. When did you ever taste meat I'd raised?"

"That ham and shoulder you give Pap that time your man was gone, he butchered for you."

But she had given Haddon only liver and loin and the head.

"Oh." She nodded slowly. And all these years she and Aunt Tildy and anyone else she had told of their loss, they had all taken for granted that it was the Bludsoes who had stolen the ham and shoulder from her smokehouse.

"Mrs. McQueen . . ." Tilmon Haddon's tongue was thick, the words would not come. His children were staring at him. Even his wife on the pallet in the corner, momentarily easy from her labor, was looking at him. "Mrs. McQueen . . ." His silly repeating of her name, remembrance of the fright he had given her that night and the injustice he had caused her to do in her mind to innocent people all these years, angered her. But before she spoke she saw the girl Ruby's eyes. They were wide and hunted and helpless as a doe's.

"Mrs. McQueen, we were hungry!" the man finally blurted out.

"I'm glad you thought that meat was good, boy," she said to the little fellow. He nodded in agreement.

"Mrs. McQueen"—it was the woman this time—"I think the baby's coming for sure."

"Ruby, give your mother your hands to hold on to," Lydia said. "And the rest of you get in the other room. Mr. Haddon"— she couldn't resist prodding him to some usefulness—"why don't you go and chop a stack of wood ahead for your wife?"

So she brought the Haddons' eleventh baby into the world, and after that there were other families who came to her for help. As the years passed, her name became known among those who could not afford to have a doctor from the county seat. And there were always those who preferred a midwife to any man doctor. Her list of babies grew. Soon now she might even be helping with a grandchild, her own and Mark's grandchild. She laid the white cap in the sun to dry.

A little worry nibbled at her mind. She thought about it while she emptied the washpot and carried the tubs and buckets back into the kitchen. A few days ago, when she and the girls were molding candles to use at the infare, Martha had said, "Maybe Tom will give up sawmilling after we're married. Maybe he'll be a farmer instead."

"Did he name all these 'maybes' to you?" Lydia asked.

"No. I was just a-wishing out loud."

"Do you be planning to change a man's way of living," Lydia said, after a pause, "appears you may be letting yourself in for disappointment."

"But I know Tom, Mama."

"Yes, you do," Lydia agreed. She wondered what right she had to be speaking so to Martha. Mark had changed since their marriage; she had changed. Could two strangers come together and live together and each not be changed? What, then, might not happen to Tom Thurston, too?

It was Martha's expression of hopefulness and longing, when she spoke of a farm, that troubled Lydia now. That longing might be the hint of an unsuspected difference, deep as a chasm, between her and the boy she was going to wed. Lydia sighed and wondered. All her life, she thought, rearranging the curtain drying on the rose-of-Sharon bush, she had been wondering about folks she loved. She was glad there were some things you didn't have to wonder about: the mountain, its ledges, her spring, new leaves in April and old leaves dying in a blaze of color in October. People changed, the earth remained. She remembered Ecclesiastes, the Preacher: "Then shall the dust return to the earth as it was: and the spirit shall return unto God who gave it."

She saw her menfolks coming down the hill, through the young apple orchard, and she hurried inside to help Aunt Tildy get dinner on the table. As she trimmed tender spring onions and filled dishes with steaming vegetables and poured cold buttermilk into each glass, watching the tiny flakes of fresh butter rise to the top, she thought of the day her father had helped set out the orchard on the hillside above the barn. He brought apple-tree switches he had raised and grafted himself—Winterjohns, Milams, Sheepnose —and showed Mark how far apart to dig the holes, where the different varieties should be planted. They had worked two long days, Lydia and the boys carrying water to puddle around each cluster of roots as they set the seedlings, one by one, in neat rows around the hillside. Jesse Moore, slightly feeble now, had stood pulling at his neat little grey beard, surveying their finished work with satisfaction. "A tree is a pleasant thing," he said to Lydia.

During the five years since that planting the trees had grown: tall and graceful, short and limby, according to their different natures. Lydia came to like this spot better than any part of the farm, except for her spring, and sometimes in the evening after supper dishes were done she would walk out there, watch the first blossoms appear, look at the green leaves and the healthy bark, be glad that this one spot was green for most of the year, not bare and stripped like much of the rest of their land was becoming.

"Be cleanliness next to godliness, you must of scrubbed your way right up to the Pearly Gates this morning, Mama," Burn said, as he came in the door.

"Not if I'm accountable for you." She smiled, looking at the sweat-soaked shirts and grimy pants and faces of Burn and Gib and Mark.

Aunt Tildy said, "Wash up. Dinner's getting cold."

They washed in the dog-trot, splashing great draughts of cool water over face and neck and arms, drying on the big homespun towel that hung on a nail beside the water bucket and gourd dipper and washbasin.

They filled their plates with food and ate heartily. They were silent until their first hunger was satisfied.

"The corn's thinner on that north hillside this year, Papa," Burn said. "Not a good stand a-tall."

Mark chewed thoughtfully. "One of the first spots I cleared after we come here. Reckon maybe the land's running out. . . ."

"Running off," Gib joined in. "All those driving spring freshets right after we got it plowed went hard on that ground, carried a heap of it right off down Thickety Creek to the river."

Mark nodded.

"Hillside farming is an everlasting chore," Aunt Tildy said. She did not enter into conversation as she once had. Sometimes, when her rheumatism was especially bad, she did not even come to the table to eat with them.

"Well," Lydia said cheerfully, "at least the orchard is prospering. I never did see such growth as those little old trees put out last year."

"Come fall, we ought to have a right smart of fruit from them," Mark said.

"Fruit's good," Gib said, "but I never did hear of nobody getting rich from it. Now you take tobacco, that's something else again."

"That's right, Papa." Burn leaned forward eagerly. "All over the county, everybody's getting onto tobacco."

"You think I hadn't noticed?" Mark looked a little amused. He finished his second glass of buttermilk.

"Why, you go in town," Burn said, "all you see or smell or hear talked is tobacco. Last fall, after the curing season, the streets were thick with wagonloads of the stuff. There were strangers everywhere with pockets full of money come to buy tobacco, and most anywhere you turned you could hear auctioneers at the warehouses shouting out the prices. Porches of the freight depots were plumb overflowing with piles on piles of leaves and there was no getting away from under the smell of it. I tell you, it was something to behold."

"Must of been, to hear you say," Mark agreed.

"There's folks getting rich every day——"

"Like Ham Nelson. . . ."

A quiet fell around the table. Mark stopped a forkful of food halfway to his mouth.

"I don't care," Gib plunged on, "no matter whether you like him or don't, Papa, Ham Nelson's drawing down the dollars two ways: he's selling to Clay Thurston's sawmill all the fine lumber on the land he owns; then when it's cleared he's planting the ground to tobacco and getting big prices for that, too."

"It's a fact he's buying up all the land he can in the valley and on the mountains," Mark said slowly.

"Course"—Burn glanced at his mother mischievously—"it's a hard-working crop to grow. Ham Nelson says Professor Duncan's school interferes a heap with his tobacco-raising."

"Maybe it interferes with a lot of your plans, too?" his mother asked.

"Come to think about it——"

"Don't." Lydia glanced at Fayte and winked. He was her other scholar, besides Martha. He was bent over his plate now, squinting slightly as he ate and listened to his older brothers. "Your eyes bothering you today, son?" Lydia asked.

Fayte looked up and straightened out his forehead. "Just a little burning."

"I'll put a cold washcloth on them after dinner. Have you been reading up there in that dim loft?" Lydia knew the dusky loft room was Fayte's favorite place of escape from the noise and routine of the house and farm.

"Just a page or two, after I'd fetched the water and firewood."

"Well, you mustn't read another word more today."

"Ah, Mama . . ."

"You mind what your ma says," Aunt Tildy warned him. "I heard a whippoorwill under my window before daylight this morning. No need for us to go courting bad luck." She left the table and hobbled to her room across the breezeway.

"One thing about it"—Gib swallowed his last bite of corn bread and butter and pushed back from the table—"old Ham Nelson needs to be rich. Did I have that woman of his, I'd want some——"

"You mean Ruby?" his brother asked with a grin.

"Don't speak a word against that poor creature." They were startled at the sharpness in Lydia's voice, arresting the aimless flow of their talk. "She couldn't help it Tilmon Haddon was her pa and in debt to Ham Nelson. No more could she help it that Ham Nelson married her."

"From the looks of her and the way folks say he's treated her during the two years past, he was a-wanting a slavey more than a wife."

"Enough, Gib," Mark said. "Your mama said not to talk about Ruby Nelson. Well, I'm saying don't speak any more about Ham Nelson a-tall."

They were silent. The family had finished eating, but they sat resting for a moment in the cool comfort of the house before tackling the long corn rows again.

Finally Burn said, "No need to go and get so mad, Papa. You and—and *him* might be neighbors. Ain't——"

"Burn!"

"Sorry, Mama, *isn't* he a-wanting to buy the Bludsoes out?"

"That's the talk."

"But they won't sell."

"Not with those whiskey-making outfits they've got set up all through their mountains," Gib joined in.

"What do you know about their outfits, Gib?" Lydia asked.

"Burn and me, we've come across them when we're hunting."

"We sure never named it to anybody."

"Hadn't been for Morgan Bludsoe," Mark said thoughtfully, "we wouldn't a-had this place here today. I bought it from Big Matt, through Morgan, soon after the war."

"Was that after all the trouble Mama's folks had had with the outliers and you'd been in prison?"

Even under his greying hair and eyebrows the old dark hate flashed up in Mark's eyes again. It had been a while since Lydia had seen that look. He slammed his fist against the table. The dishes jumped and rattled. "Leave off this talk! Everything hateful to my soul, you've jawed about it here today. Enough of it!"

After a moment, Lydia and Jessie began to clear the empty dishes from the table. Presently the men went back up to the cornfield. Before she realized it, Fayte had gone with them. She wondered if he would have a headache that afternoon.

Well before daylight the following Saturday, Lydia was up making breakfast. There was a long day ahead. She carried hot shaving water to Mark and looked in on Martha, buttoning her new shoes for the trip to town. "Should you want to use a dab," she said, "there's some powder in the trunk in my room. Dolly gave it to me once."

"Thank you, Mama."

"Not that you'll be needing it to look pretty today."

At breakfast the boys ate and were in high spirits. Martha and Lydia nibbled at their food and finally gave up the effort, and Lydia noticed that Mark's plate was still half full when he pushed back his chair and stood up.

"Guess it's time we were on our way," he said to Martha. They had arranged for Mark to take her down to the Thurstons' where they would join Tom and his father and go on to the county seat for the marrying.

Martha went into the bedroom she had shared with Jessie. Lydia followed her. The girl was standing in the middle of the room, her little hat that matched her dress clutched tightly in one hand. Tears stood in her eyes. "I'll never sleep here again," she

230

said, "not—not the same way it's been for so many years—all my life . . ."

Lydia smoothed her daughter's hair and cupped the earnest face between her hands. The brown eyes, pleading for a certain answer to some uncertain question she could not even name, seemed enormous. "You'll always be our little girl," Lydia said. "That will always be the same."

"Oh, Mama . . ." She would have flung herself into her mother's arms, but Lydia kept her at arm's length.

"It's a giant step, Martha. But we all have to take some giant steps sooner or later. You take it and God grant it will be a good one." As she spoke she wiped the tears from the girl's eyes with her hard, cool fingers. "Now—you go with your papa and find Tom Thurston."

"I reckon it's the right thing, Mama?"

Lydia nodded. Suddenly the lump in her own throat was too large to control.

Martha kissed her, then went to the mirror where she pinned the little hat on top of her heavy coiled hair. She took up her pocketbook and gloves and a little ivory fan her uncle Robert had given her once for Christmas. At the door she turned. "Do I look all right, Mama?"

"You look beautiful."

In the next room, Lydia could hear Burn and Gib greeting their sister with laughter and teasing. Presently she heard Mark drive the buggy up from the barn and the others went outside to help Martha climb in beside him.

"Where's Mama?"

Lydia rushed to the window. She could not go out there with them. She waved and blew a kiss.

Martha waved back, and Mark waved, too. They drove out of the yard.

Lydia stood very still. A sudden memory had demoralized her: she saw a little girl whose plaited hair was loose around her tear-stained face, standing with fierce protectiveness in front of an older, puzzled brother. "He kicked David! . . . he'll hurt him!" the child screamed.

Lydia's throat ached and her clenched hands were bitten with the sharpness of her fingernails. She closed her eyes, fighting for control.

"Mama," one of the boys called. "Mama?"

"Yes?" The word squeezed out past the painful lump she could not swallow.

"Do you want us to be setting up benches around the yard for folks to use at the infare tonight?"

"Yes. Yes, that would be a mighty helpful thing."

Burn stood at the door to the bedroom. He looked at her. "You all right, Mama?"

"I'm all right." She wiped her apron across her face and went to help them.

They worked feverishly all day. Aunt Tildy and Jessie helped her as much as they could with the cooking. The rich smells of Lydia's good food kept the boys trotting in for samples all through the morning and afternoon. Jessie asked a hundred questions, more or less, about marrying. Lydia was distracted by the child's chatter, and thankful for it. There was precious little time, or silence, for thinking.

The infare was a great success. Newlywed happiness shone around Martha and Tom Thurston with the untarnished brightness of new-minted money. Sue Thurston helped Lydia with the food. "They're such young'uns," she said, "but I know my boy loves your girl, Lydia, if that's any comfort."

"It's all the comfort in the world, Sue. And Tom's a fine upstanding boy. We're proud to have him one of us."

Everyone seemed to share the gladness of this marriage. Clay Thurston had brought Weatherby Hayes and his fiddle and after the first round of eating from Lydia's heaped tables, some of the young folks, led by Paul and Dolly's Tim and Pru, began to dance.

"If Pru can dance, why can't I try?" Jessie teased her mother, and Lydia nodded for her to go ahead. It was all a frolic, in good fun, and everyone should enter in.

When Paul and Dolly came to tell her they would be leaving early because Dolly's father was sick and they couldn't leave him alone for long at a time, Lydia was troubled by the disappointment that flawed Dolly's pretty face. Dolly always loved parties, even if she had grown too plump to dance easily any more. "I'm sorry you'll be leaving," Lydia said.

"If we'd only found someone to sit with him . . ." Dolly begą

"We miss Annie Marie," Paul said, and something in his to silenced his wife. She said no more.

Kate and Alec joined the dancing. "See if you can skip as light as you could before three young'uns," he teased her.

And Kate tossed her pretty hair and called, "See if you can keep up, old man."

Harmon Duncan and Lenore stood at one side and watched the dancing. Lenore looked particularly lovely, Lydia thought, with her alabaster skin set off by the dark red richness of the dress she wore. The fine material made Lydia unconsciously finger the folds of her own blue silk, a dress she had made a long time ago from an old one of her mother's. The silk was still handsome, but she supposed the style was a little out of date. She had added a new lace collar for this occasion. And besides, what did a flounce or the new cut of a skirt matter if your family and friends were happy in your home?

"I didn't know whether you'd be asking them or not," Sue Thurston said to Lydia, nodding toward Duncan and Lenore.

"I've tried not to let it make any difference between us that she didn't marry Robert," Lydia answered. "You know, before she married Professor Duncan she came to me, asked me what to do. She said she felt obliged to Robert, but I could see it was the other one she loved."

"What did you say to her, Lydia?"

"I told her a body doesn't marry from obligation. And beyond that, I couldn't play God. I wouldn't tell her what to do. It nearly tore me in two, knowing how Robert felt about her, but dear God, that's all the words I knew to say."

Sue Thurston nodded. "Him and his sister Octavia treat her more like a play-pretty than a person." They watched the dancing.

After a while Lydia noticed that Tom was dancing, while Martha sat at one side and watched him, smiling, nodding to him. Martha, like her grandmother before her, had never come to believe that dancing was exactly right. Tom was a fine dancer, Lydia observed. He had a slim waist and his long legs and nimble feet seemed to know what the music would play before the notes fell. He laughed and waved to Martha and changed his partner and danced again. Lydia wondered if Martha might be a little too prim, too conscientious, for this high-spirited, gay man.

Before she could worry, however, Robert appeared in the doorway. He looked very elegant in his black cutaway coat and there was the stamp of town and experience in the slightly ironic lines settling around his mouth and eyes. When the music stopped he invited everyone to see the gift he had fetched the bride and groom. They followed him outside. There was a shiny new buggy, of the latest style, drawn by a sleek dappled-grey horse.

Martha kissed her uncle Robert and Tom shook his hand like a proper man, then leaped into the seat like a delighted boy. Mark told Robert he shouldn't have given such a handsome gift. Lydia only looked at her brother and squeezed his arm.

Their friends were loud in praise and pleasure. The women climbed in the buggy and examined its details while the men surveyed the horse, peered at its teeth, patted its sides, walked around the turnout, nodded and patted and looked some more.

"Guess you might say this is a throwback," Robert told them all at last, "a throwback to my days as livery-stable boy!"

They all joined in hearty laughter, and some of the men shared recollections of the time when this fine lawyer had been just a shaver at the stable in town. "Back in them days, you was throwing out horse manure instead of words," one of them called. And Lydia saw how quickly and easily Robert had made common cause with them, kept their friendship despite his success, which wasn't always easy on Thickety, where people were suspicious of anyone, especially one of their own, who might be "stuck up."

She saw Lenore and her husband speak to Robert and she watched her brother's face remain in its pleasant, slightly withdrawn, mask. Lenore was not so successful and for the first time Lydia could recall, a flush brought color to the girl's cheeks. Then Jesse Moore came up to his son and the Duncans turned away.

A little later, Lydia led Robert into the kitchen and heaped up a plate with his favorite foods. "I saved the pickled peaches especially," she said.

"I'll always remember your cooking, Lydia. You could take next-to-nothing and work some kind of magic——" He broke off, tasted one of the peaches and winked at her.

She sat down across the table from him. Weatherby Hayes' fiddle was playing again in the next room and she could hear another dance beginning.

"You know the best meal I ever ate, Lydia?" Robert asked.

"Why, no." She moved a dish of honey closer to his plate.

"It was the ham and wheat-bread cakes you cooked that morning after the outliers had been on our place. . . ." His voice trailed off. "I remember skinning up into the loft after that ham. . . ." They looked at each other.

Slowly he pushed back his plate.

"Robert," she asked, not looking at him, tracing with one fingernail a pattern on the tablecloth, "do you ever wonder, now, who it was?"

"No." Quickly he shook his head. "I'm not sure we'd want to know, if we could——"

There was a burst of laughter from the adjoining room.

She stood up and poured a hot cup of coffee for Robert. "I'd better hot up the coffee for some of the folks in there. Wouldn't ever want it thought the McQueens were skimpy on hospitality."

"Not likely."

And after the second set of dances they all came to the tables again and ate once more and still there was an abundance of food left. While most of the people were eating, Mark and Clay Thurston helped Martha and Tom slip away in the new buggy. The young couple would stay the night at the Thurstons', where they would live while Tom continued helping his father at the sawmill, at least for a few months.

When it was discovered that the newlyweds were gone, some of the young people howled in disappointment. Then, led by Gib and Burn, and joined by Fayte and Tim, they gathered up old pans and a cowbell and set out down the valley to serenade Martha and Tom as soon as they thought the young couple were alone together.

Jessie, eyes shining with excitement, begged her mother to let her go and spend the night with Aunt Elizabeth and Grandpa. "Everybody's leaving," she cried, as the wagons and carriages carrying their guests pulled out one by one. "Pretty soon all the fun up here on this old mountain will be gone, and I do so want to be down there with everybody else."

"Did you let the child come, Lydia, it would pleasure us," Elizabeth joined in quietly.

"Why, I guess she can go," Lydia agreed.

Jesse Moore and Elizabeth and young Jessie were the last to leave. "You come home tomorrow evening at the latest," Lydia called after the child. "I'll send one of the boys for you."

Aunt Tildy, wearied by the night's festivities, had long since gone to bed.

Lydia and Mark were left alone in the yard. The quiet around them seemed greater than usual because it followed the noise that had been there such a short while before. The emptiness of the yard and house seemed more complete because of the disorder of chairs and benches, the plates and scraps of food that betrayed the presence of all the people so recently there.

"You gave them a fine infare, Lyddy," Mark said, coming to stand beside her.

She was looking up at the full moon over the young apple orchard. She squeezed the hand he laid on her shoulder. They stood for quite a time, not talking, not needing to talk.

"I reckon a full moon is one of the finest sights on earth," Mark said at last.

Lydia nodded. "It starts out such a thin, empty sliver and first thing you know it's riding up there high and full——"

"Like tonight——"

"But before you can really see it or know it or get your fill of its beauty, it's on the wane. Before you've turned around, it's gone."

Mark looked at her. "That don't hardly sound like you, Lyddy."

236

"I know. I guess it's Martha's marrying . . ." She squeezed his hand again and started abruptly toward the house.

Halfway across the yard she stopped under the walnut tree, where there was a view down the mountain toward the valley. She called for Mark to come and look. There was a dim but unmistakable glow in the distance. As they watched, it shimmered and rose and fell in intensity, and rose again.

"Looks like a fire," Mark said.

"I can't make out where it would be."

The glow became brighter. "Best I can judge," Mark said, "it's the schoolhouse."

12th

CHAPTER

When the boys came home, just before day-light, they brought news of the schoolhouse burning. Lydia lit the lamp and she and Mark went to the kitchen to hear their story.

"She's gone, all right," Gib announced. "Professor Duncan will have to get him another schoolhouse."

Burn nodded. "Plumb to the ground. Those old timbers were cured out, ripe for a fire."

"Specially with a little help."

"What do you mean?" Lydia asked. She stood in bare feet and voluminous white nightgown, the two long braids of her hair falling down her back. "You aren't a-saying that somebody deliberately——"

Gib and Burn looked at each other. "Unless a gallon or two of lamp oil just naturally turned itself over and soaked up the floor of that main room," Burn said.

"You could smell it all over, no mistake."

"Well, I'll be damned!" Mark exclaimed.

Fayte went over to his mother. "Mama, who'd want our school-house burned?"

"Why, I don't know. I can't think. We need it too bad for anybody to set his mind on deliberately destroying it."

"I used to work in that old building, before ever it was a school,"
Mark said, shaking his head. "I worked there for James and John
and Ida Burke, milling, when I first come to this mountain country."

"Where was the school then?" Fayte asked.

"Wasn't any school," Mark said. "Why, you was just a little
shirttail tad when your mama got Professor Duncan's school under
way."

"Mama did that?"

"Not all of it," Lydia said. "A few others turned their hand. But
it was a long time coming—a long, long time."

"It was a short enough time going. You ought to just a-been
there and seen what a bonfire there was."

"We made out the light of the blaze from up here," Mark said.

"Folks are already talking who did it," Burn interrupted.

"You mean they know?" Lydia asked.

The boy shrugged. "They're saying it was the Bludsoes' doing."

"Any of the Bludsoes around there tonight?" Mark asked.

"None that I saw," Burn answered. The other two boys shook
their heads.

"Seemed like about everybody else in this part of the country
came to see the fire," Fayte said. "I never knew so many people
to be all together at once on Thickety Creek."

"Some still had on their clothes from the infare."

"Professor Duncan"—Fayte's young face was troubled—"he
tried to fight the fire. He was carrying water from the old millrace,
and there were a few trying to help him, but it was like throwing
rocks in quicksand, just swallowed up."

"Everybody was excited, hollering out advice, but seemed like
anything they did just made the flames worse," Burn agreed.

"Grandpa Moore finally had to take Professor Duncan away,"
Fayte said. "Everybody was afraid he was getting too close to the
fire, he might faint or something."

"Mrs. Caldwell did faint," Gib grinned.

"She came around pretty quick," Burn said. "She didn't want to miss seeing the roof cave in."

"There was a shower of sparks shot up to the sky and came down like falling stars, Mama," Fayte said.

"I'm glad Emma Caldwell didn't miss it," Lydia said briefly. She picked up the lamp. "We'd best all get to bed. This has been a day, all right."

"Reckon it will be a long time before Thickety forgets Martha's and Tom's marrying day," Gib said.

Lydia was already halfway to the door. "Tomorrow we'll have to go down and see . . ." she said. But she did not tell them what they would have to see about: the past—who had burned this school? Or the future—how could they build another?

It was almost noon the next day before Lydia and Mark could leave and go down to the valley. There was much work left over from the celebration the night before, Aunt Tildy was not as well as usual and stayed in bed for the day, and there were farm chores that had to be done before they could get away. When at last they were ready, Mark told the boys to stay at home and mind the place while he and their mother were gone. They were so surprised and chagrined that they did not have a chance to argue before their parents had left.

"I thought things might be excitable down here," Mark said, as they turned into the road. "I didn't want our boys mixed up in it."

"What do you look to happen, Mark?" she asked.

"I don't know what to look for," he said. "But it's just better if our boys aren't traipsing around."

Lydia nodded. Her thoughts had been going in circles all morning. Who in the community, in the county, would have set that fire? He must have chosen the very night of the infare, when he knew everyone would be up on the mountain. Then the other question would whirl across her mind: How would they ever get another school? She had long since spent the little lump of money Dr. Hornsby had left for a school. Robert had told them the state said all the children should have a four-month schooling every year, but it looked like the word hadn't reached some parts of Nantahala County yet.

They were almost at the foot of the mountain when they began to hear a noise on the road ahead of them. "What is it, Mark?" Lydia asked.

He listened, head tilted to one side. "Sounds like a crowd of men."

As they rounded the next curve, they came face to face with a dozen—perhaps fifteen, Lydia didn't have time to count them—men on horseback. From the looks of them they were a rowdy bunch and might be looking for trouble.

"Whoa!" Mark halted their buggy right in the middle of the narrow road. There was no getting around it unless the horsemen went single file. They reined in their mounts and greeted Mark. Lydia did not know most of them, although she did recognize the blacksmith from down along the river, and a man named Fry, who was tenant on the Hawkins place, and one or two of the hands from the Thurstons' sawmill. She also recognized the man in front, who was speaking to them now.

"Howdy, Mr. McQueen. Mrs. McQueen." Tilmon Haddon said. He made a gesture to tip his ragged hat, but his hand fell short of the brim and he did not make the effort again.

"Howdy," Mark said. The greeting took in all the men.

"You just now going down the valley?" one of them asked.

Mark nodded.

"Then you don't know what happened down here last night?"

"We heard."

Lydia did not like the undertone in the men's voices. She wished Mark had not stopped to talk with them.

"Knowing how Mrs. McQueen felt about that there school, reckon you're right torn up about its being burned," Tilmon Haddon said.

"Maybe he'd like to come along with us," one of the red-eyed sawmill hands in the rear called.

The others looked at Mark.

"Depends on where you're going," he said.

"We're riding up the mountain to teach a little lesson to some folks," Tilmon Haddon said.

"What folks?"

"The Bludsoes."

Lydia felt her heart skip a beat. This was dangerous talk.

"What lesson?" Mark pursued quietly.

"We aim to learn them not to play with matches," the blacksmith shouted. The others grinned and nodded.

"Fight fire with fire," someone shouted.

"The Bludsoes set that fire last night?" Lydia asked.

"Who else?" one of the strangers replied.

"Anybody see them around the school last night?" Mark asked.

"You don't reckon they'd be that big fools?" the blacksmith said. "They're sly varmints."

"Anybody heard them speak anything against the school?" Mark asked.

"I ain't heard them speak nothing," Tilmon Haddon said. He spat a long stream of tobacco juice into the road. "Don't have to hear them talk to know what they've got in their minds."

"You a mind reader now, Haddon?" Mark asked.

"I know they hate the guts of everybody on this-here creek," the scrawny man replied. "Ever since the smithy yonder whipped Euell Bludsoe in a fair fight down at his shop———"

"That wasn't the way I heard it told," Mark said. He sat leaning a little forward on the buggy seat, hands clasped lightly between his legs. "Way I heard it, Euell won that fracas by a mile—with two or three against him."

The men had grown quieter. They were paying closer attention and looking straight at Mark. "Whose side you on here, anyway?" someone asked.

"Didn't know there were sides," Mark answered. "Just pointing out that the Bludsoes are pretty stout fighters."

"We ain't afraid!" Tilmon Haddon said. He patted the gun lying across his saddle.

"Looks like you got a-hold of some cheap courage, Haddon," Mark said. "The kind that comes out of a bottle."

"Look-a here———"

"Maybe a Bludsoe bottle?"

Haddon's face reddened. "Are you a-saying, look-a here are you———"

242

"I'm saying this"—Lydia saw Mark's eyes narrow and darken as he stiffened on the seat—"you fellers aren't showing very good judgment, taking on the Bludsoes on their own ground. 'Specially when you're not a-tall sure they did what you accuse them of."

"They done it all right."

"Who else?"

"I don't *know* who else." Mark spoke almost patiently. Lydia thought she had never heard him so deliberate. "And I don't *know* they did it, either. But there's one thing I have had experience of, and that's being a stranger, being different. It can be mighty costy to a feller. So I'm wishing all of you would take your bottles and your matches and your guns and turn around and go home."

"If wishes be horses, beggars would ride," someone mumbled.

"I'm advising you to forget this," Mark said.

"Don't recollect we asked your advice."

"Well, I'm offering it, anyway."

Tilmon Haddon slouched on his horse. His head swayed. "Reckon you lived up here on this mountain breathing Bludsoes' air so long you all are thick as thieves."

"That'll be enough, Haddon."

"We ain't about to turn around! You get that buggy out of the road and let some men get on with men's business. . . ."

Others behind him muttered assent.

Easily, before they knew what he was doing, Mark reached under the seat beneath him and Lydia. His gun, when he brought it up, pointed straight across the horse's back. "Don't one of you make a move to reach for your firearms," he said. "Now forget about your plan for burning out Bludsoes and get back down the mountain."

"You can't scare us, McQueen . . ."

"Tilmon Haddon!" The sight of Mark's gun, the deadly earnestness of his voice, frightened Lydia. She tried to keep her voice steady. "Tilmon Haddon, you better do like he says."

The half-drunk man in front of her met the gaze of her clear grey eyes, deep-set between her high cheekbones and forehead. Her look did not falter. Lydia hoped that in the sodden mind behind that dirty face he was remembering what she was, a baby being born, and some stolen meat. A flush, hardly visible on the already mottled skin, crossed Haddon's face. "Mrs. McQueen," he began boldly, then paused. "Mrs. McQueen . . ."

"You got a habit for repeating my name?" she asked, and knew this time that her words had driven home, recalling to him that other day when he had said her name over and over, fumbling to explain his thievery.

"I wouldn't want no trouble with a lady around," he mumbled finally.

"We're going to do our job," the blacksmith said, riding toward the head of the group.

"I tell you what," Mark said, holding the gun and his voice equally level, "I'll give you my pledge to go talk to the Bludsoes——"

"Talk's no 'count. They'll say anything."

"The Bludsoes don't lie," Mark said. "You all know that. Fight and kill and make liquor, yes, but their word's their bond."

No one denied this. Lydia looked at Mark's gun and remembered, unaccountably, the time when Jessie was a baby that Mark had shot a rattlesnake right from this buggy seat. He had hit it squarely on its ugly head.

"Men," she said, "you know this school has meant as much to Mark and me as anybody. We want to find out, maybe worse than you do, who would be low enough to destroy it. We promise you, if it's the Bludsoes we'll see they get their due."

One of the sawmill men spoke up. "I don't want no trouble with the McQueens. It was the Bludsoes I come after."

Several others muttered agreement. "If Mark and Lydia McQueen will give their word——"

"We give our word," Mark said.

With surly looks, slowly, one by one, they began to turn their horses down the valley. Mark did not move.

"You a-standing up for half-breeds," the blacksmith said, looking straight at Lydia. "I always thought the Moores, at least, were fine folks in these parts. Reckon I was bad mistaken." He spat.

"That'll be enough," Mark said.

"You're damned right it's enough," the big man said angrily, "it's a crawful. I want to go home and puke." He turned back with the others.

Their horses moved gradually at first, then one by one they broke into a gallop and disappeared from sight.

Mark laid his gun back under the seat. He pulled off his hat and drew his right arm across his forehead. Then he picked up the reins. "Wasn't that something?" he said.

"It was a shame," Lydia said. "Mark, could we go back home?"

"Don't know why not. Looks like our business now is up with the Bludsoes, not down in Thickety, anyway." At the next wide place in the road he turned the horse around.

"Mark, I want to go with you when you go up to see Big Matt and the others."

"Don't seem like it's woman's business."

"I want to go. I want to know about the school. And," she added, trying to smile at him, "I want to see all those chests of riches old Vashti and the others brought with them when they came to this country."

"Tales," he said.

"They're tales I've heard life-long," she persisted. "I'd like to see some treasure."

"Don't reckon I can keep you from going."

"You kept those men from going," she said. They looked at each other. "Would they have burned the Bludsoes out?"

"They'd a-made a stab at it."

"And I reckon the Bludsoes would have killed some of them?"

"They'd a-tried. And I never heard of one of them missing an aim yet."

Before they turned into the lane under the Devil's Brow, leading home, Lydia said, "Mark?"

He waited, then looked up. "Yes?"

"I like you, Mark McQueen."

When they reached home, they told Burn and Gib about the encounter on the road. The boys' eyes shone.

"We miss all the high times!" Gib protested.

"You ought to had us along to help you," Burn said.

245

"Your papa did all right by himself," Lydia said.

"I wasn't exactly alone. Your mama put in a word or two——"

"We're your children all right, Mama," Burn teased. "You don't shy away from a good fight."

"There's few enough 'good,' " she answered briskly.

Lydia rode her sidesaddle on the mare and Mark rode the horse when they went, two days later, up to the Bludsoes'. The trail they followed wound up the mountain steeply above the Devil's Brow. It grew more difficult and rocky. They came to a rail fence, zig-zagging across the face of the mountain like a giant snake, and a gate made of peeled locust poles. The gate was fastened with a stout chain and lock.

Mark shouted. "Hallo-o-o."

There was only silence and he shouted again.

Then a young man, tall and thin and gangling, came down the ravine toward them. He wore an old hat and loose, patched clothes. Lydia wondered how long they had been hand-me-downs. He did not look at them or hesitate. He unlocked the chain, swung the gate wide and waited for them to ride through. Then he pulled the heavy gate shut again.

"I want to talk with Big Matt," Mark said.

The young man nodded.

Something in his face seemed familiar to Lydia. "Are you Young Matt's boy?" she asked. "Didn't you bring me a side of deer meat once, a long time ago?"

He nodded again. "For your mammy's funeralizing, it was," he said.

"Then I'm proud to see you again."

"They call me Black Matt," he said.

"Proud to see you again, Black Matt."

"Grandpap's up here at his house, a-waiting to see you folks," he said.

As they rode along, Lydia had the same feeling she had known the time Morgan Bludsoe came down to help her with her hog-killing: that everything they had been doing was already known to the Bludsoes. She could hardly wait to see their homes.

246

Lydia was not prepared for what she found. Much as she had disbelieved many of the stories she had heard since she was a child, she had still thought that there must be something rare and exotic about the lives of these people who lived apart from the humdrum community she knew. Now she found that they were not the stuff of mysterious legends but miserable subjects for pity. They were outcasts, and nature had not redeemed them from the wildness and poverty to which men had sentenced them.

The Bludsoe houses were a series of half a dozen huts huddled in the shelter of a bare ravine near the top of the mountain. The steep yards in front of the weathered frame shacks were beaten to the barren hardness of cement, through which hard rains had washed a gulley here and there. Every blooming bush and tree and tender plant that had once been here was long since gone.

In the open shelter under the porch and floor of each house there were chickens and dogs and pieces of old lumber or harness or other trash. Smoke curled from the clay-daubed chimneys, several of which were in disrepair. Everything about the little settlement was poor and ugly and abused beyond belief. And yet, looking at the great dark balsams fringing the mountaintop just above them, and at the bold, clear stream that plunged down the middle of the ravine, and at the luxuriant growth of rhododendron and laurel and galax on the slopes above the clearing, Lydia marveled at the beauty which surrounded this ugliness.

They stopped at the first house, the largest and oldest, weathered grey, the color of lichens Lydia had seen in the deep woods. They dismounted. Three men and a woman and several children sat crowded on the narrow porch. There were only two chairs and one of the men leaned against the wall beside the door while the woman and children sat on the floor, their bare feet dangling off the edge of the porch. The hair of every person there was black as a starling's wing, but as she spoke to each one in turn, Lydia saw that their eyes varied from the dark blue, almost violet color of the woman Callie's, to the light brown, amber of her husband Big Matt's eyes. In between, and equally watchful, were their sons' eyes—Young Matt's, Morgan's, and the children no one bothered to notice.

Big Matt offered them chairs.

"I'd as soon stand," Mark said, but the huge bearded man pushed the chair at him and he took it.

Lydia tried to draw closer to where the other woman sat, but there was no sign they had seen the gesture of friendship. As she and Mark sat in the straight-backed chairs while the three men stood above them, she felt almost as if they were on trial.

Big Matt waved the children off the porch. They jumped like startled toad frogs in a pool. Lydia was struck with the paleness of their faces, the thinness of their legs and shoulders. She wondered if they might not have pellagra, maybe even consumption, some of them. Yet judging from the bulk of these men around her here, some of the Bludsoes must grow up healthy enough.

"Not seen you for a spell, Morgan," Mark said.

"Not been in Thickety for a spell," he answered.

"You heard what happened the other night." It was hardly a question, the way Mark put it.

Morgan Bludsoe nodded. "The other night and the next day, too," he said.

Mark flushed. "Don't hold what happened there on the road against most of the valley folks."

Lydia was taken aback. Like swimmers pushed into deep water before they had had a chance to get their breath, Mark and the Bludsoes were already plunged into the talk for which they had made this steep journey.

Ever since they had come onto the porch Lydia had been aware of a low whining sound, a mixture of pain and weakness. "Is it one of your dogs?" she asked, nodding toward the floor beneath them.

"Old Thunder, Morgan's best bear dog," Callie Bludsoe answered softly. "He was in a fight last week, got part of his belly ripped open."

"Could I look at him?" She had no idea why she asked the question. The words had just come to her tongue before she knew what she was speaking.

When the woman crawled under the porch and brought the animal, howling louder now with the pain of being moved, into the

248

yard a little at one side of the house, and Lydia went to look at it, she wondered again why she had asked to see the dog.

"We'd better leave him here," the Bludsoe woman said. "Big Matt don't like no racket going on when he's talking."

"Poor thing, poor thing," Lydia murmured. The gash in the dog's stomach stood wide as the moment it was made; blood and dirt were caked around it and it had begun to fester.

"We put cobwebs on it and stopped it up with chimney soot, good as we could," the woman said.

"Do you have any hot water now?" Lydia asked.

"I reckon there's a kettle over the fire."

"If you'll bring it to me, and get somebody to hold the dog——"

"That would have to be Morgan. Nobody else can do nothing with him." She brought the water. Morgan came from the porch, where Lydia knew the men were already talking about the school and the fire and the accusations.

"If you'll hold your dog," she said to him, "I'm going to try to help it get well."

He did not answer, but stretched the dog out gently on the ground, the long angry wound turned up to Lydia. Firmly he grasped its forelegs and head and called one of the children to hold the animal's hind quarters.

With her own clean handkerchief and the hot water Lydia bathed the wound as well as she could. Then she took off the poke bonnet she was wearing and ripped the long stiff splits of the brim separate from the crown. She brought the dog's skin together over the wound, then wrapped the soft, stiffened length of the bonnet brim tightly around its stomach. She tied it in place with the bonnet strings.

"Maybe now it can knit back together," she said, as she stood up. "I have medicine at home—you send somebody down to get it and I'll make you up a salve to put on that gash. It'll keep down that festering and let it heal."

"Iffen you've helped save Old Thunder, I'll be beholden to you," Morgan Bludsoe said.

She brushed off her dress. "Call it repayment for a kindness you did me once, butchering for me when Mark was away."

"That wasn't nothing to me," he said.

"Nor this to me," she said. She smiled at him. It occurred to her that she had seen no one smile since she had come to this place. Now it was Callie who smiled back at her.

"They'd named you to me before this," the gaunt, black-haired, violet-eyed woman said. "I know they spoke truth."

The three of them went back to the porch. Lydia stepped quietly as she heard Big Matt saying, ". . . no part in any burning, ever, in Thickety Creek or beyond."

There was silence. She noticed Mark's hesitancy and so, she guessed, did Big Matt, for suddenly he said, "You know, last winter, that I shot Euell through the heart?"

Mark nodded.

"You heard why I had to kill him off?"

"No."

"He told me he hadn't been around Ham Nelson's store, not since I told every being on this mountain never to set foot in that hellhole again, what with him trying to get the very land out from under us—and when I spoke 'never,' I meant just that thing." He paused a moment. "Euell said he hadn't been there. Then I learned that he had been, trading around for chewing tobacco and trash. He lied."

"I'm sorry," Mark said.

"No need. No real Bludsoe ever broke his word. And I'm giving you my word that none of my folks harmed your schoolhouse."

Suddenly, hearing his words, listening to him speak of the son he had killed, Lydia knew she must ask him, for once and all, about the war times. She cleared her throat. "It's not easy for me to name this, Matt Bludsoe," she said, and though her voice wavered slightly her eyes did not, "but it ought to be cleared up between us for once and all. During the war, just before the fighting closed, some riders came to my mother's house——"

He held up his big sinewy arm. "I'll ease your asking. No, it wasn't any Bludsoe that stole your stock, harmed your family, while the menfolks was off to war."

She was oddly relieved, yet not relieved, either, for she still did not know, might never know now, who those outliers had been.

"It's gall to me to think you nursed suspicion of us all these years," Big Matt said.

"Oh, but I——"

"I was of the mind, when you took that side of deer meat, that you took our good faith toward your family, too. I was wrong."

How strange, she thought, that now, just as her suspicions had been buried and she and Mark were finally free to be kindly disposed toward the Bludsoes, the Bludsoes had become suspicious of them, were withdrawing into a shell of their own. "Nothing ever gained but something lost," her mother had said. But somehow she must try to set this straight.

"I never really——" she began.

But Big Matt would not listen. "No difference. That's the way things go. But you'll have to look closer home if you're driven to know the ones that wronged you. Now I reckon there's no more business between us——"

"Much obliged, Matt," Mark said, and held out his hand. He shook hands all around the porch. So did Lydia. When she came to Callie, she said, "Don't forget the salve for Old Thunder."

The woman said nothing, but she squeezed Lydia's hand.

Black Matt led them back down the ravine, through the locust gate. As they went down the mountain, Lydia felt the tenseness easing from her neck and shoulders. She looked at Mark. He was watching her closely.

"How'd you like all those treasures?" he asked, and she saw a little smile crease the corners of his mouth.

"I was shamed," she said. And, after a moment, "All these years," she said, "and none of us down here have ever really known what those folks were like. They might have been living in China on the other side of the globe."

"They've got their own ways——"

"It's more than that, much more," she cried. "We've packed off on them everything bad we didn't admit of doing ourselves. The Bludsoes were bad! We didn't have to look for any wrong we might be doing. All my life I've heard tell how black-hearted were the Bludsoes. Now I know that they're just people, poor miserable people. And so are we on Thickety!"

"It was good you could nurse Morgan's dog," Mark said. "He sets a heap of store by Old Thunder."

"Mark"—she had not even heard what he was saying—"Mark, there's so many things we need to learn here in the valley—some only a school can teach us——"

"And some no school can teach us?" he said.

"That's what I was fixing to say."

13th
CHAPTER

Harmon Duncan waited until the following July before taking Lenore and his sister, Octavia, back North. He would return to Thickety Creek as soon as another school was built to replace the makeshift building they had lost. When the men of the valley had become convinced that the Bludsoes were not responsible for the burning, they seemed to lose interest in pursuing their revenge, in seeking out the perpetrator. The fight for a new school lagged. Duncan came to see Lydia the day before they left.

The afternoon was hot and she had just finished carrying out the ashes in the big kitchen fireplace and scrubbing the hearth-stones.

"Don't you know better than to clean out your fireplace on a Friday?" Aunt Tildy quarreled all the while she was working. "Eh law, child, something in this house is bound to be stolen before another Friday comes around, the way you're flouting fate."

"No call for you to fret so, Aunt Tildy," Lydia said, as she took out the last shovelful of ashes, knowing how bitter it was to the older woman not to be able to walk briskly or work busily as she had done for a lifetime, "better a little something should be stolen than these ashes pile up in here another day. Besides, with Mark and Fayte gone to mill, we didn't need hot dinner today. I could let the fire go out."

"Do you go against the old ways, it'll sorrow you." Aunt Tildy dipped her black-gum toothbrush into her little brass snuff box. "Eh law, seems like things change too fast for a body's knowing . . ." She muttered on to herself.

When Harmon Duncan arrived, Lydia was half relieved to talk to someone who was not living in the past.

"It's cooler in the dog-trot or out in the yard under a tree," she said, when she had pulled off her apron and smoothed her hair.

"The shade of that walnut tree would be delightful," he said.

Mark and the boys had already taken chairs out there the night before, and so she and the thin, intense professor, whose greying hair was belied by the eagerness of his quick, green eyes, sat and talked in the leafy coolness of the out of doors. Bees hummed in the sun-hot fields and the cows in the pasture had gathered on the shady side of the hill and were lying down, chewing their cuds.

"I'm leaving because I'm discouraged, Mrs. McQueen," Professor Duncan said. (She wondered if she would ever grow quite accustomed to the clipped precision of his speech.) "I have waited a year for a new school building. I have done all that I could to see that one was built. And you know what has happened."

She nodded unhappily.

"The people in this valley seem to like preachers better than teachers." He smiled, but Lydia thought such a smile was a twisty, unhappy thing to see.

"No," she said, "you must understand. Gentry Caldwell is one of our own folks; he grew up here, and I guess everybody's so surprised he can do anything a-tall, much less preach, that they turn out to support him. With you our professor, being from up North where there's so much more money and better schooling and all, we just naturally expect you to——"

"No, Mrs. McQueen, thank you for the compliment, but it's more than that. There's something in the people here—and not only here, I might add—something that's suspicious of learning.

254

Faith is acceptable; education is"—he shrugged—"at best, dubious. At worst, unnecessary."

"Not all of us feel that way, Professor Duncan. Please don't go away with that thought on your mind." Her hard brown hands were clasped in her lap and she clenched them tightly as she spoke. "This may seem an uncharitable thing to say, but there's only one main person that has stood in the way of our school——"

"Hamilton Nelson."

"Yes. And the rest of the people just haven't cared enough one way or the other. Ham's like a great log that falls across a bold stream. Soon as he blocks the way all the dead limbs and fallen leaves and bits of trash pile up behind and help hold the water back. For a while the natural flow of the stream is clogged, but when it's dammed up high as that log can hold it, it breaks loose. And when it does that, sometimes it carries the hindrance and everything else along with it."

"You think that will happen with our school?"

"It has to."

"I hope you're right. But a man is a mighty formidable impediment when he can burn the very school building and not be brought to justice." He leaned forward in the straight-backed chair, "Oh, I know I shouldn't make such accusations without absolute proof, but does anyone in the valley think otherwise?"

Lydia shook her head. "I reckon not—not since Tilmon Haddon packed up bag and baggage and sneaked off in the night the week after the burning. Him leading a big gang to drive out the Bludsoes, with that empty tattletale kerosene can thrown in the weeds behind his house! But everyone knows there's only one person would have put him up to such mischief: the man he was tenant and pappy-in-law to——"

Harmon Duncan gave another short mirthless laugh. "That poor Ruby. Do you suppose she knew what Nelson and her father were doing?"

"It wouldn't have mattered if she did." Lydia sighed. "Her pappy starved the spirit out of her and Ham is working it out of her; she's like a farm brute more than a woman."

"If she could testify in court——"

"I'd never ask her to," Lydia said. "He would beat her to death."

"But why is Nelson so opposed to a school here in the community? Doesn't he realize it would help him, too?" Impatience made the professor's eyes glisten.

"Not to his way of thinking, it wouldn't help him. He's got no children, at least none he claims," Lydia said. She was thinking of Dolly's Tim, who had gone in town to the private academy, and now had a job at the courthouse—recorder of deeds, or court clerk, had Robert said?—with some of Ham's cronies. She looked at her hands. "Ham's been thinking school hindered work in his tobacco fields. He's afraid it will get his taxes raised. And I should admit it, he'll be eternally against anything I'm for in this valley."

Professor Duncan looked at her sharply.

"We had our differences, a long time ago," she explained lamely.

He asked no questions. "Well," he said, straightening up and tilting his chair back toward the walnut tree, "don't you ever stop working on the school officials in there at the county seat. They'll have to appropriate money for a building out here sooner or later. State law provides——"

"That's what I told Robert not long ago," she interrupted, "and his answer to me was, 'State law may provide, but local men decide.' Robert says that Ham Nelson is in so thick with the politicians at the courthouse that we may get an improved road out here next year—and never get any school till next century."

"It's a damnable shame," Duncan said. He stood up and paced the ground a moment. "Excuse my language, but I grow angry——"

She smiled. "So does Mark. Never mind, we'll keep pestering the men in town."

"There are so few here in the valley who seem to care about their children's minds—care the way you and your husband do, I mean. So few to help you."

"And *we* seem to be growing less account all the time. There are always so many things need our care." A worried frown crossed her face. "When Martha had her—her trouble, losing her baby this spring, I had to go and stay with her, over in Henry

County where Tom is lumbering, for nigh onto a month. Then when I came home and found out that two of my boys had decided to go up to the mining country in Kentucky or West Virginia, or wherever it was they could get work, well . . ." Her hands were clasped like a vise. She pressed them to her mouth.

"I know," Professor Duncan said. "I know, Mrs. McQueen. I assure you, I don't see how you do all that——"

"Everyone has work and trouble," Lydia said. "I'm not special." She laid her hands in her lap again and looked directly at him. "I'm just fretted because I can't do more. There are so many things I want to do, one especially besides the school that I've had on my heart for a year now."

His eyebrows rose.

"The Bludsoes."

"But I heard you at Christmas, down at the church, explaining to the people how they had misjudged the Bludsoes, how poor and ailing they were. Why you got them a big basket of food and some clothes and medicine."

"And you heard what happened to that basket?" she cried. "After I took it to Callie Bludsoe while her menfolks were all out hunting?"

He nodded. "When Big Matt came home and found it, he brought it down and dumped the contents all over the porch of Ham Nelson's store and stomped them, and called out a warning against anybody ever again bringing charity up to Bludsoe country."

"I hadn't meant it as charity," Lydia said, "but I understood why he couldn't take it. I was sort of proud of what he did."

"The other valley folks didn't see it that way," Duncan said. "They took it as an insult that Big Matt didn't want their spare food. They're all waiting for Ham Nelson to buy the Bludsoes out."

She bit her lip. "He's got money," she murmured.

"Money isn't everything."

"Well, it's a lot," she said suddenly, "especially when you don't have it. Oh, I've never given overly much thought to money, the having of it or not. But I see the need of it can wear out your land and the people tending it. It can send your boys away to a country of black coal and working underground like moles."

"I want to tell you, Mrs. McQueen"—Professor Duncan sat down again and drew his chair deeper into the shade—"how much I have liked those boys of yours."

"Oh, that Burn and Gib," she smiled, "they're no scholars. I know how they must have deviled you when you were trying to hold classes."

"I won't deny that"—he nodded quickly—"but whatever trouble they gave me there, they made it up double in the fun they provided me outside of school."

"You really do mean that, don't you?" Lydia looked at him.

"Yes, indeed. Why, they thought up barrels of innocent jokes to keep this valley lively. They showed me all the tricks to hunting a raccoon or spotting an opossum in a persimmon tree. They taught me a great deal about plants and the woods."

"Aunt Tildy says Burn and Gib need breaking to the harness, but they're goodhearted," Lydia smiled. The Professor's words had pleased her more than he knew.

"They represent what we might call 'natural man,' Mrs. McQueen," Duncan said. "They're big, good-looking, hearty men of the earth who accumulate knowledge all their own through their hands, through their pores. But now your other boy . . ."

"Lafayette," Lydia said softly. "Fayte."

"Ah, Fayte is a different matter. Like your father, Mr. Moore, that boy's a scholar. You know how much I enjoyed teaching Martha and having her help in the school as a teacher herself. Well, in many ways Fayte is an even brighter child, Mrs. McQueen. That's why I tutored him last winter and this spring, since we've been without a school. And now that I'm leaving, I've come to ask that you make certain he doesn't give up his studies."

"I know." Lydia's face was troubled.

"One of the reasons I came up here this afternoon—I brought my saddlebags full of books for him to study while I'm away. These could help prepare him for higher studies sometime."

"That was a kind thing——"

"No, no." He shook his head impatiently. "It's never just a 'kind

258

thing' when we encourage brains. It's our duty, our responsibility, our privilege, if you will. I'm not trying to help Fayte just for himself, but for all the people *he* may be able to help someday, for the riddles he may be able to answer sometime."

"Professor Duncan, I don't know whether you noticed it or not, while you were still tutoring him, but Fayte's eyes have been giving him trouble."

"He seemed a little nearsighted sometimes——"

"He has headaches; sometimes he can't read for a spell."

"Then you must take him in to a doctor at once. Can't you have your brother make an appointment for you?" He stood up and started toward the horse he had hitched to the fence around the yard. "Fayte must study these books. He can't grow discouraged or indifferent now. This is a very critical time for the boy."

Lydia followed him to the gate and watched as he pulled the volumes from his saddlebags. He brought them to her eagerly, bestowing them on her as though they were a rich gift and also a grave charge. She accepted them in the same way. "Composition and oratory and geography and computation and algebra and Latin . . ."

She cradled the books in her arms. "I wish Fayte was here," she told him, "but he's gone with his papa for the day. He'll be proud to find these waiting for him when he comes back tonight."

"Well don't let him read them in a dim light. Be sure and take him to a doctor, Mrs. McQueen." Before she knew it, Duncan was on his horse. "I'm sorry to be leaving, but we'll be back."

"I hate to see you go . . ." She was not sure what to say.

Before she could choose any words, however, he said something so strange and embarrassing that she was completely tongue-tied. "I wish I were a painter," he said. "It would give me satisfaction to paint your face, Mrs. McQueen. You'll pardon my saying it, but I suppose it's the handsomest face I've ever seen on a woman. Oh, now don't mistake me, my Lenore is pretty, and there are others look well enough, but there's something chiseled about your countenance, as if time had chipped away everything unimportant and left only the essential of eyes that see what they behold, a nose that smells the wind, and a mouth that tastes the honey and

259

gall of life." The words stopped but he was still examining her, remotely, critically, with homage, too.

Lydia was overcome with confusion. She could feel the flush mounting to her cheeks like a hot brand. In the span of her entire life, no one had ever told her she was beautiful. One of the books slipped from her arms. She stooped to pick it up from the dust and dropped another one. "I'm sorry . . ."

"Maybe I was too outspoken," Professor Duncan said. "I didn't mean to embarrass you. Give Fayte my advice, and my books, and tell him I'll be back one of these days."

"Yes. Oh, yes, I will," Lydia said. She straightened up and he was starting down the lane. "Thank you, Professor Duncan——"

"You're welcome," he called.

"——for everything."

When he was gone, she walked up the path to the house, thinking about what he had said. It occurred to her that she had sent no word to Lenore. Professor Duncan had hardly given her a chance. He had not talked about himself or his wife or sister this afternoon. Lydia remembered that Octavia Duncan had once told Sue Thurston that her brother gave up a salary of several thousand dollars a year to come and teach in these mountains for a few hundred. No denying it, Professor Duncan was the most unselfish person she had ever known.

"Professor Duncan is going home till we can get him a school to teach in," she told Aunt Tildy, as she put the stack of books on a shelf behind the door. Years of habit had made it hard for Lydia to remember that she no longer had a baby around the house and there was no need to keep things out of reach. "It's a sin to let him go, when we ought to be beginning a new school term on Thickety Creek right now."

"All the men could pitch in together, have a school-raising," Aunt Tildy said, "same as they used to have house-raisings."

"They could, Aunt Tildy, if they all weren't so bird-livered about offending Ham Nelson."

Aunt Tildy snorted.

"Oh, it's not that they like him," Lydia went on, making ready to fix supper; "they're quiet because of their bread and butter.

Some of them work for Ham. Others owe him money, either borrowed outright or through old bills at the store. Several need his political nod in at the courthouse."

"Appears like Hamilton Nelson's the man to reckon with around here. The big man."

"Well, he's not big enough to log-jam progress all his life," Lydia said, and Aunt Tildy grinned to see the sudden set of her jaw. "Ham Nelson is the man the Bible speaks of who gobbles up the earth and everything that's on it, and his neighbors let him—more than that, they watch him and admire. And he takes everything he's inherited from the past, and his neighbors have inherited from the past, and he rips it out and digs it up and wastes it, and when he's through there's no inheritance left for the ones who are coming on tomorrow. But he doesn't care. Because he's greed—pure, fat, total greed, and someday, somehow, I'm going to shake loose his hold on that community, that valley. You'll see, Aunt Tildy."

"I'm watching, Lydia honey."

When Mark and Fayte came home from the mill that night, she told them about Professor Duncan's visit. She brought the books from behind the door and gave them to Fayte. Then he made her repeat again everything that the professor had said while he was there. Lydia told them everything except the words he had spoken just before he left, about her face. Those words were locked deep inside her, a buried treasure, to draw out in her mind and think upon sometime when she was solitary and had time and quiet and much need for reassurance.

"Professor Duncan says you can work toward higher education with these studies," she told Fayte, "but you mustn't read a word in them until we have gone to a doctor in town and had your eyes examined."

"Ah, Mama . . ."

"Those were Professor Duncan's last instructions to me."

"Come Monday, we'll go in to town," Mark said.

Robert directed them to "the best doctor in Nantahala County," as he described the man. "The way he talks may seem harsh to

261

you, but when he's treating you or caring for you, he's tender as a mother's love. And he knows his medicine."

The old man did not mince words with them. "The boy's mistreated his eyes. Now they're mistreating him. He must wear glasses later, but now he shouldn't use his eyes for at least six months. Then we'll have to see just how well he progresses."

"Six months——" Fayte, listening, started to protest.

"Months now—or your eyesight permanently. You can have it either way you choose."

"Well, of course, I couldn't choose a lifetime——" Fayte began, eyes wide.

"Good. Then, boy, do as I say." And he said that Fayte could not read in Professor Duncan's books, or anything else. He must rest his eyes and use drops the doctor gave him. Fayte's face was frightened and desolate as he started home with his father and mother. His eyes, so much like Lydia's, were full of tears.

"Pearten up, boy," Mark said to him, "your mama will think of something to help."

The next morning Fayte left the house early and was gone all day, Lydia did not know where. But the following day, she did think of something. She announced at the dinner table that she would read Fayte's study books aloud to him, one by one, beginning this very day and continuing as long as necessary. "We'll educate ourselves together, Fayte," she said. "No need to be downhearted. I always say if you can't go to town in a buggy, use a wagon, and if you don't have a wagon, use shank's mare. Now, where's that first book, on the world's geography?"

And so she began a schedule of reading to him every day, as soon as dinner was finished, and again in the evening after they had eaten supper. At first her throat grew tired from the unaccustomed effort and she stumbled over some of the words, but she learned to use Martha's dictionary, and when there was something she didn't understand, she asked her father about it. They saved up questions, she and Fayte, and carried them down the valley when they went for a visit or on an errand. Jesse Moore didn't always know the answer, but he was pleased to be consulted and he often knew where to look for an answer. She frequently

262

borrowed his books and read pages from them to fill out Fayte's curiosity, and her own, on the subject they were studying.

Faraway lands, foreign names, wars and wonders, and people of whom she had never heard, suddenly began to become part of Lydia's life. She was forty-one years old. Her body had been wracked and toughened by pain and work. All the dross of unnecessary flesh and fretfulness of spirit seemed to have been burned away from her. Her body was not as soft and quivering and fresh as in the days of her youth, but it leaned no less eagerly toward the daily experience and touch of life. Her mind was not as trusting and unbruised as when she was a girl, but, given a chance, it turned even more vigorously to laying hold of knowledge, not only the knowledge of the brain but of the understanding heart, as well. She had attained a measure of wisdom.

Lydia carried one day's reading with her till the following day, pondering it through dozens of chores, imagining how it might be to live in a certain country, thinking why Caesar or Napoleon had been as they were; astonished and pleased, always, at the neat, relentless beauty of numbers and all that could be done with them. Her curiosity and enthusiasm was matched by Fayte's, and each was contagious to the other.

Sometimes their conversations drew Mark and Jessie and Aunt Tildy into offering comments, and then they all talked together. Sometimes, when Robert came to visit overnight, Lydia made him read aloud to them from the book on rhetoric. And her father came up for a week, late in October, and started them on the Latin studies. Mark never tired of listening to their lessons. He would sit near the door, if it was a warm night, or beside the fire, if it was cool, staring into the darkness or the light, and sometimes there was regret in his face, and sometimes hope.

For her part, Aunt Tildy sniffed once in a while and muttered about "grown folks playing school," but she spent many an evening listening to the play. Jessie complained a few times that other folks seemed to have good times, not books day in and day out, but she settled down to making the best of her mother's "quare whims," as Emma Caldwell said, on education.

This was, in many ways, the most wonderful fall and winter

Lydia had known in a long time. The walls of her world seemed to have been pushed back and she caught a glimpse of the rich variety and vastness of the earth, not only as it surrounded her at this moment but as it had been down through countless centuries before.

"It's a marvel to think on," she said to Mark one night in November, as they sat up later than usual, after everyone else was abed.

"What's that, Lydia?" he asked.

"All the things there are to know in this world. It pleasures the mind to think it's free to lay claim to such a treasure." She was gathering up the books she and Fayte had been studying a little while earlier.

"Makes a feller wonder what reason he's got for being here," Mark said. "So much gone before, so much to come after. What knowledge or use does almighty God have of us, me, a-being here right now?"

She looked at him in surprise. She had not heard Mark speak so before. "Why, I guess a body can't say exactly. I remember old Elijah Gudger used to preach we were all a part of a pattern too big for our mortal eyes to behold."

He nodded, still looking at the glowing coals. Lydia noticed how many grey streaks were coming in Mark's dark, crisp hair. She had seen, during the summer and autumn, how often his heavy shoulders seemed to slump with weariness and discouragement. Since Burn and Gib had left, Lydia and Fayte and Jessie had tried to take their place in the fields, but they were a poor substitute. Crops had been short this fall, but even then they had barely got everything harvested before winter set in. Lydia had picked most of the apples herself, cherishing every specimen as she laid the firm, good ones back for eating during cold weather, and cooked or dried the faulty windfalls.

At least she was glad Mark had not planted tobacco, as the boys had wanted. Suddenly all those who were growing rich by tobacco were now being made poor by it. For the first time, the welfare of many of the people on Thickety Creek had become dependent on the outside world, on the habits and fashions of people living a long distance away, and their prosperity was vulnerable in a way they had never known before. All at once, it seemed, flue-cured tobacco such as they raised here in the North Carolina hills, was no longer popular. In addition, some spoke of a tobacco syndicate that had been formed and was running many of the scattered little warehouses, including those in Nantahala County, out of the business. The swift decline was all puzzling and a little frightening.

As if he had been following Lydia's thoughts, Mark sighed and stood up. "Guess we don't have to settle it all tonight," he said, and stretched his arms above his head with a wide yawn.

"I guess not." Lydia covered the fire and picked up the lamp.

"You know, Lyddy, we mustn't be forgetting about those fellers in at the courthouse," Mark said. "You and Fayte and Jessie seem to be making out pretty good by yourselves, but we've got to keep them prodded or we'll never have a schoolhouse for Thickety Creek."

"You're right, Mark." She smiled at him, across the smoky lamp chimney. "Do the weather fair up, we can go the first of the week."

"We'll ask Clay Thurston to ride in with us this time."

But their trip the following week was like all the others had been for the past year. In narrow, dingy offices, men of authority, who seemed agreeable enough and in symapthy with their need, listened to their petition and gave assurances they would "study the situation."

"Er-ah," Clay Thurston said, "you gentlemen have er-ah had a chance to study the building of a school longer than the scholars have had a chance to study their books in it."

One of the men frowned and ran a thumb and forefinger over his carefully trimmed mustache. "Well, my dear sir," he said, "that may be true. But we have more applicants for funds, too, than we have funds. The state provides us only so much money for school construction, and that is mighty little. Since the war, we're not a rich state." He looked at Mark and at Clay Thurston and smoothed the mustache again. "We were defeated in that war and we're still paying the penalty. Our taxpayers have only a token of money for schools, or anything else. You must wait your turn."

Lydia was puzzled by the man's words. Everyone knew that money was scarce, especially tax money, but she also knew that the time had long since come when Thickety Creek's schoolhouse was due to be built.

Mark and Clay Thurston needed to go to the harness shop and while they were there Lydia went to Robert's law office. After he had seated her on a new horsehair chair and she had given him the little news of the valley and their father's health, she told him about the visit to the courthouse.

"The men we see, they won't say they're against us—that's what makes it so hard to talk to them. Every time they seem to agree with us, but then they just don't do anything. They don't deny Thickety Creek should have a school. They don't appear to oppose it any way. They just don't do anything. That's all it takes to kill a school—or anything else."

"Whoa, whoa!" Robert held up his hand. "Tell me what, exactly, the men you spoke with said."

Lydia repeated the strange comments the man at the courthouse had made and she asked Robert their meaning.

As he listened, his face changed expression and when she had finished, he stood up and pushed back his desk chair impatiently. "How could I have been so stupid?" he exploded. "All this time and I didn't even think of it, but of course Ham Nelson has used that against you, all along."

"What, Robert? What are you saying?"

"The county administration is totally Democratic now. Mark's a Republican."

"But he's not in politics——" Lydia began.

"He votes," Robert said. "He votes Republican, he fought Republican in the war. You don't understand, Lydia, these things make a difference here, to men who live by politics. And I'm sure Ham Nelson has used Mark's party to work against you."

"But a school, Robert . . . it wasn't anything just for ourselves."

"Ham was against it, and he's been in thick as cream with this present courthouse group," Robert said shortly. "Of course, Clay Thurston is an outspoken Republican, too. . . ."

"Mark never thought, when he asked him to come. Clay is an upstanding citizen; we hoped he might have some influence."

"I'm sure he did, the opposite way!" Robert said. Then, seeing Lydia's troubled face, he seemed to remember this was his sister sitting before him. "Don't fret. Now that we're onto Ham Nelson's game, we'll scheme up a way to scotch it."

"Mark won't ever change his party——" Lydia began. This talk of games and schemes distressed her. The whole matter seemed so simply one of need and right.

"I'm aware of that." Robert smiled the small secret smile she had noticed for many months. "No"—he leaned back in his chair, the picture, it seemed to her, of success and a special knowledge of how large affairs are managed—"we'll point out to these gentlemen, and some of those over at the state capitol, too, if it's necessary, that your father and your brother were soldiers in the Confederate army, one was wounded, that they now vote a good Democratic ticket—that, indeed, our family lost a great deal in the late war." He's already speaking as if he's before a jury, Lydia thought.

"Will that make a difference?" she asked.

"We'll try to see that it does. We'll point out that they have been following divisive leadership from our neck of Nantahala County." He picked up a paperweight from his desk. "You know, Lydia, I've thought I might try to run for some political office one of these days."

"Then do it!" she said.

"That's my Lydia." He smiled at her, and this time it was more like the old free humor she remembered so well in his boyish face. "Always boosting me to go ahead. You almost make me believe I'd stand a chance."

She recalled his speeches at the July Fourth celebrations through the years, his ease in establishing friendliness at the infare and everywhere she had ever seen him, and she nodded. "You'd be elected."

He winked at her. She was relieved to see that the mask he seemed to wear these days could be cracked a little. "I'll help you get your school, you help me get elected. By heaven, we already sound like horse-trading politicians." They laughed together, but she knew he meant everything he had said, that he had confided to her one of his deepest wishes. The knowledge made her happy.

Robert was right about Ham's information to the county officials concerning Mark's politics and those of some of the other people in the valley. Robert told them that Lydia's family held opposite political views, however.

"We been taking Nelson's word for things out there," the man with the neat mustache explained. "He seems to keep his end of the county in the Democratic column. Not that the way people vote has anything to do with the school-building arrangements, but we have to go by community needs. We'll try to re-examine the need on Thickety Creek. We do the best we can."

"All a man can do," Robert agreed. His voice was bland.

But even in the new light thrown on the situation, there would be no more money for buildings until the next school year. Education was hard to come by in the mountains; education and money, and each waited on the other.

Late in February, Mark and Lydia took Fayte to the doctor again.

"Eyes better," he said. "Another six months and they'll be fully recovered."

"Are you sure, doctor?" Fayte asked.

"Lad, what I'm not sure of, doesn't cross my tongue."

"Then it looks like I've a heap more reading to do," Lydia said.

Through the spring and into the summer, at night after ploughing and planting and making crops, on rainy days and Sundays and during spare moments, she read deeper and deeper into the books Professor Duncan had left. She would not let the boy grow discouraged. He repeated lessons after her, memorized page after page, learned difficult spelling and how to figure in his head. They grew tired, but neither one would admit it to the other. This was an unspoken pact between them. It seemed to Lydia that she knew every expression, every line and pore of her youngest son's round, eager face, so constantly had it been turned up toward hers during this year of struggle to learn together.

"Am I doing all right, Mama?" he would ask sometimes, and

she could see herself reflected in the precious grey eyes looking into her own.

"Again Professor Duncan comes back, you'll be ready to take that examination for going into college." She admitted only to herself that it might be easier for him to pass the test than for Mark and her to raise the money to let him get even a start in college.

Times were growing hard, recalling the days right after the war. The spring season was unusually dry. Early crops failed altogether and late plantings were stunted. Crows stripped the cornfields and Mark and the other men had to take valuable time off from their work and shoot them until there were piles of the dead birds on every farm.

Lydia's flock of chickens, which she had improved and increased through the years, was ravaged by hawks. Mark finally killed or frightened all of them away from the farm—all except one. He was a medium-sized red-tailed hawk with an unusual wingspread. At first he was bold and careless, and twice at midday Lydia rushed out of the house, in response to the chickens' startled flight for cover, in time to see the shadow of those outspread wings pass across the yard. After Mark's careful aim had once come close to him, however, the bird grew wary. He attacked at different hours, picking off an isolated chick or hen here and there. Once, when she was by herself, Lydia came upon the hawk late of an afternoon in the barnyard. For a strange still moment she looked into the fierce, glittering, unflinching eyes. Then those great wings, carefully patterned as a patchwork quilt but more intricate, more delicate, spread in sudden flight and with a snap of powerful beak and a feathery rush of wind the hawk was gone—part of the high, rare atmosphere above this little patch of earth. She watched it disappear. "It's a thing of beauty," she said to herself in astonishment and wonder.

And although she could not bring herself to tell the others how she had come to feel about the hawk—no longer wanting it killed, admiring its loneliness and fierceness—she never again called Mark to bring his gun when she saw the red-tail hovering high above their farm.

Gardens were poor and Lydia's survived only because she and

Fayte and Jessie carried bucket after bucket of water from the spring to keep tender roots alive. The effort seemed worth while to Lydia whenever she saw a wilted yellow plant stand up and begin to grow again. Now that tobacco was no longer a money crop, empty fields, ragged with weeds and neglect, dotted the valley and the mountainsides. Winter rains had washed gullies down some of the steeper ones. They were an ugly sight.

That August, Gentry Caldwell decided to hold a revival meeting in the valley. He built a brush arbor on the ill-tended farm he had bought soon after the end of the war. "Damnation and hell fire, temptation and redemption, those are my subjects, good brothers and sisters," he trumpeted up and down Thickety Creek, and beyond. "Come and get yourself saved, and help set this poor old sinful world straight," he commanded, and they came from all over Thickety, and beyond.

In the hot summer nights when a breathless hush of weariness and expectancy lay over the valley, the men with sunburned arms and necks and faces, the women with sagging shoulders and freshly smoothed hair, the barefooted tough-skinned children, eager for companionship and excitement, gathered to hear the word of Gentry Caldwell. They sat on the rough slab benches, women to the front, the men toward the back. The women were calm and attentive at the beginning. A few of the men were uneasy and stood outside the arbor until the last minute when their wives motioned them inside. They sang with no accompaniment but the katydids and crickets in the surrounding fields, their voices cracked and exuberant, and they prayed simple earnest prayers. Then Gentry's voice took over.

He asked the questions that had troubled Mark one night by the fire, the questions that had stirred deep in the minds of many of these men and women as they sat beside their hearths of a winter night and heard the wind sweep down from the mountains and felt their lonely cabins shake in the icy blast; or as the fog of autumn closed in over the valley and isolated each person, each place, in a damp, impenetrable, absolutely silent mystery. They were questions of spirit as well as mind, of old, dark fears clutching toward new bright hopes, the questions that are forever answered and never answered. Why am I here? What is the meaning and fulfillment of the years between an unchosen birth and an unsought death? Where and what is the ending? At the close of this life? Or another? Or is there, after all, eternity and immortality?

They neither put the questions so precisely nor did Gentry answer them deeply, but it was the darkness of these fears he stirred and fed.

With relish and vigor in the warm throbbing nights he described the geography, the purposes, the everlastingness of Hell. With venom and some familiarity he talked of the sins of the world, which were the sins of men's appetites, and these were drunkenness and fornication and pridefulness of spirit. Gentry Caldwell's shirt was soaked with sweat and his forehead gleamed as he spoke, several times, of the dark aliens who stayed apart from other men and poisoned the valley with strong drink, which was a mocker. He described the lusts of the flesh to a motionless audience.

The night he preached on the doom of pride, Dolly Moore was converted. During the last ten years Dolly had grown too plump; her waist and stomach sagged shapelessly beneath the costly dresses she wore, and her neck and arms were heavy with layers of fat. Her face had remained pretty, however, with its pink cheeks and the petulant smile of its rosebud mouth. As Dolly had become stouter she had become more quarrelsome. Paul, working steadily, wordlessly, at the mill or at home, could never please her, and neither could Tim nor Pru. Tim, who finished school at the academy in town in the spring, refused to return home. He explained to Paul, "For you I would come, Papa. But I can't abide Mama's everlasting nagging. Ham Nelson's helped me get a job at the courthouse."

Many had gone to the mourner's bench during the weeks of Gentry Caldwell's preaching. Many had ask forgiveness of their sins and asserted their conversion to a religious life. Many were ready for baptism in the river when the revival should come to an end. Dolly's coming forward was a special triumph for Gentry. She was daughter to Thomas Hawkins and wife to Paul Moore, who owned the mill on Thickety and were known as prosperous, stable men. She was daughter-in-law to Jesse Moore, who was venerated above all other residents of the valley. And she was full of tears and shouting; her feelings were contagious, and while the gathering sang "The Old Rugged Cross," several other women and six children followed Dolly to the front.

Gentry was beside himself with astonishment at the power of his own words, with pride in the tumult of feeling swelling through this group of people, and with ambition for the meetings yet to come. He welcomed Dolly as a sister and invited her to bring others to the great fellowship of confession and conversion.

The next day Dolly gave away her fancy clothes, the hats with lovely sweeping plumes, dresses with lace insertions in the yokes and sleeves, a long velvet cloak with embroidered collar and lapels. She took Prudence to the revival and would not rest until Paul went with them; the girl was converted the next night, and a few days later Paul consented quietly to baptism in the fellowship.

Dolly went up on the mountain to see Lydia and Mark. "I declare it's a sight, the power that's been laid on that Gentry Caldwell. Never, never, never have I been as happy, have I been as content as I am at this minute, and it's because I know, I *know* I'm right with the Lord and I'll spend eternity with Him. Won't you-all come down and just hear the word?"

"I never took much to the Caldwells——" Lydia began.

"You can't be mean and little, Lydia; I've never known you to be that," Dolly said. "I'm asking you to come as a special favor, come and take supper with us and then——"

"No"—Lydia smiled at her—"we won't come for supper, Dolly. But we're laying off to go down and see Papa one day soon, and does it suit Mark, we'll stay on through the evening and come to the preaching."

"That would suit me, Lydia," Mark said.

August lay humid and heavy and waiting over the land. Crops were blasted. Folks brought their terror and their hope, raw as an open wound, to Gentry Caldwell's brush arbor. Lydia and Mark went on a Friday night.

14th

CHAPTER

"Who'd ever a-thought my boy would be the instrument of getting Mark McQueen to make a profession of faith?" Emma Caldwell, excited and triumphant, asked Lydia after the services.

But looking back, months later, on that Friday night when Mark walked down to the row of benches in front of Gentry Caldwell and joined the church, Lydia decided that it was not so much Gentry Caldwell to whom Mark had responded as to a combination of need long accumulated and mood scarce recognized.

In the twenty-six years of their marriage, Mark had never stopped asking "why"—not once in a while, in the way of most men, but as a constant prod and irritant, until Lydia had been reminded of a high-spirited horse that could not settle to the harness because of a sharp cockleburr buried beneath the hames or belly strap. For years after the war, he had asked it in awful anger; following David's death, he had asked the unspoken question in sorrow; then, as the first fruits of his laborious farming had begun to diminish and he saw his land grow thin and poor, his questioning had come from pure skepticism: was there even need to wonder why? But hate or grief or puzzlement, his dark eyes had haunted

273

Lydia—when he was far away in the West or when he was only across the table from her. She had lived with him and loved him tenderly and passionately, in the morning's work no less than the evening's rest, and yet she had not been able to answer, or even ask, this question that haunted him and drove him.

She, too, sometimes wondered, and thus she could sympathize with Mark, but the living of each day with those who depended on her absorbed Lydia so totally, in all her senses and muscles and mind, that she could not forego the pressures and pleasures of the present for need to be certain of the future. Somehow the future was built of the minutes of now, anyway, and to lose them was to lose all, both today and tomorrow.

But Mark believed he had found an answer on that Friday night in August under Gentry Caldwell's brush arbor. The night was hot, with an occasional cool evening breeze from the mountains, and the scent of honeysuckle hung sweet upon the air. Before the services began, the drone of voices in the soft twilight, as men and women greeted one another and spoke of corn and gardens and haying and the day's events, was like the hum of giant bees storing honey. Then, as they sang together, the simple tunes poured forth like soothing syrup, and old enmities and suspicions were forgotten in momentary fellowship. After the singing, Gentry spoke.

Lydia was ashamed to admit later, even to herself, that she heard very little of what Gentry said. She heard him take his text, "Vanity of vanities, saith the Preacher, vanity of vanities, all is vanity," but then she began to think of Martha, expecting a baby again: what should she do, she wondered, to help her daughter insure that this baby would go full term?

And Lydia thought of Fayte and the end of his second six months, and what the doctor might say to them at this visit. Would all her hours on hours on hours of reading bear fruit? Her thoughts rambled on, punctuated here and there by an especially loud shout from Gentry in his makeshift pulpit, and then by "amen" shouts from some of the crowd. The day just finished had been a long hard one and she rested her weary back and limbs as

274

best she could on the stiff bench and enjoyed the cool, sweet air of evening.

How the valley was growing! She remembered one of Elijah Gudger's first visits to her father and mother's, when she was a girl, and he had preached to a room full of people, all of Thickety Creek. Now there were some whose names she did not even know, and several whose homes she had never visited. She looked around more closely. Here and there she recognized babies she had helped birth.

The thought of babies coming brought Martha's grave, youthful face before her. How was the girl feeling, over in that wild country where Tom had gone to cut out a stand of virgin timber? Lydia remembered Martha's disappointment and suffering when she had lost her first baby, a boy six months along, last year. She closed her eyes and breathed a small prayer that all would go well this time.

And almost unconsciously she included a prayer, as she had each day since they were gone, for Burn and Gib. "Wherever they are, be with my boys tonight."

Even as she spoke the words over and over in her mind, "Be with them tonight, be close . . ." she felt Mark move beside her.

"I'm going up, Lyddy," he said. "Gentry Caldwell's words about a prideful spirit, maybe that's the sin that has dogged me all these years. I want to be free of it."

"Why, yes, Mark."

And there had been amazement and great rejoicing, weeping and shouting and shaking of hands, as Mark joined—for the first time since the end of the war and his withdrawal to the mountain —the community of Thickety Creek. He might be headed for the Kingdom of God, but first he had acknowledged their fellowship. This they understood.

Lydia found a change in Mark during the days that followed. At last he seemed to have found a measure of peace. He read at length in the Bible, laboriously, carefully, and he pondered on what he read. He and Lydia and Fayte and Jessie went to the all-day revival gatherings on Saturdays and Sundays when the wagons and carriages and horses were crowded thick on the road, bringing people who could not come to night preaching through the week. Families spread their dinners and suppers under the trees, some boiled or fried or roasted hot food, and the pungent smell of brewing coffee filled the field and arbor.

When they had finished eating, they gathered once more and Gentry Caldwell fed them on hell-fire and damnation. Many professed a new faith, some quietly, almost shyly, with deep conviction and sincerity, while most came with shouting and crying and hugging of neighbor and preacher and family. Then the singing might go on for hours while children fell asleep from plain exhaustion and some backslider wrestled with his soul, succumbing at last to the mourner's bench amidst new shouts and tears and songs.

On the farm the days went along as usual, from morning milking to the final household chore. The red-tail hawk made inroads on a gang of late fryers Lydia was raising; Mark threatened to leave the fields and lie in wait in the barnyard a whole day, if necessary, to get the hawk, but Lydia discouraged him from doing this. She could not explain the reason, but she did not want the hawk killed. "No need to neglect the crops," she said to Mark. "We'll need every scrap we raise this year. I expect everything will be dear."

The last week in August the doctor at the county seat told Lydia and Fayte that the boy's eyes were restored to health. "Wear your glasses when you read, even a few words. Otherwise, wear them or not, as you please. No more straining, understand?"

"Yes, sir," Fayte said. He stood up. Lydia thought he stood two inches taller than when he came into the office.

"What are you going to do now, young chap?" the doctor asked.

"Finish my studies. Go to one of the academies if I can. My mother has been reading my lessons to me."

The doctor raised his bushy white eyebrows and tilted back in his chair. "Oh? And how long have you been studying in this fashion?" he asked.

"Ever since my eyes went bad," Fayte said. "A year and three weeks, I calculate."

276

The doctor looked at Lydia sharply. He nodded. "Good luck," he said and stood up, too, "though it strikes me you're the sort of folks make your own luck." He shook hands with them and said to Fayte, "Come see me again in six, eight months. Don't fail."

"No, sir." Fayte's face, which had always seemed to Lydia so like David's, expressive and vulnerable, broke into a wide grin.

They were eager to share their relief and joy with Mark and they did not stop to see anyone, even Robert, in town or on the way home. As soon as the buggy swung into the yard and they saw Mark coming up from the spring, Fayte called out the doctor's good news.

"Thank God," Mark said. "Maybe this is a gift to us, a sign——"

"No, Mark!" Lydia cried impulsively as she climbed down from the seat. "It's all a gift, the good or bad, the living or dying, but don't say it's a sign: how could we ever bear the sorrow or the joy of it if we had to be a-wondering what we had done to deserve either?" She looked from one to the other of them and saw that neither of them understood what she had wanted to say.

"All right, Lydia," Mark said, "call it whatever you please, we're thankful for the boy's sight——"

"Merciful God, yes," Lydia said.

"And now I've got a surprise for you. Guess who's yonder in the house?"

Lydia glanced quickly toward the door. "Grandpa Moore?" Fayte asked. "Burn? Gib?"

"Pretty close. Martha it is! Why don't you get on in there and see her," he teased, "instead of standing around out here gabbling like geese?"

Lydia was already halfway to the kitchen.

After supper Martha told them she had ridden over to Thickety Creek with Clay Thurston, who had been to check up on Tom's sawmill work. "It's the most beautiful country you ever laid eyes on, over there where we're a-living," she said. "There are stands of forest look as though no human foot had ever walked in them. But, oh, it's lonesome beyond belief."

Strangely, the words shocked Lydia. The girl was like her in so many ways, yet it occurred to her that she had never been lonely in her life. There had been times, were times now, when she longed to see a certain person—Burnett's slow grin, Gib's quick wink and ready laugh—or to be with someone special, but that was not the loneliness Martha meant, a hunger simply for other people, anyone, to provide human companionship. In the woods and mountains, her orchard and her spring, Lydia had always found a deep companionship she could not name or describe. It anchored her, with a firmness and trueness she scarcely suspected, against the buffeting tides of change, of coming and going, loss and gain.

"We're glad to have you home for a spell," she said to Martha, patting her daughter's arm with a big, work-roughened hand. "You've been feeling pretty well?"

Martha nodded, and her cheeks flushed. "The baby's not due till February. I'm trying to make sure everything will go right this time."

"You'll have to come here and stay with us," Mark said. "Your mama and little sister here will look after you, and Fayte and I will do whatever we can."

"We'll see, Papa." Martha smiled at him. "I hate to leave Tom over there so long by himself."

"He's got all that timber crew," Mark said.

"I reckon I mean without me," Martha answered.

"You an old married woman now and talking any such a way!" they teased her.

When Martha left, at the end of the week, they missed her more than they ever had before. "Seems like the house has never been so quiet," Mark said the next day after she had gone.

"Why does everybody go away?" Jessie cried. "I want my sister and my brothers to come back and live with us again. Nothing ever happens up here . . ."

"Jessica, Jessica," Lydia soothed her.

"Do you be good and help your mama, we'll go down to the valley to preaching tomorrow," Mark promised her. "You'll see people a-plenty there."

In mid-September Gentry Caldwell announced that the revival was coming to a close. On the last Sunday, Paul's family and Lydia's went to their father and Elizabeth's for the midday meal. When the afternoon preaching was over, they gathered again at Jesse Moore's. Lydia was in the familiar old kitchen when Dolly cornered her.

Ever since Dolly's shouting conversion, she had seemed, to Lydia, much like a child with some new-found sweet: she wanted to seize it all at once, completely, wholly, and devour it. Once upon a time she had wanted the best dresses and hats in the valley; now she wanted the best religion. And in order for hers to be special, she was driven to question the power or perfectness of other experiences. She was worried, she told Lydia, by the quietness of Mark's conversion.

"To be downright honest, don't look like he's so different now from what he was before," she said. "I can't see Mark's habits or ways have spruced up much."

"Where his changes be, maybe mortal eyes can't look," Lydia answered.

The young folks were out in the yard; Paul and Mark had walked down to the barn with Elizabeth to see the calf her cow had dropped the day before; Lydia's father was in the next room looking through a new book Paul had just brought him from Robert. The afternoon was growing late and Lydia was eager to start back home. She wanted no long, drawn-out argument with Dolly, and certainly nothing that would upset her father.

"Course we can't see a body's heart," Dolly retorted, "or his mind, but we can tell from actions how anybody really feels. That's why I gave away all my pretty finery of the flesh, so folks would have an outer sign of how good I feel inside. That's what I'm talking about with Mark. I can't see a sign——"

Lydia sighed. "Dolly, Dolly, you mustn't be so concerned about the state of other souls——"

"And you mustn't treat me like I was a silly child, Lydia!" Dolly cried. "You say Mark has lost all that old hate that used to gnaw at him——"

Lydia nodded.

"You say the war's finally over for him and he's even forgiven the band of outliers——"

"I hope so."

Lydia wanted to get away from Dolly's prying questions and frantic face. If this agitation was any sign of her present state, surely she had not found peace.

"But how do you *know* he's different? Does he *know* if he's saved? Forgiveness is hard come by——"

"There's nothing else left, Dolly," Lydia said.

"But what if he knew who they were?"

Something in Dolly's voice arrested Lydia. They looked at each other for a long moment.

"We *don't* know," Lydia said.

"*You* don't."

"What are you telling me, Dolly?"

She gave a little toss of her head, the way she had done when she was a girl and someone had crossed her and she had determined to plunge on and do as she wished, careless of any plea or warning. "I can tell Mark and you who it was informed the outliers your mama had the best livestock and smokehouse left in the valley."

Lydia stared at her. Dolly's words reverberated through the kitchen. Then all was still.

"I've held the secret all these years," Dolly went on. "I knew it could only end in bad blood if I told you or any of your folks, or even Paul."

"Then he didn't know?" Lydia murmured.

"No," Dolly said. "But now religion and conversion has come to this valley and our secrets can be brought out to the light, our forgiveness can be put to test——"

"Who was it?" Lydia asked. She felt oddly remote and dizzy, as if she stood at the brink of some sharp precipice. Dolly started to shake her head. "Tell me!" Lydia spoke sharply.

"Gentry Caldwell," Dolly said.

"Gentry——" Lydia stopped. She did not believe it. All at once she realized that she herself had made some grievous mistakes of judgment all these years. She might stand in need of some forgiveness herself. "But why Gentry?"

"He got two gold pieces. Hadn't anybody in these parts seen a gold piece for years before those raiders come. And to save his own mama's farm and food, he told them about yours."

Lydia remembered the land, the very place where the revival had been held, that Gentry bought just after the close of the war, paid for, no doubt, by the gold. The sight of Gentry, fat with rich food, steaming and exhorting in the late summer heat, flashed across Lydia's mind. And her mother's face, too—small, pinched, withdrawn—came clearly before her.

"What about Gentry Caldwell?" Jesse Moore stood in the door, glasses pushed up on his forehead, one finger between the pages of the book he was reading.

"Papa——"

"What were you talking about?" He looked straight at Dolly.

"I was telling Lydia the revival should have made us forgive——"

"What do we have to forgive Gentry Caldwell?" he asked.

"Papa"—Lydia went to him and laid her hand on his bony shoulder. Very gently and very clearly she said—"Papa, Dolly tells us it was Gentry Caldwell who directed the outliers to our place here back in the spring of 'sixty-five."

His face grew even paler than usual, but he did not flinch. "How do you know, Dolly?" he asked, and Lydia wondered why that hadn't been her first question, too.

"Oh, I know, I know." And all at once she burst into tears. "It's hateful to me to carry the burden of knowing any longer. But now we can all truly forgive and forget. We can put our Christianity to test. I want Paul to take me home." She ran from the room, a heavy-set woman with red, tear-streaked face, but to Lydia she seemed as thoughtless and impulsive and destructive as she had been when she was still a girl.

Paul and Mark were coming from the barn. They met Dolly on the porch.

"I told them!" she cried. "I've unburdened my heart and now I'm free. The truth can make you free, too, Mark."

"Hush, Dolly, quieten down." Paul hurried to his overwrought wife and spoke softly. "What has——"

Lydia appeared in the doorway. By the look on her face, Paul and Mark knew at once that whatever was happening, it was no trifling matter; something important had taken place, or was about to.

"Mark, Paul . . ." Lydia began, saying both their names but looking at Mark, trying in the same moment to foretell and forestall whatever might happen. "Dolly says she knows who led the outliers to plunder——"

"It was Gentry Caldwell!" Dolly burst out, unwilling to relinquish her moment of drama, fearful of the consequences but excited, too. In the back of her mind, the thought struck Lydia: Why, she would have risked everything—our peace, our honor, our effort to lay hold of religion—just to be part of some excitement. That's all she understands of this revelation she's made to us.

Dolly was telling these two the same scanty facts she had already told Lydia.

Mark's face held the look of a man who is struck a vital, unexpected blow. He struggled to absorb the shock of this knowledge he had sought so long and bitterly, and finally become resigned to never finding. Now, suddenly, it was thrust upon him. "How do you know?" he asked.

"Yes, Dolly," Paul said, "all these years—how did you know?"

She stared at them, hesitated, started to speak and hesitated again. "Don't you understand a-tall?" she asked them. "It don't matter who did it, or how I know, but that you forgive them. It would be vanity of the sinfulest sort to carry on a grudge after——"

"Are you telling us truth, Dolly?" Before any of them knew what he was doing, Mark had suddenly taken the chattering, agitated woman by the shoulders and was shaking her. "Was Gentry Caldwell the one?"

"Yes. I swear. It's gospel truth." She was trembling with excitement and fright.

"But how can you be so sure?" Paul's face was full of pain and disgust. He looked old beyond his years.

282

Paul did not frighten Dolly, although she seemed taken aback at the look on his face. She stopped trembling. "I won't tell you that. I can't. There's no need."

Unnoticed, Jesse Moore had come onto the porch.

"I'll see Caldwell," Mark said, and swung abruptly toward the steps.

"Mark"—Lydia ran to him—"you can't go till you've collected your wits. Things have stood this way for twenty-five, twenty-six years now, they can stand a little longer, till you know what you're about. Come in the house, Papa, Mark, Paul, everyone. I'll make up coffee and then we'll see what has to be done." As she talked she guided Mark and her father into the house. She could feel the resistance of Mark's arm as he pulled against her, but she persisted, talking, belying the turmoil that churned in her own mind and blood. They came into the kitchen and she remembered that morning when her mother's hands had been so tender. Dear God, she must not think about it now.

She was able to divert them for a moment, but she could not make Mark wait till tomorrow before seeing Caldwell. Her father and Paul agreed with him.

"This is something must be attended to, Lydia," Jesse Moore said.

"But Papa Moore—"

"Be still, Dolly," her father-in-law said patiently. Then he added, and at any other time Lydia suspected there would have been a twinkle in his eye, "Remember there's a passage in your Good Book that says, 'Be still and know that I am God.' "

The young people, Pru and Fayte and Jessie, had come in and were watching and listening in bewildered silence. When Elizabeth came up from milking, Lydia told her what had happened. At remembrance of that dreadful night in the past, Elizabeth threw her arms around Lydia and buried her face on her older sister's shoulder. Gently, Lydia lifted her arms away and said, "Elizabeth, you and Dolly will have to look after the young'uns for us a little while. . . ."

"Mama, you talk like we were babies," Fayte began, then hushed.

"Where you going, Lyddy?" Mark asked.

"With you and Papa and Paul to see Gentry Caldwell."

"I can't let you. This is men's affairs."

She and Mark had not had a serious difference for a long while, but she answered him steadily now. "It wasn't only men's affairs the night it happened. I'm the only one of you was here that night."

There was quiet in the kitchen. Dolly, frightened and subdued, looked from one to the other of them. Jesse Moore nodded slowly, with the sadness of an old man who has met many revelations.

"You're right, Lyddy," Mark said. "Whether you go or stay, it's not for me to say."

It was dark by the time they reached the Caldwell home. As they drove back up in the yard and hitched their horse, they could barely see Gentry climb out of a hammock swung between two oak trees and come toward them with his ready greetings. He seemed surprised to see the four of them. Lydia wondered what he would have felt if he could fully see the expressions on their faces. Coming down the valley none of them had spoken. Each was locked in his own memory and thought.

"Just taking my ease in the cool of the evening, now that meeting's over." Gentry was talking to them in his "pulpit voice," Lydia realized. "A long hard meeting, but fruitful in the church's harvest . . ." He led them into the yard; they would not go to his house. A pale light outlined their faces, made them faintly visible to one another as they stood under the dome of stars that arched above them. "All up and down the creek, the good people are still rejoicing, Mark, that you——"

"We've a little business to talk over, Gentry," Mark interrupted.

The tone of Mark's voice halted Gentry's easy flow of talk. "All right, Brother McQueen," he said.

"This has taken a heap of time, Gentry. But now it won't take hardly any time a-tall. Just answer us one question: during the spring of 'sixty-five, near the close of the war, did you direct a gang of outliers to the Moore farm?"

The question hung there in the darkness.

"We've come to know," Jesse Moore said.

At last, barely audible, came Gentry Caldwell's answer.

"Yes."

One of them let out a breath. Lydia thought it was her father. He shouldn't be here, she thought. It will go hard with him, reliving Mama's agony. . . .

"You turned that pack on a defenseless household?" Mark's voice was savage. Lydia knew how he would look, if Gentry Caldwell could see him: taut and powerful as a drawn bow waiting to release its shafted arrow. His eyes would be blacker than this night, the pupils solidly, brilliantly dark. "You loosed those varmints on women and children?"

"God help me, yes."

"And yet you can get up and preach, you can mouth the word of the Bible and pretend to save men's souls?" Mark demanded. "What sort of hypocrite, what make of beast are you?"

"I'll be damned," Paul whispered.

"No"—Gentry Caldwell caught it up desperately—"I'm the one who was damned. Do you think it's been an easy knowledge to live with all these years? It's been a millstone choking me, the thorn in my flesh from which there seemed no deliverance."

"But why?"

"They threatened my mother and me and our farm"—the words were tumbling out now, feverishly, franticly—"and when they saw we didn't have anything left worth taking, they said they'd burn us out if I didn't help. And they never mentioned harming anyone. It was only food and livestock they wanted. They claimed the armies needed it."

"They claimed!" Mark said. "But you knew their habit, how they'd plundered a dozen other places through the mountains——"

"What else could I do? Are you sure you'd have done different?"

The question struck them like a blow. They were angry men, suffering from an old wound reopened, but they were fair. A sound like a sob broke from Jesse Moore's throat.

Then Lydia saw one of the shadowy figures facing Gentry Caldwell leap across the space between them and clutch him by the throat. "Monster," Paul said thickly, "to live amongst us and——"

With half-embarrassed ease, the thickset man loosed the single hand and arm holding him. He pushed Paul aside. With a stumble, Lydia's brother struck against her side, recovered himself and stood, stoop-shouldered, beside her.

Suddenly, with the speed and directness of a lightning bolt, Mark seized Gentry and held him motionless with one arm twisted behind his back. "Don't you touch another one of my kin," Mark said harshly. "Many's the night I've laid awake thinking about killing the man who's turned out to be you, Caldwell. I've plotted your punishment a hundred times."

" 'Vengeance is mine . . . saith the Lord,' " the preacher answered. His voice did not falter as much as Lydia would have expected. Her own voice seemed paralyzed, her body turned to water. She wondered if this might be a dream she was walking through, one of those nightmares so real that when she awoke she would feel heavy and depressed.

"Don't quote Bible to me, a renegade like you!" Mark commanded.

"Don't you think a man can change, Mark McQueen?" Caldwell asked. His arm was still bent behind him in the viselike grip. "You've been paying lip-service to that belief all these weeks past."

"How should a man know what to think when his preacher has played Judas to him and those he loves?"

"I wasn't preacher then, Mark."

"And you're a shameful pretense of one now."

"We're all shameful sinners on this poor old earth."

"Kill him, Mark," Paul said. Lydia, beside him, was shocked at the cruel words of her quiet brother. "Kill him for all the ruin and sorrow he brought. . . ." It seemed to Lydia that in his cry was released all the pent-up resentment and grief of a lifetime of loss and unfulfilled hope and love. She was overwhelmed with pity for him.

"Don't, Paul." She put her arm on his shoulder. "Don't."

"Like I say, we're all sinners, one way or another," Caldwell

said, growing calmer all the time as the first shock of their con-
fronting him wore off. "And I've repented whatever I——"

"That doesn't change it," Mark said.

"It can't change what's past," the other man agreed, "but it can
change me, and what's to come. It's my own suffering lets me know
how much the others need repentance, too."

"What others?" Mark pounced on the words. "Were there
others here in the valley helped that roving gang?"

"Were you of the mind that one man could a-done all the wrong
that they needed for their scheming?" Gentry Caldwell took a step
away from his captor. "Let go your hold on my arm, McQueen,"
he said easily.

"Loose him, Mark." Lydia spoke for the first time that night.
"Let him tell us all he can."

"Why did you come with them, Lydia?" Caldwell asked.

"I was in the valley that night your riders come, Gentry Caldwell. A little later I welcomed your mama when she come to sympathize with us. I've been here ever since. And now I'm waiting
for all the truth, from the mouth of Thickety Grove's preacher.
It's the least you can give us in return."

"I didn't keep the truth out of stinginess, Lydia. I didn't even
keep it all these years out of fear only. You'll understand when I've
unraveled it for you."

"We're waiting, Gentry," she said. The starlight made them all
indistinct and distant, one shadowy form talking to another.

"There isn't much more. But enough, I'd reckon." He rubbed
his free hand, where Mark had gripped the wrist. "After the outliers had robbed your place, they got scared. The army was on
their trail. They sold the livestock they stole from you, sold it off
the next day, so they could travel light.

"Are you a-saying somebody right here in the valley bought our
stock?"

"That's right."

"And who was it?" Mark asked.

"Hamilton Nelson and old man Thomas Hawkins."

"Dolly's father?" Paul choked.

"Him." Caldwell's voice was growing more confident. "Hawkins was just setting up that fine new mill and Nelson was a-helping him. Nelson was supposed to be away in the army but he was home more than anybody knew—foraging food and supplies for his outfit, so he said. Nelson had it all studied out, how they could buy cheap the stolen stock the outliers brought in, then fatten it up on their tolls from the corn at the mill, and sell it off to whichever army would pay best for it. He got Hawkins to go in with him . . ."

"They bought Papa's livestock?"

"And sold it off a couple of weeks later. By that time, none of the armies argued about whether animals they got were fat or not. If anything on four legs could make a shadow, it was taken. Nelson and Hawkins, they turned a tidy profit on the deal."

They stood stunned and silent before his revelations.

Presently Caldwell spoke again, his voice easier, finding words more readily. "Then after Paul come home from the war and married Dolly Hawkins, I kind of got to figuring justice had come a full round. Paul was in with old man Hawkins at the mill and they prospered, and it looked like part of what was taken from you folks would be going back to some of you, anyway."

"My God, my God," Paul was saying over and over.

There was a short silence before Lydia spoke. "You really meant we were all sinners together, unbeknownst or not, didn't you?"

"And all forgiven if we choose to be," Caldwell answered, as if by rote. "We cannot take these things too hard. Old wrongs can crucify us. I've done you ill and I ask forgiveness. . . ."

But, Lydia thought, there was confidence, not humility, in his voice. He betrayed a strange sort of pride in his willingness to ask forgiveness, not the brotherly sharing of pain which leads a man to cry out in sorrow for forgiveness. Mark had sensed this, too, for he said now, out of fury, "What do you know of those wrongs, Caldwell? What do you know about crucifixion? Ask old man Moore here about his wife, Sarah, or ask my Lydia here about our firstborn. . . ." The words seemed to tear his throat.

288

" 'Judge not, that ye be not judged,' " Caldwell said. "I couldn't know any of those wicked things would happen. '. . . Whatsoever ye——' "

"Words! Words!" Mark flung back. "You'd drink our blood and give us words in return."

"I got no 'returns' from the plunder of your farm," Caldwell said.

"Only your safety," Lydia said.

"Only my safety," he agreed. "But it was Nelson and Hawkins —and you folks—that finally prospered."

"Don't name it to us again, Caldwell," Paul cried, "or I'll——"

"Hold on," Jesse Moore said quietly. He had regained control of his voice. His white hair was the only clearly visible feature of any of the little group talking under the dark oak trees. He spoke slowly. "Mark has said the preacher's talking is just words. It comes to my mind that I've staked a big part of my life on words, on what men have set down in books and passed on down to me, to all of us. Yet I've never put their strength to everyday test before. And none of them is greater than the book the preacher just quoted. I reckon the time has come for me, for us, to see if we can live by the word."

They stood in a silent little cluster under the starlight.

"It's not just idle talk: 'Vengeance is mine . . . saith the Lord.' It's truth! In the gospel, where we read it over and over, calmly, maybe carelessly—or in our guts, tonight, where we feel it burning like hot coals: vengeance is with God."

"And are we to leave him scot-free then?" Mark asked.

The white head bowed lightly. "Could you think of a way Mark, to make him pay for all that's past?"

Lydia answered. "Dear God, no. There's no payment——"

"Then if there can be no repayment," Jesse Moore said, "we must forgive the debt."

The simplicity, the enormity, of the word they had heard mouthed and believed they lived by all their lives, swept over Lydia. The impossibility of their total achievement by any man, coupled with the wonder of every man's effort, staggered her mind.

This, then, was what a glimpse of truth might be like: hard as stone, beautiful as stars, satisfying as bread.

"Mark, Paul, Papa," she said, "let's go home."

"You too, Lydia?" Mark asked. His voice was uncertain.

"Me and you and Paul and all of us. Don't you see? This is why Robert went into law, and why Papa read his books, and why Professor Duncan came to Thickety Creek—and maybe why Gentry Caldwell finally went to preaching: to help us find a way to live together, whether by law or knowledge or instinct or the love of God. And it's part of the reason you went up to the mourner's bench in Gentry's brush arbor, Mark."

"Maybe so, but I never meant to pledge away my manhood."

"Why, you only pledged away your selfhood, son," Jesse Moore said, "your narrow little self for a larger manhood. And now you're up to the lick-log: you've been called to keep that pledge."

For the space of a breath they all stood as still as a tableau, then abruptly, Mark turned and walked out of the yard. Slowly Paul followed him. Lydia and her father were left facing Gentry Caldwell. Lydia put her hand on her father's arm.

"God help you, Gentry Caldwell," Jesse Moore said.

"Mr. Moore, Lydia"—Caldwell's voice was on the verge of breaking; the confidence, the pious tones, had vanished—"I don't know . . ."

Lydia and her father followed the others across the grass and back to the road. They would have a long ride home at this hour of the night.

Along the way they said little, but Lydia finally broke the silence to tell them of the last time she had talked with her mother, when Sarah Moore had asked her if Mark and her father were yet free of hate. "She warned you'd have to let it go," Lydia said.

"It's harder, now we know who it was," Paul said.

"Like a tick buried in the flesh for years and nigh impossible to pluck out, bringing blood as it comes, that's how this hate is with me." Mark rode slightly slouched, talking as much to himself as to the others. At last he added, "But the time for revenge is long gone, I reckon."

As they reached Jesse Moore's house, he spoke. "I'm grateful you told us Sarah's words, Lydia. We wouldn't do aught to mar her memory."

They said good night.

The next morning Mark did not go to the fields. Fayte fed the livestock and went to cut fodder in the upper cornfield. Lydia and Jessie milked and did the household chores. Mark sat in the breezeway and looked up toward the mountain and the woods behind the house. The sourwoods were already turning first red; a warm autumn haze hung over the land.

In the sun-drenched stillness just before noon, a shadow crossed the barn lot. It was the red-tailed hawk. Slowly he swung across the clearing and disappeared above the distant treetops. Mark went into the house and returned with his gun. Carefully he loaded it, then scanned the horizon. The sky was empty. There was no sound anywhere. Chickens wallowed in the dust of the barnyard. He leaned against a porch post, motionless, alert.

Then the shadow drifted down the mountain and across the farm again. Mark lifted the gun to his shoulder slowly and took sight along the barrel. Suddenly the bird wheeled on its course of flight and with a plunge swooped toward one of the pullets on the ground below. Just as its talons were buried in the startled chicken, Mark's shot rang out. The great wings crumpled.

Lydia, down by the spring, heard the shot and came running up to the house. She followed Mark out into the barnyard. The frightened chickens had raised a commotion of feathers and cackling. The red-tailed hawk lay in the dust.

"Well, that settles him," Mark said. With the toe of his boot he turned the bird over.

The wings were an intricate design of white and brown and black. The small head was partially shattered from the shot but one fierce yellow eye remained in its socket, and the beak was like a sharp, hooked slash of steel. The powerful talons were still curved for their last thrusting grasp. In its absolute fierceness the hawk seemed still alive.

As she had known she would be, Lydia was sorry to see this vitality and hunger extinguished. She was sorry to think of the wings brought low that had once lifted so proudly on the morning wind. She looked at the squawking, scurrying hens. Chickens were witless creatures: always frightened, huddling together, losing their senses at the slightest threat, rushing around in a fuss of noise and feathers. To protect these silly fat things, Mark had killed the wild, lean hawk.

She went back to the house and sat down by the kitchen table and put her head in her arms. Mark came, too, and laid his gun on its rack above the door.

"I feel better," Mark said. "At least I've rid the valley of one varmint."

"Yes," she said. Presently she got up from the table and began to fix their dinner.

After they had eaten, while Aunt Tildy and Jessie were clearing the table, she said to Mark, "You remember telling me once that those outliers ruined our lives?"

He nodded.

"I've been thinking, they brought us trouble, all right, but nobody can plumb ruin your life, nobody but yourself. Nor save it, either."

He nodded again, slowly.

No one spoke.

"Well"—she stood up—"I reckon the best we can do then is salvage all we can from any ruins we come across."

"Where there's anything left," Mark said.

Lydia did not look at him. "If you'll not be using the mare tomorrow, I'd be much obliged if you'd saddle her up for me soon tomorrow morning."

"You be going somewhere?"

"I've got an errand down the valley. I'll be back after noon."

With the knowledge Gentry Caldwell had given them last night, she must see Hamilton Nelson once more. Out of their past loss might be reckoned some future gain, as her mother had often said.

15th
CHAPTER

As she rode down the valley in the early morning fog, Lydia marveled, as she had in the past, at the vast indifference of nature to her little human turmoil. Two nights ago, hearing of the treachery and deceit of neighbors she had known almost all her life long, remembering the grief of her mother's broken spirit and her oldest child's broken mind, she had wondered if she could ever feel at home in this place again.

And yet here she was, at the beginning of a fine day in September, with the first rays of the sun burning away the moist fog, revealing familiar trails bordered by thick clumps of shining green galax leaves, tall Solomon's-seal, running partridge vines. The blue jays cried high and lonesome in the distance as they had on hundreds of other mornings she remembered; ground squirrels scurried over the leaves; a wood thrush nearby made the forest ring with its clear melody; the wet smell of rotting logs and leaves and spongy earth rose strong and bitter all around her. She was at home in this woods world that had always been familiar and at the same time always unknown, inviting more exploration.

The fog lifted and Lydia turned in the saddle and looked back at the grey precipice of the Devil's Brow, looming there behind her on the mountainside. Hate and despair, vengeance and satisfaction, all the jagged, cutting, upthrust moments of life—were they, too, worn down by time, sanded by the weather of days and years, like the Devil's Brow, to a smooth hard surface? What was it Robert had said to her once? "You're like one of those insects has too many crawlers and pincers and whiskers, Lydia. You've got too many feelers out into the world. You can get bad hurt that way."

"You can know you're alive that way," she had answered.

Sometimes, as in the past two days, however, you knew you were alive because of the puzzlement and pain. Yet a curious reaction of relief had come over Lydia last night. She knew now, completely and certainly, that the taint of hate and revenge would no longer be eating at Mark's mind. He was, as Dolly in her fanaticism had said he must be, a changed person.

She had pondered her meeting with Hamilton Nelson today, trying to think of some·way it might be avoided, yet certain that only so could anything lasting and good be wrung out of the ugliness of that night long ago. The dread of facing Ham Nelson lay like a stone in her stomach, hung like a millstone around her neck, but she had a plan—and it might work. She prodded her horse. She must meet this bad moment and put it behind her as quickly as possible.

Hamilton Nelson was not at his store. The boy taking his place at the cash drawer explained in a nasal, timid voice that Mr. Nelson was at home, reckoning some lumber accounts. Back in the dim recesses of the store, Lydia saw Ida Burke's old copper apple-butter pot still gathering dust. She thought of the pride the old woman had always taken in the butter she stirred and cooked and spiced in that caldron, and how it must have grieved her to part with it. Lydia resolved to buy Ida Burke's kettle sometime when she got a little extra money ahead.

She had not been on the Nelson farm since the time she and Mark had lived there when they were first married. She was shocked to see how barren the place looked now, and she realized it was because all the trees above the size of a sapling had been cut. Instinctively she looked toward the spring down near the field where the tenant house had been. The tall, straight poplars were gone. From this distance she could make out only a clump of second-growth sprouts and briers, most likely blackberries, around the spring. She wondered what had happened to that bubbling vein of water since all its protection had been taken away.

Ruby, scrubbing the porch with a new corn-shuck broom she had made, flushed with pleasure when she saw her visitor. While Lydia fastened her horse at the hitching block and dismounted, Ruby took the broom and bucket of water into the house. She was untying her threadbare, dirty apron when she came back out.

"Step right in, Mrs. McQueen. It's so little company we have, I'm plumb ashamed to——"

"Never mind, Ruby," Lydia said quickly. "This isn't really a visit. I've come to see Ham on some business. Is he at home?"

The girl's face went bleak with disappointment. Lydia thought she had seldom seen a more worn, more miserable-looking human. "He's home, all right. I'll fetch him." She did not leave the porch so eagerly this time. Lydia felt guilty that she had not taken the time and effort to talk with Ruby a little before asking her to call Ham—the girl obviously dreaded him. But Lydia herself was anxious today. Perhaps later she would find another time to talk with Ruby and be pleasant and neighborly and help her forget the drudge's life she lived.

"Well, now, if it's not Lydia Moore," Ham said, walking through the door slowly, as if he had not completely made up his mind whether he would come and talk with her or not.

"It's Mrs. McQueen," Ruby said carefully behind him.

"I know who it is! I don't need your corrections, girl." He snapped the words at her. "Get on with the churning or whatever it is you've a mind to do back in that pigsty of a kitchen. Get!"

Like a stray cat accustomed to making quick escapes from casual kicks and cruelties, the girl disappeared. Ham came out onto the porch. Lydia was surprised to notice how paunchy he had grown. His stomach sagged over the top of his trousers and strained at the old suspenders he wore. The plumpness of his cheeks had been transformed into jowls and they gave his cynical face a dejected,

295

dissipated look. She wondered if he had ever, even for a moment, seemed handsome to her.

"Well, now, Mrs. Lydia, did you come by to see how I'm a-looking these days, or was there something else on your mind?" She started, realizing she had been staring at him, remembering too how quick and shrewd he was beneath that ponderous manner.

"There was something—on my mind," she said.

"I figured so. Do you want to deliver it standing up"—his eyes looked at her from foot to crown in the old calculating way—"or will you take a chair?"

She started to flush and sat down too hastily in the chair he pushed forward. "Thank you."

"Why, you're welcome." The narrow eyes looked watchful and amused. He settled in a chair just opposite her.

"No need to beat forty ways about the bush. I've come asking you to use your influence, and maybe some of your wealth, too, Ham, toward getting the valley a new school."

He brushed a fly away, annoyed by its buzzing and by Lydia. "Now that about my wealth, everybody seems to forget about the bottom dropping out of the tobacco market hereabouts. And about that school, seems to me we already been through this a time or two, Lydia. You always stirring up some ruckus about a school."

"I wouldn't have to if the school we had was left alone."

He pretended not to hear her. "Again we get good roads in here, we'll find ways to go in with other communities, build one school 'stead of two. It takes time——"

"And all this time a lot of young'uns are growing up without any schooling a-tall. What about them?"

He shrugged. "No school here when I was coming up. I'm not doing the worst in the world."

She bit her tongue, hesitated, and said, "But your mother was educated. I remember her telling my mama once that she'd taught you the multiplication sets a week or so before. Lots of folks hereabouts can't do that for their young'uns. And besides, we want the ones coming on to know more than we——"

"They'll not likely find it in books," he said with disgust. "It's common old horse sense, hard work, a little luck along, that puts a man ahead."

And sometimes, if his name is Hamilton Nelson, doing things other folks wouldn't do, Lydia thought. Aloud, she said, "Books won't rob anybody of his common sense. They'll just give him tools to help him use whatever sense he's got."

"I don't hold with all this public schooling nonsense—and that's that!" He slapped his knee. "No need for everybody to get an education. I don't aim to lift one little finger to help another school open on this creek and keep good tobacco hands out of the field, raise land taxes, get things stirred up."

"Maybe you'll change your mind," Lydia said. She could feel anger warming the chill in her stomach and hands.

"Do you aim to try to make me change my mind?" His eyes were bold.

"Maybe." She rubbed one thumb against a callus on the palm of the opposite hand, trying to determine how she could tell him what she had to say.

His laugh was a short loud crackle of derision.

"We talked with Gentry Caldwell night before last," Lydia went on. "We learned that he was the one directed the outliers to our house the night—the night we lost so much, near the end of the war."

Ham was sitting very still, watching her. He said nothing.

"We asked him if it was true, and he confessed it. But he said he never took any of what was stolen." She paused. Still he did not move. "He did know who had traded for our livestock, though, who fattened it up and made a profit a short spell afterward by selling it to one of the armies."

"Caldwell must be a pretty knowing man, to know all that," Ham Nelson said evenly.

"I'm not trying to play games with you, Ham," Lydia said. "I'll speak plain out. We both know you took our stock and sold it. You made——"

"Me? I heard it was old man Thomas Hawkins. Didn't Caldwell mention Hawkins?" Ham asked, watching her closely.

297

"Yes, Mr. Hawkins: my brother Paul's father-in-law," she said. "He—and you—bought the cattle and horses."

"I just want to make sure you keep all your big news straight," he said.

"Ham"—she was determined to finish this as quickly, as cleanly, as possible—"go in to see your courthouse cronies and tell them you'd approve of a school out here. Then trade us a little corner in that field next to your store, or somewhere around there where it's central to the community, where you've bought up all the land."

"What would you trade?"

"Our mill site. It's too out of the way for the children."

"Why should I take that no 'count land?" he demanded.

"Because we need this place," she said.

He grinned at her and shook his head.

Then she said, "Because if you don't, I'm going to ask my brother Robert to bring a suit against you at the county seat, a lawsuit accusing you of trafficking in stolen livestock. We'll ask full repayment—with interest."

His eyes were fixed on her face and his jaws, for all their wattles, were tight with anger. "Well, now, of all the fool plans!" he exclaimed. "Why, you wouldn't get anywhere with a lawsuit like that. Even if it had happened like you say, it's all been too long ago."

"It happened like I say. Gentry Caldwell would testify that."

"Fool preacher!" Ham Nelson spat across the porch.

"And it may have been a long time ago," she went on, "but you know well as I do, Ham Nelson, that you couldn't find a jury of twelve men anywhere in this county who wouldn't be glad to see you have to pay, who wouldn't help convict you. It wouldn't make too much difference who you paid or why."

His face was purple with a fury that acknowledged better than any words the truth of what she had said.

"You've gouged too many people, Ham."

"So now you're gouging me, is that it, Lydia McQueen?"

He spoke truth. She felt little and mean for bargaining with his greed and fear. But she had to be sure of a school. She stood up. "You think it over, Ham——"

"Don't be so hasty, Lydia," he said. The words wrenched from him with effort. "I reckon I could speak to the fellers at the courthouse."

"This week, Ham."

"But if they put the school here, let them use the old millsite for the land. Do I get their favor toward the school, that ought to be enough for you."

"It isn't. Robert has already won some of their favor. But I don't want any more excuses they can hide behind. You trade us your piece of land, and they'll be forced to set aside enough money to put us up some kind of a decent building."

"But that land is valuable. Your pappy's puny livestock wasn't worth——"

"Don't speak another word, Ham Nelson." She stood trembling with a greater anger than she had ever known before in her life. "Don't you compare the value of what we lost that night with any parcel of land!" Had she a weapon, she could have struck him.

"All right." He stood up, too. They faced each other. He was panting, as though he had just finished a long, useless race. "I'll find another piece of ground for you——"

"Not for me, for——"

"Although it wouldn't throw such a nice light on your own family if you brought your suit and I testified about Hawkins, about his money your brother Paul lives off of——"

"My brother didn't know about Dolly's father until two nights ago. There's much he doesn't know, Ham Nelson, the better for you. But he earns his living. You know he's a master miller!"

"So I do. But his pappy-in-law's trouble would be a juicy tidbit to pass around for the valley's talk. Tear me down, and he goes, too." Ham was growing calmer. He had found he had a lever on the situation after all.

"Help get our school and we'll never name that night to anyone again."

"Well, now, I've said I would. Seems like I ought to have a little favor, though, for all I'm doing."

"What are you driving at, Ham?" All at once she was very weary; her legs were weak and shaking.

He latched his thumbs through his suspenders; his face was no longer purple. "I'd say at least the school ought to be named after me."

She looked at him in surprise.

"Everybody called the other school 'Professor Duncan's School,' that was all I could hear morning till night. Well, by thunder, if I'm supposed to provide everything——"

"Everything but the teaching," Lydia murmured.

"I want this school named after me."

"All right." She wanted to have done with this bargaining. She wanted to get far away from that bloated face, that greedy grasp that left its mark on every field and hill it touched and would leave its name on the very school it had choked for so long a time.

So the Hamilton Nelson School came to Thickety Grove. It was a one-room building, but it was made of sawed lumber sold cheaply to the county school committee by the Thurstons, and the hickory shingles of its roof had been carefully split in the dark of the moon by Mark and Fayte so they wouldn't warp and curl. There was a box-supper celebration and a dedication after Professor Duncan returned, the night before the new school term was to commence. The superintendent of education came out from the county seat and made an address. Professor Duncan talked of how good it was to return to the mountains and to have an opportunity to teach again. Hamilton Nelson, in a black suit, sat with the speakers at the front of the room.

Lydia was not present for the school dedication. Two nights before, Martha had lost her second baby. She was too ill for Lydia to leave her bedside.

16th

CHAPTER

Summer thunder rolled through the hills, rumbled across the valley and faded away in the distance. "Somebody up yonder rolling those old pumpkin wagons," Lydia's father used to say.

After the thunder, the night was quiet. Outside Lydia's window there was not a sound. Black darkness seemed to have swallowed up every cricket and peeper and night creature in the fields and woods. The stillness and the heat were suffocating. She lay alone in bed and watched the window, waiting for another streak of heat lightning. Was the night really this warm, Lydia wondered, or was she simply having what Aunt Tildy called hot flashes?

"After all, a woman your age," Aunt Tildy had said a few weeks back, "forty-nine, going-on-fifty, it's high time you had hot flashes and nerves and any of the rest of it you're a mind to."

"A woman your age." The words rang bleakly in her ears. What was her age? How was it counted? By date of birth only or by the freshness, the anticipation that still welled up like a spring in her spirit? Her age. She had glanced in the mirror that hung over her washbasin and for the first time in a long while she had really looked at herself and seen the stark planes and lines of her own face, sharp and clear under the sun-baked, wind-burned skin drawn so taut it seemed to have been purified in some furnace where all excess of flesh and discontent and frailty was burned away. She touched her hair, so much grey mixed with the rich brown, drawn tightly back from forehead and cheeks into a smooth heavy knot. The years of her age were branded on her face, but the youth of her spirit still shone in her eyes.

Ah, well, she would not listen to Aunt Tildy's female talk. Time passed and people changed and she would endure, as others had, and enjoy as she always had.

Time passed—it did that and no dispute. Sometimes lately, especially with the autumn of the year coming on, Lydia thought back to the days when she was a girl, or when she was first married and David was a baby. How long the days had seemed. Then, at midmorning, with the cackling of hens and crying of guineas out in the pasture and sunlight pouring down on the shingle roofs and the empty woodyard and the sparkling creek, the afternoon and evening had seemed to stretch out before her like an endless spool of silk. Now, by midmorning, she could feel the pressure of the approaching night, and it often seemed to her that the day was ending before she had even begun to recognize its presence.

Unconsciously, lying in the darkness, she listened for the ticking of the clock. Then she remembered. Of course. The clock hadn't been in the house since Fayte was in the first finishing exercises at Professor Duncan's school. She had traded it for some store cloth to make the boy a new suit, not a reshaped hand-me-down but one cut to fit only him. And when he stood up there, thin and awkward as a rail, eager and intense, and gave his oration, the first scholar on Thickety Creek to receive a diploma signed in the Professor's classic script, she had known his new suit was worth any clock on earth.

She knew, too, that those long hours of reading together had been worth every minute. When Fayte mentioned Julius Caesar and the Rubicon in his speech, did he look at her and give a faint nod, acknowledging those special evenings when they had read and talked about the Roman until he became like a long-lost relative to them? Her heart had been full to bursting that night.

302

She had cheated a little on the trading for the suit, anyway. Much as she had disliked the idea, she had not really sold the clock, but had finally taken it to Ham Nelson's store. He would never sell it cheaply, of that she was certain, and she would buy it back one of these days when she and Mark had a little money ahead. With Fayte needing help to go to the academy in town after a while, and with the Cleveland Panic, as Clay Thurston called it, still tightening its grip, she had not wanted to mention clothes money to Mark. Casting around for some way she could buy Fayte's suit she had discovered that the clock was just about the only possession of any value at all that she alone owned. There were other things she set great store by, oh, many things— the trundle bed her children had used when they were little, her mother's spinning wheel, Aunt Tildy's midwife satchel, a copy of Dr. Hornsby's last will and testament, the little hat Martha had worn when she was married—but what cash value had any of these? The clock had meant much to her, too. The night before she slipped it down to Nelson's she had not slept at all, thinking, remembering, figuring. But living people had living needs, and she knew that a new suit now for shy, oversensitive Fayte might mean more than a mansion later.

Tonight, however, it would be nice to have the clock back on her mantel again, ticking off its tidy seconds, keeping her sad, implacable company. A wave of light shimmered across the sky, brightening her room briefly in one feverish flash. She wondered if Aunt Tildy and Jessie were awake. She hoped not. She hoped that the old woman's knotted aching joints were relaxed in deep peace for the moment, that Jessie's sturdy legs and arms were resting for new chores to do around the farm tomorrow while her father was away. Seventy and twenty, Aunt Tildy and Jessie stretched on either side of her life. She thought of a long chain— and she was in the middle—reaching from yesterday to tomorrow.

Ah, but the bond with an even farther tomorrow was here in the room with her, in the worn trundle bed just below where she lay now so wide awake. Sophronia: it seemed a rather strange name Martha and Tom had given their first living child. Everyone called her Frone. And now little Frone was thirteen months old and when Lydia had come back, more than a week ago, from helping Martha give birth to a second girl, she had brought this peart-faced oldest grandchild home with her.

"It don't seem natural not to have a little one around the house," Lydia had told Martha and Tom as she made ready to leave them alone with their new baby. "Mark and me need to borrow Frone awhile. And you'll have an easier time getting little Ivy started off right."

"Do you think it's a pretty name, Mama?" Martha had asked, looking very small and large-eyed as she took up her household work for the first time since she had borne this easy, gentle baby.

"Ivy Thurston," Lydia said it over to herself. "It has a nice sound."

"I've always thought the ivy was about the prettiest thing growing here, the way it clings to the mountains, the way it comes in the cutover places and covers up the scars with blooms in spring. I thought it would make a special name for a girl."

"And this-here's a special girl child, all right." Lydia laid the bundle of blankets and two big brown eyes down on the bed and made ready to change a diaper. Eh law, as Aunt Tildy would say, let a woman name her baby anything she'd a mind to, if it brought her satisfaction or a special meaning. She'd earned the right.

Lydia listened, wondering if the last crash of thunder had wakened little Frone. She moved to the edge of the bed and raised her head from the pillow. The child's breathing was quick and regular. Lydia listened to it in deep content, thinking this rhythm could take the place of her clock's voice in keeping her company. Steadily, steadily, the breath came and went and came again and. . . .

Dear God, it was a warm night. She did not ever remember so warm a night up here on the mountain before. She loosed the buttons on the yoke of her nightgown. What would she give to bury her face right now in the crystal coolness of her spring? She could veritably taste the sweetness of its water on her parched tongue. So different it was from the sluggish water she had found in the old spring on Ham Nelson's farm.

On her way home from Martha's, as Tom took a short cut from

the new road and came past the field where the Nelson's tenant house had once been, where she had once lived, she had asked her son-in-law if he would turn aside a minute and let her go down to the place in the pasture where she remembered the spring. While Tom and little Frone waited, she climbed through the fence and walked across the sprout-stubbled field. As she had noticed three, four years back when she went to bludgeon Ham into helping them get a school in the valley, the great virgin poplars were gone. Only their decaying stumps remained. Nearby rose a pyramid of rotting sawdust, signifying where the mill had stood while this part of the Nelson tract was being lumbered out.

Years of rain seeping through that mound of sawdust had turned the water in the spring brackish. The spring itself was full of leaves, abandoned and diminished. She cleaned out handfuls of the leaves, down to the sandy bed, and waited for the water to flow clear again. The trickle came so slowly she could hardly believe this was the bold, fine spring she had once dipped into with deep buckets. When the sand had settled and the stream seemed pure again, she cupped her hands and took a drink of water. It was tepid and tasteless.

She had gone back to Tom and her grandbaby. A weary sadness and sense of age had settled over her. "Let's get on up to the mountain," she had said, trying to smile at them lightly.

The very next day she had cleaned out her own spring and the springhouse where she kept her milk and butter and cream, and the vessels for milking and churning. With Jessie helping her, they had trimmed the shrubs and vines twining in the tree roots that sheltered the spring. When they were finished, only the fresh new growth of luxuriant leaves and ferns hung over the moss-covered stones. Then they cleaned the spring-run, swept down the cobwebs and mud daubers from the walls of the springhouse, scrubbed out the long trough where crocks and jars, covered with white cloths and slabs of wood, sat in a cold, flowing stream. When they finished, she had smiled at Jessie and said, "I reckon I'm plumb foolish about this spring."

"Well, Mama," Jessie teased her as they walked toward the house together, "I confess right out, I'd hate for you to be put to

305

the test to have to choose between it and"—she cast around for
a startling comparison—"and me!"

Lydia kept her face straight. "A good spring *is* mighty hard to
come by," she had said gravely.

"So is a good daughter." Jessie tossed her tomboy head.

"Now that's a fact," Lydia said. "I'd have to take that into con-
sideration." She laid a sweaty arm around her youngest child's
shoulders. "Which do you say has done the best job of looking
after the other this afternoon, little Frone or Aunt Tildy?"

"About even, I'd say," Jessie replied. "And what with Papa and
Aunt Tildy, to say nothing of you and me, being so foolish about
that young'un, I look for her to be rotten spoiled inside a month."

"I'm just a-hoping Martha and Tom will let her stay with us
that long."

She hoped anew that little Frone would be sleeping alongside
her here in the trundle bed for many a night to come. And ever
since Mark had gone, the first of the week, to take a wagonload of
apples down to South Carolina, she had been especially thankful
for the child.

She wondered how long it would take Mark, how far he would
have to go, to sell his load of fruit. He took only red apples to the
Low Country. "No matter the flavor, folks down there don't think
they've got an apple if it's not red," Mark had said. "You give
them a white one, like a Maidenblush, or a green Horse apple, or a
yellow Belle o' Buncombe, three of the finest ever I tasted, and
they won't even try it. Think you're cheating them if it's anything
but red."

So they had dried these early white apples with an eye on winter and picked their red fruit to get it on the first market down in
the hotter lowlands where only peaches thrived. Lydia hoped
the load of apples would bring a good price. This would be Fayte's
last year at the Nantahala Academy in town and he had had a lot
to mention lately—she had noticed, and so had Mark—about
medicine and doctors.

"What would you say, Mrs. McQueen," Mark asked her, not
long ago, "if we had a boy turned out to be a doctor?"

She smiled at him. "I'd say it was a worth-while thing."

Mark's pride had been something good to behold. The next day he had announced he would try to sell their master crop of apples for every penny he could get this year. "Education for a doctor takes a long time, I've heard tell," he said. "Most likely costy, too."

Yes, it would be an unbelievably fine thing to have a doctor in their family. "Folks have to look up," her mother had always said. Well, if Fayte wanted to look way up, she and Mark would do what was necessary to help him.

If Fayte had been a doctor two years ago, maybe he could have saved Kate's and Alec's baby. The child was only two and a half, their third and youngest; Kate was rendering lard one day in early winter and the boy had pulled over a kettle of the boiling fat. The bubbling grease had poured over his little body until the skin and flesh fell away from his bones in sizable pieces. He had died the next night.

Thinking of how the hot liquid must have burned, Lydia was aware again of her own warm body. There was another streak of lightning, closer and sharper this time, followed by a quick bolt of thunder. Perhaps it was building up to rain in a few minutes and then the air would cool. She listened for some sound outside, but there was only silence. She remembered other times she had lain awake here waiting for the sound of her oldest boys, Burn and Gib, as they returned late in the night from a fox hunt or their rambles up and down the valley. Why was it that whenever she thought of those two, she always smiled to herself? Even though she felt close to tears, as she did now, with longing to see them, with memory of their muscled arms and work-hardened faces when they had come home for a short visit from the coal fields, she still had to smile a little at memory of them. Because they were so gay, so full of the sap and enjoyment of life from one moment to the next, because between them seemed to glint the humor of some vast secret, common to all yet best known only to them. Their wit was easy and contagious and turned strangers into ready friends.

A year and a half it was now since they had been home. They

had appeared unexpectedly at breakfast one morning, carrying two pails of milk still warm and foamy from the cows' udders.

"Here's your morning's milking," Burn said, setting his pail in the middle of the table.

"We done finished up the chores for you," Gib said, and set his pail alongside Burn's.

"What in thunder——" their father began, taken aback with surprise and pleasure.

"Wanted to make sure we'd be welcome," Gib said, and grinned at them from his clean-shaven man's face.

"Such a way to talk!" Lydia had just finished making biscuits and was wiping her hands on her apron. Her face glowed with a light brighter than that reflected from the fire.

"Burn, Gib . . ." Fayte fumbled for words to welcome these brothers again. Jessie, less restrained, threw herself into their arms.

"Eh law, I always foretold those boys would come to no-count ends," Aunt Tildy began, but her quavering voice broke and denied her gruff words and she dabbed happily at her pale old eyes with one end of her shawl. Lydia was glad to have to go to the chair and look after her, so that no one would see the tears in her own eyes.

They had stayed home seven weeks, Gib and Burn, recounting tales of disaster in the mines, of frolics and fights in the coal camps, of hard-earned money in rough country. Lydia had pleaded with them not to go back. "It shrivels my soul to think of folks burrowing underground like moles all day long, away from sunlight and air. I can't think I brought chaps into the world to spend their strength hacking away in darkness all their young years."

They had agreed and told Mark and Lydia they were setting their sights on the West now. "Tell us what the country was like when you were out there, Papa," Gib said.

"Where, to your way of thinking, would be a likely place to stake a homesite or a ranch maybe?" Burn asked.

And so there had been talk of the West around her fireside again. And when the boys left, slipping out one night as unheralded as they had arrived, they took with them the same high hopes she had sent West once before.

Perhaps, one day before long, when she was least expecting it, Burn and Gib would surprise them again and she would look up from cooking or sewing or rocking little Frone to see them standing in the door. Then she would learn whether they had found that homesite or that ranch and settled down. . . .

Another clap of thunder, so close it made her jump. And then she discovered a warm wetness running down her chin and neck. She groped for the lamp. When she finally got it lit, she saw the blood on her gown and pillowcase. Her nose was bleeding. Cupping one hand over her face and carrying the lamp in the other, she hurried into the kitchen. Jessie had brought up a bucket of fresh water just at nightfall. Lydia sloshed dippers full of it into the washbasin and rinsed her face. The water turned pink, then red, as blood continued to gush forth. She squeezed a towel out in the cool water and pressed it over her face, holding it tightly against her nose. After a few minutes she wrung it out again and repeated the process. Gradually the bleeding stopped.

She emptied the basin of bloody water out in the yard. A sprinkle of rain had set in. The lightning and thunder seemed to have stopped. Suddenly she felt no longer hot, as she had in the bed. In fact, she was chilly. She put the washbowl back on its shelf.

The kitchen was dim and empty. There was the heavy smell of food left over from supper, still on the table under a long white cloth to protect it from flies or other insects. Outside, the sound of the rain was growing louder. The indoor smell of the food mingled with the outside smell of the first raindrops settling the summer dust. The mingling of rain and dust made a good smell peculiar to deep summer.

Suddenly she shivered. The front of her gown was damp with blood and water. Her legs trembled. She could feel the goose flesh rising on her arms and shoulders. Lydia could not understand this sudden cold. Only the faintest breeze stirred outside. The rain was not part of a blowing storm, but quiet and steady. For the first time, she wondered if she might have a fever.

She recalled Aunt Tildy's words, yesterday when they were

finishing dinner. "You haven't eaten a thimbleful at table any meal the last two days. You coming down with something?"

"Nothing but plain old laziness," she had replied, trying to laugh a little. "Seems like I been no-count ever since I came back from Martha's. Reckon having another grandbaby aged me?"

But Aunt Tildy had not laughed. "Eh law, seems like late summer's the treacherous time for all manner of complaints."

Summer or not, Lydia's bones this night felt as if the chill of winter were upon them. She had to warm herself some way. The fire from cooking supper had left a handful of coals on the hearth. They were almost gone out, but she scraped them into a little heap with the shovel and laid a few ends of wood across them. With great effort she blew the coals back to life. A flame caught hold of one of the bits of wood. Presently there was a fire.

She crouched close and held her hands to it. Then her fingers were warmed, but the rest of her body remained cold. Her teeth chattered with the chill.

There was a sound in the doorway. She looked around and saw Aunt Tildy, grey hair hanging wildly around her stooped shoulders, eyes peering feebly through the dim light. "That you, Lyddy?" she asked.

"Yes, Aunt Tildy," Lydia answered. And either her voice told more than she knew or Aunt Tildy's ears were keener than she had thought, for all at once the old woman came across the kitchen swiftly.

"What's wrong, child?"

"Nothing." As Lydia stood up, her head grew dizzy. She reached out and caught hold of Aunt Tildy's nightgown. "I don't know. I was lying in bed and I was so hot I thought I might suffocate, then my nose began to bleed and when I came in here I began to feel chilly——"

"Eh law, eh law." Aunt Tildy shivered, as if she had glimpsed an old and mortal enemy.

"I don't know what it could be . . ."

"Get back to bed, child." Aunt Tildy, suddenly erect with a new-found strength, took Lydia by the arm and guided her into the next room. "Jessie, Jessie," she was calling all the while, "come quick as you can." And when the sleepy, startled girl stood in the door, Aunt Tildy said, "Your mama's sick."

"Mama?"

Lydia heard Jessie speak to her, but just as she was ready to answer she fell onto the bed and a heavy weakness and whirling dizziness engulfed her. She heard the baby Frone wake up in the trundle bed and commence to cry, and then Aunt Tildy answered Jessie. "Yes, your mama. She's bad-off sick."

Typhoid fever. The name had struck terror at one time or another to almost every family in the valley. Word circulated that Robert Moore had brought the doctor out from town up to the mountain and Lydia McQueen had typhoid. Many memories were stirred.

"It was typhoid carried away my pappy over forty year ago," Emma Caldwell told a neighbor.

"My folks had the fever once when I was a young'un," Ruby Nelson told her husband, Ham, as she served him his supper one night. "It killed off one of my baby sisters and Mama come through it, but she never was the same afterward . . ."

But Ham made her no answer.

"Typhoid fever took two brothers older than er-ah Alec or me either one," Clay Thurston said to Sue. "I hate to hear that er-ah Lydia . . ." His stammering had overcome him for the moment.

Sue Thurston was combing her hair and winding it in a fresh, tight knot. She was preparing to go and help look after Lydia. "I just dread to see Martha and her other children," she said. "They set such store by their mama."

"Er-ah"—Clay Thurston could hardly speak, but he kept on trying—"er-ah, there's a heap of people set store by Lydia McQueen. If there's anything you thought er-ah I could do up there——"

"Not now," she said, wanting to relieve his concern and keep him as long as she could from the drawn-out sickness that might lie ahead. "I'll ride on up with Tom and Martha, as they come by, and if there's aught you can do, Tom will bring you word."

"Make sure he does."

"I may be gone quite a spell," she said, jabbing her last hairpin in place. "I don't know who there'll be to look after her."

But the whole valley, it seemed, would look after her.

During the next few days, despite their dread of the fever and the press of their work, the people of the valley went up the mountain to offer their help to Lydia McQueen.

They stood in her green yard under the walnut trees, beside the rose-of-Sharon bush, among the little flowers and vines she had brought from the woods and planted all around her home, and they spoke in hushed tones.

"I remember when my woman was having her first young'un and there was nobody else I could get to look after her. I come after Mrs. McQueen and she brought my woman and young'un both right through."

"She never was one to say 'no' to a body in need."

Ruby Nelson came. "The last baby Mama ever had, Mrs. McQueen helped her bring it. Papa was plumb at the end of his wits and he came after her."

"There was a time at the sawmill one of the men nearly cut an arm off. Lydia was visiting nearby and I recollect she tied that feller's arm up, stayed with him all the way into town. The doctor said it saved his life. He'd cut an artery."

Callie Bludsoe came. "I'm a stranger to you'uns, but I be no stranger to her that's laying in yonder. She saved a dog for my boy, Morgan, once. And just a year past, she come up on Stony Ridge and nursed me five days when I was abed. Any chore I could turn my hand to, I'd be proud."

"Aye God, we all stand ready to help."

"I think back on it now, when she was putting up such a fight for our school here, I didn't lift a hand to strengthen her. And I can't rightly say why, either. But my little ones are down there getting learning right now, and it plagues me there's nothing I can do to show her my gratefulness."

"I recollect when my first baby, Tim, was born . . ." Dolly wept and grew hysterical and had to be put to bed.

Lenore Hornsby Duncan came and refused to be set aside. "She's been more than mother and sister to me, and I mean to help

312

nurse her now." The pale, lovely face was set with grief and determination. And in spite of her fragile looks, Lenore turned to helping Kate and Elizabeth, and Martha and Jessie, and Sue Thurston, with a will of iron and a body that would not admit fatigue.

"It's the nursing counts for everything," the doctor said to Lydia's daughters and sisters and friends, as he came day after day, fetched by a Robert whose face was set in shocked unbelief. "Someone must be with her all the time. You must give her this medicine at regular intervals and you must sponge her off and keep her temperature down if possible. I will show each of you how to wash her mouth and keep that yellow fur from coating her tongue. Her bed will be foul sometimes and must be changed often and she must have all the water she will drink, quantities of it. If her fever makes her delirious, you must comfort her. . . ."

And so he instructed them how to look after Lydia McQueen's tortured body.

"Isn't there something else?" Robert asked the doctor, but the old man shook his head wearily. "We do our best, son," he said.

As Robert took him back down the valley, he was halted as he passed Nelson's store. Someone called his name. Ham was coming down the steps to the store, an object in his arms. When he reached the buggy he handed something up to Robert, an object wrapped in an old quilt. "Be obliged would you take it on back home tomorrow," he said.

"What is it?" Robert asked.

"Her clock."

Robert was surprised. He turned back a corner of the quilt and made sure of the contents. "I don't understand. How did you come to have it?"

"She brought it down here to trade off for cloth for a suit. It was when her boy Fayte was a-finishing school, gave his oration. I've had it since."

Robert's face was stricken. "I didn't know. I wish she had come to me. She prized her clock . . ." He paused.

"Reckon she was always mighty independent."

"Was?" Robert cried. "Is! She *is* this moment." He took a grip

313

on the reins. "I'll settle with you later on about this, Ham. I'm much obliged."

The next morning Robert replaced his mother's clock on Lydia's mantel.

The women arranged for shifts and two by two they cared for her night and day. Whenever possible, Lenore insisted on taking Martha's turn, leaving her free to care for her baby and nurse it when there was need.

Lydia's fever climbed and held. The women bathed her in cool water. They swabbed out her parched, coated mouth. At the doctor's instructions, they cut her hair, the long brown hair once rich with amber high lights, streaked now with grey. Yet the fever held.

Lydia thought of winter. A fine season, winter, with frost on the windowpanes in the mornings, icy frost—and sometimes snow: pure, cold snow covering every fence post and frond, every field and pasture path. A cold white blanket of snow. "And dogwood winter yet to come," she heard her mother saying. They were talking about Mark, she and her mother. But she did not want to talk about Mark. She wanted to see him, to be with him. His arms were strong and brown with sun, she had seen them at the Burkes' mill when he was lifting a turn of corn up to be ground.

"Mark!" Her voice sounded very dim and far away.

"He's not here, Lyddy," someone said to her. "He's gone with apples to South Carolina, you recollect. But he ought to be back any day now. . . ."

The voice became blurred in her fever.

A night and a day and another night dragged by. Once she thought she heard her clock ticking. Most of the time, however, she was barely conscious of the light or dark. But at last there was a voice that said, "Thank God, somebody sighted his wagon down the road. He's on his way."

"I wouldn't want to be the one to break the news to him."

After a while there was a voice she knew.

"Lyddy."

"Mark." She could feel the good firm arms under her and around her.

314

"Mark, there was an owl come and perched on the comb of the roof last night. I heard its calling."

He looked at Lenore Duncan and Sue Thurston and they shook their heads silently.

"Never mind, Lyddy, I——"

"Don't shoot it, Mark," she said. Her tongue was too large, too dry; it was difficult to make the words. "I was always sorry we killed that red-tailed hawk."

"Lyddy."

Wherever they said that he had been, she was glad he had come back. "Was it prison where you've been, Mark?"

"Why, no, Lyddy, I've been to——" He paused, and then she heard him say, "Oh, yes, in Andersonville prison, a long time ago——"

"I'm glad you're free at last, Mark."

"Lyddy," he said in a strange, choked voice.

There was more she wanted to say. There were a great many things that had to be finished, but her very bones seemed to melt with weakness and fever.

The next day, while Sue Thurston was sponging her face, Lydia hemorrhaged. Before Robert arrived with the doctor, she was dead.

It was six months before Mark and Jesse Moore and Robert and Paul could get a proper stone cut. Below Lydia's name and the dates enclosing the years of her life, 1846-1896, there was a single line on the slab of gray granite: "Precious above rubies."

In the spring, when Martha and Tom moved back to the valley, Martha often took her baby and walked up on the mountain where the little graveyard was. The child, Frone, liked to stay with her grandmother Thurston and play with blocks from the sawmill. But the baby, Ivy, seemed to love the woods best. She clutched at every leaf and vine and flower they passed. And her hands were already Ivy Thurston's worst feature—and her best: long and large-boned hands that would hold loosely and give generously and build well, strong, like her grandmother's, Lydia McQueen's.